Looking on Darkness

Looking on Darkness

a novel by André P. Brink

WILLIAM MORROW AND COMPANY, INC.
NEW YORK   1975

Published in the United States in 1975.

First published in Afrikans under the title *Kennis van die Aand*
by Buren Publishers, Cape Town, South Africa, copyright © 1973
by André P. Brink.

English translation copyright © 1974 by André P. Brink.

Published in Great Britain in 1974.

Printed in the United States of America.

1 2 3 4 5   79 78 77 76 75

Library of Congress Cataloging in Publication Data

Brink, André Philippus (date)
  Looking on darkness.

  Translation of Kennis van die aand.
  I. Title.
PZ4.B8583Lo3 [PT6592.12.R5]   839.3'6'35   75-4515
ISBN 0-688-02924-9

In Memoriam
ROB

Nothing in this novel has been invented, and the climate, history and circumstances from which it arises are those of South Africa today. But separate events and people have been recast in the context of a novel, in which they exist as fiction only. It is not the surface reality which is important but the patterns and relationships underneath that surface. Therefore all resemblance between the characters and incidents in this book and people and situations outside is strictly coincidental.

... la noticia vespertina, que es sabiduría de Dios en sus creaturas y obras y ordenaciones admirables; la cual es ... más baja sabiduría que la matutina.
— ST JOHN OF THE CROSS.

The day will not save them
and we own
the night.
— LEROI JONES.

Toute vraie liberté est noire et se confond immanquablement avec la liberté du sexe qui est noire elle aussi.
— ANTONIN ARTAUD

Looking on darkness that the blind do see.
— WILLIAM SHAKESPEARE.

Ed è subito sera.
— SALVATORE QUASIMODO.

Das ist eine Nacht des Unglücks, wo der Mensch die Wahrheit sieht.
— BERTOLT BRECHT.

Sur une même chose, on ne pense pas de même façon le matin ou le soir. Mais où est le vrai, dans la pensée de la nuit ou l'esprit de midi? Deux réponses, deux races d'hommes.
— ALBERT CAMUS.

Looking on Darkness

One

I

To know who I am. To define myself through the why and the how of her death. To enumerate and name it all, trying to determine not what a man can know of man, but simply what I dare to know about myself.

To preserve this body with all its parts – including the bruises and the scars, including the persistent pain – and keep it intact, virginal for its inevitable death.

In the early-morning shower I contemplate myself with a sense of amazement, almost awe; sometimes of an evening I take off my clothes and stand with my back pressed against the wall of my cell, or lie down on the narrow bunk, studying and touching this body, strange and familiar as that of a beloved. Even when I know they are watching me through the peephole in the door it doesn't upset me. I'm taking stock, over and over, of everything which, visibly and tangibly, has remained my own. These feet and knees and thighs, this vulnerable sex which seems to shrink from touch like a small scared animal, this pale brown belly and chest, these arms, these hands, each nail so intimately known; this face modelled under my fingertips. This is mine. This, at least, is the topography of that sad certainty which has been left to me.

For the rest – the rest is a muddle of memories and words, dreams, possibilities, names.

I can say : Jessica.

I can say : I love you.

I can say : Willem, or Dulpert, or Richard, or Jerry.

And then I can proceed to recall them and describe them in detail. I can say : Jessica Thomson, with dark blonde hair and stubborn chin, with peculiar grooves in the nails of her thumbs, with the small, definite, round breasts of a portrait from the innocent age preceding Raphael, and with a skin smooth and starkly white against my brownness, making love in the dark light of the dawn.

7

But it isn't enough, it remains a list of Shakespearean items, a catalogue of small separate moments. I'll have to do better than that.

They are looking after me very well nowadays, providing me with all the paper I require, the way one pampers a child or a madman. I suppose that is what death does to one – some do become madmen, others children. Or perhaps they're hoping to get something out of me in this way, some 'light on the subject', clarifying the many doubts undoubtedly raised by the trial. But that is irrelevant, really. I'm not writing this for them but only for myself, here, now, in the days or weeks before I'm taken by the deep dark lady, death.

It is important that I take my time. As the end approaches and my heart contracts, it becomes more and more imperative to write it down very calmly and very clearly. So that I can empty myself completely, in order to return into myself. It's a form of discipline, like the meditations of St John of the Cross, or Hamlet's game of madness at court. To fight my way through a web of syntactic certainties towards a final, possible glimpse of truth.

We're on the beach with several other people, an open white beach stretching for miles between surf and dunes, occasionally broken by a line of rocks. We're trying to get away from the others, picnicking and frolicking and playing with enormous plastic balls. But they won't let us escape. Laughing, they hold on to us and force us to join their games. Then, suddenly, we're free. Hand in hand we run across the white sand, both naked, her hair flying in the windy wind. Beyond the first line of rocks, finally isolated from the world, we stop, panting. There is an oval pool in the sand, its water still and lukewarm from the day's abundant sunshine; and it is very clear, almost brilliant, in spite of the approaching dusk. We wash the sand from our bodies and suddenly I'm kneeling in front of her, my face between her thighs, in the ozone of sea and woman. But before she can be moved to ecstasy I notice, with a rush of primitive fear, a fleet of green ice-cream trucks approaching across the dunes. She turns away from me, towards them. I try to call her back, but my voice is soundless. I try to follow her, but cannot move. The great green trucks come to a standstill; men in white overalls emerge from them. She is running now. The convoy leader is waiting for her. I want to shout: 'Jessica! Jessica! Jessica!' He is now spreading his arms, catching her, embracing her, glistening, nude and wet against his white coat. I can see her eagerly talking to him as she follows him

8

back to the truck in front. Slowly the long convoy starts moving away again, away across the ribbed sand, gone.

I am walking back now, alone. It's getting dark. All the others have gone. There is a single wooden cottage on the beach and I know it belongs to Richard and he's waiting for me at the door.

'Joseph,' he says. I want to walk on, but he says, 'Joseph.'

It is quite dark now and there is nowhere else I could go so I'll have to stay with him.

'She went away with the green ice-cream trucks,' I tell him, and he says, 'I know, I saw.'

'I can't stay here. Not with you, what can we talk about, we've got nothing to say to one another.'

'We can talk about her,' he says.

So we sit down at the table, on either side of the oil lamp, with bread and wine before us, talking about her. We talk endlessly, hating each other. Through that whole night and through the next day and through many more nights and days we go on talking about her. Until eventually hate subsides into weary resignation, and resignation into acceptance of what has happened and of each other. Then, one morning, as we wake up and look out through the open door, we see the green convoy returning over the distant dunes, like slow sea-creatures crawling across the sand, and we realise that she is back, that she can once again be ours, his or mine, his and mine, but neither of us makes any move to get up. In the end I simply lift my hand very calmly and push the dark door shut.

And then I wake up with a sense of serenity I cannot define even to myself, for why should I have excluded her in my sleep when all my waking hours are so utterly open towards her, even though it is during these waking hours I realise so acutely that I can never grasp her hand again or with my lips caress her secret mouth?

We arm ourselves to the teeth against a thousand threats which never materialise, but against that one thing, death, which always happens, we have no defence. I must be wary, I must protect myself, lest they use my very death to finally get hold of me through what I've written.

What I'm writing here, I shall destroy as I go on. Otherwise they may get hold of it, and that may implicate too many others. Fortunately the paper is very thin and it will be easy to flush it, page by page, down the toilet. In that way it will remain my own, which is all that matters now.

9

But I'll fool them all the same. I know they're constantly spying on me through the peephole as I'm writing, those vultures, awaiting their prey. For them, especially for them, on separate sheets, I'll write out and save the ten or twelve or however many of Shakespeare's sonnets I can remember. If necessary, I'll do it over and over, to exercise my memory and my mind. It may be nothing but a gesture. But in this extremity, in these nights of writing under the bare bulb, I'll allow myself the luxury of a last theatrical gesture. I was an actor, after all. In the repetition of memorised words and the rehearsal of roles I must discover the fleeting self : where else?

'Good morning, Malan,' he said. 'I'm your counsel. Let's see what we can do.'

Under different circumstances he would have addressed me as 'Mr Malan'. In fact, it was my impression that he regretted not being able to do so, but it wouldn't be seemly. Misters don't commit murder. And in a way I actually felt sorry for him, because I know he would have liked to take advantage of my presence to convince himself of his own broadmindedness. One of the younger generation who radiates the new images of its nationalism with as much conviction as sectarian converts trying to impress the world with their chronic smiles. Isn't a smile just another way of baring one's teeth, a prefiguration of the skull?

He entered with the trim brief-case (genuine leather) and sat down on the bunk beside me. Apart from the toilet that was the only seat.

'Name's Joubert,' he said.

'Also a Huguenot name.'

He gave a forced smile. 'Listen, Joseph, I appreciate your feelings. And I can assure you . . .' He looked at me. My eyes remained on his. Not in anticipation or accusation, and without antagonism. Just – well, peacefully. After everything that had happened, after all those terrible months, after I'd so nearly broken down in their hands, this was all that remained : this peace. As if nothing else mattered any more in the face of the anticlimax of a formal conclusion.

He resumed. 'Joseph, I want . . .'

I want. The way one says : *I want a kilo of sirloin, and some calf's liver.*

'I want you to trust me. I'm here to help you. If you are prepared to co-operate.'

It was strange. Like a film from which the sound has suddenly disappeared. I could still see his mouth move, and occasionally his hands as well, but I wasn't conscious of sound. Fascinated, I sat watching him. His rather narrow face, tanned and yet pale; a neat gold-filling in one front tooth; his hair longish and fair, but trimmed in a very straight line at the back, and with a tendency to fall across his forehead so that he constantly had to push it back with a combing gesture; it tended to make him look younger than the twenty-eight or twenty-nine he must have been. He wore a very modern suit but without being conspicuous. The purple handkerchief in his breast pocket matched his tie and the colour of his socks. There was a wedding ring on his left hand, and another ring with a large onyx on the little finger of his right hand.

'I want you to tell me everything in your own words.'

Did he expect me to repeat someone else's, as in the theatre? But he was probably unaware of the implications of his questions.

'It's really not important any more,' I said.

'Oh no, it's most important. Your life depends on it.'

'Did *they* hire you?' I asked.

'I've been appointed Pro Deo. Surely you realise: in a case like this . . .'

'I didn't ask for counsel.'

'But the law demands it.' I could detect a hint of irritability in his voice: 'Don't you realise where this is going to end if you refuse to co-operate?'

'It'll end there whether I co-operate or not.'

He took a packet of cigarettes from his pocket. 'Smoke? It'll calm you down.'

'Thanks, but I haven't smoked for several months now. I'm afraid I'll feel sick if I did.'

I watched him light his own: the whiteness and dexterity of his hands.

The smoke seemed to relax him. 'I realise it must look pretty hopeless to you, Joseph,' he said. 'But I want you to pull yourself together. Nothing is lost yet.' He shut the briefcase which he'd opened a few minutes earlier, and leaned closer to me. 'Some Pro Deo advocates regard their cases as a matter of routine and assume that they've lost before they've even started. But I want you to know that I regard every case as a personal challenge. I won't let you down. Look, the evidence against you is pretty overwhelming. But some aspects haven't been cleared up at all yet. For example, we know the sorts of people Jessica Thomson associated with. If we can prove that there was something she tried to draw you into – some sort of subversive activity – a plot or something she tried to force you into – something completely foreign to your nature as an artist, so that you felt cornered, you know, desperate. . . . That will mean extenuating circumstances. In fact, if we can prove something like that and you're prepared to co-operate to implicate the others, it's not unlikely that you may be used as a State Witness against them. You see? There's a very real chance. If you can help me . . .'

'I thought you meant to help *me*.'

He was put out for a moment before he changed his approach : 'Listen, I can understand that you're feeling bitter and suspicious. But this is your last chance, Joseph!'

Mr Joubert, my last chance was the day I met Jessica Thomson.

But all I asked was; once again : 'Who hired you?'

'I told you it's a matter of procedure. I'm taking your case Pro Deo.'

I couldn't resist it : '*Do* you believe in God, Mr Joubert?'

For the first time he looked really ruffled. 'I can't see that that has anything to do with it.'

I shrugged.

Then he asked, aggressively : 'Do you believe in him?'

'I'm Coloured, Mr Joubert. Surely you don't expect me to believe in God.'

With great agility he once again changed his approach : 'You've been tortured,' he said. 'That explains your attitude. I want you to tell me all about it. Then I can really press them.'

A train whistled in the distance, then the sound was blown away. It meant that there was wind. One of these days, in a week or two or three, after the case, I would also leave by train, for Pretoria, and early one morning there would be the closed courtyard and final jerk and then peace, and then peace. And the wind bloweth where it listeth.

'What have they done to you?' he insisted. 'I promise you, it can become one of our major points of attack. You've been confined by the Security Police for nearly three months before they charged you. Usually that happens only in political cases. But after three months all they could bring in against you was murder. And look at you! I'll see to it that you're examined by the District Surgeon before this day is out. We'll give them hell.' He leaned over again. I must say that I found his small repertoire of gestures disappointing. 'Please don't be scared. You can talk freely now.'

'I'm tired. And it no longer matters.'

'But how can you expect me to get up in court and . . .' He controlled himself, reopened his case, took out a pile of papers, arranged them on his lap, and then got up and went to lean against the door. 'Just to refresh your memory. The facts of the case . . .'

The case lasted a week and at every session a number of people had standing room only. There was a notable majority of women. Sturdy old ladies who would probably have brought their food baskets with them had it been allowed. Younger women, married to civil servants, hair 'done' for the occasion, hips already matronly: at home, one could well imagine, there would be, on mahogany-and-plastic bedside table, the twenty-sixth impression of a Christian sex guide, the Bible, and the latest copy of *Reader's Digest*. And then there were the newly emancipated young ones, with self-assurance of the Pill in the brazen expression of their eyes, the tilt of their chins and the impudence of their bra-less breasts. Several social workers, clergymen's wives, the students, including some of Stellenbosch. In spite of individual differences they had in common a dignified sordidness in their general antagonism towards Jack the Ripper and in the equally general regret of his capture.

A theatre critic would have judged it a successful production, I presume. The tall, emaciated judge had a most elegant manner and thanks to his quips the proceedings were never allowed to lapse into dreariness; there was a well-balanced struggle between the unruffled middle-aged Prosecutor and brilliant young Pro Deo counsel; a few times there even was active audience participation, mainly caused by a lady with a floral hat who regularly interrupted the first day's proceedings by exclaiming very loudly and adamantly: 'Hang him!' until she was escorted outside, with considerable difficulty, by two burly court sergeants.

The only criticism, I think, one could offer would be that the accused remained too passive throughout. It is possible that his unbroken silence allowed more scope to one's fantasy than, say, an emotional outburst, a series of obscene gestures or a charge in the direction of the public galleries – but basically he was betraying the unwritten rules of the game. It is part of the conditions of the set-up that good be recognised as good and evil as evil, with all the unflexible certainty of a distinction between black and white.

There was no applause at the end. One unmarried pregnant girl fainted, but that might be attributed to other causes. Afterwards she was interviewed by several Sunday newspapers. Among other things she

13

was a firm supporter of capital punishment as an effective deterrent in a multiracial society.

I don't want to be disloyal to the 'truth' of the case. But how could the case itself be other than disloyal to the truth of what had gone before? I can remember how often in the course of that week, listening absently to the 'facts of the case', I asked myself: Was that all? Was that all that remained of the agony of all those months, of that eternity of struggling and groping and pleasure and pain? – this series of 'facts' conveyed in the court jargon which, through many years, had been counted and sifted, until one was left with nothing but the coarsest? And then I looked up at the eyes, the vulture eyes of the old ladies, the implacable eyes of the matrons, the naked eyes of the girls – and the only difference between them was the degree of their greed (the cold Calvinistic ecstasies, the masturbation of the mind). The only thing confirmed by the eyes was the inevitability of what had to happen – not as a result of the murder, for that was commonplace, but as a result of the only immorality acknowledged by their society: that a white girl and a brown man dare make love. I looked up at those eyes, thinking: here you've got me now, naked, like those others before you in their cells and stations and torture rooms: take me and tear me to pieces, eat my body, drink my blood. For the first time, in that lofty courtroom, did I catch a glimpse of the mystic ecstasies of a St Simon Stylites. What had happened had to happen, and in no other way but that in which it happened: this was only another station on my way, and I had to get through it, impassively and with humility, because it formed as much part of the whole as the months and years preceding it. No drop of the cup could be left undrunk, not even the most humiliating or banal. That was the very *raison d'être* of the new station reached in court: that the most intimate of what happened between her and me, everything exclusively ours, had to be delivered and exposed to the randy eyes of the world. For that reason I had to endure it, without the luxury of masochism, simply endure it, the way a bird endures the air through which it flies, the way a flame endures itself in the act of burning, caught up in the utter necessity of itself, unaffected by will or reason.

For long spells I heard no word of what was said, just like during Joubert's first visit to my cell. Or else there was a distance between the process and myself, as if I really were nothing but a spectator at a rather commonplace performance. Even when what was said affected me in the most vital and immediate sense I experienced it in the way I used to look at foyer photographs of myself. Perhaps one develops a form of immunity to 'facts', not by excluding them, but, on the contrary, by opening oneself completely to them.

'Your lordship, we shall lead evidence to the effect that on the night of 13th April the accused was noticed in the building in Kloof Nek where the deceased, Jessica Mary Thomson, had her flat. Shortly after his arrival, at about 10 p.m., he was seen in a café near the building in the company of the deceased. From there, we hope to prove, they returned to her flat. That was the last occasion on which the deceased was seen alive. The next morning at about 11 a.m. a friend, Mr Richard Cole, arrived at her flat. He had an appointment with Miss Thomson. When there came no reply to his knocking he borrowed a duplicate key from the caretaker. Mr Cole will testify that he felt worried, as on the previous day he and the deceased had had an argument about her relationship with the accused.'

Commotion in court. 'Hang him!'

'What do you understand by "a relationship", Mr Mostert?'

'We shall bring witnesses to say that it was a sexual relationship, m'lord.'

'And for how long did it go on?'

'Our evidence will show that it lasted for at least a year.'

'They never tried to leave the country?'

'Not as far as we could determine, m'lord.'

'It would have been a logical solution, wouldn't it? It seems probable that the accused would have continued his career overseas. And the deceased, I believe, was British in any case?'

A murmur of voices. 'Hang him.'

The Public Prosecutor rearranged his documents while my counsel got up, obviously annoyed: how often had he not put these same questions to me during our interviews?

'M'lord, I . . .'

'Continue, Mr Mostert.'

'So on the morning of Good Friday, 14th April, Mr Cole entered the flat of the deceased accompanied by the caretaker to find her on the bed in the bedroom. She was naked, covered only by a sheet.'

'Hang him!'

'Our forensic experts will testify that death occurred as a result of strangulation at least twelve hours before the discovery of the body, and that evidence was found of sexual intercourse before death.'

15

'Hang him.'

'The State will point out similarities between the accused's hair and some discovered on the fingers of the deceased; in addition, traces of blood found under her fingernails were identical with the accused's blood group. There were marks on his back which may have been caused by the deceased's nails.'

'Signs of a struggle?'

'Not in the usual sense of the word, m'lord.'

Nervous giggling and whispering. 'Silence in court!'

'The police will testify that several possessions of the accused, including letters, books, records and items of underclothing were found in the flat of the deceased, and some of her books and letters in the rooms he occupied in the Malay Quarter.'

'Is all this necessary, Mr Mostert?'

'With respect, m'lord: we shall try to establish the nature of the relationship between the deceased and the accused.'

'This court is more interested in the end of that relationship, Mr Mostert.'

'As your Lordship wishes. The State will testify that the accused's car was discovered, hidden under some branches beside the road in Bain's Kloof Pass, on Saturday, 15th April. On the next day, Sunday, 16th April, the accused made his appearance on the farm 'Skadukrans' in the Bain's Kloof area, where he was subsequently arrested.'

'Did he offer any resistance?'

'None whatsoever, m'lord. Neither did he make any effort to deny anything. In fact, he made a full statement to the police.'

'Voluntarily?'

'Completely so, m'lord.'

'If your Lordship will allow me . . .'

'You shall have an opportunity in due course, Mr Joubert. Please proceed, Mr Mostert.'

'We hope to establish beyond all doubt that the relationship between the accused and the deceased had reached a point beyond which it could no longer continue within the framework of the laws and the traditional way of life in this country; that the accused, furthermore, became jealous of a possible relationship between the deceased and Mr Cole; and that he resorted to killing her because he could not bear to part with her.'

'The Court will draw its own conclusions after all the evidence has been heard, Mr Mostert.'

'M'lord, with your permission I shall now call the first witness . . .'

There was a whispering and shuffling on the public galleries where the women settled in more comfortable postures. For now the prologue was over and the programme announced; now they could sit back to see the case run its course. There was an air of satisfaction about it all, not unlike the atmosphere in a theatre where Shakespeare is performed: the play was familiar, each phrase could be anticipated, each new moment expected – hence the 'tranquillity' Anouilh speaks of, the calm resignation to the fate slowly fulfilling itself. The Public Prosecutor might well have added: with our evidence we shall prove this, and then that, and then that; and then you will adjourn the Court and return to find the accused guilty, and with him will be done according to your verdict, and society will once again be purged by the expulsion of an antibody from the collective organism.

And while all this was slowly being fulfilled, I remained motionless under many eyes, hardly conscious of what was said around me. Occasionally one could hear something from the streets outside, but only very vaguely: a rumbling truck, a car hooting angrily in Keerom Street, the sputtering of a motor-cycle. These sounds recalled others which were more eloquently, more distinctly Capetonian, richer in texture, more subtle in meaning: the chattering of the flower sellers in Adderley Street; a Salvation Army Choir on the Parade, bravely singing: 'Onward, Christian Soldiers . . .'; the earsplitting voices of newspaper vendors at the entrance to the Gardens; the hoarse complaints of the foghorn at Mouille Point like a sick ox lowing in the distance; children playing among fruit-carts and jumbled shops in District Six or high up against the mottled slope of Signal Hill; the cannon booming at noon and the pigeons flying up with the harpsichord sound of their whirring wings; ship's-horns grunting bluntly in the harbour; the entire grey totality of sound from the city far below Jessica's balcony in Kloof Nek.

The balcony played a central role in the year we shared. It was a starting-point of our excursions, a sanctuary to return to, a landmark. To a large extent its role was determined by the fact that it was the place we went back to after we'd been to Bain's Kloof for the first time.

Strictly speaking, it is wrong to talk about a 'first time' for there was no other. Yet it would be wrong to call it the 'only time', since we returned to it so often in the mind. In every relationship there are such places, like music, or books, or colours, forever claimed by the couple as 'ours'. But to us Bain's Kloof was really much more than 'our place'. In fact, in the course of one year it became much more than a place: it was the name of a state of mind, a dimension of existence. From my earliest years, when the Bible still mattered, I can recall one episode which left an indelible impression: that occasion when Jesus sent his disciples away across the lake so that he could withdraw into the mountains alone. That quality of isolation, of remoteness from the world, Bain's Kloof acquired for me and Jessica. Perhaps because it meant the birth of something which hadn't existed before, the creation of an 'us'.

I had offered to show her the Boland. At that time she'd been in the country for six months or so, overwhelmed by impressions and not quite sure whether she should pack up and return to England. She was still in bed when, at eight o'clock that Thursday morning, I knocked on her door. In my ancient blue Austin we took the road to Stellenbosch, and French Hoek, and Paarl. It was April 18th, with autumn in the vineyards and poplars and, barely perceptible, in the oaks. The mountain folds still lacked the mists of May, but the landscape already had that lucidity characteristic of an April in the Western Cape, when the sun grows clear and still, less harsh than before, and the days seem to open up, cool at the edges but caressingly warm in the middle; when voices begin to sound more precise among the trees, and the patterns of leaves dissolve into the innumerable colour specks of a Seurat painting. It's as if people become more vulnerable then, and more dignified in their stark isolation as they move along the dusty country lanes; the air has the sadness of grapes, and in the tall trees the turtledoves call with uncompromising clarity. On the farmyards of the whitewashed houses pigs are grunting in the acorns; there are chickens in the patches of sunlight among the trees; and in the vineyards the straight lanes are speckled red and yellow and blue with the shirts and skirts of the labourers. Empty boxes stand piled up against barn walls and everything is redolent with heady must and young wine.

I took her to where I'd grown up in one of the small white labourers' houses behind a Cape-Dutch homestead near Paarl. The house was still there, smaller than I'd remembered it, narrower, with starker windows. There was a string of dried fish under the oak tree at the front door, and a crowd of exuberant brown children were recklessly chasing a dilapidated box-cart down the incline. On 'our' threshold a small girl in a red checked dress was sitting, with several spiky plaits sticking out in all directions from her head, an open pomegranate on her dusty knees.

Meticulously she broke the pips away and popped them down her throat, one by one.

I suppose I'd planned the visit as a test for Jessica. I wanted to see, I wanted to make quite sure, how she'd react. And after a few minutes I said, deliberately: 'I could have been any of those children.'

I was watching her very intently. She continued to follow the game for a while, then looked at me with those disconcertingly straightforward eyes. And all she said was: 'Did you have a cart like that, too?'

'Yes. Painted bright red in the beginning, but that soon peeled off; we got the wheels from an old pram in the backyard of Kahn & Co. Their chickens used to roost on it, but they refused to sell it to us, so one night we stole it.'

She laughed, with that small bubble of inner glee in her voice, putting her hand on mine. I remember that so well; the very real need she constantly felt to be touching people. To her it was as natural as eating or sleeping, a confirmation of being alive.

'You must have been happy.'

'I was poor.'

'Happy. With your red cart and all your pals. I wish I could change places with you.'

'But you told me how happy you used to be.'

'Yes. But it was different.' As she spoke, one of her fingers was tracing the outline of my hand, and I was more conscious of her touch, I think, than of her words. 'It was always just me, you see. My brother was so much older, he was already at Harrow when I was born. My parents only came out to the estate at weekends and then it was a very special favour to have a meal with them. For the rest there was only Nanny.'

'But you said she was a wonderful storyteller.'

'Oh yes. In the nursery in the mornings, or else at night, in my narrow white bed with the high posts.' Her small laugh. 'Above my head there used to be one of those Victorian plates with a text on it: *Thou God seest me*. And Nan never missed a chance of reminding me of that. Some nights I woke up terrified, imagining an eye like a hot coal of fire up there above my bed, but I was too scared to look.'

'But in the daytime you were happy. You said so. You told me all about your kingdom.' The fantasy castles under the birch trees, and your own playhouse in a corner of the garden, and the fairies dancing on the croquet lawn.

'Yes.' Her hand tightened on mine. 'But lonely, Joseph. Don't you

19

understand? So terribly lonely. And it does something to one, in the long run. It becomes almost impossible to share with someone else, ever, if you want to. One always seems to be holding something back.'

'Didn't you have any playmates at all?'

'Sometimes. The gardener's son.' An impish smile. 'We must have been ten or so.'

'What did you do?' I asked with an inexplicable rush of jealousy.

'What all children do, I imagine. Chased each other among the trees, played around, fought like hell. Took off our clothes and examined each other with great interest. Then back to *Thou God seest me*.'

'I wish I could wring the little bastard's neck!'

She laughed. 'It didn't last long.' More subdued. 'After all, there was nothing really to keep us together after that first bit of curiosity. And it didn't matter much either. Not then. But when the same sort of thing happened again, later, with others, when I was older, then it became worse: a little curiosity, a little sharing, but without ever reaching one another. And gradually one becomes scared. You begin to fear that it may be a sort of fate, and that it won't be different.'

'I love you.'

She shook her head slowly, almost reluctantly, almost with amazement. 'How can one be sure? How can you know so soon? We hardly know each other. Ten days.'

'Time has nothing to do with it, Jessica. I – we . . .'

'Let's go,' she interrupted. 'You said there was still a long way to go.'

We had already gone several miles on the Wellington road, she with her sandals kicked off and her bare feet on the edge of the seat beside me, when she suddenly said: 'You know, I wish I'd bought some sweets for those children. But then I thought: suppose I gave them sweets, it would feel as if I were trying to give *you* something.'

'Why don't you want to give me something?'

She was looking straight ahead. 'Because I think, if ever I get so far as to start giving, I'd like to give you everything.'

I didn't look at her. I simply knew she was there beside me, with the purple scarf covering her dark blonde hair, her brown eyes large and inscrutable, the line of her profile drawn with such clarity and confidence: small straight nose, gentle curve of mouth, aggressive chin – for however far she might have strayed from her upper-middle-class world, she had retained something of the implacable dignity of her background.

20

From Wellington we took the road to Bain's Kloof. It was half past three before we reached the hotel on the summit, where we stopped to look out over the autumn slopes and valleys. Neither of us spoke. Without asking, she got out to buy us cans of beer at the hotel and brought them back to the car. The matter-of-fact considerateness of the gesture, since we couldn't enter the hotel together, touched me. One becomes hyperconscious of these small moments to which the heart can never quite resign itself.

When I put out my hand to turn the ignition key again, she said: 'I don't want to go back yet.'

'There's a beautiful kloof behind the hotel,' I hesitated. 'But it's almost four o'clock.'

'We're not in a hurry, are we? Please take me there.'

Leaving the car at the hotel, we followed the narrow path leading to the ravine behind it, and down the rocky slope to the river bed below. There were no other people around. We took off our shoes, jumping lightly from boulder to boulder, zigzag across the narrow stream. We didn't speak. Sometimes I would scramble up a rock and hold out my hand to help her up; then she'd say, breathlessly: 'Thanks.' Or else she would go on ahead of me and wait for me, squatting beside a tiny rock-pool, looking up as I approached: 'Look,' pointing out minute fish, or a frog, or multicoloured pebbles on the rocky bed below.

Half a mile, a mile. On either side the slope was steep, almost perpendicular. Occasionally a bird would call. Otherwise it was completely silent, apart from the sensual sound of the water. The mountain air was heavy with the warm odour of buchu and wild herbs.

On a large grey boulder we finally sat down, she with her chin on her drawn-up knees and her narrow hands on her feet. I lay back on my elbows, watching her.

I can remember it all with such precision, as if it had been preserved in quartz.

'We've brought nothing with us,' she said after some time.

'Are you hungry?'

'I don't mean food or anything.' She remained quiet again, the patterns of light reflected from the water playing across her face. 'I mean: we haven't brought anything at all from the world down there. Nothing. It's only us.'

It was uncanny. As if history had suddenly been suspended and everything was waiting in a womb to be born: as if nothing except this kloof had ever existed, without form, and void; with darkness upon the face of the deep; the world waiting for us in order to start happening and become conscious to itself.

She got up. And once again, with that complete matter-of-factness so characteristic of her, she began to undress. I watched her body emerge from shirt and jeans and black pants. She took off her scarf and shook her hair over her shoulders. There was sunlight on her small white breasts and the dark gold of her love hair. Then she dived in. I got up and stripped and followed her. The water felt voluptuously cool, caressing us. With easy, even strokes she swam towards a shallow cave on the opposite side of the pool, where light reflections danced fantastically across the surfaces. I turned towards a different formation of rocks and for a while we sat basking in the late warm sun, separated by the amber-coloured water. Then dived back, laughing and cavorting, our bodies touching. For a brief moment she clung to me with a sense of urgency, then, embarrassed, we separated, like children caught in a forbidden game.

I reacted like a young boy, diving away from her, deep down, to pick up one of the small smooth pebbles from the bottom. It was perfectly round and white, with a slight groove across one of the ridges. I took it back to her, up on the high boulder where we'd left our clothes, and laid it in her hand. For a moment we were both intensely interested in the pebble. There was an awareness of anguish, because we'd never been so completely exposed to each other – an exposure which had nothing to do with the nakedness of our bodies. With a strange intentness she started stroking the groove cutting into the smooth round edge of the stone.

'It's a girl,' I said.

She looked up. 'I wish one could be like this,' she said. 'Like this pebble. So smooth. So whole. If I let it drop, it'll endure it, for it has no pride. It's so completely itself.'

'Jessica.'

She lifted her face towards me, still wet with water, newly born in the late light. We kissed. Not passionately at all. Almost chastely. Her eyes were shut. She dropped the pebble. Both of us were calmly conscious of its fall. And then we followed it down, to the grass below the rock, where it was softer.

'Yes,' she whispered after a long time. 'Come into me.'

And after the raging of our bodies had subsided, I lay down beside her, holding her in my arms, in the last generosity of the day's excessive sun, and slept. I don't know for how long. The sun was down when I woke up to find her awake like me, her eyes exploring mine.

I whispered, the way one does in the hours of love: 'Are you frightened?'

'No.' Her brown eyes were peaceful. 'Not now. And it's the first time for I don't know how long. But when we get back, Joseph . . . ? I'm scared that I may be frightened then.'

'Don't think of that now. Don't limit the future by forcing into any specific direction now.'

'But the future has already started.'

'We needn't exclude anything which may happen,' I pleaded. 'We needn't deny anything awaiting us. But now – is now.'

'Yes.' She sat up. 'I want it to stay now.' Then kissed me. And in a leisurely way began to caress my body, until I finally brought back her mouth to mine and entered her again, with more confidence and more passion than before, and slowly she began to moan under me, the small helpless sounds of love growing and increasing, changing finally into tears of joy as my own joy rose to meet hers in her secret depths; and when at last we separated the first stars were already out.

We remained sitting, just sitting, and the moon rose over us with quiet, mat light on her cheeks and shoulders. We knew we'd have to return soon, but we kept on postponing it until it was no longer possible, for by then the moon had grown old above the mountains.

We got up. In the dim night light I held her face between my palms. I didn't even kiss her. Her fingers were on my wrists. That was all. And yet it was the most intense contact I've ever had with anybody in all my life.

'This is you,' I whispered, with an extraordinary feeling of discovering an overwhelming truth.

And she, more softly than a whisper, barely a sigh, said: 'This is you.'

We helped each other dress; started back, reluctantly and slowly, for by now the numb fear had begun to grow.

Thinking back now, I know that nothing in my life has been more beautiful than that first innocent kiss, that first serene conversation of our bodies. But beyond that kiss and that conversation lay the night and all the wildness of the world. *Thou God seest me.*

23

Richard was called to the witness box immediately after the police evidence had been heard. He seemed thinner, and certainly much older than when I'd last seen him in April. And when he took his stand opposite me I suddenly regretted not knowing him better, and that he'd always been such an enigma to me, whereas, of all people, he might have become important to me. He looked as impressive as ever with his grey mane and the rather too deliberately chosen tie – above all things, the arrogant and slightly dishevelled gentleman. I'd always been surprised by his tendency to wear expensive modish clothes in which his large loose limbs never quite looked comfortable. And then there was that quality of what I can only describe as 'physicality' and which is, para-doxically, peculiar to some people who deliberately try to deny their bodies. In any conversation one was immediately struck by Richard's intellect and his faculty for abstract reasoning – but I could never reconcile that with his physique, his splendid mane, his angular and big-boned limbs, and above all his hairiness. However immaculately he might be dressed, like that day in court, I always remained uncomfort-ably aware of the shaggy fleece covering his arms, his chest and stomach, even his back down to the very bulge of his buttocks. Although I saw him naked only once I constantly recalled his body through Jessica's eyes. Perhaps my fascinated revulsion is the natural reaction of a hairless man to a hirsute one ('My brother Esau is an hairy man, but I am a smooth man'); or perhaps my reaction would have been the same to anybody familiar with that, so smooth and beautiful, of the woman I loved myself.

During the cross-examination Joubert soon steered the questions in the direction of our relationship :

'Mr Cole, you said that you had an appointment with the deceased on the morning of Good Friday, 14th April. But we already know that there was a relationship between her and the accused.' There was a moment filled with eyes. 'I'd like to know more about your exact role in this matter. Surely, as a writer, you must be aware of the dangers implicit in the eternal triangle?'

'I met Miss Thomson soon after her arrival in this country. She had an extremely open interest in South Africa and I undertook to acquaint her more fully with circumstances here.'

'Undoubtedly with the noblest of intentions,' said the advocate quietly. 'How unfortunate that this sort of interest should so often be open only at one end.'

24

Richard's face flushed, causing the fine network of veins across his nose and cheeks to turn a darker purple.

'Miss Thomson was a Social Anthropologist, which was the subject I used to teach at University. She regarded me as a mentor.'

'Was your relationship with Miss Thomson completely platonic, Mr Cole?'

'I cannot see that this has anything to do with the case,' Richard retorted angrily.

'On the contrary, it is of great importance to the Defence,' Joubert insisted.

The Judge folded his long thin hands. 'The Court would like to hear your answer to that question, Mr Cole.'

'I was in love with Miss Thomson from the beginning, my lord.' He stood quite still for a while, his hands tightly clenched on the railing of the witness box. 'But for a very long time there was no suggestion at all of what you are insinuating'

'The Court has asked a question, Mr Cole: it did not make an insinuation.' The Judge adjusted his robe. 'So we may assume that Miss Thomson was not interested in changing the nature of the relationship?'

'If you insist, yes.'

'But *you* would have liked to see it on a different basis?' prompted Joubert.

'I've already said that I loved her.'

'And you kept on trying to persuade her?'

Richard turned towards the Judge to protest: 'Your Lordship . . . !'

But the Judge smiled very coldly and said: 'The mentor in the role of tormentor, Mr Cole?'

Joubert: 'Were you aware of the nature of the relationship between the accused and the deceased?'

Richard: 'Only much later.' He didn't look at me. 'In the beginning I simply regarded Joseph Malan as a friend of Miss Thomson. In fact, it was I who introduced him to her. She had many friends. She always seemed to attract people to her.'

Joubert: 'And you found nothing extraordinary in such a friendship?'

Richard: 'Not where she was concerned. Of course not. I've got many black friends myself. I've never allowed my friendships to be dictated by unreasonable laws trying to keep people apart.'

The Judge: 'Please reply to the questions only, Mr Cole. This court is not interested in political speeches.' A short pause: 'I seem to recall that your political activities have landed you in trouble before. And in jail.'

Richard: 'Because three years ago in the Transkei I . . .'

The Judge: 'That is not relevant to the present case.'

Joubert: 'If your Lordship will permit me: we may find it necessary to return to that aspect at a later stage when it may be relevant.'

The Judge: 'The court will decide on that when the time comes.'

Joubert: 'Well, Mr Cole, we have now established that the friendship did not disturb you in the beginning. Can you tell us at what stage you changed your mind about it?'

Richard: 'In the course of last year I spent six months in Johannesburg doing research for a book . . .'

Joubert: 'Did you keep in touch with Miss Thomson?'

Richard: 'We corresponded.'

Joubert: 'The ordinary sort of correspondence between master and disciple?'

Richard: 'If you wish to call it that.'

Joubert: 'No love letters?'

(Whispering among the women on the gallery.)

Richard: 'Our correspondence was of a private nature.' A pause. 'All right: I did mention love in my letters.'

Joubert: 'What about her?'

Richard: 'She never said anything which made me suspect . . .'

The Judge: 'And then you returned to Cape Town. When was that?'

Richard: 'At the end of October.'

Joubert: 'And you discovered that there was something going on between Miss Thomson and the accused?'

Richard: 'I did. Quite soon.'

Joubert: 'You were shocked?'

Richard: 'I was upset.'

Joubert: 'Because Joseph Malan was Coloured?'

Richard: 'Because he was a rival.' Turning to the bench: 'Your Lordship, I am a writer. I'm interested in man, not in the colour of his skin.'

In the monotonous afternoon, a stray bee buzzing against one of the high windows, I heard Richard repeat all the statements I'd so often heard him formulate in identical words. Here in court it all sounded unreal and pretentious: his interest in 'man' had so very little to do with separate, living, moving men with hands and feet and faces. Even I – and I sometimes think even Jessica – was nothing to him but a set

26

of ideas and abstractions, created to the measure of his convictions and opinions. There was a time when I hated him, a time when I was wildly jealous of him; there was a time when I pitied him. But that day in court everything had fallen away as if it had never existed.

The advocate was as indefatigable as that bee against the window-pane. He alternated his attacks with apparently innocent questions, and these with a show of sympathy. And all the time he was boring inwards to expose all the particles he could incorporate in his system. The audience was fascinated, not by the game but by the small intimate details brought to light. Joubert persisted. He had to attack Richard's credibility and undermine all his respectability in his efforts to force him into a corner where he would have to admit something in my favour or something which might create some uncertainty about my behaviour. And so he hammered on those last few months.

Joubert: 'What did you do about the relationship between them? Did you never discuss it with Miss Thomson?'

Richard: 'Of course I discussed it. I tried to persuade her . . . What's the sense of digging it all up again?' There was a weary and desperate tone in his voice: 'It was hell for all of us, those few months.'

Joubert: 'Who were "all of us"?'

Richard: 'Jessica – Miss Thomson – and Joseph and myself. We were all at the end of our tether.'

Joubert: 'Exactly what do you mean by that?'

Richard: 'Just what I'm saying.'

Joubert: 'What happened?'

Richard: 'Nothing happened. That was what made it so unbearable. Nothing happened, but all the time we were waiting for it to happen.'

Joubert: 'For what to happen?'

Richard: 'Some sort of explosion. After all, it was quite inevitable.'

Joubert: 'Was it?'

Richard's voice was sounding more and more strained: 'Surely you realise it was an impossible situation. We couldn't bear it indefinitely.'

Tirelessly Joubert went on: 'Why do you call it an "impossible situation"?'

'But don't you understand?' For a moment Richard lost his temper. 'I loved her. I wanted her. And they . . .' He groped for words.

'Why didn't you give up when you realised it was hopeless to go on trying?'

'Because there had never been any future in her affair with Joseph.'

'And your motives for helping her were completely altruistic?'

'I loved her!'

He leaned forward across the brown railing, his heavy body supported on his hands, his elbows turned outwards. And once again the old dichotomy in him struck me, and I remembered thinking: *Oh that this too, too solid flesh would melt . . . !*

'And so it went on until April before something finally happened?'

'No. It started before then.'

'Ah, you mean you made some progress?'

'From the middle of January until late in February Joseph was away from Cape Town on a theatre tour. Miss Thomson stayed behind. She wanted to have some rest. We thought it would be a break for all of us . . .' There was perspiration on his forehead. 'It couldn't go on like that, your Lordship. We couldn't bear it for much longer.'

'And so, while the accused was away . . . ?'

He looked down. His hair covered his eyes.

'Well, Mr Cole?'

Richard pushed his hair back and for a few seconds studied his hand as if he felt surprised to find it moist. 'I can't talk about it.'

'What happened during that month, Mr Cole?' A long pause. 'You tried to comfort one another, I presume?'

He looked up slowly. 'When one reaches such an extremity, my lord, there isn't any comfort left. We only . . .'

'You made love.'

The clean blow drew a gasp from the gallery. He stood looking at the advocate for a long time before he nodded.

'So you certainly used the opportunity. Behind his back.'

'One doesn't always choose what happens to one.'

'Nonsense, Mr Cole!' Joubert was only a few inches away from him now, his eyes glittering fiercely. 'For the last half an hour you've been telling us how you were trying for months on end to get her into bed with you: don't pretend you were caught unawares! You very deliberately awaited your chance.' He rearranged his documents and when he resumed his voice was deadly calm again. 'And so, when the accused returned late in February as you indicated . . . ? I want to know what happened between you then.'

He shook his head.

'Did Miss Thomson return to him or did she stay with you? I want an answer, Mr Cole.'

28

'She went back to him.'

'And you couldn't take that.'

'I tried to accept it. I tried.'

'But it didn't work.'

'I didn't want to . . .'

'What didn't you want?'

'Please,' Richard said, quite suddenly, almost whispering. 'Have you no respect for anything?'

'I want to know what happened, Mr Cole.'

'No.'

'Shall I tell you what happened?' Joubert flung his documents down on the long table in front of him, with a sharp smacking sound like an electric shock in the courtroom. 'I put it to you that you were desperate. That you'd reached a stage where you were prepared to do anything to anybody in order to get her back. And that you approached the accused to threaten him.' It was very quiet now, only the bee went on buzzing. 'Is that correct, Cole?'

And then he broke down, in front of all those eyes. I'd previously noticed this strange phenomenon in older men who, like him, fall in love with a young girl and then become quite extravagant, almost adolescent in their reactions. But even that hadn't prepared me for this public spectacle.

'Yes,' he admitted, 'I went to warn him. I . . .' His voice broke. 'It was the only thing I could do. I had to, for all of us. I told him to stick to people of his own colour.'

'A good liberal, Mr Cole,' Joubert said dryly.

'I did it to save *him*, to save *her*. I told you it was hell. I loved them both.' He was sobbing now. And suddenly he started exclaiming melodramatically: 'I hate this country! I hate everything in this country which forces people to betray each other. For how many months have you been persecuting me? What have I done? You wanted me to break down. Well, now you have succeeded. Break me, tread on me, do anything, but for God's sake get it over. Go and tell everybody, tell the world: yes I did it, I betrayed everything I've ever believed in. But I loved her. And he was my friend. I swear it! I swear it to God!'

'That will be all for the moment, thank you, Mr Cole.' Joubert bowed towards the bench. 'If it pleases your Lordship . . .'

It must be deep in the night, but it makes no difference to the light in my cell. I've even got used to this naked bulb staring down on me like the unflinching sun-eye of God on primitive man. One does become primitive in this refined hollow of civilisation. One's need grows less, reduced to the innermost, prenatal peace. It is the form of Hindu peace into which Dulpert so often, as on that day at the morgue, withdrew himself, sitting crosslegged on his bed and intoning over and over the sacred word : 'Om. Om. Om.'

In the days of my detention before the case started I was worried by the needs of the body. I was constantly hungry, I suffered from stomach cramps, I was never without headache. But not any more. Now they're fattening me, it seems, like Hansel and Gretel.

My only real need, and that is very intense indeed, is quite illogical. In fact, I'm surprised by it myself. It is my deep need for the dark. Perhaps it is caused by the bulb burning throughout the night so that I never see the dark any more. And I'm lusting after it like – in earlier days – after a woman : a consummation, a sensual ecstacy. Often, while I'm filling my writing-paper or flushing it down the toilet, I stop to get on my bunk and touch, with my fingertips, the high barred window, trying to sniff the night outside – no longer a Cape night with an imaginable sea, but the Transvaal darkness where I'm now awaiting the dawn of the last day. Years ago primordial night would have covered the small fires of traders on this open plain filled with the mad laughter of hyenas or the deep moans of a lion. All I can hear is the occasional sound of cars approaching the city from the freeway. Yet Africa is not far off. It's as close as the night.

Even as a child I was never scared of the dark. Our nights used to be brimful of sound in the wide backyard, with the strumming of guitars and sonorous voices singing or talking; laughing. And very late, as it grew quiet, there would still be the whispering behind my mother's floral folding-screen, and the creaking of the brass bed, and the muffled moaning of her joy which excited me long before I could understand the meaning of it.

In later years there were the Cape nights in the turbulence of District Six, conversations and love in the dark, Dulpert's meang sticks, rehearsals in the backyard. And then, of course, the theatre, shifting the centre of gravity from the day's light hours to the dark: the only meaningful common denominator between Cape Town and London. Only it was so different there, those shimmering wet streets on winter

30

nights, growing more and more quiet and dark as one proceeded eastward, with sleepy faces against the windows of passing buses, like molten wax running down the glass – and then the nightness of my distant district.

There were other nights, on the boat trip back, lost in space, and yet with an awareness of the continent slowly unfolding beyond the horizon, with jungles and deserts, rivers and wonderful Ngorongoros.

Or our theatre tours: those nights after the audience had gone and we were left alone to bed down in the combi, here tonight and gone tomorrow.

The night in Bain's Kloof, and Jessica with me.

No, I've never been scared of the dark at all, after that first experience.

The night I discovered the night, I was a mere child. The Baas and his family were away for the weekend and on the Saturday there'd been a funeral: Uncle Juts had died early in the morning after a long illness and all day the men were digging away at the grave to get him laid to rest before the Sabbath dawned. In our parts funerals used to be great occasions, and when they happened during a weekend no wedding could match the festivities. By the time Uncle Juts had to be buried there was no man fit to carry him. The pig slaughtered early in the morning had already been devoured, together with dripping sweet potatoes and yellow rice with raisins; and the normal quota of wine had been augmented with a fair supply from the cellar after an unidentified guest had managed to force the door. The accordions were wailing, the guitars singing; someone had even brought a fiddle. On one side, balanced on trestles, the open coffin was waiting, more or less unattended. And it was hard on midnight when the people began to remember about the burial part of the festivities. By that time most of the fires had burnt down to smouldering ashes and there was much fumbling with the coffin in the dark. Several times on the tricky way to the little square graveyard below the vineyards the bearers stumbled and fell, without, however, interrupting their hearty singing of Psalm 136. And when, finally, the coffin was lowered and the grave filled up, most of the bearers remained sprawled across the mound, the only difference between them and the deceased being the sonorous snoring accompanying their sleep.

The next morning there was an outcry in the yard: Uncle Juts's body had been discovered lying among the protruding roots of an oak tree where the procession must have stopped after one of its many falls. With great anxiety the grave was dug up again, the coffin heaved out

31

and opened – to reveal the fiddler, Willem Gom, loudly snoring and more than half suffocated, but nevertheless saved through the inscrutable mercy of the Lord. Without much ceremony he was thrown out of the coffin, the corpse substituted, and for the rest of the Sabbath the people enjoyed the deserved rest as prescribed by the Scriptures.

Then it was evening, that Sunday night. I couldn't sleep. I waited until my mother's bed grew silent and crept out to the unearthly silent yard. There was no moon and in the light of the stars everything seemed stranger than usual. I was terrified. But with almost perverse glee I forced myself to walk across the emptiness of the yard where, the previous night, people had been celebrating the death of a man quietly lying in his coffin among the oak trees, and where, suddenly, now, there was no one but myself. In that silence the absent din of their carousing seemed louder than when it had actually happened. In the dark I felt my way barefoot over innumerable corpses across the limitless expanse of that backyard, until I finally reached the house.

The whitewashed walls were a barely perceptible smudge in the night, the windows a blacker black. I knew it was empty; the Baas and his family wouldn't return before the next morning. I stroked the smooth hard surface of the panes, the rough plaster of the walls, the oiled grain of heavy doors, the cool secret shapes of knobs and knockers. Unexpectedly, the kitchen door gave way. There was no reason why that should surprise me: the house was always left open for the coming and going of servants, the carrying in and out of milk pails, the fetching of flour and sugar, the depositing of eggs. And yet it came as a shock to feel the door opening under my hand. It was as if, on opening night, walking across the stage before the performance for a final check on props and positions, one suddenly heard a swishing sound and swung round to find the curtains opening to the waiting audience.

It was like a sign. I could do nothing else but enter and explore. My journey through the night had brought me there and I couldn't turn back.

I entered the kitchen. It smelled of burnt coffee and blue soap. Step by step I went on, bumping against strange objects, confronted by menacing walls. I wasn't looking for anything, I didn't want to get anywhere, I simply went further and further.

Here and there I caught the faint glimmering of porcelain or silver or brassware behind the glass doors of stinkwood and yellowwood armoires. But nothing was recognisable. This was Ultima Thule, the

32

House of the Baas, the heart of the great *Thou-shalt-not* which dominated my childhood years.

It was a large room, blacker than all the others because the curtains were drawn. I bumped against a heavy object and heard invisible strings reverberating in my ears. I couldn't breathe, from pure shock. But I stretched out my hands to feel all over that smooth, strange thing. Even after I'd realised that it was the piano on which Hermien used to play in the daytime, my brain refused to accept or admit it. It remained: The Thing. I lifted the lid, removed the cloth, and silently ran a finger down the row of notes. There was no sound, but with every inch my finger moved there was a *possibility* of sound. Only when I reached the last note did I dare to press it. I listened to the deep bass sound booming in the night like a stone falling in a pool and causing ripples, expanding and fading circles of sound, more and more distantly, diminishing into the barest whisper on the far horizon between sound and silence; and then I pressed the note down again, and again heard it gently vibrating, not only away from me, but right into me, through flesh and bones, to where the body itself stopped and something more remote began. And in that silence, in that sound which made the silence audible, I discovered the night. Then, with a strange feeling of contentment, I picked up the cover and placed it across the ivory notes, and closed the lid, and found my way back to the world of the dead and the living outside.

And now the night is my constant guardian, a great fish which has swallowed me. I find a form of comfort in it which the day lacks, an innocence like that I knew with Jessica: for the night used to be our domain, it was the landscape of our love. To us the night meant safety and protection against the dangerous world with the innumerable eyes.

Dulpert once told me: if one is a Brahman or some other nobleman in India, the quality of one's courage is determined by heroic deeds or one's power to sacrifice; but for a man belonging to a lower caste courage is synonymous with *kshatriya*, the word for night – because among the pariahs the only conceivable form of courage is the courage to endure.

After the verdict, and just before I was led out to the police van, Mr Joubert visited me in the cell below the courtroom. I suppose it is normal procedure, and in a way I appreciated his acting so correctly until the very last.

'Well . . .' He was standing with his robe draped over one shoulder. 'So now it's all over.'

'Yes,' I admitted, since I couldn't really deny it. From his point of view it was, indeed, all over, and at that precise moment, neither sooner nor later.

'I've tried my best.' He sounded annoyed. 'If only you'd been prepared to say something yourself. Just once. If you'd made the slighest effort to help me . . .'

'I'm sorry.' At that moment it was the truth. The Judge had complimented him on the way in which he'd conducted a difficult case, but with my co-operation he could have made an even better impression. In his profession that sort of thing carries weight.

They came to take me away. For a moment we remained facing each other. He shoved his brief-case under his left arm and offered me his right hand, 'Good luck,' he said.

And for his sake I played the game and said: 'Thanks.'

With a final and somehow unexpected hint of hesitation, as I was already walking towards the door, he said: 'There are a few points I'd really like to have cleared up . . .' Then he lit a cigarette and shrugged. 'Not that it would have made any difference, I suppose. We had all the facts of the case before us.'

In the back of the police van, and soon afterwards in the train to the North, his words remained with me, and I still can't get rid of them. The facts of the case. Everybody was so concerned about that, and so sure about that.

That is what I now have to sort out and weigh again. Because one forgets, one forgets, even a body forgets. And yet it must remain hidden somewhere, secret in the blood. That is what I must rediscover to find its arcane meaning.

But where does it lead one? Truth is not a collection of facts which can be narrated but a landscape through which one travels in the dark. And my particular journey has its origin far beyond Bain's Kloof, beyond Jessica, immensely far beyond myself. I am really an almost incidental moment in a pattern fulfilling itself over generations and centuries and in infinite space.

Two

The story of our family which my mother so regularly told me in my youth, with endless variations and additions and embroideries from her active imagination, was usually interspersed with stories from the Bible, with the result that those two worlds often fused in my mind, all the more so since the names from both were so similar: Adam and Moses, Abraham, Rachel, Leah, Daniel and David, Jacob, down to Joseph. It is more than likely that she exploited the parallels with the Jews of the Old Testament, although I doubt that she ever did so consciously. To her, our story, despite the twists and turns she gave it in her manifold renderings, was the one abiding thing of comfort and pride and respectability in a life which all too often experienced the defeat of the spirit by the flesh.

My father had gone to the war when I was a mere baby, so I have no personal memories of him at all, only a dim photograph with an enigmatic smile, and then, of course, the facts and fiction of my mother's many stories. 'You must look up, Joseph. Remember your Fa'rer and his peoples. I'm nothing, I'm a orphan born and bred. But he's different, he's got a hist'ry jus' like enny white man. Don' forget that.'

She never tried to find a larger pattern in the chronicle of our family and it may be presumption or wishful thinking on my part to do so. In fact, the very effort, over the years, may have prompted manipulations and inventions in my own gradual reconstruction of our story, so that, by now, every episode in it seems to have become a station on an endless *via dolorosa* – as if it had been destined that in each new generation all the sin and suffering of an entire society should find its sacrificial victim in our tribe. It is certainly no reason for pride! In fact, it is in the very ordinariness and the unexceptionalness of our chronicle that I find the agony which propagates itself from century to century, assuming new avatars according to the demands of each new age.

What has been delivered to me, distorted by retelling over many generations, reshaped, and re-created by myself through the years and through my months of imprisonment, is no longer history at all but mythology. Yet how often in the course of time has mythical possibility not proved more valid than historical fact?

I don't even know where it really started. The first my mother could recall was an episode like the one in Genesis when the sons of God chose wives from the daughters of men. Only, in our story, the son of God was a giant of a man with a tall plumed hat and black eyes and a pointed black beard visiting a wine farm on the outskirts of Stellenbosch late in the eighteenth century; and the daughter of men was a young slave girl of thirteen or fourteen, Leah by name and presumably Malay. He pressed a rix dollar in her small yellow hand after he'd had his way with her behind the haystack, his hair and beard and cloak dishevelled and covered with straw. Soon after, it seems, her master got word of the money and accused her of stealing it from the house. It was confiscated and she was led to the yard where her clothes were ripped of and she was tied, naked, to a pole, after which the farmer's two young sons took turns to flog her with a rhino whip until the blood streaked down her legs. She finally lost consciousness without uttering a sound. Nine months later, again without a sound, she gave birth to a boy.

With a fine sense of history she christened him Adam, adding the surname Malan. It was, of course, customary procedure at the time for slaves to assume the surname of their masters, but our chronicle excludes that possibility, insisting, instead, that Leah deliberately named the boy after the man with the tall hat. Hence my claim to Huguenot descent.

That is all I know about Leah. Whether she finally died a violent death or whether she died in extreme old age, toothless and desiccated, her head a small baked apple on a frail bundle of skin and bones, after a lifetime of patient, passive suffering, I cannot tell.

If one thinks of it: a child's fear in the dark, her barefoot excursions across fields white with frost, her games in a vineyard or at a riverside; the dread of growing up in the budding breasts and the first sight of blood; the cycle of work and sleep and work, the slow maturing of a woman and the process of ageing when the grasshopper has become a burden, the fear of death or the longing for it, the rough or tender game with men who want to humiliate or honour her body; probably hunger, worries about children, the short pleasures of a birth here, a wedding there, the plodding of feet in the thin procession to the graveyard: if one thinks of all the pleasure and pain of threescore years and ten, of the pitcher broken at the fountain and the song of bride and bridegroom falling silent . . . if one thinks of everything happening around the insignificant axis of her life : a Dutch East India Company going bankrupt while the colonists celebrate the French fashions; conflagration in Europe and British Occupation of the Cape, revolts in the interior, negotiations and quarrels with tribes beyond the mountains; wars and bribery, the extravagant parties of Lady Anne Barnard, the military parades in the Cape's broad streets . . . if one thinks of all this, her life dwindles into obscurity, reduced to those three moments : a struggle in a haystack, the contortions of a body under a whip, a night of birth. God, it's so little. But that is all I have of her after two hundred years, all I can honour. The reckless son of God took the shy small daughter of men, and something was born from it, an agony of futility which can never subside or die away.

Not much more is known about Adam, although, at least, our mythology includes his beginning and his end. The first years of his life seemed to have been spent more or less uneventfully on the wine farm. I can imagine a man with skilful hands, and my mother felt sure that he could read and write as well, no mean achievement in that age. So I presume he was valued by his master and treated kindly by a Godfearing man who must have appreciated that servants deserved food and punishment at the appointed times.

In due course he acquired a wife, but when at the age of twenty or so he was sold to one Claassen, a frontier boer from Graaff-Reinet, she had to stay behind. My mother's romantic imagination led her to believe that the separation caused a grudge in him but I can't vouch for it — after all, one doesn't expect a slave to indulge in the luxury of feeling or thinking and if he really had so much temerity it certainly served him right to suffer for it.

Claassen wasn't a very rich man and after paying a high price for the new slave he probably treated him particularly well. I can't imagine him ever working for more than fourteen or fifteen hours a day, except, of course, during the harvest time or while the ewes were lambing. Adam was given enough flour, he was allowed to have his own vegetable garden, and whenever a sheep died of bluetongue or worms or something else the labourers were generously allowed to have the meat.

A few years after his arrival on the farm he took another wife. Her

37

name was Martha, or Miriam, or Maria – my mother usually mixed them up. She was a slave like him, apparently more Hottentot than Malay, and several years older than Adam. In spite of the age difference one gets the impression that the relationship between them was of a particularly intense nature, and if they hadn't been slaves one might well have used the word 'love'.

Their first child died soon after birth and the mother very nearly didn't survive. The second child lived, but once again the mother's health was severely impaired. It was a particularly busy time of the year, so the Baas couldn't very well afford to give her a few days off, which may account for the fact that she never quite recovered.

When the baby, Moses, was two years old his mother fell pregnant again. According to my reckoning that must have been around 1810 or 1812. Martha (or Maria, or Miriam) was five or six months gone when the farmer's eldest son, approaching the age of discretion, chose her as the object of some experimentation to prepare himself for matrimony. Whether the youth was particularly violent in his clumsiness or whether Miriam's condition was precarious anyway, is difficult to make out. The 'facts of the case' simply reveal that she died of a miscarriage a few days later, whereupon Adam approached the young Claassen and would have strangled him but for the father's timely appearance on the scene.

Adam was tied between two wagon wheels, flogged, and left for dead; but our people are tough and after a few weeks he was ready to resume his work on the farm. Claassen called him to the stone house on the hill, subjected him to a long reading from the Scriptures and then, as token of his magnanimity, offered him a small *sopie* of home-made brandy. In return for his generosity, right there beside the Bible and the barrel in the voorhuis with the dung-plastered floor, Adam killed the Baas.

He spent the night in his own mud hut with his small son, waiting for them to come for him. They arrived the next morning, farmers from all the neighbouring farms, and after testing his toughness with sjamboks and thongs for a couple of hours, which fortunately landed him in a state of near-unconsciousness, he was laid down spreadeagled on the ground, his wrists and ankles tied to four horses, and then, in the presence of all the other labourers and slaves, including his two-year-old son, the horses were suddenly lashed very violently on their rumps, causing them to start off towards the north, east, south and west respectively. It's not a neat way to die, but very quick. And afterwards, as always when some animal had died on the farm, the meat was given to the labourers, this time for burial. The Lord gave, and the Lord hath taken away.

II

Moses was an enigmatic character, possibly as a result of what he'd been forced to witness on the farm that morning. Soon after the event the farm was sold, together with all the cattle and furniture and slaves and other movables. An elderly slave woman took Moses in her care. He was a difficult child, and she used to have only one remedy for every problem – a proper thrashing; but in our chronicle she fulfilled the important function of telling Moses the story of his parents.

He must have been about ten when he ran away for the first time. The Baas brought him back driving him out in front of his horse; and the old woman forced his wanton feet into a newly made fire to prevent future escapades of that nature. But as soon as he'd recovered, he was off again, this time trying to reach the Mission Station at Bethelsdorp, probably unaware of the fact that after the Black Circuit not much help could be expected from those quarters.

He was brought back once more, and this time all the labourers were punished with half-rations to ensure that they would keep an eye on him. He survived their wrath with considerable difficulty and escaped as soon as he'd regained the use of his legs.

By this time the Baas seemed to have accepted that the boy was useless; so he took him to the Drosdty at Graaff Reinet to be flogged and branded, and sold him to a travelling trader.

The few years he spent in the company of this *smous* became the only peaceful period of his life. There were only the two of them : once a year they came to Cape Town for provisions, then turned back on the long rough road of the interior and the frontier districts. It was during that time that he picked up his astounding knowledge of Cape laws : every new slave regulation he could recite by heart. He was completely illiterate, of course, but had a prodigious memory for songs and rhymes, and wherever they came he was called upon to reproduce his repertoire to buyers and visitors. It was good for business and being a reasonable man, the trader never failed to reward Moses with a few rix dollars.

He never spent the money but saved it all in an old scarf. The day the slaves were freed, he used to say, he wanted to be a man of means. That such a day would come he never doubted. All the signs were favourable: the never-ending amendments to the slavery laws, the clamorous meetings of owners from year to year. Heaven knows how, but he also got hold of odd strands of the prevalent philosophies overseas – overhearing a group of farmers here, eavesdropping on a meeting of townsmen elsewhere, listening to the small talk of the *smous*, something of Dr Philip, something of Wilberforce, something, belatedly, of Jean-Jacques.

Moses started addressing his own gathering wherever they stopped over. After reciting his verses and singing his songs for the trader's crowd he would disappear to address small groups of slaves or labourers from the vicinity: strange, confused words about liberty, equality, fraternity; about a Promised Land in which he believed as implicitly as his own namesake. Oh, dangerous ancestor of mine!

I can't imagine anybody taking him seriously, least of all the slaves in his audience. But *he* believed, and a fire was kindled inside him. Gradually the rumours spread, until the people approached the *smous* to complain. Did he know he was sheltering an agitator? Was he a member of Philip's crowd? He laughed it off. Nonsense, Moses didn't mean it seriously. Who paid attention to a slave? But the rumours persisted. Less than a year later it was common cause that the *smous* was a foreign agent who'd come to incite the slaves against their masters. On a dark night his wagon was ambushed in a ford near Swellendam. They probably hadn't meant to do more than give him a good scare, but the sudden attack convinced the *smous* that they were a band of marauders and he promptly grabbed his gun. In the violent battle that followed he was shot dead.

Moses ran off with his scarf full of rix dollars, and for the next few years he disappeared completely from our annals. The first that was seen of him again was in the early '30s when he made his appearance on a farm at Bruintjieshoogte looking for work. He presented himself as a free Hottentot and presumably appeared reliable and skilful enough to be hired on the spot.

The farm belonged to the Greeff brothers, all three youngish, with a great reputation for their home-made brandy and their success with the frontier ladies. They had little time for the laws of the Colony and made a habit of raiding cattle from across the frontier. Not that they really needed more cattle, but they were game for anything which involved a contravention of the Englishman's laws.

Before the end of his first year on the farm Moses, with his talk of freedom and his very attitude, had stirred up a restlessness among the other labourers. Then, one evening, they came upon him swimming in the river and saw the old scars of the cat-o'-nine-tails on his back and the weals left by the branding iron on his buttocks, and before the day was out everybody on the farm knew that he was a runaway slave.

The three brothers sent for him, inspected his body and then, with some trouble – they had to knock off his jaw – managed to get the whole story out of him. After dealing with him in a fitting manner they dragged him back to his hut where they ransacked everything and discovered the rix dollars tied up in the scarf. These were duly confiscated and Moses was informed that henceforth he'd have to work without wages, as befitted a slave.

Three weeks later he ran away – or tried to, for he was still rather weak, so that they caught up with him in a few days. The brothers didn't bother to deal with the matter personally. One of them casually gave him a blow over the head with a piece of wood, which may have been the reason why he never fully recovered his wits; for the rest, two of the house slaves were instructed to punish him. They did a thorough job as Moses never tried to run away again.

This was, more or less, the state of affairs when the eldest of the Greef brothers decided to take themselves a wife. On the eve of the wedding all the neighbours, some as far as two days' travelling away, were gathered on the farm for the festivities. The womenfolk huddled inside while the men were drinking and cavorting in the farmyard.

There happened to be a young black woman on the farm, a particularly attractive girl called Sbongile. A few months earlier the brothers had brought her back, with a herd of cattle, from a tribe across the Fish River, with the intention of preparing her for kitchen service after the projected marriage. And as the sport reached a climax on that evening, with Sbongile serving the men from huge platters of venison and pumpkin, and Moses keeping the brandy glasses filled, someone had the brilliant idea of getting the two to 'perform' for them. Sbongile tried to flee, but was caught and forced to the ground amid great shouts of glee, and Moses, encouraged with a sjambok, was forced to rape the loudly wailing Sbongile.

For the wedding guests that was the end of the affair and the next

41

day the eldest Greeff brother and his bride were duly united in holy matrimony. But for Moses and Sbongile it was only a grotesque beginning. When their baby was born nine months later he called the child Daniel, and she Dlamini. Moses didn't know a word of Xhosa, and Sbongile was completely unfamiliar with Dutch. Yet they stayed together and, according to our family tradition, especially in my mother's sentimental version, they were pathetically fond of each other. She protected the crazy Moses from the taunts of the other men, and he looked after her. As she slowly managed to learn something of his language, he recited all his old rhymes to her and sang his silly little songs.

People passing by their shack at night regularly heard Moses addressing Sbongile and the baby in the language of Wilberforce and Rousseau, on man born free and now in chains, and on the day of liberation drawning near. Wide-eyed and patient, Sbongile listened to his harangues while Dlamini/Daniel slept or gurgled or stared. Moses asked no more. And in the daytime he did his work, as thoroughly as any ox or ass, so that the Greeffs were satisfied and he was left in peace.

Slowly, as time passed, the rumours about liberation became more and more persistent. The other labourers were dumb with disbelief: this man in their midst must surely be bewitched to have predicted the event so long ago. December 1834, December 1834, December 1834: that was the magic word from the Cape to the Great Fish River. And Moses became more and more inspired in his sermons on the Promised Land.

But early in October he became delirious – something in his head, they said, which had never properly healed – and before the end of the month, before he could witness the liberation he had preached, he quietly died one evening. The Lord gave and the Lord hath taken away; blessed be the name of the Lord.

III

It was as if, with the appearance of Dlamini/Daniel, a darker and more secret stream of African passivity entered our blood. I find him stranger and more stubborn than any of the others, more difficult to fathom. Yet, I must admit that I sometimes feel myself closer to him than to any of my other ancestors. I can remember how his name used to intrigue me as a child, how the doubleness and strangeness of that Dlamini/

Daniel excited my imagination, so that it is difficult, today, to distinguish between what I was told about him and what, in the course of time, I thought up for myself.

He is the only man in our chronicle who ever grew old. None of the others was his match in years; I myself am thirty-three. And this is our end. The possibility of a future has died in Jessica's womb.

The Greeff brothers decided to keep Sbongile and her son, presumably on the assumption that, never officially a slave, she couldn't be liberated with the others either. Sbongile didn't complain. A few months after December 1834, while the brothers were off on a new raid across the border, she simply took her child and a bundle of clothes and went off. I can vaguely remember my mother talking about some time spent in the Kat River Settlement, but I'm not sure about the particulars. All I know is that she finally reached Cape Town. And there she disappeared for good.

Dlamini/Daniel was eight or nine at the time, living with his mother in a shanty of boards and thatch in the Upper Cape, when, one afternoon, she left for the harbour where she often found something to do. But that afternoon she didn't come home and when he set out to look for her he lost his way. For weeks he barely managed to survive. Grabbing a few oranges from a stand on Green Market Square one morning, he was caught redhanded by an officer on horseback. Dlamini/Daniel was convinced that his last hour had come, but fortunately for him the officer belonged to a younger generation of liberal-minded men. He felt pity for the miserable urchin, took him back to his own house and offered him food and a bed in a ramshackle storeroom. He was washed and scrubbed, his hair meticulously cleaned of lice, and then he was dressed in livery and put in the care of the cook. The children soon became fond of him, taught him to read and write, and treated him as combination of playmate and household pet.

One Christmas he was given a guitar. It became a turning-point in his life. Music opened up something inside him of which he'd never been aware before.

Soon afterwards the officer's term at the Cape expired and the family made preparations for their return to London. They wanted to take Dlamini/Daniel with them, the noble little savage from Darkest Africa, and musical as well. But in the chaos of getting everything on board the guitar was mislaid and when the boy raced back to retrieve it at the last minute, the gangway was hauled up and he had to remain standing on the quayside as the ship heaved and swayed past the rollers, churning out white foam from under the high rump. And then he went back into the dusky city on his own. All his other possessions had disappeared on the ship; but he had his guitar.

He managed to get odd jobs from time to time, but most employers were sceptical. He was much too smart for their liking, he wouldn't know his place. In at least one respect their distrust may have been well founded: Dlamini/Daniel wasn't a reliable worker. One might order him to do something in the garden, but if one came back an hour later he'd be sitting somewhere strumming his guitar.

Later he started wandering through the land with his music, the thin boy, the thin young man, always half-hungry, always tattered. Today in Cape Town, tomorrow in Tulbagh, in three months' time in Uitenhage. He must have been twenty or so when he became *mantoor* or overseer on a farm in Klapmuts district. The farmer, a widower, was getting on in years and didn't care very much about anything, which suited Dlamini/Daniel.

The man had no fewer than five nubile daughters, of whom the youngest was fifteen; the others were sixteen, eighteen and nineteen; the eldest, from a previous marriage, being much older, about twenty-five. The younger ones were fine and full-breasted farm girls, blonde and brimful of energy. But the oldest, Jacoba, poor thing, had a severe squint and more than a hint of moustache on her upper lip.

Every weekend the farm was crowded with suitors on horseback visiting the four younger girls from many miles around (Dlamini/Daniel had to look after the horses), and the nineteen-year-old was already engaged. But at fully twenty-five poor Jacoba had never known a beau. Apparently she had on one occasion tried to drown herself in the duckpond, but it so happened that a suitor of one of her stepsisters passed by and dragged her out, dripping wet, to the merciless mirth of the four young bitches.

What happened next is an almost classical situation on which I've often imagined endless variations of detail. Dlamini/Daniel was sitting on the broad whitewashed wall enclosing the farmyard, fitting new gutstrings to his guitar. The farmer had gone to town, the labourers were far away chanting on the fields, three of the blonde sisters were occupied in the house while the fourth, still untamed, had gone riding on her stallion. The yard was a peaceful expanse of shade and sun-patches, with occasional interruptions of sound: a strident female voice

44

shouting on the lands, the creaking and moaning and splashing of the watermill, pigs grunting or squealing, the contented clucking of a hen with a brood of chickens. A Stanislavsky *mise en scène*. Dlamini/Daniel was patiently testing his strings, strumming with a thumb, stroking with a forefinger, when Jacoba approached through the trees. He glanced up and went on tuning the guitar.

'I heard you,' she said, after watching him in embarrassed silence for a while. 'I often listen at my window when you're playing.'

His thumb moved along the deep droning bass of the lowest string.

'You never mix with anyone,' she tried again. 'You must be very lonely.' With intense concentration she pried a bit of bark from the tree beside the wall.

'So what?' he said, starting on the second string.

'It's hell for me too.' She looked down at the bit of bark disintegrating between her busy fingers. 'Have you noticed how they're treating me? Like dirt. But I'm a person too. Just like them.' She looked straight at him. 'Just like you.'

His eyes swept across her face, but he said nothing.

She came closer, took the half-finished guitar from his hands and studied it. 'How do you get it so smooth?' she asked.

'Takes a long time.'

'D'you like it?'

'I like it.' He took it back and started fastening the peg holding the second string.

'I've often listened when you're playing,' she repeated.

She leaned closer to watch his hands more attentively. For a long time they were silent. Then she moved. Her breast brushed against his arm. They tensed. He went on working, more jerkily than before and conscious, with every movement, of her breast pressing against his elbow. He could hear her breathing faster and when he looked up again, briefly, he could see small specks of perspiration on her hairy upper lip. His eyes shied away, but he had to look up again. She fascinated him like a sore, like a wound.

She stared straight at him, one eye slightly off course. 'I've never had a man,' she said hoarsely.

'I'm busy. You must go home.'

She touched his leg where he sat on the high wall beside her.

'You needn't be afraid, they won't know,' she said. God knows what it must have cost her. 'And I know you're lonely too.'

45

He swallowed, and shrugged.

'These youngsters calling on my sisters – they're not my size. I don't want to have anything to do with them. But you . . . I've heard people say . . .' More drops of perspiration on her lip, her eyes greedily watching him, with a terrible insistence now that she couldn't turn back any more. 'They say – a brown man is more . . . manly.' He stopped working and stared at her. Her fingers were moving across his thigh, upwards. 'People say you're bigger there . . . better than white men, they say, more . . . more manly. Is it true?'

The guitar was silent between them.

'Is it true, Daniel?'

It was as if the lighter half of his name broke the spell, as if withholding the darker half, she set something free in him. With hate in his eyes he looked down on her white face, now a feverish red, the mouth half-opened and panting, her breasts still pressing against his arm.

He lifted his leg and kicked her.

'My God, Daniel!' Instead of going away she grabbed him.

He hit out with the guitar, shattering it on her head.

She stumbled out of reach and started tearing her dress to shreds. He watched her hair cascading over her shoulders, her breasts tumbling out. Screaming, she ran home, blundering over the protruding roots of the trees in the yard.

Dlamini/Daniel waited until he could no longer hear her, then picked up the guitar and, with shaking hands, tried to repair the damage. After a while the younger sisters appeared at the back door, with Jacoba sobbing and gesticulating among them. But they didn't come nearer, merely stood there staring at him; and he looked down and pretended to go on working feverishly.

It was dusk before he saw the farmer returning on his horse. Shortly afterwards the old man came out to him from the house, gun in hand.

Dlamini/Daniel didn't move.

Ten yards away the old man stopped. 'Bastard!' he shouted. 'I'm going to shoot you to pieces!'

'It wasn't me.'

At the first shot Dlamini/Daniel abandoned his guitar and fled. From the top of the wall the farmer fired again. He took the shot in the hip, but in some miraculous way still managed to reach the fringe of the wood beyond the yard. It was equally inexplicable that they didn't pursue him – perhaps the old man was scared of being surprised in the dark.

46

For a few months Dlamini/Daniel kept to the woods like an animal. When he finally emerged, he was skin and bones, with a lame hipbone jutting out at an awkward angle. He made his way back to the Cape and started working on a new guitar.

One night, as he was playing on the corner in front of the old theatre, a group of Coloureds struck up a conversation with him; and when they finally went home they took the musician back with them.

There followed a short spell of peace, the last he knew in his long life – for very soon he fell in love with the neighbour's daughter Anna, whose father, not at all in favour of a lame son-in-law, tried to force a break-up: and when friendly reasoning or angry threats proved useless, one night in a drunken frenzy he hit Dlamini/Daniel in the face with an iron pole and threw him out of the house. In the small hours Anna came to pick him up and together they disappeared into the night. For him the night was endless now, for the blow had damaged both his eyes.

They used to stay over wherever Anna could land a job, sometimes for a year or even for three or four, sometimes for a matter of months or weeks: then it was back on the road. Across the new Outeniqua Pass to George, following the brass bugle of the mailcoach to Grahamstown and the frontier. When life became dangerous there,they would pack up again, to Graaff-Reinet, back to Cape, and then off on another inland journey, this time following the Cedarberg coach, past Britstown, into the vast arid spaces of the interior. Anna looked after the children, coped with kitchen work, took in washing, even worked as a field hand in harvest time. Dlamini/Daniel, growing thinner and thinner through the years, shrinking away into himself, learned to make new musical instruments with a pocket-knife, guitars and flutes, to amuse him through the dark days; or else he would simply sit there, unmoving, contemplating the invisible world.

In due course they produced four children, two boys and two girls. The oldest girl died of the croup before she'd reached the age of two. It was a bad winter, which also ruined Anna's health: at night Dlamini/Daniel could hear her coughing with such violence that it sounded as if her thin body was torn to pieces, but she never complained and got angry if he mentioned it.

When the oldest boy was ten he had to step out and help earn some money for the family. As they were up in Namaqualand at that time he was booked in with a fisherman of Lambert's Bay. A year later they were

47

told that his boat had capsized in a storm and the whole crew drowned.

After that Anna seemed to decline more rapidly. The boy had been her favourite. One night Dlamini/Daniel heard her coughing again, but when he spoke to her, she said: 'It's awright, don' worry.' The next morning she was dead beside him.

Things were really bad then. The second boy was only nine, the smallest girl no more than four, and Dlamini/Daniel wasn't fit for any work at all. What they couldn't get through begging they had to steal. So back to Cape Town where the boy could help out on the market and Dlamini/Daniel could rely on the occasional christening or wedding to entertain the guests with his music. Else he would take up position at the entrance to the Gardens and his precocious little Rachel would dance while he played the guitar: a few more pennies.

Strange to think how little of the country's official history appears in my chronicle, as if we've always existed apart from it. During Dlamini/Daniel's lifetime the Great Trek took place, and then the battle of Blood River was fought against the Zulus of Dingaan; Natal was annexed by the British and new Boer Republics were founded in the interior; Bains Kloof Pass was built by convicts, and the Xhosas were exterminated through the tragic dreams of Nonquasi; a thousand miles of railways were built, there was a decisive battle at Rorke's Drift, the Cape evolved from Representative to Responsible Government; Barney Barnato grew rich in Kimberley and on the goldfields of the north, and Rhodes began to dream of a highway through Africa; in Paarl a small group of patriots launched a movement to promote a new language, in the Orange Free State a President tried to placate King Moshesh with a barrel of gunpowder, in the north a first Boer War was fought and the name of Kruger became a household word.

Of all that there is no mention in my chronicle. It surrounds our story but forms no part of it. For my tale is not history, but, at most, the shadow-side of history.

When Dlamini/Daniel's son was fourteen he got a job at the Cape railway station where he landed under a train seven months later. The blind man took his daughter Rachel, then nine years old, and left for the diamond fields. How he'd make his fortune there, he couldn't tell, but everybody took that road in the '70s. And as it turned out, he managed to make a reasonable existence playing in pubs and canteens, at balls and weddings and amateur theatricals.

The money kept him alive, but he was deeply worried about the effect of the wild digger's life on Rachel. She was a quiet and unassuming child : and beautiful too, but that, of course, he didn't know. They must have formed a singular pair, with him so dark, his negroid head disproportionately large for his weak frame, his hip lopsided and his hands enormous – and the small girl so gentle and reserved, with her large black eyes and grave face.

He'd never been much of a talker, and now he spoke even less, only to Rachel. Over and over he told her the story of his father and his father's father, back to where I started, probably in the same way my mother used to tell it to me, only more seriously and slowly, with a greater sense of ritual.

Rachel was sixteen when she ran away with a man – a white man, they said. Dlamini/Daniel packed his few possessions on a rickety donkey-wagon and set off, with only a skinny dog to keep him company, looking for Rachel.

From time to time he heard rumours of her, but even those died away. Still he went on trekking through the vast land, from pure habit, because he could no longer stop. Where shall we sleep tonight, here or there? It doesn't matter, not at all, the night is the same everywhere.

There's not much more to tell, because for the account of his last years Rachel later had to rely on rumours and hearsay. She only knew about the donkey-wagon and the dog. And that the dog also died in the end, all flesh being grass; and that even then he went on trekking.

On through the limitless land, across the dusty plains of the Karoo where the heat lay trembling, through the Cold Bokkeveld in winter, the wheels crushing the hard snow, across impossible mountain passes, up to the Great River and beyond, past the Big Hole, through the merciless wastes of the north-west, then back along the ribbed dunes of the coast to the undulating wheatfields and vineyards of Swartland and Boland. The wagon began to fall apart, the voice of the guitar grew thin, the donkey died. And where he died, the story goes, Dlamini/Daniel sat down at the roadside : I usually imagine it high up in Bain's Kloof where the dead convicts had been plastered up in the concrete walls. When people stopped to offer him lifts, he shook his great grey head above the thin skeletal body and said no, he was all right just there, and hadn't they seen his daughter Rachel anywhere?

There he died. Not of old age or suffering or illness, but simply because it was too much trouble to go on. And history went its inexor-

able way and nothing changed and no cock crowed, not a thistle-seed
was disturbed in the wind. For, really, he was less than a sparrow and it
must have been easy for the Lord to take away what he'd given.

IV

It was remarkable how my mother always, when she reached Rachel's
part of the story, switched to the first person. As what I'm saying mos.
To leave him jus' like that. Must've been med I was, but what do you
do when love take you? It's not, no, as what I didn' love my fa'rer, but
jiss, one's only swiet sixteen once in a lifetime hey, and it's not as if it
was all roses and moonshine. So this men come en' he's white en' oll, so
what could I say! Thisaway en' thataway, but there I was, full in the
flower en' it's mos flower what he's looking for. Irishman they sed he
were, en' suts a nice men too with that red beard. But what about my
fa'rer, I said to him. Don' worry men, he said, I'll fix yo' fa'rer. Jus'
come with me to Port Lizbit en' we take the shippietjie beck to Ireland,
then we send yo' fa'rer money like he never sawed befo'.

En' so he take me away from the Diekens oll in the night, jus' stars
where you look men, en' he speak so sof'ly en' he take me so gen'ly, so
how could I say no? No, he didn' break in, it was with consent, I said
yes take me. I'm yours, make with me what you want, men, en' if it
must break my poor old fa'rer's heart, it's ok maar just too bed for I love
you.

So we get on the road oll the way to Port Lizbit, it give one a chance
to think, en' when we got there I ask him : What now 'bout my fa'rer?
I ask. Bogger yo' fa'rer, he say. You coming with me or not, hey? The
Lawd God know if I made a mistake there, but I said : So awright, I
said, I stay jus' here. You go to hell, he say, blerry hotnot. En' there I
sit, I didn't even go to the harber the day he took his shippietjie, praise
de Lawd.

Awright, I thought, now I go to my fa'rer. But it's jus' then what I see
I'm in trubble, men So what can I do now? I'm in trubble. How can I
go beck en' tell my fa'rer I got a men's child here in me? En' he with
his bline eyes en' oll

Latertimes I thought yes, I must maar have gone. Ollytime he gave
me the word of don' you do as those other skollies, my chile, you got
class, yo' body is a temple of the Lawd. But he would hef taked me beck.

Ennyway, it's now too late and I'm not complaining. So I go to Grahams-town, barmaid is what I was in one of the canteens there in the New Street until as what I couldn't stand on my two legs enny more. En' that's where Braampie was borned. I thought I was dying out that night, hell, men, it's mos a bed to be alone en' me not quite seventeen, jiss.

Thet Braampie, men! So pretty it made one afraid jus' from looking, you could see the mark of de Lawd on him. Quite, newwe' even cried, jus' lie like thet en' look at the world with that big eyes he got. En' white! Got it from his fa'rer of course. There's not meny whites what is as white as thet, en' then that blonde hair en' blue eyes, men. Abraham Malan I beptised him inne name of de Lawd, 'cause he was mos mine, name en' surname de lot, he was not a demn that blerry Irishman's chile, it's tog mos I what walked with him oll the months, en' who's going to kerry on our name inne world if he can't take it?

Meantime I cared fo' him. It was helltimes, men! Where could I now get work? I can't let my chile look like a hotnot, he must get clothes en' he must get good food, he's mos white. So we go to Cape Town, it's more open there for work. I put on my one decent outfit en' I walk myself dead. Five days, then I find a dressmakery en' the men say yes, he want a seamstress, but where's yo' references? Try me, I say, praise the Lawd.

We'll see, he say. We'll see. En' he give me a lot of dresses to sew. Big room where we all sit together, high windows, not so good for the light, but ennyway, we work on to sunset. The others get going, but the men come en' stend inne door en' he say: You come a bietjie to the office, Rachel.

I go. Big office what he hed, papers left right and centre, en' a long sofa inne corner. Remem'er it to my dying day, thet sofa with the red upholstery. He close the door en' now he's bigger than ewwer in his life.

Come here, he say. I won't bite you.

I stay where I am.

You want the job? he ask.

I want the job, Master. God, I got a chile. Now don't let a poor . . .

Shaddap, he say. Lie down.

There's a spider what I saw on the ceiling, one of the sort with long legs, you know mos. First I think it's a crack, he sit so still, but then I see no, it's mos a spider en' he watch everything down there. Through that whole week he sit en' look et me, en' only when it's Friday what shall I see but that the blerry thing is mos dead a long time ago.

Gimme my money now, I say to the Baas, my week is out.

What money? he ask. I paid you in services rendered.

So on my way back home I got to steal a bread in a bakery near the Parade. I give it to my chile to eat, en' I go to wash my body with water, oll over.

Now I'm not saying that's how it went ollytime. I'm not complaining en' I thenk the Lawd fo' his mercy en' his showers of blessings. Oll I'm saying is that it wasn' easy. To bring up det chile so he won' be ashamed of his mo'rer. I'm not asking ennything fo' myself, I'm not greedy – it's jus' thet I want thet chile to be white when he grow up, so as what he can get on in life. So as what he can take me out of the sheddows of the Lawd with him, beck to the sun.

I get a job in a laundry now, oll de smart peoples send their clothes to us. Twelf hours a day I stend there widde steam coming from de irons, hevvy irons they was for oll de littel pleats en' things. But I'm not complaining. Not much food we got, for the chile must go to school, hey, en' de Lawd is his Sheppid, he shall not want. Lots of things he's learning in thet Boys' High School, praise the Lawd, espeshully English.

At night I watch him there where he sit with his books, en' then he brings me littel thingetjies what he wrote, poetry en' so. Jus' go on writing, I say to him, en' I tell him of his gran'fa'rer en' de poetries he made music from in his blindness.

Hard work in the laundry, don't worry. Mondays I fetch the di'ty bunnels at the houses, Thursday I take them back, clean. But that Thursday the blerry Bleck Southeaster he greb me en' put me down in the mud of Edde'ley Street, washing de lot. En' then thet men come en' pick me up, Hendrick. I jus' keep thinking about de washing, a whole week's work in de mud, men, but he put it on his shoulders en' he keep a arm round me for de wind, en' he laugh that you can hear him far away. Lot older then me he was, forty or so, en' he got a good job. So I think of Braampie, thirteen soon en' things getting dearer en' me not getting healthier, praise de Lawd. En' so we get married. In a office, it was. I was a bietjie sed, ollywhile I was mos thinking of a white wedding, but God knows best en' so be it, amen.

Now life will be better, I think. But jus' one month, then Hendrik sits out of work. Got a wife mos, he says, to bring in de money, so why de hell must he be a slave? En' weekends, jiss, then he jus' break out en' then it's murder when he come back. For myself I didn' mind so much, I can take it, but there's Braampie. He wasn' used to it, en' ollyways such a quite chile. So the only way is Braampie must go out boarding. I'll sommer die if he go on seeing Hendrik's medness.

But boarding is not a cheap thing, men, en' I want only the best for him, 'cause he's mos white. So now I mus' take in extra work for nights. Sewing, smocking, things for brides en' so. Midnight en' much later, en' de light is maar bed, it's hell on the eyes, but it bring in money for the boarding, en' a littel bit extra fo' Hendrik fo' the weekend.

A year it goes awright, only the eyes don' see so good no more en' the head is like a fire, praise de Lawd. Hendrik stay home ollytime now en' Fridays he takes de lot, so I begin to worry about my chile, you see. En' if I complain he take of his belt en' he moer me, en' den it's worse.

So I leave my money with Mary Pieterse, for it's Chris'mas month en' Jennewary it's Secondary time fo' Braampie, thet's a blerry lot of money I can tell you.

Three months I save up, then I fetch my money from Mary, one We'nsday, so I can go pay Braampie's school early inne morning. I sit there on my bed counting de money to hide in my stocking en' I newwe' heard him befo' he was right there inne room beside me. It's jus' something what suddenly say to me : Rachel look up. En' when I look up, it's Hendrik there, swaying on his two feet like a grass inne Southeaster.

I put de money in my dress up here but he got my hend, it's like a snake so fast, praise de Lawd.

What's thet money? he ask me.

It's Braampie's money, I say.

You got money for yo' white shit en' I got blerry nothing, he say. He twist my arm. It hurt.

I gave you all what you wanted, I say. It's mine this. Lemme go.

Hoer! he shout.

He want to grab the money from my dress, so I pull away en' I jus' near it tearing en' it's oll onne floor. I go down to get it, but he's too fast, drunk en' oll, en' then he hit me, jiss, en' I see his boot coming down to my stomach, en' then I throw up. But he jus' go on, he jus' go on, praise de Lawd, en' den I stop.

It was the neighbours, they tole me, as what took me out there. Half-dead I was, but how can I now lie in bed like a blerry medem if my chile needs money? So I get up en' I go ask my Baas at de laundry, a bietjie edvance money fo' Braampie.

Edvance? he say. I know you hotnots. I give you edvance en' I newwe' see you again.

Well, jiss, what can I do? I know where he keep the laundry money, so I wait for him to go out en' I take what I need. There is lot more then what I wanted, but I didn' touch it, jus' what I need fo' Braampie, en' so I go home.

They came nog de same night, the Baas en' some poellies.

Where's de money?

Paid for Braampie's school, I say.

So they take me en' one of them show me a stick en' he say: *Meid*, where's de money?

I took it, I tell him. I can't give it beck, for I hevven' got it no more. But I'll work it oll in, de lot. I swear by de Lawd God.

Where's de money? he ask en' he hit me.

I tell him again.

Where's de money? he ask en' he hit me again.

I got no more crying left in me, not after Hendrik's thing: I mean, one's got so much here en' then it's finish en' klaar. I'm not complaining. But they was big men, all three of dem, en' I'm maar bietjie small, not even a hunne'd on de scale, it's of this years of work en' not enough to eat.

It was still pain oll over when the Juts sent me out to the stokkies. They didn' send no doctor to me but it was a bietjie rest, the Lawd look after his chillun. Not much to eat what they gave me, but then I wasn' really used to much, so I'm not complaining. Ricewater, porridge, coffee. One don't need more.

The one arm was sore fo' a long time, the one they broke with de stick, but he grew on again. Not straight, but awright, en' it was de lef' hend, so there's always reason to praise de Lawd. It's jus' that a year is a blerry long time, men, en' there I was worrying myself sick for Braampie. Did they beat him there in de smart school if he speak Afrikaans? Is he still writing his poetries? Has he still got thet way of staring so far away when dere's people, as if he can see things we others newwe' see, jus' like my ole blind fa'rer? Shit, Lawd, I mus' get out of here to look after my chile. Jus' look at me here, good fo' nothing, sitting on my arse getting fat from other people's food.

They gave me some pasella fo' good behaviour en' so I got out befo' my year was out. Braampie sitting on de streets, for he got no more money fo' school. En' there's Hendrik at home, no-good drunk like a old dry tit, en' he want money.

There was darem a undertaker what gave me a job to sew the long clothes-things for the dead people, en' on Sa'rdays, if we was lucky, Braampie rang de bell for de funerals. So slowly it get better again en' in de new year he go back to school. I take extra work so Hendrik also shut up. It's only in de wet weather that I got trouble with that left arm, en' then the rheumatism got into the right hand, jiss. Now if Hendrik hadn't focked me up so much I think I could have menneged, praise de Lawd. But God is a wonne'ful men in his way. Jus' when I was now thinking it's tickets with the meid, there Hendrik got a stroke en' he's condemn'. He can move his foot a bietjie, en' his eyes, thet's oll. So he lie there watching me, watching me olly time, day en' night, en' I must look after him like a blerry littel baby, but God hear me, I'm not complaining. It's only thet it took him so long to die altogether, three years en' seven months before we could dig the old shit in. Thet time Braampie was through with school en' off my hends, thenk God, for my hends was useless then, ennyway.

En' jus' after Hendrik went down unne' de cypresses, Braampie got married with that smart white girl, one of the Cape Van Reenens, jiss. Now I can't of course mix with those guests on de wedding, nobody knows old Rachel with the crooked hends is Braampie's mo'rer – det Braampie with his whiteness en' his blue eyes from his fa'rer. He was sed thet day but I say to him : Braampie, I say, don't worry about me, you stick to white en' follow the Lawd. En' so he got married en' I can retire a bit in my old age.

But now how could I know about de baby? Just one year after de wedding, en' this brown chile in de smart Cape family, praise the Lawd. Came to me that night, late-late, with this baby in his littel white blanket. En' he's crying, Braampie is crying. Twenty-two years ole, but he's crying like a blerry baby himself. Chased out by his new white family en' there he is now, halfway med, men, en' he wants to go drown the poor littel thing like a dog. So I take him away. I'll look after him, I say. Give him to me. It's the will of the Lawd God.

Braampie went away that very same night en' I newwe' sawed him again. I also got out of de Cape, out of de Van Reenens' way. To Gordon's Bay it was I took de babytjie. The fisherman made a littel hut fo' us there on de beach, en' there we lived on, me en' de baby,

Braam's baby David. When the boats come in, we go and help them clean the fish, so we get de heads for free, en' sometimes a bietjie extra. Jus' de two of us, me en' David, en' I could feel my time coming on, but how can I now die like thet and leave the chile? Brought him up in de fear of de Lawd, jus' like he was my own, so I can give him off to life when life gives me death. I'm not afraid to die, no. It's jus' like sleep, the pastor says, like sleep what got no end. En' so I'm thinking: God, give me thet sleep to rest this tired old heap of bones a bit, jus' a bietjie rest without end, for jiss, one gets tired, men, the sort of tiredness what creep into you like the salt wind of de sea, yes I'm blerry tired, God, I don't think I can go on much longer, so see thy handmaiden en' gimme thet rest where I newwe' got to open my two eyes again on de hungryness en' de sorenes of a new day, gimme, Lawd, thet sleep what got no end.

V

With Abraham Malan (18??–1902) the male line of our family is resumed. The irony has never escaped me that during the sole White moment of our chronicle the bearer of our fate had to be a member of a nation despised and rejected in its own country and by many of its own people. For that one moment when we had the right colour, our language was wrong.

From my mother's interpretation of Rachel's life I already knew that Abraham was a sensitive little creature, without any friends, and given to dreaming; at the same time I know that he must have possessed, from very far back, a form of determination, a fierce will, which must have made an impact on those crossing his path. Not that it could have made life any easier for him, especially during the time he spent in the English school.

Things were aggravated by Hendrik's maltreatment, but then, of course, Abraham was soon sent away to boarding school. The 'facts' of our history obviously are more concerned with the external manifestations of suffering. But the more secret, hidden suffering of a young boy who from an early age had to take refuge in an inner existence to escape from the incomprehensible threats of the outside world, was probably as significant as any form of physical torture experienced by my other ancestors.

What happened to him during the year Rachel spent in prison no one has ever learnt. Not even to her did he divulge any hint, and it is quite possible that an essential clue to his life might have got lost in that way.

At the beginning of the year following her release she enrolled him in a new school, less exclusive than the previous one; the anti-Afrikaans spirit was less vicious and extreme, which must have given him more self-confidence, so that he resumed composing his poetic trifles, some of them published in the pioneer magazine *Ons Klyntji* – either anonymously or under pseudonyms. It has given me endless pleasure to page through anthologies of that early language movement and choose from the hundreds of nameless verses those I feel I should like to associate with Abraham. I have no ground whatsoever for my choice, so my imagination can create much of the man and his work in complete liberty.

After school he was enrolled as an articled clerk with a lawyer in town. Quite a leading firm considering his background : but then, of course, all his acquaintances regarded him as an orphan whose parents had been killed by Xhosas. He received a very small salary from the lawyer, but at least there were prospects of fast promotion; and every month he managed to save something for his mother.

In the Van Reenens' large Victorian home he met the lawyer's daughter. True to the style of the turn of the century Afrikaans *nouveaux riches* she bore the name of Charmaine and the home language was English. Still, she seemed to have been a particularly fine girl, much sought after by suitors from Cape Town and even farther afield, so that it was no mean achievement for Abraham finally to win her hand. The wedding was a glittering affair, by far the greatest social occasion in the history of our tribe; among the guests were Onze Jan Hofmeyr, and John X. Merriman, and God knows who else.

I wish I knew how Abraham *really* reacted all the time. Did he appreciate why his mother tried to pass him off as white? Did he share her determination, or did he simply acquiesce for her sake? Did he deliberately exploit the situation to further his interests? Did he cynically accept Charmaine and their marriage as part of his 'fate'? Did he use her to fulfil his own ambitions? Did he, perhaps, really love her? Was he upset that Rachel was not allowed to mix with the wedding guests or did he find it an easy solution to an embarrassing situation? Abraham, father Abraham, there is so much of myself I'd like to discover and sort out through you!

And then the baby was born, the brown child of two white parents. God knows what happened that day in the impressive mansion in Oranjezicht. All that has been passed on to me is his arrival, in the dark of the night, in his mother's cottage in Claremont, with the child rolled in a blanket. There was madness in his eyes; he said nothing to all Rachel's questions. All he could do was sob, over and over: Look, look, look! Past midnight she took the child to a friend who'd given birth the previous week so that the baby could have something to drink. When she returned, exhausted, Abraham had left. It was near the end of September, 1899. What happened to him afterwards, came filtering back to the family through the years, much of it unreliable, but gradually sanctioned through retelling from generation to generation.

On the 11th October of that year Kruger's ultimatum to Britain expired and war broke out. In the Cape Colony the development of the first offensive was followed by a barely restrained fever of excitement. Old Commandant-general Piet Joubert warily penetrating into Natal until, to his own utter amazement, the whole section north of the Tugela was in Boer hands, with the key town of Ladysmith occupied; De la Rey coolly capturing the armoured train at Kraaipan, followed by the almost casual siege of the British troops at Kimberley and Mafeking; the arrival of the poor gentleman soldier, Lord Buller, and his miserable efforts to save the situation; and all this topped by Britain's Black Week in early December, with the three great battles of Stormberg, Magersfontein and Colenso. Small wonder that the Colonists were in a state of eager turmoil: during those climactic weeks thousands of them must have prepared to take up arms themselves. Just wait for the great breakthrough, they resolved – Ladysmith, Kimberley, or Mafeking – then they'd rise up and chase the Rooineks back to where they belonged.

These were, roughly, the circumstances under which Abraham left for the north. While hundreds of others were still waiting for a final sign to prove that God was really fighting on Kruger's side, Abraham took the plunge. I feel reluctant to talk about heroism. It may well be that he simply had less to lose than those others; perhaps he was in such utter distress that he used the first opportunity of escaping from his impossible situation. But it is equally possible, of course, that he saw with terrible clarity exactly what lay ahead and rode out to meet that fate with open eyes. It is characteristic of our family to foresee the destructive end of an action and yet to continue, with a sort of restrained joy, trying to discover how far we can venture into the landscape of the impossible.

With a few bits of clothing in a leather suitcase and a small amount of money Abraham departed from Cape Town by train, in search of history. In slightly different circumstances it might even have been comical. In Beaufort West he got off the train, spent most of his money to buy an old hack from a farmer enriching himself from the war, packed provisions for a few days, strapped on a bandolier, slung a gun across his shoulder, mounted Rocinante and rode off towards the enemy.

As far as he went there were rumours of forces converging on the Modder River, of Cronjé joining De la Rey to finally stop the march of the British troops towards Kimberley. But Abraham made little headway, for his horse was hopeless, he had no knowledge of the countryside, and he had to steer clear of roaming Government scouts. On his way he ran into an ancient Boer, a lean Oom Joggie who, by his own and oft repeated accounts, had fought in the First Boer War and God knows how many Kaffir Wars – and the old man convinced him that he knew the Jacobsdal district like the palm of his own sunscorched hand. It gradually transpired that he hadn't been there for over thirty years, but even that doesn't explain how they managed to wander through the area for more than two weeks before they finally reached the Boer forces, unless the old man had deliberately tried to lead Abraham astray.

By that time the battle of Modder River had already taken place.

However, it soon became clear that the really decisive battle was still to come, and for that occasion I can imagine Abraham preparing himself with cool passion. It had to compensate for the mess he'd made of his life. Violence itself would become his true wedding feast. And there must have been something ecstatic about discovering that he finally found himself on the brink of history.

But then his Field-cornet ordered him and another burgher, a Transvaler, to take a report to Botha who'd just been appointed officer in command of the Natal forces. It was a personal message from Cronjé, but why Abraham was chosen to deliver it, I find difficult to explain – unless they preferred to keep all the more experienced men at hand for the coming fight.

He and his companion, Kolbe, left without delay, if rather grudgingly because they'd been denied the expected climax, drawing meagre comfort from the fact that their mission had some importance in its own right.

Three or four days later they heard that the great battle of Magersfontein had, in fact, started without them. By this time there was a new expectation of taking part in another decisive battle in Natal; even a raw recruit could sense that something was brewing in at Colenso.

Alas, they missed that too, for Abraham's horse trod in a hole and it took three days to find a replacement. At the same time they had to be so careful to avoid the troop movements on the main roads that the battle of Colenso had ended a week before they even heard of it. They were at a loss about what to do next, since the message in Abraham's knapsack was certainly irrelevant by now. Should they push on or turn back? The decision was taken from their hands when, a couple of days later, Kolbe was surprised by a detachment of soldiers while he was out trying to find something to eat.

Hearing the burst of fire Abraham, with the bravado of the utterly impractical, gave chase to liberate his companion; but on a long decline his horse stumbled and fell, sending his rider tumbling downhill. As he landed his gun went off, and the horse galloped off into the distance.

For days on end he struggled on foot until he reached a farm inhabited by an old man of nearly ninety and his crippled wife, their daughter, and the daughter's children – four girls, and two boys of under ten years of age. The men had all gone on commando. Abraham wanted to continue on his way, but it was nearly Christmas and they persuaded him to stay. A decisive factor was that the wheat was ripe on the billowing lands, so at least he could help to bring the harvest in.

Shortly after New Year's Day a small commando arrived on the farm. Abraham wanted to join them, but he still had no horse and they were rather discouraging: a horseless man would be useless in Natal – they were on their way to capture Ladysmith, and only cavalry could do that. So they left without him.

Abraham packed his knapsack and went to the nearest station. He simply had to be there if something great was to happen. The train took him as far as Volksrust, from where he had to continue on foot. But barely one day's trek away he got news that Botha's efforts to break the siege of Ladysmith had failed, so he turned back to the Transvaal. In this way he also missed the battle of Spioen Kop.

From here the chronicle becomes more confused. It would seem that, in the company of a group of other homeless souls, Abraham spent a long time wandering aimlessly through the country in the hope of finding a commando they could join. Every man in the group had his own bright ideas, with the result that they never got anywhere. By mid-February Abraham couldn't stand the uncertainty any longer and broke away on his own to return to General Cronjé.

Again he was just too late. Less than three days from Kimberley he heard of Cronjé's surrender at Paardeberg, and the next day the Union Jack was hoisted in Bloemfontein. Once more history had by-passed him.

The only solution seemed to be to return to the Transvaal. There, too, things were deteriorating. But somewhere, somewhere, surely, his opportunity would come. Perhaps his very eagerness to get involved in the war thwarted his efforts, for instead of staying with one commando he would constantly join new groups – until, sometime in May, a band of adventurers persuaded him to accompany them to Moçambique where they hoped to join a larger force of volunteers reportedly gathering from a variety of overseas countries.

On their way through the Eastern Transvaal Pretoria fell behind them. But they kept on. Each day brought new rumours and mirages. They reached the region of the pale fever trees beyond Komatipoort. Although it was nearly winter it was still oppressively hot. A few horses were stung by tsetse flies. That was the beginning of the end. But nothing could induce them to turn back : now they were heading for Armaggedon, they were on the trail of God.

Then came the mosquitoes. Abraham was one of the first to go down with malaria. The survivors struggled ahead on foot, lugging the stretchers with the sick and dying. From day to day their numbers dwindled. Abraham was already delirious by the time the Portuguese came to their rescue among the fever trees, consequently we know nothing about the next few months – except that in November or December that year he disembarked from a ship in Port Elizabeth. Even that was probably a mistake : he must have meant to go back to Cape Town, but through some accident, some misunderstanding, some fluke, he got off the boat too soon, and that really sealed his fate.

According to my mother's story he was already 'strange in the head' at the time of his landing in Port Elizabeth, and for many months he wandered through the Eastern Cape without any conceivable aim. Then, suddenly, he stole a horse outside a grocer's shop at Uitenhage : a few nights later he lodged with a farmer in the Long Kloof and when the family got up the next morning, he'd disappeared with one of their guns and almost all their ammunition.

61

According to the stories filtering back to Rachel, years afterwards, from people who'd met him on the way, his conversation was quite confused: he would talk incoherently about Cronjé and his friend Kolbe and his mother, but mostly about a son he'd left in the Cape and to whom he wanted to return. I have a suspicion that Rachel herself might have introduced this romantic angle, or my mother, but I can blame neither. Abraham wanted to go back to his child, the David he'd left with his mother, that night of madness. For him the war was already a thing of the past, only the child was real.

But why the gun and ammunition then? I don't know. Remember, he no longer had his wits about him, he was seriously ill. Remember. For if he'd really meant to go back to the war, surely he wouldn't have taken the road to Cape Town?

There were numerous small bands and commandos roaming through the Colony at the time, as far south as the Peninsula. But the end was in sight. It was April 1902, and negotiations for peace had already started.

In all that confusion he went on, giving his stolen horse hell. In less than a week the animal was lame.

Abraham had already crossed the Little Karoo and reached the outskirts of Robertson when they caught him with his crippled horse and his gun and his bag of ammunition. During the interrogation he kept on talking about his son, about Cronjé and everything he'd missed: Modder River, Magersfontein, Colenso, Spioen Kop, Paardeberg, Pretoria. In his feverish mind those places had become the names of battles in which he'd actually fought; finally he was accepted by history. And now he was on his way back to his son.

The military tribunal obviously had no choice. And at six o'clock on the morning of 20th May 1902, eleven days before the Peace of Vereeniging, he was executed by a firing squad in Worcester. He was twenty years, seven months and three days old. The Lord gave and the Lord hath taken away, blessed be the name of the Lord.

VI

With David our lifeline resumes its customary course.

He was only six, living with his grandmother in the little hovel on the beach at Gordon's Bay, when he had to start doing small jobs to help keep body and soul together. Carrying messages, working in gardens, stealing fish from the harbour to sell at back doors in the village. There was no time for school. In the beginning Rachel did her best to teach him the rudiments of reading and writing; and I can picture her reciting to him, day after day, her account of his history, until he must have known it pretty well by heart. But that was as far as her efforts went. With Braampie it had been different: he had to learn, he was white; her grandchild needn't be burdened with so much.

He came and went like the wind. When the schools of herrings came in, he was down on the beach, otherwise he'd haunt the bushy mountainside or the line of rocks beyond the village. Most of his time he spent drawing. He really was obsessed by drawing. And he had the strange, almost morbid habit of tracing his drawings on the beach just within reach of the tide; with the patience of a gull he'd wait the six hours from ebb to high tide until the last lines of his drawings had been covered by the foam of the gentle and remorseless water.

His urge to draw was directly responsible for the premature termination of his childhood when he was barely twelve. He used to go on drawing beside the oil lamp until long after Rachel had gone to sleep at night, and he'd normally burn up the evening's work before going to bed himself. But on that particular night, as he was still watching, spellbound, the spasms of the burning paper, the fire got out of hand. Before he could stop it, the table was burning. Trying to beat down the flames, he upset the lamp and a jet of fire streaked out across the narrow bed where Rachel was mumbling and moaning in her sleep. Suddenly the whole wooden shack was burning. He tried to drag his grandmother from her bed, but she was too heavy. From the door he saw her sitting up soundlessly, clothed in flickering flames; and then the hut collapsed on her.

David bore the scars of the fire until the day of his death: but of course he didn't grow very old, so perhaps it is irrelevant.

There was no one to look after him. He roamed along the beach spending his nights in three or four different hideouts on the mountain. As time passed he explored the entire stretch of coastland from the Strand as far as Koeël Bay, until he was familiar with every rockpool and mountain path, every movement of current and tide, every sign of changing wind or weather.

Sometime during those years he met Katryn, a brown girl from a fishing family – decent people in their way, the father the leading singer of his congregation, the mother from Malay descent but converted to Christianity at a tender age: hence a tendency towards exaggeration in virtue and good works.

They used to play together beyond the rocks at the far end of the village. That was where he showed her his drawings, and where they fished and talked and swam; on the endless fine days lasting from spring to a late autumn, they'd take off their clothes and spend whole mornings or afternoons naked in the nearly waveless water: she much paler than he, and with long hair reaching down, when she was standing, to the dimples above her small round buttocks. Basking in the sun on the white sand, she would gently touch the scars the fire had left on his thin body; and gradually, as he grew more confident, he'd respond by touching her, exploring her differentness.

He must have been about fifteen, she fourteen, when she fell pregnant. It took more than four months before she realised what was going on. Actually it was her pious mother who made the time-honoured calculations and informed the righteously furious father. The day after they'd made their discovery, the Godfearing man brought an ashen, dead-scared David back home and hauled the two children before the Church Council, like two panic-stricken chickens at an auction. With evil, loving glee every detail was wrung from them, every excursion and caress exhibited to the damning eyes of the good sanhedrin. Then a long prayer was said, and afterwards two of the church elders went home with them to lend a hand with the prescribed chastisement. The two children were tied across two empty barrels in the backyard and flogged in turns by the father and the two helpful brethren.

David was sent off into the dusk with a final kick under the arse, and Katryn was given up to the tender care of her mother. Next morning both were gone. They searched high and low, but no trace was ever found. Everything happens for the best, the stricken parents assured themselves, going down on their knees to confess their sins and praise the Lord.

The children hadn't gone very far. David knew the coast so intimately that they managed to live in a cave immediately above the village for a full fortnight, so that the uproar could first die down and their bodies recover from the bruises. Expecting the townsfolk to concentrate their searching in the direction of Cape Town, they followed the opposite way as soon as Katryn was fit to move on. It was February then, in the heart of a fierce and windless summer, so David had no trouble finding food in the wilderness. In a strange way those following few months had an idyllic undertone. They kept to the sea, swimming in the diaphanous warm water, sleeping under trees or in caves, playing with carefree abandon, catching small fishes, dreaming for hours on end.

But the season of grapes passed and the first breath of autumn coolness came into the still air; the winter rains started earlier than usual. Katryn wasn't well. Her pregnant belly had swollen to an enormous size; when she huddled close to him for a bit of warmth on cold nights, the fear of what lay ahead kept her awake. From their short-lived paradise they were driven back to the world of men.

David had to find work to support his wife and coming child, but he knew no craft or trade at all. He could draw, of course, but that was as useless as the music of his great-grandfather Dlamini/Daniel. And even Katryn began to blame him for landing them in a mess and for being incapable of saving them from it.

In the vicinity of Knysna her time grew full. It was night, and it was raining, and in the anguish and suffering of labour she was like a mad animal turning against him. He listened to her moaning and screaming, he watched her convulsions; and being no more than a child himself he fled to look for help. An old black woman came. Through the night and the next long day and through most of the second night she hindered and helped as Katryn struggled with the unborn baby, half strangled by the umbilical cord.

They were sure the child would die. After the first tentative wail it seemed to stop breathing. Delirious, Katryn insisted that he must be baptised, else he'd go to hell. David caught some rainwater in a tin and christened his own child: Jacob, in the name of the Father, and of the Son, and of the Holy Ghost; and then turned back to Katryn, who had lapsed into a coma. At daybreak she began to breathe more peacefully. And only after they finally woke up did they discover that the child was still alive.

What happened during the next five or six years conforms to the general pattern of our story: an aimless trek through the hostile or apathetic land, three months in one place, seven in the next, a year elsewhere, looking for work and a place to settle. But it was wartime, the world was in uproar, and there was no lasting place to rest their heads.

They ended up in Queenstown where they spent a year with the weird sect of Enoch's 'Israelites', who, near Bulhoek, had assembled round their tabernacle to await the end of the world and the salvation of the Black race. Some of the members of the sect, mainly Fingoes, may have had political undertones to their religious zeal – a late incarnation of Nonquasi's dreams of power for the Xhosas – but for most of them Bulhoek seemed to be an escape from work and worries. What led David and Katryn to the sect, I don't know. More likely than not they were simply trying to find a temporary haven far from the world which had threatened them for so long.

Late in 1920 there was a first brush with the police, not without comedy. One can imagine it on a stage: the battalion of police approaching from one side, the 'Israelites' from the other clad in flowing white robes and brandishing ancient rusty swords; the police falling back in disarray. Followed, of course, by the firm conviction that God's chosen were bulletproof. But David felt restless, and if Katryn hadn't just given birth to their second child, a girl, they would probably have moved on in time.

As it happened, the baby was only a few months old when the police returned, this time almost a thousand of them, supported by artillery. The 'Israelites' attacked as before, their robes flapping in the wind. The police opened fire. It was the first Sharpeville of Jan Smuts. A hundred and sixty or seventy were killed and numerous wounded, I can't remember the exact figures. Among the dead was Katryn who'd been feeding the baby in front of their hut; the child got shot through the head. David and his five-year-old Jacob escaped.

They eventually turned up on the Witwatersrand, looking for work in that impossible time of unrest and strikes and unemployment when the tension between mine owners and labourers was becoming so serious that there was open talk of a Bolshevist Revolution.

In a shanty on the edge of Sophiatown, David and his son found lodgings with an old man called Samuel. Timelessly old and blind, with his long white beard, I find it impossible to divorce him from his Biblical counterpart – in fact, he may well be one of the products of my childhood fantasies. He took in the two pilgrims and treated them like his own son and grandson. In the long evenings he liked nothing better than to listen to David's account of our tribal history.

During the day David ransacked the Reef for work. Occasionally he found temporary employment, but never anything lasting or substantial. And his body, maimed by the fire of so many years ago, was unfit for the mines which had been his real aim.

66

By the end of the year things were beginning to look very bad indeed. More and more white workers were laid off, and when their wages were drastically cut at the beginning of the new year, black labour being so much cheaper, the strikes began. All that is history, but once again our family passed by on the shadow side.

Day after day David dragged his weary legs past mine compounds and back streets looking for jobs. He circled warily round groups of strikers; sometimes he heard shots in the distance; at the end of February he was nearly caught in the crossfire between Smuts soldiers and miners. But he was barely conscious of it all : it only entered his world because it made things so much more difficult for him.

There were outbursts of arson; in the shopping areas vandalism was rampant. But he went on doggedly, lean and ragged and determined, because that was the only way to keep his child and himself alive.

Early in March he was on his way back home rather later than usual, his tin of food under his arm. The morning's bread was still untouched, for he hadn't earned anything that day and wanted to take the food back to his child. Near Kazerne he heard a din of voices and instinctively swerved to avoid it. But suddenly the voices were all around him, and furious stubbly faces were swirling and eddying past him; hard blunt hands were grabbing his tattered clothes.

'Blerry Hotnot! Who do you think you are, hey? Taking our jobs, shitting on us, hey? Think you're baas in a white man's land, hey?' Ad lib.

He tried to break away. They grabbed him and jerked him back. He struggled to get free. A fist caught him in the neck. He staggered. A knee bruised his back. He turned round. A large boot kicked him in the stomach. He half collapsed and lost his tin. 'Got bread with you, hey, and we must *vrek* of hunger!' He was on his knees. Fists and boots and elbows everywhere. And voices. He dropped on all fours and tried to crawl past the vicious legs. A blow broke his nose, he could see nothing but blood. But rolling, crawling, ducking, scurrying, he managed to break from them and started running in the deep dusk. Then the first stone caught him on the shoulder. He gave a jerk, but went on running, trying to wipe the blood from his face with a backhand. The second stone broke his head. He stumbled. Another stone. 'Got him! Kill the focken Hotnot!'

They stoned him there like a young Jew from the Old Testament. He wasn't fully twenty-three yet. Blessed be the name of the Lord.

67

VII

And then Jacob. My story is becoming monotonous, I know. In the course of the seasons, through autumn and winter, one reaches spring again; the rhythm of nature takes one beyond night back to dawn and day – but it seems to me as if our tale represents a journey more and more deeply into the night, into ever-increasing darkness: a way of suffering which doesn't purify or purge or break through to tragic wisdom, but which remains true only to its own futility. So that after eight generations all one can say is not that one has learnt something or gained something, but only that it has all been quite useless, and that the darkness now is more than in the beginning.

Jacob, they say, was a handsome boy and quite light-skinned too. If *he* had been Abraham's child, nobody would have batted an eyelid – but, of course, his time and place were wrongly chosen. The old blind Samuel looked after him for seven years and it must have been during this time that the boy learned something of his past. Whenever my mother told me the story she insisted on Jacob's extraordinary faculty for remembering the smallest detail. She, of course, compensated for the lack of this faculty in herself by relying on her equally extraordinary fantasy.

His hunger for memorising and learning extended to much more than his own history. He devoured whatever reading matter he could find: crumpled newspapers in dustbins or on pavements, the odd discarded book in a backyard – such formed his library. But his favourite was *The Pilgrim's Progress*, a very old edition with the cover missing, but he took it with him wherever he went, even to the smoking rubbish dumps of the city where old women and emaciated piccanins scrambled and fought for broken loaves and half-eaten bones and rotten fruit. Strange that he should have chosen that particular book, because even at a very early age he was wildly and blasphemously antireligious.

Jacob had one remarkable gift and that was his ability to mime and impersonate. Whatever joy he knew in his miserable childhood was derived from that. But in the end this very gift was responsible for most of his suffering too.

When he was about fourteen, soon after the death of old Samuel, and after saving up every penny for more than two years, he was able to go

68

to school for the first time. But in the third term of that year he was caught giving a realistic and most embarrassing impersonation of the principal, which promptly led to his expulsion.

From then on he had to fend for himself. He read and re-read *The Pilgrim's Progress* until he could quote long passages by heart; other books he bought second-hand, or borrowed, or stole. But since man cannot live by words alone and it became more and more difficult, during the Depression, to find bread, he suffered agony in the hereditary process of drifting from job to job.

For a year or so he polished shoes in front of the Gents' at the station. There he found time not only for reading but for studying people whose eccentricities he could mime to appreciative audiences. For his clients soon discovered his talent and in due course started rewarding him with quite substantial tips.

After one of his successful improvisations a distinguished-looking gentleman invited Jacob to take up employment in his house. He started as kitchen help, but as soon as his patron, Mitchell, discovered that his trust had been well placed, Jacob was promoted to majordomo and eventually to chauffeur, with a very natty uniform. And whenever the Mitchells had guests, he had to entertain them from his growing repertoire of impersonations. In the life of each of my ancestors there occurred such a period of peace – every time with disastrous consequences.

Elise appeared on the scene. Over many years her family and the Mitchells had been business associates and house friends, and since her childhood there had been playful references to the possibility of a marriage with one of the Mitchell sons. After her sixteenth birthday she was sent to Britain and Switzerland to acquire a polish still thought to be lacking in South Africa. And then she came back, nineteen years old, beautiful and impulsive and passionate, on a long visit to the Mitchells. It soon transpired that the real object of the holiday was to explore the possibilities of an engagement to the elder son.

In due course it was celebrated. But at the same time she met Jacob. They fell in love, and the affair was facilitated by the fact that Jacob had to give her driving lessons.

Their relationship was based on a strange perversion which may have been the result of my mother's imagination or partly of my own: Elise and Jacob fell in love, but they acted out their love as if it were a play: whenever they were together she would urge him to assume the role of her fiancé, young Mitchell, and she would respond in the role of mistress

69

. . . God alone knows how it started. How it ended, on the other hand, is only too well known in our family.

They were surprised in Jacob's small room behind the kitchen. When she saw her fiancé and his brother on the threshold she started screaming rape.

The police were called after they'd finished with him. When he came out of jail shortly after his twenty-second birthday, not in the best state of health and still bearing the marks of the cat-o'-nine-tails, he left for the Cape without wasting any time. All he took with him from his first life – and where on earth could he have found it? – was *The Pilgrim's Progress*, and a conviction, more passionate than ever before, about the absence of God from the world.

In Cape Town he got work in the harbour and during the fruit season he was transferred to the warehouses where a farmer from Paarl recruited him. His new employer, Frans Viviers, was really an officer in the Defence Force, but after the death of an older brother had recently acquired the old family farm and was having difficulty in coping with everything.

By that time Jacob was a sullen and solitary man, but a particularly good worker, and, unlike the other labourers, he wasn't fond of drink at all. He found little time for reading on the large fruit farm, working from dawn to past sunset, but he seemed resigned to it. Jail had broken something inside him.

On the farm he met Sophie, the beautiful, exuberant girl with the full round breasts, by nature so utterly unlike himself. She'd started life as a foundling at the Mission Station of Genadendal and eventually landed on the farm as kitchen maid. All the men were after her, but it was Jacob she finally chose. To her he was an irresistible man from a distant world, a man of books and deep thoughts, a man of Johannesburg, and an artist in his own way. They got married – in church, what's more, although I can hardly accept the interpretation that it presented some sort of conversion; at the wedding reception, in fact, he amused the crowd by impersonating the parson. Afterwards, while Sophie and the others were thoroughly enjoying themselves, he quietly slipped away and went to bed.

Their son was only a few months old when the war broke out. Frans Viviers, using his prerogative as an officer, ordered Jacob to accompany him to North Africa as his batman and so wife and child had to be left behind.

70

In a downstairs corridor of the Cape Castle the recruits were weighed and measured, followed by a hand in the air and a mumbled So-help-me-God; next thing they were on a train to the bitter Highveld winter of the Transvaal, for preparatory training at the Premier Mine. Jacob contracted pneumonia but recovered just in time to leave with the First Division from Durban. And suddenly it was war. Jacob accompanied the troops from Nairobi northward, through Italian Somaliland, across the Juba River, into the mountains and rift valleys of Ethiopia. He never fought in the trenches, of course: he was only a batman and carried no weapons. His job was to keep his master's rifle clean and his clothes in order; he had to pitch the tent and help dig trenches and load the lorries. Sometimes he and some of his colleagues had to do some reconnoitring to make sure there were no land mines on their way.

Throughout the campaign, while dysentery and malaria claimed as many victims as the battles, he looked after Frans Viviers. He travelled through Ethiopia with *The Pilgrim's Progress* in his knapsack and two chameleons on his shoulder – the latter being his only protection against the flies.

After the battle of Addis Ababa they marched on to Egypt where they had to mark time until the offensive towards the Western Desert got under way. For Jacob it was a schizoid existence: in the Continental Savoy in Cairo, and afterwards in Alexandria's Cecil Bar, he could come and go as freely as he chose; in the rabbit's warren of back streets he was accosted, like any white soldier, by urchins offering for sale bracelets and paste jewels, fake scarabs, embroidered coverlets, and very clean, very cheap sisters; but back at the base he was brown and had to obey the bosses. Admittedly, the atmosphere was much more relaxed than at home and through his talent for mime he soon became popular among the men (his impersonations of Churchill and Smuts, Hitler, Mussolini and officers of the First Brigade earned him quite a reputation) but, in the final analysis, he remained 'that smart Hotnot', 'just like a white man', the clever batman of Frans Viviers.

Slowly they began to move towards Matruh where the limestone hills broke against the sand and the salt shrubs; beyond lay the stone desert, stretching on to Alamein. It was a time of boredom and flies among the dunes and barren plateaux and desolate wadis; sometimes there were bomb attacks, but mostly there was nothing but that nerve-racking waiting in the terrible heat.

During that period of comparative safety Frans Viviers got his wound.

71

As an officer he had access to a private latrine; and as he was sitting there one morning a lone Stuka came diving out of the blue and blasted their trenches with a hail of bombs. The narrow building collapsed and Frans Viviers's buttocks were partially destroyed. It left a permanent scar on his character, for he was a proud man who loved to blow his own trumpet, and now he couldn't even show his wound to anyone.

Soon after he'd left the field hospital the moment of destiny arrived, quite unexpectedly and without glory. Viviers and a small convoy were on their way with provisions to one of the farthest posts along the Gazala line where the Eighth Army had started digging its heels in to cut off Rommel's advance. Resting in the shade of their trucks at noon one blazing day, they were surprised by an Italian patrol. A few days later they were on their way to Italy in a rickety open freight plane.

Life in the camp near Perugia was not unpleasant at all; but late in September 1943, after the allied landing in Sicily, the prisoners were loaded in cattle-trucks and taken to the north. In the confusion a few men, including Frans Viviers, managed to escape; the rest were too closely guarded. And when Italy declared war against Germany a fortnight later the convoy had already crossed the border.

The German camp was another story altogether. It was a particularly severe winter and most of the prisoners were without shoes. Many of them lost toes or feet. The sleeping bunks were infested with vermin. Food was scarce. Compared with those in Buchenwald or Dachau they were still fortunate, I suppose. But Jacob and a few of the other Coloured prisoners had to bear the brunt of the Herrenvolk's ideals of racial purity. In fact, Jacob was one of the first to have his shoes confiscated. But it was only after they'd discovered his tattered copy of Bunyan that life really became unbearable. The SS refused to believe that he'd had the book with him all the time: they tried to force him to confess that it had been smuggled in to him, and that the underlined passages contained a coded message.

He denied it. They beat him till his trembling body was black with blood.

He denied again.

They crushed his testicles in a wooden vice. When he came round, he denied again.

They forced him to dig a grave in the snow, and made him stand up on the edge of it while a firing squad took up position. The guns rattled, but they deliberately shot over his head. He fainted.

72

When he came to, he was interrogated anew, but once again he denied that there was any sinister message in the Bunyan. This time they probably believed him, for he was sent back to his barracks.

That was the only time he ever spoke about his past; confused, delirious ramblings about Elise and his wife and child, interspersed with passages from *The Pilgrim's Progress*. Yet he had an incredible staying power, and when, late in 1944, he had sufficiently recovered he entertained his comrades with an impersonation of the SS Commandant.

After the applause had died down, someone touched his shoulder from behind. He looked round. It was one of the guards. In shocked silence the other prisoners watched as he was led away. A revolt seemed imminent. But before the insurgents could reach the Commandant's quarters there was an outburst of machine-gun fire and six or seven men fell down. The whole camp was placed on short rations.

Exactly what was done to Jacob, no one found out.

Three days after his arrest the other prisoners simply saw his bleeding and broken body dragged out of the main building by a couple of guards. He was laid on his stomach behind the Commandant's jeep and his wrists fastened to the back of the vehicle. The Commandant got in behind the wheel and started driving along the outer road along the barbed-wire fence and the searchlights, round and round.

The prisoners gathered in the centre, like animals brutally beaten into stupid submission. On the watchtowers the guards were waiting with their machine-guns. And the Commandant went on driving round and round, dragging the small bundle of flesh and bones after him, until nothing was left, dust unto dust.

For Jacob that was the final deliverance from all the paradoxes of his pilgrimage, the end of his own futile life and the long history behind it : the slave girl Leah and her Huguenot; and Adam killed because he'd dared to avenge the humiliation of his wife; the dark prophet of freedom, Moses, who'd engendered his son for the sport of his white masters; the wanderings of Dlamini/Daniel until he died in Bain's Kloof; Rachel's struggle to bring up her white child, her long sufferings, her death in the burning hut at the seaside; Abraham galloping in search of history, executed as a Cape rebel on his way home; David growing bitter after his childhood love for Katryn, and his end at the hands of the strikers; and then he, Jacob, who had to die for imitating his superiors, a clown who'd dare to ape the king. Done; all done. And yet handed down, beyond his death, to my mother and to me.

73

And now my own chapter is added to it. Then it will be over, for I have no son to go on after me. That is my one comfort. And that is the anguish I have to suffer all these nights.

On the day we finally got word of his death, from a letter Frans Viviers wrote after he'd heard from one of his comrades in the P.O.W. camp, my mother asked the pastor to arrange a funeral service. Even though it was many months too late, even though most of the labourers on the farm regarded it as madness, she insisted. And I can still remember the impressive drone of the pastor's voice reading the death-letter :

'It hath pleased Almighty God of his great mercy to take unto himself the soul of our dear brother Jacob Malan. The Lord gave and the Lord hath taken away; blessed be the name of the Lord. Mourned by his wife Sophie and his son Joseph.'

Three

To the contrary notwithstanding. It booms like a great bell from the dawn of my childhood years. These four words, isolated from whatever preceded or succeeded them, primitive sound reverberating through time like that lowest bass note of the piano in the dark. To the contrary notwithstanding: I don't even know where they spring from. They have acquired an almost religious intensity, like those other liturgical phrases: steadfast, unmovable, always abounding; or by his one oblation of himself once offered. To the contrary notwithstanding: and the cool, chaste whiteness of the church with its rows of pews, the Whites up front and we Coloureds at the back against the wall, and the parson with his black wings, suspended in heavenward flight on the high pulpit. Watching from a distance the white table of the Lord, the deep sounds of the organ vibrating through benches and buttocks, the chalice brimful with wine, the shining plates with broken bread – miraculously white in spite of the rationings of war – everything concentrated, somehow, in the sonority of those four words. And prayers in the dining room of the big house of an evening, me and my mother and the others huddled on the floor near the kitchen doorway. Let us pray. For those near and dear to us, fighting in Thy name in distant countries against the forces of Evil, that they may return safely into our midst, not because we deserve it, but purely in Thy unfathomable mercy, amen. My mother exorcising her deep feelings of guilt through passionate prayers and terrible admonitions: *Thou shalt not . . . thou shalt not . . . thou shalt not.* And the missionary work of Hermien, blonde daughter of the house, quietly but grimly insisting on the mechanical repetition of Commandments and Beatitudes, the names of Judges and the Prayer of the Lord.

Our Father.

Our Father.

Which art in heaven.

75

Which art in heaven.
Hallowed be thy name.
Hallowed by thy name.
Thy kingdom come.
Thy kingdom come.
Thy will be done.
Thy will be done.
On earth as it is in heaven.
In heaven.
Give us this day our daily bread.
Give us this day our daily brown bread.
God can hear you, Joseph. *Our daily bread.*
Our daily bread.
Forgive us our trespasses as we forgive those that trespass against us.
Trespass against us.
And lead us not into temptation.
And lead us not into temptation.
But deliver us from evil.
What is evil?
Close your eyes. *For thine is the kingdom.*
The kingdom.
And the power.
And the power.
And the glory.
And the glory amen.
For ever and ever.
For ever and ever amen.
Amen.
I already said amen.

Hermien was the angel of my childhood, the untouchable. On Sundays, when her plaits were combed out, I was dumfounded by the smoothness of that long blonde hair. If your sins be as scarlet I shall wash them whiter than snow. Or the movement of her hands when she sat down at the piano in the *voorhuis* and with throbbing heart I dared to peep over the window-sill. The graveness of her eyes in which I often, during Bible lessons, became so absorbed that I'd even forget the words of the Lord's Prayer. Surely this was the kingdom expected on earth, and she the blessed among women, ten years old when I was six, and gradually growing older. On the back stoep one Sunday, an afternoon with the

sound of fowls clucking as they lay in the shallow hollows they'd
dug in the dust, with red combs and yellow beaks and spread wings, she
read to us, with great conviction, the story of Noah and his sons and
cursed be Canaan a servant of servants shall he be unto his brethren.
Then she shut the Bible on her lap and with her chin propped up on
her cupped hands, her elbows on her knees, sitting on a box in a pool
of sunshine, she said : 'You see, that's where it comes from. We Whites
are the children of Shem and Japheth and you are the children of Ham
and his son Canaan. That's why it is like that.' And we listened meekly
and took her word for it. If that was what Hermien's Book said – look
at the light shining on her hair, look! – then there could be no doubt, it
was the truth of truths, cross your heart.

The drunkenness of Noah was revived on weekends by the unholy
fathers of my playmates, whereas mine only existed as a faded snapshot
on my mother's washstand; and at night when she had a visitor in her
brass bed she would reverently turn the photo face to the wall so as not
to offend or be offended. And so, praise the Lord, I knew less of
drunkenness than the late Canaan or his father Ham; but of eating bread
in the sweat of my face I had my fair share.

At daybreak we were called to work by the slave bell which, after
two hundred and fifty years, still did its morning duty, Sundays ex-
cepted, with praiseworthy efficacy, come spring, summer autumn or
winter, in sun and rain and wind and even in memorable snow. I can
still feel that early-morning shudder creep through my body like a negative orgasm whenever I remember that sound shattering the peace of
the farmyard like a Last Trumpet; and then the last huddling in the
comforting rustle of the reed mattress before my mother would appear
round the edge of the folding screen to shoo me out of bed. While I'm
dancing on one foot trying to find the right trouser leg with the other,
she is moving about in the kitchen trying to light the primus stove,
singing hymns to atone for last night's sins, interrupted by oaths if she
breaks a match or upsets the meths bottle, or, sleepy-eyed, fails to find
the hole with the pricker. Stand up, stand up for Jesus – shit – ye soldiers
of the cross – blerry baste'd – Lift high his royal banner – come en'
help me with this focken thing, Joseph – it must not suffer loss – Jissis-
gott!

I knew the words of her hymns at a very early age, just like the Lord's
Prayer which I learnt so reverently from Hermien; the primus words
were equally easy to memorise, but for those I had my mouth rinsed with

blue soap. After that I was more careful and only tasted them on the tip of my tongue when I was behind the mud bank of the irrigation dam.

All words fascinated me. I would sit on a slab of slate watching the yellow-beaked ducks diving in the water and say: 'Duck.' And then: 'Dam.' And then, with elation: 'Hermien. Sophie. Joseph. She is Hermien. My mother is Sophie. I am Joseph.' Walking to and fro along the broad bank, the mud forming slithery worms between my toes, I'd say aloud: 'I am Hermien. I am Sophie. I am duck. I am water.' I would try to walk like my mother, I'd imitate the way Hermien held her head, I'd waggle like a duck or lie down in the mud to get the feel of water.

Hermien's two brothers were my closest friends. Willem was the same age as I, Thys a year younger. When the time came for them to go to school – I had to get up with the clanging of the bell to break wood for the stove and kindle a fire – they used to say their lessons with her in the afternoons. Then I would squat behind the low stoep wall, listening and repeating the *c-a-t – cat* and *m-a-t – mat* they were spelling from their blue reader.

Willem had trouble memorising his lessons, especially English. I can remember an afternoon when after Hermien's third patient effort he still got stuck with 'Little Miss Muffet sat on her tuffet . . . sat on her tuffet . . . little Miss Muffett . . .' For a moment I'd completely forgotten where I was and that they weren't supposed to know of my presence behind the wall, and I started reciting:

> 'Little Miss Maffett
> Set on he' tuffet
> Eating he' cirts en' whey.
> Dere came a bick spaider
> En' set down besaider
> En' fraiten Miss Maffet awhey.'

Surprised, Hermien looked over the wall. I was petrified.

'Where did you learn it, Joseph?' she asked. I was ready to flee: 'I'm maar jus' sitting here, Miss Hermien, 'scuse, I won' do it again, Miss Hermien.' From that day I was allowed to join them with their lessons.

I had no idea of what the words meant and even after I'd seen the picture in Hermien's book I still was none the wiser about *tuffet* or *curds*

78

or *whey*. But I couldn't care: it was the words themselves that mattered, like the liturgical phrases which came later, like *to the contrary notwithstanding*. And Hermien's praise moved me so deeply that I thought I was going to cry.

Afterwards it sometimes happened, when there were guests on a Sunday afternoon, that I'd be called to recite for them. I felt like running away, but that was out of the question – one had to obey when the Missus ordered something, my mother had taught me, or else the terrible dark woman Antjie Somers would come at night and wring my balls, – so I would stand in the circle of white visitors, head hanging, big toe digging into the ground, rattling off whatever was asked of me.

'Clever little bastard,' I once heard the Missus say after I'd finished my recitation; and before I was out of earshot one of the guests, a fat woman with a minute and perfectly round mouth, answered: 'Lucy, if you go on like this, that *klonkie* is going straight to hell. One of these days he won't know his place any more, let me tell you.' And with an embarrassed laugh the Missus said: 'Don't take it so seriously, man. After all, his father is Frans's batman.'

That night I lay awake on my rustling mattress for a very long time. *That klonkie is going straight to hell.* From my mother I'd heard all about hell, the devil with his fork and cloven hooves, and his furnace worse than last February's mountain fire which scorched the beaters' eyebrows when the wind suddenly changed. – 'Thet fire burn you until the fet drip out of you, Joseph.' – But why was I on my way to hell? What did my recitations have to do with it? Just one swoosh, and there wouldn't be anything left of this little mattress. *One of these days he won't know his place any more.* Where was my place then? Surely it was here, this room with its bright floral screen between my mother's side and mine, this row of whitewashed cottages under the oaks, this yard enclosed by the wide stone wall, that homestead half-hidden by foliage, with its thatched roof and the steep ladder leading up to the attic where the bush-tea lay spread out to dry after being braised in the outdoor oven, and where dried peaches and apricots were stored in fat barrels; fourpence was the fee one got for pressing and preparing one tray of apricots, while old Daniel kept a falcon's eye on all his workers, distributing tokens for every finished tray; and on Friday afternoon these were exchanged for money. Wasn't this my place? Surely I knew it, I could traverse it in the dark without stumbling over a root or falling into an irrigation furrow, even without stepping on the chickens' droppings. God, that was how I knew my place. Wasn't that enough? So how could I stop knowing it one of these days? And go to hell, drifting into that fire on my burning mattress like a walnut boat in a stream, flaming water, and Satan a fat woman with an arse-shaped mouth and a fork in her clammy hands. Sobbing, I crept across the dung-floor to my mother's bed.

'Fockoff, Joseph,' her deep voice threatened me.

'But I know this place, Ma. I don' want to go to hell.'

'The devil's already got you in his grip. Go beck to bed.'

In the hostile darkness I returned to my inflammable mattress, filled with terrible longing for my father – *After all, his father is Frans's batman* – gone to war so many years ago and never a word from him since the day the wireless spoke his name: Malan, Jacob – missing, presumed dead.

I sat up praying on my bed, my eyes wide open because I was much too scared to close them and hoping that God wouldn't notice it in the dark. 'Fa'rer,' I prayed, 'please tell Lawd Jissis I don' want to go to hell en' I know my place and please come back to me not because I deserve it but in thy endless mercy amen.' And then I slept until the fearful clanging of the slave bell resounded over the dawn-dark yard.

It made no difference to my love of reciting. In fact, the episode enhanced its fascination – the spell of something dangerous and dark, something evil, something forbidden, a game with unimaginable power: to go on, to see what would happen, to see how far I could go. My mother encouraged me. ('You got it from your fa'rer, it comes from way back') and resumed her narrations of our history with more religious fervour than ever before. That created a whole set of new possibilities for my dam games:

'I am Adam. I am Moses. I am Dlamini/Daniel . . .'

Sometimes the game was extended to make room for Willem and Thys. Normally they were the ones who commanded me when we went out to shoot finches with our catapults or to chase up hares with the dog – especially after they'd discovered that I couldn't stand the sight of blood. But when it came to play-acting I was allowed to dictate the rules. Our acting usually had war as its theme, and even though I was never allowed to be anything but batman, at least they left it to me to devise the situations and direct the general action.

Soon after Frans Viviers came back from the war, a very thin, deeply tanned cripple, a new element was introduced into our games. On

Christmas Eve that year the white children of the vicinity produced a Nativity play in our yard, mainly for the edification and amusement of the grown-ups who fed their ardour from the cellar : but we brown children were there as well, huddled on the periphery of the circle of light with its paper decorations.

Hermien, of course, was the Virgin Mary, with scarlet lips and cheeks, Jesus was a baby from a neighbouring farm, who very early in the evening was scared out of his wits by the enthusiasm of the performance, with the result that he bawled throughout the play, in spite of having his nappy changed halfway through. It made no difference to the devoted attention with which I watched the performance. On that sacred evening the screaming, peeing child was the promised Messiah himself; Hermien was transfigured into the Blessed Virgin; the sheet-swathed children were shepherds following the route of the star; and Willem was Joseph–not me–Joseph, but Bible-Joseph, the word made flesh. Then the Three Magi arrived, played by Thys and two friends, to offer their gold and incense and myrrh. Thys carried the gold, his face unrecognisably blackened with boot polish. In a strange way it came as such a shock to me that I nearly burst into tears, without knowing why.

For days I remained in something of a trance. It was past New Year's Day when I finally cornered Thys and asked him : 'Did you give all the gold away? Didn' you keep nothing?'

'What gold?'

'Chris'mus Eve when you had the gold.'

'But it wasn't gold, it was just little pebbles Hermien painted.'

'I saw her paint them but Chris'mus Eve it was gold. You said gold en' incense and myrrh.'

'It was just a play, man!' Thys laughed, but I thought he was pulling my leg. I'd seen the gold with my own eyes that night when Jesus was born in Bethlehem, and Hermien was his mother.

'Why'd you make your face black?' I asked him.

' 'Cause one of the Wise men *was* black!'

There was a lump in my throat. 'Well,' I said, hoarse with eagerness, 'if you play again nex' year . . . c'n I be the black men?'

' 'Course not,' he said scornfully. 'How can you? You're not white.'

I accepted it without a murmur. It fitted in with the entire pattern of life on the farm which determined that Frans Viviers and his family should live in the large Cape-Dutch homestead and we in one of a row of cottages in the backyard; that they should ring the slave bell for us in the mornings to get up and work; that I should break the firewood for the kitchen stove, that my mother should serve them coffee in their bedroom, and that afterwards we should go down to the vineyard or the orchards or the fields to hoe or pick or harvest under the watching eyes of the crippled Baas; that Hermien and Willem and Thys should go to school in the bus and that in the afternoon I should squat on the stoep with them when Hermien helped them with their lessons; that my father should have been a batman who hadn't returned after the war while his Baas was back on the farm; that I should be Sophie's barefoot boy and Hermien the Mother of God.

But that Christmas Eve kindled something inside me. I kept it secret for months before I dared to mention it to Hermien :

'Miss Hermien, when it's Chris'mus again, c'n I also do something?'

'What, Joseph? '

'Like las' Chris'mus, Miss Hermien. Of Mary en' the Chile en' so.' Adding hastily : 'But I won't bodder you, I'll make my own play.'

'Of course, Joseph. Do you want me to help you?'

God, she was so close to me, I was quite flustered, her hair was so long and silky, her eyes like the heaven of God and all his angels. I could see the fine hair on the gentle roundness of her forearm. And I wondered : What would it feel like? How soft would it be? I swallowed and said : 'No, Miss Hermien, is awright, I'll mennidge,' and ran away.

Within a week I'd recruited a cast for my play : the story of Paradise. Jonnie Katkop was Adam, a sturdy bullock with bandy legs; Eve was Aunt Katy's daughter Lisa, a precocious little dish; and with great enthusiasm and a total lack of humility I took the parts of both God the Father and the Serpent. In addition, there were a dozen or so angels. Mondays were rehearsal days, because then we were assured of enough sheets from the washing-lines for the robes of God and his heavenly host : Jonnie and Lisa, of course, had to be naked, not without indignant protests to start with, but with great gusto once they understood the pious motivation and been threatened with eternal torment in hell if they refused. The apple caused endless quarrels between Adam and Eve about who was entitled to the largest share; and in the course of one long rehearsal in early December, when there were no apples available, Lisa devoured so many green apricots that she got the squitters and nearly died. I insisted on a replacement, which offended Lisa so deeply that she promply spread her own version of their naked acting, with the result that the entire cast, including the angels and the poor replacement who'd never been to a rehearsal yet, were soundly thrashed – and that was the end of my first production.

On Christmas Eve the white children entertained us once again with their Nativity play. But somewhere between the two performances an important change had taken place: in the first, the transubstantiation had been complete: in the second, from which I was specifically excluded, the gold and incense and myrrh remained painted pebbles, smoking twigs, and ground cinnamon in a Nugget tin.

I was nine or ten years old when we went to see the circus in Cape Town, Hermien and Willem and Thys and I, in the family's vast old '38 Hudson long past its prime. Their mother dropped us on the Parade, for she had shopping to do in town; after the show she was to pick us up again. For a while we inspected tractors and caravans and cages until somebody chased us away. Then Willem gave me money to buy my own ticket at the Non-Whites office; they went to the front entrance with its bright lights and coloured ribbons, while I had to queue at the back of the tent where an irritable man with a fearsome red face examined our tickets and jostled us inside with a volley of curses and thundering imprecations. Inside we were packed until there were two of us for every seat. On the opposite side of the tent, where Willem and the others sat, there were large open blocks. But I didn't mind. It was like a view of Heaven itself, infinitely more wonderful than the Christmas shows on the farm. The ordinary world was transformed into something miraculous. Nothing I saw that day could be explained in terms of anything I'd ever seen before and yet it was happening in front of my own eyes. Horses dancing with plumes growing from their heads, elephants standing on their hind legs, lions jumping through a burning hoop, a bear chasing a dwarf, divine creatures in sparkling costumes flying high above our heads from trapeze to trapeze. The red-faced man who'd shoved us inside devoured glass and razor blades and swallowed large mouthfuls of fire. And everything happened to the accompaniment of music.

It was so loud and dazzling that it irrevocably changed the perspective of my ordinary life: it was more real than the reality I'd known; it peopled my world with the impossible, so that I could never again successfully escape from it.

For at least a week afterwards I kept to myself. Later, yes, later I would gather my friends and organise our own circuses; for months I would draw nourishment from that vivid dream. I would get bruised all over trying to somersault from a rope dangling in a tree; I'd singe Flappie's hair trying to force him to swallow fire; I'd be thrashed for plucking the feathers from the dusters in the house to bedeck my 'ponies'. But during that first week I kept everything inside myself and found no peace at all. I went on pestering everybody on the farm until the foreman offered to take me back to Cape Town when he had to deliver a load of boxes at the harbour. High up on the back of the truck I watched the vineyards and orchards streaming past on the long road to the Cape. Slowly Table Mountain grew before us, blue against the blue; and then the city around us. On the Parade, where the circus tent had been, I was deposited and threatened with certain death if I didn't keep my eyes on the Town Hall's clock tower and wait for them at four o'clock.

But the circus was no longer there. The cages had gone, the wagons and caravans had gone, the tent had disappeared. There weren't even tracks or traces left, no sawdust or manure, nothing. Only the madness of people streaming and jostling past, tables and stalls packed with strange wares, an enormous brown woman with bundles and packets of herbs and spices and roots on the pavement in front of her, newspaper vendors with trumpet voices, pigeons, cars, bicycles, pushcarts filled with fruit; and on the corner near the City Hall, under a tatty palm tree, a man standing on a box intoning over and over : 'Woe unto you, woe unto you, woe unto you!' Once a fishcart dashed past with the glistening smooth bodies of snoek and geelbek, kabeljou and mackerel, accompanied by a bugle which penetrated to the very marrow of one's bones. And lunchtime an orchestra with shiny brass instruments and an enormous drum, and a group of shrill women's voices (and one little man in their midst, with a moustache and tearful eyes and blue veins on his nose and a startling bass) bravely singing :
'Onward, Christian soldiers . . . !'
But the circus, the circus had gone. There was nothing left of the flying gymnasts, the plumed horses, the jumping lion, the magicians, the dwarfs, the clowns, the camels, the elephants. *And it had been there!* I knew it had, I'd seen it!

Timidly I ventured into the streets. In front of the station I hesitated : perhaps the circus had passed that way, into the interior. But I was too scared to ask. Later I proceeded downstreet, past Van Riebeeck's statue, in the direction of the harbour. Rows of ships were lined up against the quays, some covered with smoke and flags; and far away in the open sea one white ship was on its way out into watery space, perhaps on a trip round the world, and maybe the circus was on board, with flatfooted clowns and men eating fire and monkeys riding bicycles, gone, gone, sailing towards nowhere, world without end. My throat was taut. I couldn't swallow. I didn't want to be left behind without my circus. I felt abandoned by God and man. And I wetted my pants because there was nowhere to pee.

'One day I'm goin' to run away,' I told Willem when I got back on the farm. 'I'll run away to the circus en' I won' ewwe' come beck again.'

He snorted. 'You know what happens to people who run away, hey?'

Yes. I knew. Sagrys of Uncle Jakes had run away once. For months he'd threatened to do so: he was sixteen and sick and tired of the farm, and so he left. For three days they looked for him; then he was brought back on a van. The foreman asked him: 'Sagrys, must I take you to the police, or shall I give you a hiding myself?'

'Baas can hit me,' he mumbled, looking down to his feet, and suddenly his legs seemed so grey and thin in the floppy khaki shorts. They took him to the shed and shut the wide door behind him. I knew how dark it was inside with that door shut and only a few small holes to let in long nails of fierce light. I was with Willem and Thys and Hermien on the back stoep. It was she who said. 'Let's go. I don't want to be near.' We went to the far side of the house. But we couldn't escape the sound of the blows falling slowly and regularly, a dull, smacking, rhythmic thud, and Sagrys howling. He didn't cry like a human being, it was the howl of a night thing, of an animal, a high, monotonous sound torn from him like an intestine. We stood among the oak treees trying not to hear, but listening with sickening intensity. Hermien's face was pale, there were drops of perspiration on her forehead, and she was breathing deeply. On the other side of the house the beating went on and on and the howl continued. Hermien was uttering strange small sounds but she wasn't laughing. Still it went on. Now she was crying. And suddenly she grabbed me by the shoulders and started shaking me till my teeth were chattering: 'D'you hear that?' she cried. 'D'you hear? Don't ever run away, Joseph! Don't you dare!' I broke away from her and bent down and was sick. It went on until it felt as if there was nothing left in me, and still I belched as if my stomach was trying to get rid of myself. When I finally stopped the farm was very quiet, only the finches were chattering in the trees.

Behind the foreman's house we used to set our home-made trap to catch the red and yellow finches. That was where the poultry were fed at night, beside the privy in the backyard, and in the long afternoons, when the fowls were flopped out in the shade of the trees, swarms of finches would come down to peck up whatever food remained for them. As time went on they got wise and it became more and more difficult to lure them under the wood and gauze trap, but provided one had enough patience it still happened. We usually lay behind the privy, Willem and Thys and I, taking turns to pull the string and bring the trap down, and we carefully kept count of our scores. In the late afternoon we would go home with our string and trap and the birds we'd caught. Sometimes Willem and Thys sold the finches at school, but it happened very seldom for I usually returned to the back stoep after dark to set the caught birds free. I had no particular reason for doing so. It happened once, and then it became a habit. They never caught on. We would spend hours repairing the cage and blocking up every possible slit or hole, and I helped them very conscientiously, but the birds continued to escape. Perhaps it eventually became a ritual for Willem and Thys too. And anyway, there was always a tomorrow to catch new birds.

That afternoon began like all the others. Twice we'd pulled the trap down, the first time too soon, the second time catching a single sparrow which escaped when Willem tried to remove it. Once a bird has got away it's hell to lure them back under the trap. But the day was warm and languorous, with children's voices shrilling in the vineyards far away, and cicadas in the trees, and we had nothing else to do. When the afternoon grew yellow over the yard, we would go up to the dam for a swim, and milk the two cows, breathing deeply the smell of udder and urine and grass; and then we'd carry the heavy buckets to the dairy where Paulus would separate the milk : I can still hear the monotonous tinkling of the little bell on the red handle and the foamy sound of the milk and the thin cream-coloured trickle of cream; and afterwards Willem and Thys would disappear into the big house and I would walk across the darkening yard with my small pail of skimmed milk to where the oil lamp formed a splash of orange light against the checkered curtains and across the lower half of the pine door. But all that was for later. At the moment there was still sunshine and the afternoon seemed endless where we lay on our stomachs waiting for the birds to come back.

The foreman's wife approached from the kitchen door. We heard the gauze door slam and looked up, and watched her coming towards the privy : a fat woman wearing a man's hat and walking with a rowing motion of her heavy arms. On other afternoons we'd also seen her in the yard, and we used to curse because she'd scared the birds away, but that was all. Why was this day different, then? The privy door squeaked and was pulled shut, and from the inside we heard the scraping sound of the wooden latch.

Then Willem whispered : 'Hey look.' And he lifted the back flap where the bucket stood. Whispering and giggling, we peered inside, overwhelmed by the warm, bodily stench. We watched with bravado and disgust and dark subdued hilarity – but just for a moment, for Willem lost his balance as we pressed against him and the flap slammed shut. Inside we heard a muffled shout, and then the door was opened. We'd never in our lives run quite as fast as that. Racing across the backyard, grabbing the trap in passing, we dived in among the first fruit trees just as the foreman's wife came hobbling round the corner with her bloomers round her ankles. We ran over the ploughed earth along the narrow lanes among the trees, ducking so that she wouldn't recognise us : we stumbled and fell and got up again, until, panting, we reached the farthest plum orchard from where we could go home in a wide semi-circle. On the edge of our own yard we stopped, completely out of breath. We looked at each other and tried to laugh, but it sounded strained and we avoided one another's eyes.

'Ag well . . .' said Willem.

We stood fumbling. Thys picked up a stone and threw it as far as he could, high over the thatched roof of the farmhouse.

'I got work,' I said.

We parted; I had a weary sense of discomfort like a lump in my stomach.

I walked past the house to the irrigation dam and sat down on the other side of the bank, throwing small stones into the water. The ducks quacked and protested with indignation. I went on throwing stones, angrily, viciously, gleefully. She sat there, I thought. I saw her. She a white woman. And there's no difference, none at all, it's exactly the same, God, and it smells just like a Coloured's.

Last night, after I'd finally stopped writing and gone to bed, I dreamed a variation of the old recurrent dream : of me and Jessica and the warm pool on the beach where we wash the sand from our bodies and I kneel before her hiding my face between her thighs and she turns away and

runs to others : but this time it wasn't a fleet of green ice-cream trucks –
it was a circus train, and the man she went with had a blood-red face
and a mouth filled with fire. I woke up shivering with cold. They never
give one enough blankets and as night advances the cold creeps up from
one's feet. Above me the eternal bulb was still burning but outside, I
knew, it was night, more hospitable than my illuminated cell. I thought :
when I write again tomorrow night, I must write about Jessica, to fill
my loneliness with her. But now I realise the time has not yet come. I
must first rediscover and organise the origins of all the later patterns.

I'm groping for some sense behind my random memories. I know it
must be there, somewhere in the constant efforts – even while I was a
child – to determine my place in the midst of shifting truths. All of
them syndromes of one central complex of questions : Where is my
place? Who am I? I could spell out my questions before God or the
irreverent ducks of the muddy dam, telling my words like the beads of
a rosary : *I am Joseph. My mother is Sophie. She is Hermien.* But did it
bring me any closer to solutions? I was still too young and impatient,
too much of a stranger on our yard and in the world to realise that there
are some questions whose only sense lies in the fact that they cannot be
answered. And usually my mother had to bear the brunt of my uncer·
tainty.

She did try her best to provide me with answers, even though most
of them were negative, a pathetic set of certainties starting with : *Thou
shalt not – thou shalt not – thou shalt not.* She could recite the Ten
Commandments with such profound enjoyment; then everything seemed
simple and convincing to me. But it never lasted long, for how
could I accept her rules if she herself transgressed so openly and so fre-
quently? Yet, when I dared to question her about it, she had several
explanations ready : 'The Commandments only say thou shalt not covet
thy neighbour's wife, it says nothing about wanting a man, look it up.'
And often her sermons would end with : 'Joseph, look, inne daytime I
work my blerry arse off fo' the white people, but when it gets dark it's
our turn. The Lawd give us the night to have a bit of happiness, for
the days are hell.'

But whenever I took up her words literally and went off to have
some fun on my own, she would tear strips off me, threaten me with
eternal damnation, and end with the sombre admonition. 'God don't
sleep.'

So gradually I resigned myself to 'my mother's truth' as part of the incomprehensible order determining my life. And I even felt proud when some man or other said to me: 'Joseph, yo' mo'rer is the finest woman the Lawd ewwe' made with his two hends. Lookit her walking away, lookit her coming this way. There isn't another one like her. One fo' you en' one fo' me, jis!'

Still, I often found it disconcerting to discover in her my own uncertainties, in spite of her unwavering knowledge of good and evil. It was only too evident in her Sunday moods when she'd sit down, get up, walk about in the room, sit down again, get up again, walk about again, finally to stop at the door, leaning on the lower half, looking out, and sighing: 'I'm feeling like a blerry fly in a blerry bottle again today.'

'What's wrong with you, Ma?'

'Sundays is jus' too bad.' Another sigh.

'Is it because God isn't working today?'

'God's got nothing to do with it.'

'What's he doing these days, Ma? He finished the world so long ago.'

'He give us time to bogger it up so he can come en' put it right again.'

'How do we bogger it up, Ma?'

'Ag, gwaan, men.'

Then perhaps, I would suddenly ask: 'What we doing here, Ma?'

'How d'you mean? We living here. It's our place.'

'What makes it our place?'

'Yo' place is yo' place.'

'That other Missus said I don' know my place.'

'The hell.'

I would venture closer to her, where she stood leaning with her full round breasts over the half-door. 'I'm not talking about the farm, Ma.'

'What you talking then?'

'Why we *living* Ma?'

'Too menny questions en' you jus' see yo' arse.' And while I stood fumbling with the latch, irritable and dissatisfied, she suddenly added: 'Ag ja, we're all squatters on the beckyard of Baas Life.'

This is my lasting image of our Sunday sadness: to stand beside my mother looking out to the still yard where the cicadas were screeching and the lizards lay motionless on the flat stones, where a wagtail was hopping along pertly on the dark patch left by the dishwater, and a butcher-bird sat on the fence beside the pergola where the grasshopper he'd caught was still struggling feebly on the thorn piercing its green body; and where, as the sun grew older, a bokmakierie might call its terribly pure and sad notes in the high trees: *Bok-bok-makierie! Bok-bok-makierie!* And then my mother sighing and shifting her weight to the other foot and repeating her old adage: 'Ag, ja, we're all squatters on the beckyard of Baas Life.'

But towards nightfall her Sunday depression would begin to lift, after her ritualistic ablutions at the tap behind the house, wearing only her white petticoat, rubbing her long brown legs till they were smooth and shiny. She would put on a clean dress for the evening and tidy the house smiling and humming. For she was at home in the dark, and soon the visitors would arrive, perhaps one with a guitar gently complaining in the night, and many voices tuning in on the sweet sad songs; and after they'd left, one would stay behind with her, and I would hear their voices behind the floral screen for many hours of the night, hers and his, and the creaking of her bedsprings as she slowly shed her sadness: but mine would persist as I lay awake in the dark listening to the oak branches scraping on the roof, and a dog barking, and perhaps an owl moaning in the chimney like the wind.

The only way to exorcise my loneliness would be to lie whispering words to myself, until it ebbed away in their soothing sound: 'Genesis, Exodus, Leviticus, Numbers, Deuteronomy, Joshua, Judges, Ruth . . .' or phrases from Holy Communion, or random phrases: 'To the contrary notwithstanding . . .'

Holy Communion was one of the certainties I could hold on to. Not a certainty of any definable meaning, but something familiar and trustworthy because the ritual never changed and because a miracle was involved: wine changing into blood, white bread becoming the white body of Christ. But even this truth was shaken, part of the endless process of disillusionment.

It happened not without some vulgar comedy for which Oom Koot the verger of the Missionary Church, was responsible. The Missionary Church was several miles away, so we seldom went there except for a christening or first Communion – for the rest we usually went to the White church, which, in those days, was still allowed. I remember Oom Koot mainly because he had such a remarkable way of singing. It so happened that he was the proud owner of a set of large false teeth, bought second-hand on the Parade by some of his relations and presented to him for Christmas one year: they didn't fit very well and to prevent their falling out during the singing he had the habit of closing his mouth after every syllable: 'Rock. Of. A. Ges. Cleft. For. Me . . .'

One Saturday Oom Koot and a truckload of other members of his congregation went to Melkbos Beach where they thoroughly enjoyed themselves until Oom Koot was washed off his feet by an unexpectedly large wave, losing his upper set of dentures in the wildly foaming sea. For a while he furiously ducked and dived, grabbing left and right in the water, but without success. And so, being a rather temperamental old man, he became so mad that he plucked out his lower set of teeth and threw it into the sea as well, presumably according to the principle that from him that hath not shall be taken away even that which he hath.

He returned home with his bare mouth, refusing to speak to anyone. That evening there was a church service preparatory to Holy Communion, but he didn't sing a word. Next morning, immediately before the Communion service, somebody brought the news that Oom Koot's upper dentures, the ones washed away by the wave, had been found on the beach. The Lord took and the Lord hath given again. One can understand why the old man felt grudging. He sat through the long service. But after the congregation had gone home he blasphemously tried to avenge himself on God by consuming the entire stock of Communion wine in the vestry. When he was discovered shortly before the evening service he was completely beside himself, uproariously singing with his tooth-less gums, like an old tortoise masticating.

What upset me about the whole thing was the role of the wine. According to my childlike faith the wine should have been changed into blood by then, and one can't get drunk on blood. So if Oom Koot had really got pissed on whatever he'd drunk in the vestry, it meant that a serious doubt had been cast on the entire process of wine and blood, bread and body. As one grows older and loses one's grip on the Absolute, one became less vulnerable; there soon came a time when, looking back, I could laugh at myself. But something of the initial shock, something of that loss of faith, persisted deep inside me, a potent secret.

In those years my only defence against such events was to withdraw ever more deeply into the imaginary world I'd created for myself behind the bank of the irrigation dam, either alone or with friends. For instance, I acted out the whole story of Oom Koot with Willem and Thys and a few others – a performance which caused some of our audience to howl with laughter and others to conclude with absolute conviction that we were irrevocably on our way to hell. All that mattered to me was that, in a curious way, the play provided me with a grasp on what had happened. By transforming myself into that same toothless Oom Koot, I could exorcise his desecration: and that already meant something more than merely sitting on the bank with closed eyes and repeating to the ducks: 'I am Joseph. I am Hermien. I am Sophie. I am my father.'

My father, in a completely unexpected manner, became a decisive factor in my life. It happened one afternoon while I was reading *Robinson Crusoe* beside the dam. I was so totally immersed in the book that I forgot about anything else, and so I was scared out of my wits when, suddenly, a long shadow fell across me and I looked up to see Viviers appearing on the bank above me.

It was no ordinary reading session. The only reading matter I'd known before was in the lessons I used to share with Willem and Thys on the back stoep under Hermien's firm and gentle guidance. I'd never known a book: that belonged to the White world, like Christmas Eve concerts, and going to school, and sweets after lunch, and new clothes. Then Willem bought *Robinson Crusoe* in the Cape, paying out half the money he'd earned that summer by packing apricots. It was a large illustrated edition – Willem always loved beautiful books – and once he allowed me to page through it with him. For the rest I hovered in the background whenever, after lessons in the afternoon, he lay down to read among the geraniums. But one day unexpected guests arrived and Willem and Thys took the boys to the dam to build a boat. The book lay forgotten among the blood-red flowers. Ten, twenty times I walked past without daring to touch it. Hours later Willem and the others came down from the dam, the visitors left in a cloud of dust, we went to milk the cows, the supper bell rang through the large open window of the dining room – and by the time I went home with my pail of skimmed milk, *Robinson Crusoe* was still lying in the flower bed. Late that night I crept across the yard. The book was still there. I convinced myself that I had to save it from wind and falling dew, that I would only keep it overnight and return it to Willem the next day; and while my mother was out to visit the neighbours I hid the book under my mattress. I hardly slept that night. Next morning, for the first time, I could appreciate my mother's habit of singing hymns.

That afternoon the whole yard was searched for the lost book. It would have been so easy to tell Willem: 'You forgot it outside, so I kept it for you.' But I remained silent. In fact, I even helped them look for it. I found it incomprehensible that he hadn't immediately suspected the truth; at the time it increased my guilt. It was worse than common theft (*Thou shalt not kill, thou shalt not commit adultery, thou shalt not steal*): what I'd taken, came from a world totally different from mine, a region of absolute taboo.

Long after Willem had finally accepted the loss of the book, I remained too scared to take it from under my mattress. It was lying there and at night I was conscious of it, like the fairy-tale princess who felt the pea hidden under God knows how many mattresses. A month or more must have passed before I finally, trembling and short of breath, removed the book. I wouldn't have been at all surprised if it suddenly burst into flames in my hand. But nothing happened, and the fever subsided. With the book neatly wrapped in a newspaper I'd found in the dustbin, I hurried off to the dam. From then on my days were transformed by the magic of *Robinson Crusoe*. Here, between my very hands, a whole new world was being born, bearing all the authority of the printed word.

And then the lean figure of the Baas appeared on the bank that afternoon.

Ag, God, I thought, now it's tickets. It's worse than Sagrys running away.

'Don't you say good afternoon, Joseph?'

' 'Scuse, Baas. 'Af'ernoon, Baas.'

He didn't move, and with the sun right behind his hat it seemed as if all the light was coming, unbearably, from him, his shadow a long black line down the length of the bank, covering me. He stood watching me and I didn't look away, I couldn't move my eyes. High up on that bank he was as great as God.

'What are you doing here, Joseph?'

'Not'ing, Baas. Dunno, Baas. Jus' sitting.'

'Is that a book you're reading?'

My throat was dry. There were tears in my eyes. I remembered the slow rhythmic blows in the shed and Sagrys's never-ending scream. He came down the bank, slowly because of his lame hip. The sun blinded my eyes.

'Hermien told me you were such a good reader,' he said as he stood beside me.

93

I could feel the book trembling in my hands when he took it to have a closer look.

'Is this Willem's *Robinson Crusoe?*' he asked.

I couldn't utter a sound. Take me to the shed, I wanted to say. You can blerry well kill me if you want to.

'I didn' want to take it, Baas. I wan'ed to give it back to him.'

He stood very still and I watched him lighting his pipe, the whole ceremonious process. After the third match, as the smoke started puffing from his mouth, he suddenly said. 'Your father also carried a book with him wherever he went.'

'Ja, Baas, *The Pilgrim's Progress*, Baas.'

'How do you know about it? You were a baby when he left with me.'

'My mo'rer tole me, Baas.'

'What did she tell you?'

I looked up cautiously. He didn't seem angry. Still uncertain, but with great relief, I said : 'Everything of my fa'rer en' of his people, Baas, way back.'

'Your father was a man who had the world against him.' He shifted his stiff leg. 'He didn't want to go to war, but I made him go.' He pulled at his pipe and used the dead match to press the top ashes into position. 'One can't foresee the future. And there are things one can't repair afterwards.'

I saw him watching me as if he expected an answer, so I blurted out : 'Can't repair them, no, Baas, yes, Baas.'

'I've been watching you for a long time now, Joseph. You Coloureds are a godless lot. But your father was different and he never drank like the rest of them. It looks as if you may be taking after him. I want to give you a chance in life, Joseph. I've discussed it with my wife, and she agrees with me. I want to give you a chance to study.'

I stared at him open-mouthed. 'Baas?'

'From Monday you'll be going to school. We'll see how you get on. Perhaps you can learn a trade and do something useful. I hope you won't let me down, Joseph.' And then he added, to make quite sure that I'd understood him : 'It's for your father's sake that I've decided to do this.'

'T'enk you, Baas.'

Just before he turned to walk away, he hesitated and looked down to the *Robinson Crusoe* in his hands. 'About the book . . .' he said. 'Come to the house after milking time to get your punishment.' Then he walked stiffly up the bank, towards the sun.

I remained sitting there, watching the afternoon slowly ebbing away from me.

From as far back as I could remember I'd been terrified of pain, of all forms of physical suffering. My mother's narration of our history hadn't served to make me immune, in fact it had made me more vulnerable. My reaction on the day of Sagrys's thrashing had been quite spontaneous, uncontrollable. And now it was waiting for me, after milking time. Suppose I ran away . . . ? But that would only make it worse. All I could do was wait, sit through every painful minute of that endless afternoon.

When at last the sun was hovering on the edge of the mountains, I got up, my legs numb under me, and went to give a hand with the milking. I felt dizzy.

'You sick or something?' asked Willem.

I didn't answer, my head hanging, hoping the cow's udder would never get empty. As slowly as possible I carried the bucket to the dairy. All afternoon time had been suspended. Now, suddenly, nothing could hold it back.

Would I also, half an hour from now, be screaming in the shed like Sagrys? I shut my eyes and clenched my fists. No, I wouldn't. I swore to God I wouldn't. They could kill me, but they wouldn't get a sound from me. I'd show them. Through the throbbing of the blood in my ears I could hear the separator bell tinkling, tinkling, and stopping. It was time.

And suddenly the fear left me. Now that the moment had come I felt terribly calm. When I took up my pail of skimmed milk and put it down beside the steps leading to the stoep my hand wasn't even trembling. I allowed Willem and Thys to go on ahead, then approached the back door alone. The dark figure of the Baas was awaiting me, leaning against one of the white pillars of the pergola. I went to him and stopped.

' 'Evening, Baas. Here I am, Baas.' He said nothing. 'Now you c'n hit me, Baas.'

He moved away from the pillar. 'It's all right, Joseph. I've thought about it. You may go. But from now on you'll remember, won't you? — when you want something, you must ask for it, you can't just take it. It's time you got rid of your Coloured manners.'

I was crying as I walked across the yard with my little pail of milk, a soundless crying no one could hear. I didn't mean to cry, but I did. Tears and snot streaked down my face and I couldn't restrain myself.

95

'Where you been so long? What'se metter?' asked my mother when I finally stumbled through the doorway.

'Nothing,' I said with quiet rage. 'I'm going to school on Monday en' the Baas kep' me waiting oll fo' nothing, he didn' hit me, en' here's yo' blerry milk.'

II

When did it happen? – sometime during those years of innocence or ignorance (one's respect for the one is tainted by one's contempt of the other). We went to Bain's Kloof on the back of Frans Viviers's small van. He had to see a farmer in the Tulbagh valley about new vines for the patch where they'd chopped out the old pear trees, and he'd promised to drop us children in the mountain. Hermien and Willem and Thys, and seven or eight of their friends, and a few brown boys to carry the food and things. We were left near the hotel, with firm instructions to stick together, to be careful with fires, to look out for baboons, and to be back there at six o'clock so that he could pick us up again.

We followed the course of the water deep into the kloof. Where the stream widened into a series of deep, clear pools among high boulders we stopped for a swim – we boys in a pool on the near side of a tall white formation, the girls in a shallower pool on the other side. For an hour we frolicked and swam and dived and laughed, before we scrambled out of the water, smooth as otters, and stretched ourselves out on the flat and round rocks to bask in the sun until the last shiny water drops had disappeared from our brown or white skins. And then we played boys' games : sending pebbles scuttling across the water, imitating bird sounds, climbing on a rock to see who could pee the farthest, and making the inevitable anatomical comparisons to decide who had the biggest, who was sprouting hair, who had the hardest biceps.

Finally we became conscious of hunger, and started yelling to the girls on the other side of the rocks to find out whether we might come over.

'Wait!' they shouted.

We waited for a few minutes and yelled again.

They were still not ready.

It was repeated three or four times, until we got fed up with their cheek.

'We're coming!' shouted Willem, always the gangleader – and without waiting any longer we scambled over the tall rock formation to the girl's pool. Screeching and screaming they scattered to all sides, most of them only half dressed. They'd been swimming in their underclothes, and vests and pants were spread out everywhere on the rocks to dry as we made our appearance. Most of the girls promptly sat down just as they were, their dresses selfconsciously tucked in under them. We mischievously showered them with stones to try and chase them up, but they remained where they were, blushing with embarrassed anger. As the teasing and jeering went on, I couldn't keep my eyes off Hermien. She was sitting on one side, her face crimson, her hair hanging down wet and slithery across her shoulders so that her oval face appeared smaller than usual. Here and there the wetness of her body stained her light cotton dress. It struck me like a blow in the solar plexus: there was Hermien, and underneath that floral dress she was naked on the rock, and there – look – through the damp material clinging to her, her young nipples were darkly visible.

The holy Hermien I used to worship was, suddenly, not different in any way from all the little brown girls whose tits and slits I'd fondled behind the muddy bank of my dam.

'Well, we're going to have lunch,' Willem said casually after a while. 'You can stay here if you want to.' And he started leading the boys farther upstream to a picnic spot under a cliff. The girls followed soon enough, but something about the morning's carefree air had been disturbed: there was a suggestion of deliberateness and exaggeration in our laughter. I didn't look at Hermien once.

Most of them were too lazy to climb any further after lunch and remained spread out in the shade. But Willem quietly came to my side and whispered: 'Coming with?' – and like two lizards we scaled the cliff.

From far below us Thys or someone was calling: 'Where you going?'

Willem called back: 'Just up to that ridge!'

'Don't go too far!'

'We'll be back soon.'

'You're bladdy mad in that heat . . .' The voice trailed off in the distance.

We went higher and higher up the slope. For Willem it probably was a climb like any other, but for me it was an opportunity to withdraw from the world and come to peace with myself again. Therefore I didn't pay much notice to the route we followed: over the first ridge, and the second, and a third, and yet another, each time expecting to see the summit before us – that summit towards which one is driven so illogically, hoping to be able to look down from there and discover a comprehensible pattern in the world below. But on that day we never reached a summit and never discovered a more comprehensible pattern.

The first time I became conscious of our surroundings was when Willem suddenly stopped and asked: 'Why's it getting cool?'

There were clouds coming on over the mountains and the tough green grass was swept by a strong wind. The sweat on my forehead and between my shoulders changed into pinpricks of cold.

'There's mist coming down,' I said. 'We better go back.'

'Just a short way now, then we're there.'

But it wasn't the real summit and by the time we reached the ridge above the stony slope, another cliff was towering above us, disappearing into white fog.

'I s'pose we'd better go back, then,' Willem admitted with obvious disappointment.

We started the descent, climbing and sliding and stumbling. Even before we'd reached the bottom of that first slope, the fog was swirling all round us in huge humid whorls like the breath of an enormous cow.

'Shit,' said Willem.

'We mus' be careful now, there's cliffs down there.'

Very slowly we went down the slope, which grew more and more stony and uneven as we progressed.

'You sure it's the right way?' I asked after some time.

' 'Course. D'you think I'm stupid?'

By that time the fog was so thick that we couldn't see more than five yards. And in less than a quarter of an hour we stopped abruptly, and just in time, on the edge of a sheer cliff.

'Jiss!' I said. 'I do'no this place.'

'We'd better shout so they can hear us,' he suggested, still sounding confident, with the barest hint of a wavering in his voice.

'Hallo!' we shouted thinly into the white world. 'Halloooooooooo!'

The mist lay wrapped around the mountain like a shroud and no sound from the outside penetrated to us. In unearthly silence we went on groping, away from the cliff. After what seemed like miles we stopped again and yelled:

'Halloooooooooooooooo!'

There wasn't even an echo in the heavy mist. Things weren't looking well at all. Slowly the moisture was seeping through our clothes. Our teeth were chattering. Halfway through a stonefield we stopped to survey our situation, our hands thrust deeply into our pockets, folding protectively around our minute numbed pricks.

'I've got matches here,' he exclaimed, removing a hand from his pocket. 'Brought them to make the fire for lunch. Now we must just find some shelter.'

'Then we mus' look fo' the cliffs again, there's always caves.'

'Give me your hand,' he said, carefully hiding the box of matches again. 'Before we *donner* down somewhere.'

Hand in hand, as helpless as Brueghel's blind, we wandered through the wilderness. Darkness was approaching through the white fog. Every now and then we still stopped to yell, but without much conviction.

Through what miracle it happened I still don't know, but just before it grew too dark to see we found shelter. Not a cave, but a small hollow under a leaning boulder. The ground was very uneven and in times of rain a stream probably washed down that way, for there were bits and pieces of driftwood among the stones. We gathered as much as we could and made a fire. With much patience, and using up more than half the matches, we finally managed to coax a small flickering flame into being, then we sat back with our shoulders leaning against the rough stone, and slowly felt the heat permeating our shivering bodies.

'You think the others got beck to the road?' I asked when my teeth were no longer chattering.

'Oh, long ago. It's easy to get back there. I'm sure my dad is already looking for us.'

It was indeed a comforting thought. Our conversation began to flow more freely. For a while we played noughts and crosses on a patch of sand we'd smoothened among the stones.

'They're taking a long time,' he said once.

'They can't see inne mist. P'raps they won't come befo' tomorrow.'

'Shit. But I s'pose it's OK. We've got enough wood.' He sat drawing with a twig for a while. Then he suddenly asked: 'Have you ever heard of Rachel de Beer?'

'Who's she?'

'In the Greak Trek she and her brother got lost in the snow. So she dug out an antheap and put all her clothes on him and lay down outside the hollow till they found her there. Her brother was still alive.'

'En' she?'

'No.'

'Was they white?'

'Of course.'

I thought of Hermien in her moist dress, Hermien naked in front of a caved-out anthill, and my pants tautened.

We talked sporadically in the dark, the words drifting like the fog surrounding us, like the bitter smoke of our fire.

'Once, after my dad escaped in Italy, they were also trapped in the mountains like this,' Willem once said. 'It went on for a week and it was snowing too. But if it hadn't snowed the Germans would have found them.'

'My fa'rer wasn't there.'

'They were swine, those Germans, hey?' he said. 'Is it really true that they . . .?'

'It's all true.'

'If there's war again, I'll give them hell and you can go with me. You can be my batman.'

'You think there'll be war again?'

'My dad says one can't trust the Russians.'

'It'll be nice to be here in the mountains if there's war. You'll hear the cannons far away, but they won' get you here.'

'In the war they get you anywhere.'

'I'll find a spot where they won't.'

'Ha, where?' he jeered.

'Won' tell you.'

'It's because you don't know.' He changed position. 'Jiss, I'm getting hungry now. Haven't you got anything with you?'

'No.'

'I once read about people in a shipwreck. In the end they ate one another.'

'Will you eat me?' I asked.

'Hell, no man, you're mos my pal. Will you eat me?'

'No.'

'Cross your heart?'

'Cross my heart.'

We shook hands gravely, pledging ourselves to a mutual abstention from cannibalism. And then we started discussing Robinson Crusoe and what he would have done if he'd been here in the mountains instead of an island where he had all his provisions handy; and how we would like to find an island like that and live there for the rest of our lives.

Afterwards, lying huddled together, ready for sleep, I lazily said: 'It's all sommer maar make-believe, man. When you grown up, you'll be a farmer like your fa'rer.'

'Never!' He tensed his back against my stomach. 'Thys can farm, I won't. I'm going to see the world, I'm going to be rich.'

'I also going to see the world,' I bragged. 'En' all the people will know me en' say: Thet's Joseph Malan, thet outjie.'

'Why will they know you?'

'Jus' because I'm me.'

We grew more and more sleepy as the fire burned lower and lower in the silence of that white, dark night. We clung to one another and slowly drifted off to sleep. But it didn't last long, for the coals were still smouldering when we were awakened by the rain. The wind had turned. Soon the last ashes were blown away; and in the terrible cold we pressed ourselves against the stone, in a tight embrace, desperately trying to keep a last glow of warmth alive between our bodies. Thoughts and images began to merge confusedly. Hermien, always Hermien. The way she'd been that day, with her body visible through the dress, and her vest and underpants spread out on a rock. And earlier, the Hermien of our lessons, the Sunday Hermien praying for us and teaching us to sing:

> *All things bright and beautiful,*
> *All creatures great and small ...*

The Hermien of that first Christmas Eve, in her long white sheet. Round yon Virgin, mother and child, Holy infant so tender and mild. Willem was Joseph. I am Joseph. And now we're both here, Joseph and Joseph, in the vastness of the white world just the two of us alive, and we won't eat one another, cross my heart, because the war will pass and my father will come back from Robinson Crusoe's island, smiling like that snapshot on the washstand, and at night I'll listen to them together in the brass bed, my lovely mother and my distant father, and they won't send me away if I come to them, because I'll know my place and be saved from hell, and the slave bell will never ring again and all the birds will escape from the trap and naked Hermien will be clothed in white, in whiter than snow, and ascend to heaven high above the dam where I'm playing with the ducks and girls, and the power and the glory for ever and ever, in spite of notwithstanding, Joseph and Joseph together.

They found us there, late the following afternoon as the mist was clearing, both benumbed and delirious, clinging so tightly to one another that they had some difficulty separating our arms.

III

Who was M. J. Nel, who was Kerneels Bothma? Below their names, in the faded and dilapidated red edition of *The Tempest*, I signed my own, a new signature with the two swirls I'd first tried out on innumerable sheets of paper. One day someone else would wonder: who was M. J. Nel, who was Kerneels Bothma, who was Joseph Malan? And so, provided the book could last long enough, the title page would slowly be filled with names and dates, and the only thing remaining unchanged through all the years would be: *The Tempest, A Play by William Shakespeare, Edited by* I no longer know whom, probably Verity. And long after all of us had passed through the school's brown desks and the book itself had landed on the rubbish dump, Prospero would still be striding across his island with robes and magic wand speaking poetry, and Caliban would blaspheme in the darkness of his cave and Miranda, blonde like Hermien, would listen to the songs of Ariel:

> *Full fathom five thy father lies;*
> *Of his bones are coral made;*
> *Those are pearls that were his eyes;*
> *Nothing of him that doth fade*
> *But doth suffer a sea-change*
> *Into something rich and strange.*

Even whether M. J. Nel and Kerneels Bothma had been white or brown I would never know. They might have been my predecessors in that very classroom, or the book could have formed part of a donation by some White school. Often books which became too old or tattered for their use were passed on to us. Sometimes a White principal would arrive with those boxes of books and then we were all assembled in the red-brick hall to listen to speeches by our own principal, the visitor, the chairman of the School Committee and the local missionary, followed by a few concluding remarks once again by our own principal, 'to express anew our heartfelt appreciation', afterwards the anthem would be sung and we'd remain standing until the guest of honour had been escorted outside by the principal.

Mr Pieterse was a stout man who always gave the impression of wearing a corset, and on such days he wore his best striped Sunday suit. In my young mind he was soon associated with Mr Toad of Toad Hall, an impression enhanced by the way in which he used to comb his hair, divided neatly in the centre, like an open Bible on his head. He had unusually small hands for such a big man, with signet rings on both little fingers and they always felt clammy (I discovered that at prize-givings); and he always seemed particularly eager to shake hands with our White visitors.

After the anthem the pupils returned to the classrooms – to Frikkadel who used to pinch all offenders in the groin, boys and girls alike, when we made grammatical mistakes; or Blackie with his threatening divider in the maths room (his wife was eventually picked up for immorality); Baselisk's history lessons; Mr Toad for biology and Latin; or, if we were fortunate enough, back to Miss Mostert for English, to *Alpha of the Plough* and *Poetry for Boys and Girls* ('Laura stretched her gleaming neck, like a rush-embedded swan . . .'), back, oh joys of joys, to *The Tempest*, to M. J. Nel and Kerneels Bothma, my unknown brothers in Shakespeare.

It is strange that almost all my school memories should have to do with Secondary School: probably because I didn't spend much time in Primary, where I was allowed to start in Standard Four, having learnt such a lot during the back stoep lessons with Willem and Thys. My only lasting memories are of the overcrowded classrooms and how we had to take turns sitting on the floor; and how the prettiest girl in the class, Jubilee Jansen, who always sat on a bench, one day wetted herself so that a thin stream ran down into her tin mug under the seat. The mugs were meant for milk at playtime, poured from large cans under the oak tree near the boys' gate, and I can remember how we used to bet on who would get the janitor's tobacco quid in his mug. One summer we received apples too, when there was a huge surplus and somebody suggested that we should be allowed to share it with the pigs.

My Secondary School memories are different, more intimate, more exciting, each part of a process of discovery which completely entranced me. We continued with the familiar sort of work, of course, grammar and South African history and arithmetic, but in addition there were whole new worlds: not merely Van Riebeeck, Van der Stel and Hottentot Pass Laws, but also Columbus and Napoleon, and the civilisations of Egypt and Greece and Rome, Caesear and Gaul-of-three-parts. And instead of readers we had real books – short stories and essays and novels and poems.

Above all I loved the English classes of Miss Mostert, probably because the new language immediately challenged my mind with possibilities and associations. I was enthralled by adjectives and the billowing movement of long sentences; I compiled endless lists of words which stimulated my imagination: *primordial* and *somnolent* and *acquaceous* and *heterogeneous* and *euthanasia* and *sanctification*. I memorised Alpha of the Plough's entire essay 'On word magic' and could move myself to tears with :

> *And hear about the graves of martyrs the peewees crying,*
> *And hear no more at all . . .*

Poems of death – all those anonymous ballads, 'The Wife of Usher's Well', and then 'The Rime of the Ancient Mariner', and Poe's 'Raven' – moved me sensually, made my balls contract, and sometimes left me in a sweat of fear lest the bell would go too soon and I be caught with an erection.

And always back to *The Tempest*. The very first passage caught me in its spell, with those strange words still incomprehensible to me : *boatswain* and *yarely* and *bestir*, which even Miss Mostert's painstaking explanation could not rob of their magic. She had a wonderful way of reading, and in the afternoons I used to spend hours at the dam trying to modulate my voice like hers so that it could dance with Ariel and curse with Caliban and come to rest with Prospero :

> *We are such stuff*
> *As dreams are made on; and our little life*
> *Is rounded with a sleep; and our little life*
> *Is rounded with a sleep; and our little life*
> *Is rounded with a sleep; for ever and ever, amen.*

Under Miss Mostert's energetic direction we even produced the play, and I was Prospero, wearing a large striped beach towel for a cloak and using a brass fire iron as a wand. I doubt whether she'd realised beforehand what she was letting herself in for, but she was still young and school hadn't got her down yet.

We rehearsed for three months, from the cold of late July through the winds of August and September's hesitant spring until the full-blown summer heat of October was upon us. It meant we had to stay in after school and that afterwards I had to walk the six miles back home. I was still fortunate – in the mornings my mother gave me a piece of bread for lunch – but several of the others (and there were many of us, at least thirty, including the nymphs and reapers and spirits) had to go without food all day, and there were some who'd even started without break-fast in the morning. By the time we'd finished they were ashen grey in the face; and one afternoon Jubileee Jansen, who played Miranda, fainted halfway through the rehearsal. From then on Miss Mostert used to bring us something to eat, bread or fruit, which couldn't have been easy on her meagre salary.

The few rostrums we needed for the play we boys made under Miss Mostert's direction, and the girls painted the series of simple backcloths she'd designed. Since that work had to be done after rehearsals, I often didn't come home before evening. And then I still had to milk the cows, because that was part of the Baas's philosophy: 'I can ask someone else to do the milking, Joseph, but one doesn't appreciate a thing which comes too easily. I'm giving you a chance to study, but in exchange I'm expecting you not to neglect your duties on the farm.' Only after these 'duties' did I find time to do the day's homework, much to the annoyance of my mother who had already started feeling the first effects of her illness. Uusually it was past midnight before I could blow out the brass lamp; and five o'clock the next morning the slave bell would be clanging in the dark outside.

It sometimes felt as if I was wandering through the days in a trance. But it didn't matter. I was Prospero, I was part of a play, and in an inexplicable way the stumbling, fumbling rehearsals attained a sharper reality than the world surrounding them. For three months we formed part of an esoteric brotherhood, glowingly aware of the jealousy and admiration of all the other kids.

And suddenly it was opening night. Two hours before the time we arrived to be made up: there were no dressing-rooms, of course, so two classrooms had been temporarily set aside for us. The make-up was plastered on our faces like death-masks, starkly white, with round red cheeks and rosebud mouths, and my hair was sprinkled with baby powder to make it look grey. For Jubilee Miss Mostert managed to find a motheaten old wig covered with curls and locks and hanging down to the shoulders; I couldn't keep my eyes off her.

At last we were all fighting and jostling on stage for a vantage point at one of the peepholes in the curtain to watch the audience. The hall was overflowing; even the windows and aisles were packed with people. The front row was reserved for White visitors – a couple of Dominees, two vice-principals from schools (the principals having been prevented by 'unforeseen circumstances'), a few lecturers from the Teachers' Training College.

On the appointed moment Mr Toad came to the stage, in front of the curtain, and waited for the noise to subside. Just before he could start there was the sound of a resounding slap, a woman's voice said: 'I tole you to sharrap!' and a child started howling blue murder. Only after mother and child had left and her chair had been taken over by someone sitting in the aisle Mr Toad could start with his welcoming address.

After him one of the White visitors, a Dominee, took the floor. He didn't actually want to make a speech, ladies and gentlemen: just on behalf of our small group of visitors in your midst, thank you, thank you very much for the honour and the privilege. He found it a truly exceptional occasion. He'd also had Shakespeare prescribed as a child and he knew how difficult it was, and for Coloured children it would be even more so, but for that reason it was all the more praiseworthy. Praiseworthy and laudable, ladies and gentlemen. And he felt he'd like to add, if they would allow him to say so, that tonight might serve as an example to many. One so often heard of such bad ways among our Coloureds, of moral and social decay and such things, but an occasion like this renewed one's faith. He would like to appeal to the parents and children present here tonight to take it to heart and to build on it, to help their own people rise from their squalor, for that was the only way in which, in this fair land, the Name of the Lord could be . . .

Then the curtain opened.

It was Abdul Moolman, we heard afterwards, Abdul Moolman, the matric boy playing Caliban, who'd got fed up with the talking and decided to open the curtain. The actors of the first scene were already in their positions on the 'boat'; but I was there with them, right in the middle of the stage at the largest peephole, and of course I wasn't supposed to appear before the second scene. I didn't know what to do. For a while I simply stood there, aiming this way and that; then with a flourish of my striped cloak I rushed off. By that time the first bit of dialogue was already past, for the actors had been conditioned to start speaking the moment the curtain opened. And Alonso, Sebastian and their friends had already appeared on deck by the time the Dominee recovered from his surprise and crept back to his chair, which he missed because the seat had been turned up in the dark. Then the curtain was hastily drawn again, amid deafening applause and whistling and stamping of feet.

Half a minute passed. Mr Toad rose to his feet again to just, ladies and gentlemen. . . . But he was interrupted by the opening music suddenly blaring forth at full volume, and shortly afterwards the curtain went open again.

This time it went as smoothly as one might reasonably have expected. Characteristically, Miranda fluffed several of her passages, but nobody was any the wiser; in the second act Caliban stumbled over a rostrum and, to the enormous enjoyment of the audience, fell flat on his face with his load of wood; in the fourth act my robe started slipping off my shoulders and in my frantic efforts to pull it back I never realised that I'd missed my most important soliloquy; and just before the end there was a heated argument between Ariel onstage and the prompt in the wings because she'd given him the wrong cue.

There were many other interruptions because of untimely applause by the audience, which gradually grew worse after two long intervals had allowed a certain section an opportunity of emptying several jugs of heady farm wine behind the hall. In the course of the performance I was alternately upset, terrified, depressed and furious because of everything that went wrong; I was in the depths of misery after missing my soliloquy; but when the final curtain closed and the hall seemed to burst with applause, we became half mad with excitement. We embraced and kissed each other, and laughed, and cried, and babbled stupidly until we were once again surprised by the curtain opening. In utter confusion we grabbed each other's hands and tried to form a row like Miss Mostert had taught us, but by that time the curtain had already closed.

Back in the classrooms we removed most of the make-up with toilet paper, and took off our costumes, and prepared to go home with half-washed faces. In the dark quadrangle our voices reverberated among the brick walls. But once we'd passed the entrance we scattered in all directions; and suddenly it was quiet, suddenly everything was gone, and the night breeze felt icy on my burning face.

For a long time I stood outside the gate, filled and depleted at the same time, with that *tristitia post coitum* peculiar to the theatre. For three months we'd worked on the play, for one night we'd performed it, and now it was done. Together with the other actors I would probably continue, for another week or two, to quote liberally and irrelevantly from the text; we'd go on addressing each other as 'Prospero' or 'Ariel' or 'Ferdinand'; and in a year's time, perhaps, we'd still say: 'D'you remember that night with *The Tempest* when the Dominee was still talking and the curtain opened?' But then that, too, would fade and disappear and be gone. For all the others. But not for me. For me it was just the beginning of something. All my past excursions, all my games at the dam, all my confused dreams, yearnings, wishes, all the doubts emerging in my world, had been channelled in a specific course during those three months, and it would be decisive for everything that happened afterwards.

On the first street corner, after I'd finally started walking, a black figure moved against the shadow of the hedge. I stopped in my tracks.

'Is it you, Joseph?'

'What are you doing here in the dark, Ma?'

'Jus' waiting fo' you.'

I tried to make out her face in the dark, but couldn't distinguish anything. I knew that she'd been to the play, of course, but she hadn't come alone and so I wasn't expecting her there.

'Where's your boy friend then, Ma?'

'Gone home. I thought it's mos a special occasion fo' you, en' I waited fo' you, so we can walk toge'rer.'

'Thanks, Ma.' We took the long road back to the farm. After some time I asked: 'You like the show?'

'Was a bit high fo' me, but it was a nice concert. Thet cheppy what fell with the bunnel of wood, he was very funny.'

There was something secretive and shy about her which I couldn't fathom.

'Why don't you say anything?' I insisted.

'Ag, Joseph, yo' Ma is out of sorts tonight.'

'But what's the matter?'

She stopped under a street light. For the first time I realised how much she'd aged. She would be one of those who got old very suddenly, without the transition of autumn.

'You look' so jus' like yo' fa'rer tonight, Joseph, I got a fright.'

'But I'm his child.'

'You his chile, awright. God knows. You his chile en' I don' know if I mus' be gled o' sed.' She walked on and it took some time before she spoke again. 'I'm so worried, Joseph. What you going to do once you finish school, hey?'

'I'm going to be an actor, Ma.'

'But thet's not a job!'

'That's what I want to do.'

'En what about yo' learning en' all? You mus' get on in life, Joseph. When I'm no longe' there to help you.'

'Why are you talking like that? You're still young.'

'Everybody got his time. En' I still wan'ed to help you.'

'How can you help me?'

'I been putting money away fo' you from the time you was small. So you c'n have a chance inne world.'

'I told you I want to be an actor. You'll be reading in the papers about me.'

'You mustn' try to manure a whole land with one fart, Joseph.'

'I'll show you. I'll show everybody.'

Her rich voice came back to me like a bell tolling in the dark, the one sentence I'd heard so often in my life: 'You Coloured, Joseph.'

'The Whites also applauded me tonight.'

'So what? Tonight they clep hen's fo' you, en' tomorrow they kick you unne yo' arse.' We walked on. 'Remem'er yo' fa'rer's hist'ry,' she said quietly. 'Remem'er what heppen to Braam. The Lawd shell visit the iniquity of the fa'rers upon the third enne forth generashun.'

'I'm not trying to play for white, Ma. I only want to be an actor. I don't care about the rest.'

'You think you don' care. A Coloured care fo' everything, you'll fine out.'

'I thought you wanted to help me. Is this help, standing in my way like this?'

'I want to help you so you don' get hurt. You got hurt in yo' blood en' I don' wan' to see as how it get too much fo' you.'

'How can I get hurt when I'm acting? I'm not in anybody's way.'

'You trying to get into the light, thet's what. En' we people mus' stay out, it's not our place. The Lawd made us fo' his sheddows, we his night people.'

I can recall almost every word we said on that long walk home. I can do so because we didn't often speak our minds so freely, and also because it was the last proper conversation we had before she became seriously ill.

She'd been complaining for a long time and I could see her losing weight, she who used to be so proud of her body. There came fewer visitors to the brass bed. And sometimes at night I could hear her moaning and sobbing; lighting the primus in the mornings she sang more hymns and swore less. But when I inquired about her health all she said was : 'It's the Lawd what punish me,' or curtly : 'I'm awright.'

It took a long time before her condition had weakened so much that I had to insist : 'You must go to see a doctor, Ma.'

'Why?'

'You're too thin.'

'I'm slimming.'

'You're not well. You must let the doctor look at you.'

'I don' let strange men touch my bory.'

'But you can't go on like this!'

'I c'n go on like I wan' to, gwaan.'

But one morning while I was at school she collapsed in the kitchen and Mrs Viviers took her to a doctor in town. When I came home in the afternoon my mother was still in hospital. It shocked me. I could remember how often she'd said : 'When they take a Coloured to hospital, it's jus' to die.'

But a few weeks later she did come home again, with her left breast removed.

'Why didn' they finish me?' she asked bitterly. 'Now, they send me beck all lopsided en' secon'-hend en' shop-soiled.'

It was only much later that I began to understand the agony she must have been suffering all that time : the daily awareness of a body dying away from her – and what else did she really have to believe in? The only joy she'd ever known came to her through the body; it was her safeguard for the future, her key to the present. To come back home after she'd had a knife in her confirmed the worst she could conceive : that her wholeness had been wounded, that death now formed part of her. And it was almost with a sense of glee that she repeated : 'He tole me I was finish' en' klaar, it's no use, I'm rotten with the cencer.'

She refused to go back to hospital. 'My place is here. If I got to die,

I die jus' here.' The doctor sent her drugs, which she emptied in the chamber pot.

One Sunday a Malay healer arrived from Cape Town, blocked up doors and windows, and spent an hour with her while we waited anxiously under the trees outside. At sunset he reappeared and sent the children out to collect frogs. From the irrigation dam, from the fountain, from every stream and *vlei* on the farm, frogs were brought that evening. The healer tied up twelve of them in a muslin bag and lay it on my mother's chest. An hour later the frogs were replaced by fresh ones, the first group having 'sucked themselves to death', and so it went on throughout the night until at least a hundred and twenty of them had been sacrificed. At daybreak the healer dug a hole on our threshold, buried all the dead frogs and some *doepa* in it, and carefully flattened the earth again; and as my exhausted mother drifted into sleep he put the fat wad of notes she'd paid him in a brown wallet and drove off in his ancient Buick.

The amazing part of it was that her condition did, in fact, improve. For a month she was able to do her housework again. But with the approach of winter she rapidly deteriorated. In less than a fortnight she looked like a woman of sixty, as if her skin had dried out, clinging to the skull like parchment. She didn't even have the energy to curse the Malay healer. In the daytime we propped her up in the thin wintry sun where she spent her hours huddled in a tiny bundle, smoking dagga. The bittersweet smell permeated our little cottage from floor to ceiling, but I was thankful for it because at least it camouflaged the smell of death. Grass was the only remedy against the pain; in addition she used to rub nicotine into her emaciated body, 'so the cancer roots c'n grow out'. But in the more secret hours of the night, when the effect of the dagga was declining, she would start moving and moaning in her bed: a thin wailing sound, shockingly similar to her earlier sounds of love, and hour after hour it would increase with the pain; by the time the cocks started crowing one couldn't hear them for her screams. It was a relief when the slave bell rang and I could cross the pale yard to perform my early-morning tasks before setting off to school. It became more and more unbearable, and the whole farm was beginning to prepare for her death. The funeral people arrived to measure her for shroud and coffin, and the men started hoarding wine for the occasion.

Shortly before the end there was a period of peace. At the time I was amazed by her serenity, and by the way she even renounced the dagga and all other comforts, attaining a sort of virginity in the face of pain and death. Today it no longer surprises me.

During her last days we spent much time together. The present was no longer important to her, only the past. For hours, for nights on end, I had to listen, with dull resentment, to the long litany of my father's people which I already knew so well.

Once we also talked about the future.

'I tole you I put money away fo' you, Joseph.'

'Yes, Ma.'

'The hospittul took some of it en' the blerry Slams took some of it, but I got a bietjie fo' you. Look in the suitcase unne' the bed.'

It was a plain brown cardboard suitcase, but it contained several hundred notes, all her savings from God knows how many years.

'I was a orphan, Joseph, they pick' me up at Genadendal. Bare-arsed I got into this world en' bare-arsed I'll go out of it. But I got this fo' you so it c'n go better with you.'

'But where did you get all the money?'

'Save it up, I tole you. I made *gazat* fo' you.'

'Ma!'

She looked at me without moving an eyelid. How much did she earn a month? Perhaps five pounds, with board and lodgings, and the odd bits of old clothing for herself and me. From five pounds a month she couldn't possibly have saved that amount. With all the shock of a new discovery I thought of all those years, all those visitors in her bed, her vulnerability and anguish in the early morning. I wanted to ask her about it, I *had* to know, but her silent eyes silenced me.

'Jus' you make sure you walk inne way of the Lawd en' you don' lick the arses of the Whites.'

In my bewilderment I could only stammer out banalities : 'But I don't want money, Ma, I want you. Why don't you stay with me instead of trying to be good to me?'

'I'm not good fo' you, Joseph. I was a shit mo'rer en' I know it.'

'But, Ma, I . . .'

'Sharrap. Go call the pastor, I wan' to go out.'

I went to Frans Viviers for help, for the pastor lived a long way off.

'You people are so inconsiderate,' he said. 'You know very well I need everybody in the vineyards to prune and fertilise and hoe. Can't you wait for the weekend?'

'I think my mother is in a hurry to go, Baas.'

'All right, I won't stand in your way. Call Dirk and ask him to take you on his cart. If you really must.'

There was a fine drizzle when we left in the Cape cart passing under bare branches, the squelching wet mud slushing and spattering under the wheels with the fancy red spokes. The clouds were low and whitish grey and wet, and the tree-trunks very black and still in the smudging rain. All the world was inhospitable and dead. The sound of the horse's hooves and the swishing of the wheels made the silence even more silent. Next to me sat old Dirk April, holding the wet reins loosely in his lap, his hands drawn into his tattered sleeves like tortoise heads; singing monotonously:

> *My bonnie lies over the ocean,*
> *My bonnie lies over the sea . . .*

With every word a small cloud of white breath escaped from his mouth, and to this very day I find it the saddest song in all the world.

Halfway through another repetition of the song he suddenly broke off and said: 'Joseph, you mustn' let ennyone ewwe' say a bed word about yo' mo'rer. There is no woman what could give it to a men like her.'

'Yes, Oom Dirk.'

He started again with *My bonnie.*

'Oom Dirk.'

'. . . *over the seaaaa.* Ja?'

I stared straight ahead. 'Oom Dirk, did my mother ever – I mean with a man – did she ever ask money – I'm just asking.'

For a while he didn't say anything. The horse's hooves clattered on the muddy road and the cart swayed and danced with us. 'Joseph,' he finally said. 'Joseph, when you go to church: do the Lawd ask you fo' money or do you give it on yo' own, from de gledness of yo' heart?'

When we returned with the pastor she was waiting for us, patient and still. After the freshness of the air outside the little room was fetid with the heavy smell of death. The brown pastor sat down on a straight-backed chair on one side of the bed and I on the other. All the married women of the farm filed in after the pastor, most of them barefoot, and squatted on the floor. There was no hurry or curiosity in their manner: with an ancient earthy dignity they took their places and it was remarkable how the warm, moist smell of rain and the heavy human odour of their bodies subtly dominated the closeness of death. The oil lamp was already burning, turned to a mere glimmer, and the brass chain had been pulled down as far as possible so that the ceiling and corners of the room were dark, with the shadows of the human bundles motionless and stark on all four walls.

What I can remember of that long deathwatch is above all the disturbing dichotomy I felt in myself : part of me was moved by my mother dying, by the forever unfathomable process, by the sad discovery of how remote and strange she really was, how impossible to reach – while another part was fascinated by the scene as pure spectacle : the chiaroscuro of the room, the many faces in the murky yellow light of the lamp, my mother shrinking away smaller and smaller in the enormous double bed, the pastor opposite me with the neatly plaited golden chain of his pocket watch draped over his round belly, and the small scar on his chin.

I wanted to mourn for my mother, I wanted to lose myself in her dying; through her I wanted to grope towards my unknown father and the long row of shadows behind him. I wanted to mourn for myself, I wanted to give myself up to fear and loneliness : but something withheld me and forced me to contemplate the scene from a distance, with strange amazement and dispassionate analysis, as if it were taking place far outside myself and could be judged purely as theatre. It was the first time I became so acutely conscious of something which remained an inalienable part of myself.

Soon after the pastor's reading and praying she closed her eyes and lay motionless for the rest of the night, although I sometimes got the impression that she was peeping through her eyelids and smiling faintly. On the floor the women shifted and moved from time to time, and occasionally one would get up and go out and come back again. Even when the slave bell went they didn't leave. But the sound must have penetrated very deeply into my mother's sleep for she suddenly moved her head on the pillow and mumbled :

'Time to gerrup, Joseph.'

I got up from my chair and sat down on the bed. 'I'm here, Ma.'

'It's ringing, Joseph, it's ringing, move yo' arse.'

'I'm not sleeping, Ma. I'm here.'

With a sigh she opened her eyes. She was quite lucid.

'It's time fo' me to go,' she said. 'But I want Communion first. It's a long way to go en' I'll get hungry en' thirsty.'

'But, Sister . . .' the pastor protested.

'You useless. Why can't you jus' give me Communion?' She tried to sit up, but it was too much for her.

'Joseph,' he said, with some hesitation. 'Perhaps you can find us some wine and bread . . .' He seemed to hope that it would prove impossible, but one of the women rose and said : 'I got wine in my house. But jus' brown bread.'

'Go ask the Baas fo' white bread,' whispered my mother.

I didn't want to. Everything inside me rebelled against it. I got up and went out. It was still dark. The damp air made me gasp for breath after the brooding warmth inside. I walked towards the farmhouse; there was light in the window of the main bedroom.

Baas, my mother needs some white bread so that she can die in peace, it's too long to wait for the weekend. Please, Baas. Thank you, Baas. I won't trouble you again, Baas.

I stumbled over a box-cart in the yard and fell down. On the frozen ground I could feel the skin of my knees and palms breaking. I began to cry. I sat in a tight bundle and sobbed, the sound breaking from me like a living, bleeding thing. It was as if something had given way inside me. On hands and knees I crawled among the trees, vomiting out every filthy and blasphemous word I knew, until, exhausted, I lay trembling on the ground.

Slowly the revolt subsided. I got up. The day was breaking over the farm now, desolate and hard and cold. I didn't go to the farmhouse but retuning to the labourers' cottages where orange lights had started flickering amid a murmur of sleepy voices. In one of the cottages I borrowed half a loaf of brown bread and went back with it. The pastor had nearly finished the ceremony. My mother was waiting with open eyes.

'They didn't have white bread,' I said.

The pastor glanced towards her. 'In the eyes of the Lord it's all the same,' he said.

He poured some sweet red muscadel and handed it to her, and broke some bread; and slowly and deliberately she ate and drank, and choked on the bread, a cough much too violent for her weak body : I sat watching her and saw her swallowing that morsel of brown bread, and shivering and trembling, half out of my mind, I thought : I dare you, Lord, I dare you : turn that wine into your blood and that brown bread into your own body, come on Lord, I dare you. I thought it over and over in

115

my feverish mind, for minutes on end, and while I sat there dazed and shocked thinking it, I never even realised that she had already died.

IV

Much against the wish of my Baas Frans Viviers, who'd been expecting me to enter some 'useful trade' after matric, Mr Toad managed to get me a bursary to study at the University of Cape Town. He also arranged lodgings for me with some of his relatives in Observatory, but I found them too interfering to my liking and soon moved out. And after I'd packed my suitcase of clothes and my box of books two more times, moving this way and that, I finally settled in the small room in District Six which was to remain my home until the end of my Cape Town days.

Gran'ma Grace lived high up in the District, on the lower slopes of Devil's Peak. Escaping from the bustle of Hanover Street and picking one's way past romping children and reckless fruit-carts and junk shops, up towards the steepest, narrowest streets and lanes, one finally reached Oxford Place where the houses stood huddled together like a group of oxen at the abattoirs, not really knowing which way to escape. There wasn't much method in the architecture: through many decades the buildings had simply grown together, supporting one another to prevent premature collapse. On the street side there were verandahs and railings, Edwardian and Victorian and possibly even older, some badly patched with corrugated iron or wooden boards or cardboard sheets, but others still maintaining the last vestiges of dignity in spite of the all too obvious ravages of man and nature. Gran'ma Grace's was one of those, with a delicate wrought-iron pattern on the upstairs balcony. From there one could look out over children and stray dogs and scattered papers, over delivery vans and battered cars parked at random or simply abandoned in the street, causing regular outbursts of furious hooting and shouting whenever an intrepid outsider tried to pass that way. On wet or misty nights the street scene had something unreal from that high stoep: then the houses seemed to lose their solidity and become painted cardboard façades, the ochre and blue and green and off-white of a stage set, a stylised *Carmen* – or – grimmer and grimier – *A Streetcar Named Desire*. A rowdy district where one could never escape from one's neighbours, and where the entire cycle of life unfolded itself in front of my rickety window : rickety because the sashcords had broken long ago so that the frames had to be steadied against the wind with wads of folded paper. At the back of the house was a small court-yard surrounded by neighbouring houses, privies and a double row of dovecotes. There all the little girls from the neighbourhood used to play hopscotch or skip with flying plaits and bobbing dresses, while the cooped-up pigeons passionately cooed and called and courted and mated; and later I used it as an open-air stage to rehearse my own small company at night, watched by a smoking, drinking, jeering audi-ence who turned up without invitation and never left before the end.

Gran'ma Grace was a very frail, almost bird-like little woman, age-lessly old. For aesthetic or erotic reasons she'd had her front teeth re-moved in her early youth, and her caved-in moustached mouth had the appearance of a very worn-out vaginal fold. By the time I made my appearance in Oxford Place she'd already finished three men. The first two had been buried with the necessary show of grief; the third she'd got rid of after catching him in bed with another woman. She often told me the story in the most vivid terms. That their adultery had been committed in the very room I rented from her ('There's the bed, he's my witness, God don't sleep') added piquancy to the incident. 'I stood there watching them, she said, 'en' jus' there I got grey all over' – after which, without further ado, she'd thrown the goddamned couple out of her house, 'jus' like thet, with their bare bums en' all'.

One by one her children had left home – the daughters getting mar-ried; the sons pursuing their careers as fishermen or bricklayers, one of them a policeman – and Gran'ma Grace began to take in boarders. She occupied a singular place in the neighbourhood. There was no com-plaint or disease for which she had no remedy, and she was called upon, at all hours, to lend a hand at births, illnesses or deaths; in every funeral procession she was a conspicuous mourner, possibly because she had the most penetrating voice I've ever come across in my life.

Most of her income was derived from smuggling dagga, under the unofficial protection of her policeman son. There existed a highly prac-tical and rewarding relationship between them, for whenever she was cheated or developed a dislike for anyone, her son would come and pick up the person; if, on the other hand, she took a fancy to one, he could automatically count on police protection.

She spent several hours in church every Saturday, being an active mem-ber of an obscure sect, the Church of the Seraphs and Cherubs, and ru-

mour had it that she was in direct and constant communication with
several saints, the Virgin Mary, and God himself. Consequently it wasn't
advisable to rub her up the wrong way on a Saturday : she'd lam into
you, straight from church, till the neighbourhood smelled of sulphur
and saltpetre.

For some inexplicable reason this dour old Mother Courage took an
instant liking to me – perhaps because I was so completely lost in the
city, but also because she regarded me as what she called 'a lighty what
can catch the wire'. Whenever I had to work late of an evening, she
would bring me a large blue cup of tea and, without invitation, sit
down on the bed to have a chat. It made irritating inroads on my precious time and I tried to switch off as much as I could, especially when
she was telling fortune : she studied my cup, she read my palm, consulted
my stars, shuffled my cards, checked my 'numbers'. Whether there
was some Cabalistic streak in her religion I don't know, but she attached
particular value to the reading of 'numbers' : 'You jus' watch out fo'
de seven en' fo' de di'teen,' she regularly warned me. I wish I'd paid
more attention. As far as I can remember, seven was the figure of religion (always a good start when she tried to convert me), and thirteen
of birth and death (her first child had been still-born on the thirteenth
of some month).

Usually I simply went on with my work while she was chatting away
in my snug little room. There wasn't place for more than a bed and a
table and a home-made cupboard to house both clothes and books.
Originally the room had been much larger, but she'd had it divided
with a wooden partition in order to fit in more boarders. There was a
door in the middle of the partition, but it was insecurely attached to its
hinges and eventually, after Dulpert had moved into the next room, we
usually left it open for the sake of extra space.

When I'd just arrived at Gran'ma Grace's there was a girl living next
door, Ursula, a very carefree and earthy person who also managed to
irritate me considerably by turning on the volume of her transistor radio
as soon as she came home, and bursting into song whenever anything
familiar was played. Late one night it made me so furious that I started
hammering on the partitition door. The catch gave way and I surprised
her in a petticoat, studying herself in a broken mirror. Embarrassed,
I tried to apologise, but she simply looked at me over her shoulder and
asked :

'Why you looking so blerry silly? You never seen a girl before?'

'I only wanted to . . . about the noise . . . I'm sorry, I didn't mean to . . .'

'Ag, come off it!' she laughed. 'What you doing this time of the night thet one can't play a bit of mewsic?'

'I'm working.'

'What sort of work?'

She was struck dumb when I told her about University. 'You? Jiss, but you're a deep lightie, hey?' She came closer and stopped right in front of me. I became conscious of her odour, cheap scent and musk; and of her vital and touchable nearness. 'You better look out,' she taunted me, smiling. 'If you work too much it'll jus' fall off.'

'What'll fall off?'

'This.' With her provocative eyes unwaveringly on mine, she put out her hand and touched my sex. I grabbed her hand. She burst out laughing, her head thrown backwards, exposing the smoothness of her throat, and we started grappling; caught in the spell of her loud music, the room began to whirl round me. And then we fell down on her narrow bed.

My memories are usually very vivid and precise; I don't easily forget a gesture or a tone of voice. Yet I remember little of any coherence on that night. I was overwhelmed by her full breasts, her greedy mouth, her hair between our wet lips, the thrashing and wrestling of her limbs, her nails, her moistures and unrestrained animal sounds. Her orgasms were a series of volcanic eruptions. I simply went on wrestling blindly, long after I'd come and come again, for in my utter inexperience all I could do was to go on, completely abandoned to whatever she desired of me. In the early dawn she finally began to calm down, relaxing under me with lazy, whispering moans, as if she had no more will or energy left. Later she got up, wandering aimlessly through the room for a while, wet and naked, until she found her crumpled petticoat on the floor and stooped to pick it up, and put it on, and went down to the backyard. When she returned she stripped off the petticoat and came back to me, shivering slightly. I felt desire mounting in me again. With my hands entangled in her sticky hair I forced her down and returned to her warm, hidden wetness : this time my movements were slower and more confident, with a pure, arrogant insistence and completely different from the bewilderment with which I'd allowed her to seduce me.

I was bruised and sore all over when I went out on the balcony late that morning, blinking my swollen eyes against the violent sun. I'd missed an early lecture, but I couldn't care less. Ursula had left hours before – she was a seamstress in a Salt River factory – but my whole body was still conscious of her, my mouth filled with her taste.

Gran'ma Grace appeared beside me on soundless slippered feet. Guiltily I said good morning, avoiding her eyes. She took out her pipe from one of the pockets on her faded blue dressing gown and started puffing. I recognised the bittersweet smell of grass.

'Rooster's on his dunghill today,' she said at last.

I uttered a brief, embarrassed laugh.

'I don' say nuthing,' she said, puffing away. 'I don' say nuthing.' Then, suddenly : 'How ole are you?'

'Turned eighteen last month, Gran'ma Grace.'

'Ole enuff to look after yo'self. I don' say nuthing.' She was surrounded by clouds of smoke. Turning round to go back into the house, she said with unexpected aggressiveness : 'If thet djentoe ewwe' try to bogger you up, you jus' come en' tell me, hey?'

'Why will she bogger me up?'

'I'm jus' saying.'

For a while I felt crestfallen, but as soon as I shifted my legs into a new position I once again became conscious of the voluptuous aching of my body, and all my newly found confidence and exuberance returned. Like a general, like one of Lawrence's lords of life, I went down the steep, dirty, narrow lane surrounded by tall houses to the open sun of the wider streets below. Everything was more violent than other days : the yells of the fruit vendors, the jeers of labourers on scaffoldings or trucks whenever a girl came past with swaying hips, the collages of tattered posters on walls and palissades, the smell of herbs and spices from the dark interiors of small shops crammed with wares.

Feeling completely reckless, I entered one of the numerous barber shops to have my hair cut and to listen to the small talk and slander blowing in from all points of the compass. The haircut lasted for a full hour, because whenever something interesting was happening outside the barber and all the waiting clients went to the door to watch or to offer loud and libellous comments.

Every few minutes a new visitor would arrive to buy something, or to deliver or fetch contraband in small parcels, to pay off debts, to collect *fafeh* bets, to borrow money without security, or simply to chat. I was astounded by the generosity of the barber, Hassim. He must have noticed it, for just after another borrower had left with a handful of notes he said: 'Don' worry, boytjie, I been here di'teen years now en' noborry's cheated me.' And when I left, he wanted no more than half his normal price: 'Gwaan dwaal, man, you're a first-timer en' I cen see it's a speshul occashun.' Winking. 'Look's if you was using the snot sjambok las' night, hey? Jus' close yo' fly befo' you go, else they pick you fo' public excitement.' The shop roared with laughter when I hastily touched my fly to find that it was done up anyway.

On to Hanover Street, and then in to the central city, past the Parade, to the flower market. I didn't go there intentionally, but when I got there I took two shillings from my pocket – the amount I normally allowed myself for a day's food – and bought a bunch of carnations.

Ursula looked at me with a strange expression in her eyes when I offered her the flowers that evening. She took them almost brusquely and turned her back to me. For nearly a minute she stood like that before she began to untie the string to put the flowers in her pink toilet pitcher.

'What's the matter now?' I asked.

To my astonishment there were tears in her eyes when she looked round. But she only shook her head angrily, sniffed, and said: 'You're a softy. Why don't you leave me alone?'

Bewildered I returned to my room and sat down at the narrow table where my books had been lying unopened all day. Ten minutes later I heard the door in the partition open, but didn't look up. Coming up to me she put her hands over my eyes from behind.

'Guess who?' she whispered.

When I turned round she was naked. She pressed my face against her breasts. A book fell from the table. I didn't pick it up before the next day.

It was a chaotic, ecstatic, dangerous time. She was nine years older than I and although she constantly refused to talk about her past it was obvious that there was very little in the spectrum of human experience which she hadn't lived through. Sexually she was indefatigable and with sly hands and subtle lips she could rouse me, even from a state of utter exhaustion, back to aggressive potency. There was no end to her inventiveness and variety, and many times we saw the sun come through the open window without having slept a wink all night.

It couldn't go on like that, of course. My work lay heavily on my conscience. The June exams were at hand and I was struggling to find my feet in the new world. In the beginning of the year it had demanded specific concentration not to address my professors as 'Baas'. From the secluded existence of the farm I'd suddenly tumbled, wholly unprepared, into a chaos through which only will-power could keep me going, driven by the fierce determination to 'become something'. On Mr Toad's advice I hadn't registered at the School for Drama after all, but for a straight B.A. I was enthralled by the new languages, French and German; I was prepared to work day and night, but it was hell to get a grasp on it all. Everything was simply too new, too different, I had so very few landmarks on my way. The other students seemed so sure of themselves, they knew so readily where to find a book, how to arrange the material for an essay. Not I. I'd never even seen the inside of a library before. With the handful of other Coloured and Indian students I occasionally discussed my problems, but they'd all grown up in cities and regarded me, not without some condescension, as a backvelder. But the more insurmountable the problems appeared, the more determined I became to solve them. I would show them. I would show them all. I would show the whole wide world.

On the Parade flea market I bought a second-hand green alarm clock which I regularly set for five in the morning, when, long past midnight, I wearily crawled into bed. I simply couldn't afford more than five hours' sleep at night, and even that seemed like a waste of time. I tried to read at least one play or novel a day, in addition to my regular studies : I was so insatiably hungry.

The tens of thousands of books in the library completely overwhelmed me. When I got there the first time I had to lean against the wall among the shelves for several minutes to recover from dizziness. My own store of knowledge seemed so ludicrously insignificant beside those mountains of wisdom; my eighteen years were less than nothing measured against the concentrated thought of so many centuries. But after the dizziness had left me, I stood up and stretched out both hands to touch the row of books on the highest shelf; and I closed my eyes and, long before I knew of the very existence of Balzac, I thought what amounted to : *A nous deux maintenant.*

My efforts to find suitable lodgings made it even more difficult to get on with the work. But now the city had finally washed me ashore in Gran'ma Grace's pert little house; now I could finally begin to organise my life and sort out my work. And at that very moment Ursula made her appearance.

In the beginning I flung myself into her like a child discovering a huge puddle of mud, but after ten days, after a fortnight, I became panicky and tried to find some sort of equilibrium between her and my work. She was too demanding. She wanted to devour and possess me, and there was something about her excessiveness which first fascinated me but later put me off, until I began to find it positively frightening, a form of hunger which I couldn't satisfy and which forced me to rebel : it was simply too voracious, too blatant, too uncompromising. She refused to accept that I sometimes had to withdraw myself in order to get some work done. Partly it was my own fault for devoting myself so completely to her in the beginning : I've always had this tendency for the absolute, this aptitude for excess in me, however much I've tried to restrain it through the years. My enthusiasm for the play of Adam and Eve long ago, my preoccupation with the circus, my devotion to *The Tempest*, my immersion in studying and reading – everything revealed exactly the same unrestrained enthusiasm with which I now experienced Ursula. And when my work forced me to rearrange my life more sensibly, it upset her : to her it was a sign of distrust.

'It's jus' because I'm ol'er 'n you. It's because I'm twenny-seven en' one of these days I'll be thirty. You think I'm old awready, admit it!' With pathetic greed she would parade in front of her broken mirror, holding out her breasts to me, taunting : 'I'm too much fo' you, hey? You not really a man, thet's what!'

With that she sometimes succeeded in forcing me back to her, but grudgingly, resentfully. At other times I tried to reason with her. Mostly we simply shouted at each other. And when I did sit down to do some work she retaliated by turning up the volume of her radio or by sitting on my bed complaining, accusing, nagging, moping.

It went from bad to worse until I was right in the middle of my exams and faring disastrously. Our quarrels grew in direct proportion to our despair; we used our bodies to humiliate and hurt each other, until it finally became too much for me one night and, in a fit of uncontrollable rage, I flung her bodily from my room, slammed the door and returned to my studies with a blinding headache.

Although I was consciously listening to catch up every sound from next door, she slipped out so quietly that I never heard her. The complete silence made it even more difficult to concentrate. It must have been very late when I heard her coming upstairs. There was a man's voice with hers. Furiously I pressed my clenched fists to my ears, but the letters were dancing on the page in front of me and I couldn't read a thing. I wanted to break something. But I sat there until her voice next door started uttering the familiar sounds which had been exclusively mine for over a month. Then I got up and fled.

Gran'ma Grace awaited me on the stairs as if she'd known that I would come out. I tried to slip past, but she blocked the way.

'What'se metter with Ursula?'

'She can go to hell for all I care!'

Gran'ma Grace allowed me to pass. The next day I stayed away from Oxford Place. I sat in the library till late afternoon, then wandered aimlessly through the streets, sick with uncertainty. When I finally reached home, Ursula's door stood open and all her belongings were gone. In the light of the bare bulb on the landing there wasn't the slightest sign that she'd ever been there.

Gran'ma Grace came up behind me, soundlessly as always. 'P'lice mos come to fetch her,' she said nonchalantly.

'But why . . . ?'

'Stolen stuff or something, I dunno. I don' want to be nuggeted with it.'

I looked straight at her, but the old sinner stared back without batting an eyelid.

'What happened to her things?' I asked.

'Taken away. After all, I mean, she's going to bath fo' a few months now, en' de room can't stend empty olly time. What'll become of me if I don' get my boarding money?'

I suppose I should have felt relieved. Gran'ma Grace had done it for my sake. Instead, I felt miserable and it took a long time before I could rid myself of a feeling of complicity. And that night, as I lay sleepless on the ungodly bed of Gran'ma Grace's third husband, I had to find relief with my own hands, yearning for Ursula's full, ripe body forever lost.

After her an enigmatic man moved into the room next door. According to Gran'ma Grace he was a khalifa, but that must have been a camouflage, for surely no holy man would leave, as he did, one night three weeks after his arrival, taking all his baggage with him and without paying his rent. This time the small room stood empty for fully ten days before a pale, shuffling shadow of a woman came to live there. Judging from her appearance she was an Oriental, probably Chinese – in District Six one never knew: all the pariahs of the world seemed to converge there in one bedraggled brotherhood. My neighbour couldn't have been more than fifty or so, but she seemed to be suffering from T.B. and at night the wooden partition shook with the violence of her terrible coughing. We never spoke to each other apart from a brief greeting when we met on the staircase; and she never raised her voice, with the result that I, too, started addressing her in a whisper. While I was preparing for a test on the Romantics one morning, she quietly died next door. According to Gran'ma Grace it was one of the most beautiful corpses she'd ever seen, but I declined her invitation to have a look myself.

That is how Dulpert came into my life. Two days after the death of my consumptive neighbour he moved in with a carton of clothes and books and an enormous black metal trunk.

The first evening he knocked on the interleading door. I was lying on my bed reading *Rosmersholm*, after discovering Ibsen a week before, and the knock made me jump up : for such a long time now I'd never communicated with anybody next door that for a moment, completely losing my sense of time, I thought it must be Ursula. When I opened the door he was standing there, at least six inches taller than me, and extremely thin. His smooth black hair hung down over his forehead, brushing against his thick-rimmed glasses; what immediately struck me was the exquisite modelling of his high cheekbones and the stark whiteness of his teeth against his olive-coloured skin.

'I'm Dulpert Naidoo,' he said without ceremony. 'I know you're busy, the old woman warned me not to disturb you. But I can't open my trunk and I wondered whether you might be able to help me.'

As he opened the door wider and stood aside for me to pass, I noticed his hands. I'd seldom seen such expressive hands on a man, long tapered fingers, neatly trimmed nails, and a way of gesticulating which was both indolent and flamboyant.

The trunk stood in the centre of the floor : an old-fashioned marine trunk with two locks, rather the worse for wear and age, with, on one side, several holes drilled through the metal.

'I lost the key on the train,' he explained. 'I was a bit high when I got on.' It was the first time I heard him laugh, coming from deep inside him as if his whole body enjoyed it. But not boisterous at all : quiet, with an intense inner joy which forced one to laugh with him.

By the time he'd come to ask my help, he'd already broken a pair of plate-shears and two of Gran'ma Grace's tin openers on the heavy metal, and he'd just returned with some welding equipment borrowed from someone but which he didn't know how to use. I was as clumsy as he was. In experienced hands, I'm sure, it would have worked, but we only managed to melt down all four corners so that they looked like the downtrodden heels of old shoes.

I went to fetch a crowbar from under my bed and we took turns to assault the trunk with it, but apart from adding several new dents and scars it proved useless.

It became one of those evenings when everything is funny. With every blow of the crowbar we laughed until the tears were streaming down. At one o'clock that night we lugged the thing to the balcony, heaved it on to the railings and shoved it down into the cobbled street below. Two cats screaming amorously under the nearest lamp-post fled into the night with blood-curdling yells. From all the windows in the neighbourhood angry or scared voices shouted at us. When we reached the street the trunk had a very curious shape, but otherwise it was still intact. And so we had to carry the bloody thing up the staircase again.

'Tomorrow I'll get a hacksaw,' Dulpert said when we finally reached his room, wiping off perspiration and tears of laughter.

He often promised to do so during the following weeks and months, but for some reason never got round to it. And after a time strange, etiolated shoots came sprouting from the holes in the side of the trunk. There were mostly clothes inside, Dulpert said, and old newspapers, but also the remains of fruit and vegetables he'd packed in there before coming to Cape Town. The shoots might have been potatoes or pumpkins or beans, but they died before we could make sure.

When I finally returned to my room that first night the middle door got stuck. We grabbed it on both sides and started pulling and shoving. One of the hinges broke.

'Well, at least we've done something,' Dulpert said philosophically. And from then on we almost never shut the door again. In fact, shortly afterwards we rearranged the furniture to form one bedroom and a study; and throughout the years we lived together we stuck firmly to one rule: a person sitting down in the study was not to be disturbed. The only occasions on which the rickety door was ever closed, kept in position with a table, were the rare nights when either he or I brought a girl home for the night. For that purpose we bought a 'love bed' on the Parade one Saturday morning, and set it up in a corner of the study. On a paraffin box next to it Dulpert used to burn the meang sticks he bought in the District's obscure spice shops; and when the bed, a delightful Victorian thing, all curls and knobs, wasn't serving as a sturdy altar of love, Dulpert used it for his meditations. That, like studying, was an activity never disturbed from outside.

Dulpert was six years older than I and he'd already graduated from Natal University. When he arrived in Gran'ma Grace's boarding house he'd just come to the end of what he termed a 'free period'. These periods formed a very important part of his life pattern. The idea was that after a time of intense study or work he had to 'break out', or withdraw, or travel somewhere, to refreshen and open up the mind.

His most recent 'free period' had been spent in India, mainly in the footsteps of Gandhi, whom he revered. He'd travelled from the Mahatma's birthplace in the west to the park of his death in New Delhi, but most of the time – more than nine months – he'd spent in the holy man's sanctuary outside Ahmedabad.

I could listen for hours to his accounts of that *ashram*, enclave of silence and devotion in the turbulent world. He read me Tolstoy's letters to Gandhi and fed my imagination with long descriptions of the Russian's settlement on which the Mahatma had based his own. Patiently he initiated me into the world of words, *satyagraha* and *ahimsa*. . . . Their very sound fascinated me, like *boatswain* and *yarely* at school, or *tuffet* and *whey* in those back stoep afternoons so long ago. They were magic words: this 'truth-seeking power of the soul', this 'force of humility', opening windows to new landscapes in my mind.

Throughout the entire process of discovery Dulpert was my steady guide. I could listen breathlessly to his accounts of the Ganges and the pilgrims bathing in the sacred waters of their Mother, and the pyres of the dead on the banks, and the long processions of the priests. He brought me stacks of books, including some with reproductions of Hindu temples adorned with erotic art, in which the glorification of sexuality was in itself an experience of the sacred, the bodies united through lingam and yoni transfigured into the true temple of God. With him I undertook the journey through the *Upanishads* and the *Baghavad Gita*, until we reached the Tantric Buddhism of Tibet, and finally Zen. (What was he? Partly Hindu, partly Buddhist, mostly devout heathen.) He made me read treatises on the Zen way of gardening and arranging flowers, on the symbolism of the Tea Ceremony. We sat together in lotus positions, and laughed and meditated and read koans or hai-ku. To him there was nothing abstract about it at all, it formed part of the fabric of his daily existence.

On the shelf which, much to Gran'ma Grace's indignation, he'd hammered to the wall above his bed, there were, among many others: Gandhi's autobiography, the *Kama Sutra*, a dilapidated edition of the *I Ching* which he consulted before every major decision in his life, and *Das Kapital*. And, guru that he was, he saw to it that I worked through every page of them. His own subject was Political Science, and during his stay at Gran'ma Grace's he was working on a doctor's thesis. I must admit that I cared less for that than for most of the other subjects he'd introduced me to, but he refused to let me off: 'You're going to share everything you discover with me, and I'll do the same to you: that's the least we owe one another while we're living together.'

Two of the books were regularly missing from the shelf above his bed. Gran'ma Grace used the Marx, which was the heaviest of them all, to prop open her kitchen door on windy days. And the *Kama Sutra* was in great demand among friends. Dulpert used to pick up people the way a dog picks up fleas: every time he went to town he came back with two or three companions – some of them 'old friends' he'd run into, others complete strangers he'd taken a liking to. And when the conversation sooner or later turned to women or to love, the *Kama Sutra* would be discussed and a visitor would go off with it. Dulpert used to rant furiously about it, because he hated to part with his books, but he couldn't refuse either: he was one of those people who would ruin himself to help his friends.

About a year after his arrival he once again brought home a group of guests, mainly colleagues from the Department of Political Science, Coloured and White. After the others had left – it was about two in the morning – one quiet, introverted chap remained, Jim Wiley. A highly intelligent person, he was almost pathologically antisocial. Reddish hair, very pale blue eyes, and an almost transparent white skin, as if he'd spent years under a wheelbarrow in the greenhouse. That night he just sat there without saying a word. Dulpert and I could hardly keep our eyes open, but Jim made no move to go. And it was only when Dulpert asked him point-blank whether he meant to sleep there that he blushed and jumped up and asked, stammering with embarrassment, whether he might borrow the *Kama Sutra*. Dulpert was so astonished that he immediately thrust the book into Jim's hands.

'You see,' Jim tried to explain, 'I'm getting married in a fortnight and I thought . . . I mean, I've read Van de Velde and Johnson and Masters and so on, but . . .'

'D'you want to tell me you've never fucked a woman?'

Jim gulped. 'No. You see, I . . . you'll probably laugh at me, but I regard marriage as something sacred, and . . .'

'Quite,' said Dulpert. 'I can't agree with you more.'

'We're determined to make a success of it,' said Jim. 'And I do think sex is important. She thinks so too. We've been doing exercises for months now to get fit, and . . .'

'All you need is a few push-ups,' said Dulpert.

Jim blushed more deeply. 'Yes, yes, of course. But apparently variety is very important and it seems the *Kama Sutra* . . .'

'Keep the book for a wedding gift,' Dulpert interrupted him. 'And may Siva bless you.'

But a month later Jim came back, as pale as ever, with the book, wrapped in newspaper, under his arm : his left leg was in a plaster cast. 'I brought it back,' he said meekly.

'Did you try it out?'

'Yes, I . . . That's how I broke my leg. We . . .'

After he'd left, Dulpert peeled off the newspaper and threw it in the wastepaper basket. Through the window we watched Jim hobbling across Oxford Place. 'Lo and behold!' said Dulpert. 'There goes one of the best brains in our Department. *The Decline of the West.*'

In spite of his customary calm the silly little episode seemed to have upset him in an extraordinary way. How much, I only discovered a few days later when he unexpectedly broached it again :

'Incidentally, I saw Jim's wife this morning when she came to fetch him. She's really beautiful, you know.'

'I would never have expected that.'

'Neither would I. She looks anaemic. Perhaps it's just a lack of sunshine. But she has something – well – ethereal about her. The largest blue eyes you've ever seen.' Suddenly he exploded : 'God! To think that a girl like that will never know what love really means.'

'It's her own fault. She chose him.'

'But it's such a waste of potential, Joseph! Just think of it, all over the world : how much gets wasted simply because people are too shit-scared to be *human*. Can you imagine Jim when he comes out of the bathroom at night? – with Van de Velde in one hand and a pep pill in the other, Mum under the arms and zinc oxide between his toes and an

FL on his limp little prick – and probably wearing a vest so that he won't catch pneumonia. "All right, darling, tonight we start on page 69 . . ."'

I collapsed with laughter.

'You're laughing!' Dulpert was seething. 'But that's the sort of white maggot we've got to say Baas to! The master race with their white vests! And look at you, look at me . . . I could have taught her to feel, I could have shown her what it meant to be human and alive, not just a lump of pale flesh between the sheets . . . !'

'But, Dulpert!' I couldn't understand his vehemence. 'It's no concern of yours at all.'

'Why not? Because I've got a black skin?'

'Neither you nor I can do anything about it.'

He came right up to me. 'Have you ever desired a White girl, Joseph?'

'No,' I said stubbornly.

'I think you're lying.'

How could he have known about Hermien?

'What does it matter whether I'm lying?' I was vexed. 'Whatever you or I may have to say about it remains irrelevant.'

'I want to marry a White girl one day,' he said with shocking directness. 'Do you regard that as irrelevant?'

'Yes. Because as things are at the moment it's impossible.'

'As things are at the moment! Do you think things *have* to be like this?'

'What can you do to change them?' I was more cruel than was necessary. 'Do you want to start fasting like Gandhi?'

With that he unexpectedly regained his self-control and smiled: 'Joseph, Joseph,' he said, 'I think you still don't understand the Mahatma.'

'Perhaps not. But one thing I know, and that is that Gandhi's opponents were the British Government – a foreign power, and one which desperately wanted to remain a gentleman in the eyes of the world, whatever might be happening behind the screen. Against such people a public fast may be effective. Our circumstances are different.'

'If you believe in *satyagraha* you must also believe that it will conquer in the end, whatever your opponent.'

'It's no use discussing it again, Dulpert.'

'Shall I tell you why you prefer not to discuss it?' A short pause. 'Because you're scared.'

'Why should I be scared?'

'You've got your little world: you've got a place to sleep, you don't often go hungry, you can take a girl to bed from time to time; and you've got your acting. You know damn well how easily all that can be threatened if you expose yourself to the world. You know it, and you can fear it.'

I didn't reply. I thought back to what I'd memorised about my father and his father, and his father's father, and I knew that Dulpert was right: I *wanted* a different sort of life, I didn't want to become a victim like them, I could see no point in martyrdom: all I wanted was to be left in peace so I could lead my life as I thought fit. I wanted to remain whole. Wholeness was all.

'I won't try to break down your defences,' he said softly. 'I love you too much to want to break you, you bastard. But it's not a matter of choice at all. Sooner or later you'll find yourself in a position where you can no longer escape from the world. Then White and Black will matter to you. And God help you when that happens.'

The vague restlessness such conversations stirred up in me always sent me back to my work. Like the irrigation dam of my childhood the theatre became my refuge from the world. More than a refuge: an opportunity to sort out the disparate elements of the world and make them intelligible to me.

Already in the course of my first year I attended every performance in the Little Theatre, and whatever rehearsals I could. Even initial plotting rehearsals held a magic quality for me. To be able to say: 'Let's pretend . . .' and then to give free scope to the imagination – surely that was the greatest miracle of all? All my life it retained something of the quality of that first Nativity play.

At one rehearsal they asked me to give a hand in moving a series of heavy flats. Afterwards it happened a few more times, until it was accepted as a matter of course that I'd help the stage crew. It didn't matter whether I had to draw the curtains, or carry counterweights, or help the electrician while he was setting the lights: it gave me an opportunity of getting in contact with all the elements and processes of theatre. I was eager to learn about everything, the way an athlete enjoys training all the muscles in his body, including those not directly involved in his particular line of sport.

During September of that year I became aware of a crisis developing inside me. However rich the world I was discovering through my degree course, I felt it more important to switch to drama, to which all my enthusiasm was directed. But such a change would jeopardise my bursary, since Mr Toad was not prepared to recommend its renewal unless I was doing something 'useful'. I still had the small inheritance from my mother, but it would be almost sacrilege to touch it : it had been set aside for 'later'. And anyway it was an insignificant amount. So what could I do?

One night, in near despair, I discussed the matter with Dulpert. He ordered me to sit down on the love bed and took place opposite me, with the *I Ching* between us. For a long time he sat with his eyes closed, withdrawn so deeply into himself that it seemed as if he'd stopped breathing. Finally he began to shake the three worn Chinese coins and threw them; he shook and threw, and shook and threw, six times altogether, without any hurry, composing the hexagram of broken and unbroken lines. When he'd done, he consulted the key, read it in silence, then looked up with a little smile :

'Don't worry,' he said. 'You can take the jump. And you can leave your mother's money in the bank.'

'But how can I ... ?'

He raised his hand to silence me.

Next day he took me to one of his White friends whom he'd already persuaded to give me driving lessons. Afterwards he saw to it that I acquired a licence to drive heavy vehicles; and all through that summer vacation I did deliveries for a soft-drinks firm to earn money for the next year.

It meant doing my reading at night, much to Gran'ma Grace's annoyance. 'If you die of overwork one day,' she warned me with her toothless mouth, 'don' you come running to me. I warn you.'

But I persevered, and when the University reopened that March I became a full-time drama student.

There were three Coloured students in our group : Barney Salomon, a man slightly older than the rest of us, whose main interest was opera and who eventually joined the Eoan Group; a slight, attractive Malay girl, Fatima, and myself. From the start there was a particularly strong sense of unity in the group as a whole, which was a new discovery to me. The previous year I'd been so far behind the other students, especially the Whites, that I'd felt completely out of my depths. But this year it was different – it was a smaller group and more tightly knit because we shared the same interests; and as far as reading was concerned, I had by now, in fact, acquired an advantage over them.

From a very early stage I felt drawn towards Fatima. The way she had of sitting in lectures with an absent little smile, as if she never really felt committed to the present; her habit of looking one straight in the eyes with an expression of absolute serenity; the grace with which she moved; the unexpected resonance of her voice – everything about her fascinated me, although it took more than a year before it led to anything. She was deeply religious and her parents had given her a strictly conventional Malay upbringing. In fact it was remarkable that they'd ever allowed her to go to University.

Her people received me with irreproachable hospitality whenever she took me home with her, yet I got the impression that I would never penetrate beyond a polite façade. She had something similar about her, as if she was withholding something even from our most intimate moments, like an actor maintaining a distance between himself and his role.

The discipline implicit in our relationship was a revelation to me. We spent long hours working together, talking, or listening to the records to which Dulpert had already introduced me – Mahler and Mozart, Bach and the Baroque. Nothing was ever taken for granted between us. Every moment, every fleeting touch, was earned with humility and patience. It was the sort of relationship which can only exist between two very young people, too delicate ever to be repeated.

It didn't mean a denial of the body, but complete control of it, a sharpening of the senses, a refining of reactions. When, after many months, she finally allowed me to take off her blouse and caress her virginal breasts, it was the most precious experience I'd ever been allowed. Today I wish it could have remained like that: it was the sort of relationship which derived its meaning from incompleteness, a lasting beginning, the purest expression of our adolescence.

Near the end of my second drama year we started rehearsing a shortened version of *Hamlet*. I had a minor part, Osrick; she was Ophelia. One night, after a late rehearsal, I accompanied her home. Her parents had left on a pilgrimage to Mecca; she'd stayed behind to look after two younger brothers. We were talking about the play, a very intense discussion as I remember it, for I'd discovered something in her Ophelia that night which had shaken me, a complete surrender to madness which I would never have expected from her; and, because she was

Malay and acting opposite a White Hamlet, the entire role had suddenly acquired added meaning. In fact, that was the night when the idea of my own *Hamlet* was born. With a Coloured prince.

Fatima was just as excited by the idea as I. We simply couldn't stop talking. It was past two when a sudden shower on the roof made us realise what time it was. We both jumped up, and then remained standing, half foolishly.

'I must go.'

'It's raining.'

The large dining-room table was between us. We looked straight at one another, for a long time, unspeaking, a measuring look of fear and hope.

'You can sleep with the boys in their room.'

'With you.'

'No.'

'Don't say no.'

'And if I promised . . . ? I won't do anything. I'll just hold you.'

To hold her naked in my arms and caress her all night long, and yet to restrain myself. To listen to her breath coming through half-opened lips, and then her dark voice pleading : 'Please, don't. Don't.' To tempt the body to the utmost, over and over, and then to hold back, to be tortured and transported at the same time. And when we rose very early in the morning, before the boys got up for school, she shyly turned her back to me to dress, as if we'd become strangers to each other.

When, three weeks later, on the opening night of *Hamlet*, we went all the way, it actually came as a disappointment, as upsetting as the conversation which followed it :

'Are you glad?'

'If it was good for you, I'm glad.'

'But what about you?'

'I don't know.'

'Surely you must know.'

'Please don't be angry, Joseph.'

'What makes you think I'm angry?'

And the strangest thing of all was that in a completely illogical way I felt convinced that it had been like that only because I played Osrick. If I'd acted Hamlet to her Ophelia, it would have turned out differently.

It was the same production which first brought me into contact with Derek de Villiers. At the time he'd just returned to South Africa after several enormously successful seasons in London, and he was regarded as one of the leading actors in the country, young, brilliant, and dynamic, a new Barrault. He presented a series of demonstration lectures in the Drama School and we students worshipped him.

After our class production of *Hamlet* he discussed it with the cast, first the whole group, then singly. I had to wait for last, impatient and miserable. After all the others had left, he and I remained alone in the theatre, on the edge of the apron. The auditorium lights were switched off and I could only dimly make out the rows of seats in the dark. I was aware of the silence and felt like an intruder – in the only place where I'd ever been at home.

After a while Derek asked: 'Well, baby, what are *you* doing in the theatre?'

Embarrassed, I stuttered: 'I've always wanted to . . . I . . .'

'It's a bloody rat-race.'

'Why are you in it then, sir?'

'God, don't call me sir!' He looked at me with those nearly black eyes of his, then stroked back his long hair. 'Look, you had a very small part, but you were fucking good. Let's face it – you've got talent. But what do you want to *do* with it?'

'Act.' I looked back at him.

'Where are you going to find a stage in this country?'

'I'll go on till I've got a stage.'

'OK,' he said, with a sigh. 'You're idealistic and you've got guts: so what? That's simply not enough. It's no use getting out of here with a degree or a diploma or whatever and then start looking around for something to do. Jesus, be realistic. Why don't you get a group together right now?'

'But what can I teach them?'

'Never mind what you can teach them. One learns by working together. If you want to, I'll help you.'

I gaped at him.

'Come on,' he said irritably. 'Don't look at me with those "Darling-it's-so-sudden" eyes. Do you want to, or don't you?'

'My God, sir.'

'Derek.'

'Derek.'

Some of the group members I recruited during the next few weeks were students, but most were raw amateurs from District Six. And at night we rehearsed in Gran'ma Grace's backyard under Derek's direction. Night and day seemed to contain too few hours for everything I tried to cram into them. Mornings were mostly taken up by lectures, afternoons by practical sessions, evenings by rehearsals; late nights were set aside for my group. And somewhere among it all I still had to find time for my self-imposed programme of reading.

Holidays I had to work full-time – as truck driver, as waiter, as messenger, anything to earn money and stay alive. And when I felt depressed at times it was Dulpert who kept me going.

He often attended our late-night rehearsals in the backyard; and just as regularly I accompanied him to music concerts in the City Hall, he came to our performances in the Little Theatre. I can recall only one evening when he didn't turn up.

It was early in my third drama year, after we'd been flogging ourselves for a month to produce a highly experimental *Richard II*, in which I played my first lead. So I felt understandably annoyed when I arrived home after the first performance.

'Why didn't you tell me you didn't want to come? I specially kept you a ticket.'

'Don't attack me before you've heard my story.'

'It'd better be a bloody good story.'

He sat down on the black trunk which had long ago become part of our permanent furniture. 'I really meant to go, Joseph. In fact, I left home with every intention of seeing your Richard.'

'But you never got there.'

'No.'

He'd walked in to town, he said. Down in Plein Street a pregnant Coloured woman had crossed against a red robot, and a car had to slam on brakes to miss her – the sort of incident which happens a thousand times every day. But that particular driver had turned down his window and started abusing the 'bladdy *meid*'. Very apologetic, she'd said : ' 'Scuse me, sir.' Whereupon he threw his door open and jumped out : 'Who the hell is your "Sir"? You call me "Baas", do you understand?'

Dulpert paused for a while.

'And then?'

'Then I went up to him and said: "Get into your car and bugger off." '
A short laugh. 'Just as well the other cars were all hooting at him to move on, else he'd probably have *donnered* me.'

'And then you were too upset to go to the theatre?'

'Not really.' He looked sulky. 'But in Wale Street I passed an old man who'd had nothing to eat all day, so I gave him my money.'

'He probably laughed at you behind your back.'

He shrugged. 'That's his worry, not mine.'

'But, Dulpert,' I insisted, 'your ticket was waiting at the theatre, you didn't need money.'

'I know. But by then I'd had too much. It wasn't the money. It was the old man, it was the woman, just about everything. I know I've often gone with you, but tonight I simply couldn't. It was too "cultural", it would have been sick. Worse than Nero playing his lute.'

'Do you want to dismiss culture?'

'If it's the sort of culture reserved for the handful of people who can afford it, yes.'

'Suppose the theatre helps a few people to forget about the world for a while, so that they have more hope to face it when they go out: don't you think that's important?'

'Forget?' He stood up. 'You must force them to *remember*, not pamper them by allowing them to forget. They must never be allowed to forget. It's from remembering that revolutions are born.'

'How do you equate art with blood?' I asked.

'Does a revolution necessarily mean blood?'

He quietly looked at me, shaming me. And I remembered a trivial incident from the previous week when he'd gone to have a bath in Gran'ma Grace's little cardboard-and-metal bathroom behind the kitchen. I'd heard him breaking boxwood for the geyser, I'd seen smoke coming from the chimney, but in the end he'd stayed away so long that I'd gone to investigate. And I'd found him kneeling beside the bath, rescuing, with endless patience, some ants from drowning.

'I'm sorry,' I said, still disturbed by his unexpected attack.

He was upset too, but he didn't say anything more. After a while he went to the study and sat down in a lotus position on the love bed as the smoke started swirling from the meang sticks. On the table a candle was burning to focus his concentration. And deep and resonant, like a gong, I heard the sacred word rise from him again and again: 'Om. Om. Om. Om.' Sitting like that for an hour or longer, intensely concentrating and yet relaxed, he slowly brought himself back to a state of peace. And at last I could hear him whispering in a new voice: 'Shantih, shantih, shantih.' When he came back to bed, he was his usual serene self.

I know it was a Saturday because Gran'ma Grace had been 'wetting her teeth' from early morning. At sunrise she'd left for the two hours' service of the Church of the Seraphs and Cherubs and from the moment she retuned all hell was loose. I suppose it must have been caused by the unsettling contrast between her service and the furious Saturday morning bustle of our neighbourhood. On Saturdays the end of the world always seemed closer than usual and the merest glance in her direction prompted her to 'spit pepper'.

On that particular morning one could hear her a block away. Oom Sassie, an old neighbour spending his days on his balcony following the movement of the sun, shouted his customary jovial greeting:

'I say, Gran'ma! How'se tomato?'

On other days she would answer good-naturedly: 'Tomato's ripe and ready!' But that morning she gave her bitchy Saturday reply: 'Tomato blerry green!' So he wisely left her in peace.

Dulpert was working in the study, and Gran'ma Grace came to join me where I sat reading on the balcony. It usually fell to me to listen to all her complaints and calm her down.

She paraded all the sins of the scarlet city in front of me. 'S'pose it's jus' because I got rust now,' she complained with her hairy mouth, 'but inne time of de fet pennies de world was differunt. I wan' to give myself up to God now, but what chance a Christian got in dis kotter?'

At that moment a police car came screeching round the corner of Hamilton Street and the watch-word 'Salt!' went up on all sides.
The car stopped in front of the house.

'Hey!' Oom Sassie jeered from his stoep. 'Who you burnt this time, Gran'ma?'

'Jus' you look in front of you,' she retorted, 'cause it's dark behine.'

She leaned over the balcony railing to talk to the constable whom she obviously knew. Within a few minutes the whole neighbourhood was assembled in front of the house. But they were disappointed to learn that, this time, no crime was involved. A man had been found dead with Dulpert's address on him and they wanted him to identify the corpse.

He agreed to accompany them, irritable because they'd disturbed his work. When he reached the car he conferred with the police for a moment, and then called up to me :

'Come with us, Joseph!'

As we drove off, sending children, cats and dogs scattering in all directions, I asked him : 'Who is it?'

He shrugged. We drove in the direction of Salt River, through the crowded Saturday streets. On the corner of Sir Lowry's Road we passed a capsized fruit cart : a crowd gathered to carry off armsful of yellow bananas and green apples while the hawker was jumping up and down and waving his arms like a marionette. And then the commotion of the streets was suddenly behind us, and a wide door slid open, and we entered the cool morgue, with a long table in the centre and dark grey drawers lining the walls. It reminded me of the wine cellar on the farm, but it was more chilly and lacked the smell of must.

The transition was too sudden. First the roar and the throng of the streets, now this cool silence through which we moved like impostors. It was as if I'd rehearsed a particular role only to discover, as the curtain went up, that I was in the wrong play.

On the long table a naked young White man lay stretched out on his back, one arm bent under his head as if he'd peacefully fallen asleep : only it was more motionless, a more absolute peace; and to the big toe of his right foot somebody had tied a card, like a ticket on a sheep's carcass in a railway warehouse.

One of the policemen opened a draw in the wall and an icy breath of air wafted over us. It was like a filing cabinet. In the drawer lay Jim, one knee drawn up, his face distorted, but without any visible damage : Jim of the *Kama Sutra*.

Beside me Dulpert suddenly began to laugh, with a suggestion of hysteria :

'Do you know him?' the policeman asked brusquely.

Dulpert stopped laughing as suddenly as he'd begun, like the technical exercises we did at Drama School. 'Yes. He's studying in the same Department as I. I mean : he used to.'

'And you?' the constable turned to me.

'Yes, it's Jim.'

'Sure?'

'Yes.'

He closed the drawer. 'If you would just come through to sign a declaration . . .' We were taken to a small office where one of the police-men sat down at a table covered with brown paper. He started filling in a form, surrounded by files tied up with pink ribbons and tins of drawing pins and clips, dipping his school pen in a flat inkwell with blueblack ink. Dulpert had to spell out Jim's full names, and finally we were asked to sign.

'Why didn't you contact his wife?' Dulpert asked.

'Was he married then?'

'Yes.'

'All we found on him was an empty cigarette box with your name and address on it. If you could tell us where his wife lives . . .'

'A flat somewhere in Gardens. Hope Street, I think.'

He jotted it down. 'Well, if there's anything else we'll get in touch with you.'

'But how did he die?'

The policeman hesitated for a moment. 'Gassed. In a car on Signal Hill. Stolen car, that's why we . . .'

'If his wife needs any help . . .'

The constable got up. 'Shall we take you back home?'

'Don't bother. We can walk.'

And then we were back in the noisy sunlit streets, but now with a new awareness of Jim lying in his drawer in the cool room, as if the morgue had become the city's subconscious, containing the body like a psychosis.

'Did you notice that even the corpses are segregated?' Dulpert sud-denly asked. 'Still, they allowed us into the White room. If it had been a restaurant we'd have had to keep out. Apartheid seems to rot away in death.'

I didn't answer. I was still too upset, disturbed by the very matter-of-factness of the scene. One would have expected death to be different, more dignified, more impressive and strange. I was shocked for the very reason that it had been so unshocking.

A few blocks away he spoke again : 'Why d'you think he left them my address? What did I have to do with him? Why didn't he leave a letter for his wife? I haven't seen him for weeks. After that *Kama Sutra* busi-ness we hardly spoke to each other. And now this.' We were stopped by a red traffic light. 'Do you think he meant to reproach me?'

'What could he reproach you with?'

'Perhaps he was lonely, how the hell must I know? Perhaps he didn't have anybody else. One must be damned desperate if one . . . And I never really cared about him. Do you think it's my fault?'

'Don't be melodramatic, Dulpert.'

'Melodramatic!' The lights were still red but he started crossing over. A car hooted; Dulpert responded with two fingers. 'He's dead. Why didn't he come and see me if he thought I could do something for him? How was I to know?' I realised that I had to let him unburden in his own way. When we reached the corner where the fruit-cart had over-turned he said: 'Perhaps I should have known. Perhaps one should always keep oneself open to others, to see when you're needed.' With a sharp laugh he added: 'See? Now I'm progressing from melodrama to didacticism.' We threaded our way through the lower streets of our quarter. Outside the public lavatories in Upper Darling Street, we awaited our turn at the urinal, under the eagle eyes of the caretaker fondling the pennies in the pockets of his outside trousers. A boy was telling his admiring friend of a 'lekke' session' he'd had with his 'goose'. There were a few Whites in the row too, and I suspected that that was the reason why Dulpert often made that particular detour.

'Well,' he said as we left. '*Inter faeces et urinam morimur.*' He laugh-ed. 'And now he's had it.' As we came nearer to Oxford Place he grew more serious: 'Strange to think of it: yesterday he pissed like us, bought his paper, had his food, did his shopping, and now he's lying down there. Isn't it terrible how little one can really say about death? One can't get away from clichés. Probably because death is the greatest cliché of them all.' He walked on silently for a few yards, then added: 'I suppose they'll tie a card round his big toe too, now that they know who he is.'

'It must make things much easier on the other side,' I said flippantly, trying to break through his depression.

He ignored me. 'It's such a limp way to go,' he suddenly burst out. 'So undignified.'

'It must require a certain sort of courage, even if you're desperate – in the last moment to *decide* to pull the trigger or swallow the pill or turn the key.'

'It requires a different sort of courage to go on.'

'I know. I've also read Camus.'

'I'm not talking about reading, Joseph!' He stopped in the middle of the street. 'I'm talking about life and death, and of people like you and me.'

'And you exclude suicide altogether?'

'Yes, I do.'

'Do you think one can ever make an absolute statement about something like that?'

'I very seldom make absolute statements. And I always try to respect other people's motives. But I do exclude suicide. It's undignified. All it leaves to others is a negation.'

'Are those others more important than the individual who must make the decision?'

'I happen to respect my neighbour.'

'If you reach your limit, you're on your own : then all your neighbours fall away.'

'There are two reasons why I can't agree with you,' Dulpert said. 'First, if you love your neighbour as yourself, no extremity can make any difference to your obligations towards him. And second, I simply don't believe that one ever really reaches one's limit. You may sometimes think that you've reached it. But if you remain true to your nature, you can always go further.'

V

All those years the idea of going overseas formed part of the 'perhaps' one needs when one is young enough to afford the presumption of illusions. But during the summer vacation following my third year as a student it became a serious possibility, after I'd won a scholarship at the Drama School, which meant that I could save all my holiday earnings.

Derek also encouraged me. He was often absent from Cape Town on long theatre tours, but whenever he was available he helped me with my group of amateurs. It was heavy going : the actors had more than enough enthusiasm, some even had talent, but it was quite raw and I was too inexperienced myself sufficiently to shape and direct it. Some of the actors were jobless and had to rehearse without a proper meal all day; our stage manager was resourceful and energetic, but during the weekends when he was on the bottle he became completely unreliable. At one major production in the Athlone school hall to which all the so-called 'leaders of the Coloured community' had been invited, he was so sozzled that he let the final curtain down ten minutes before the end, in the very middle of the climax scene. When he realised what he'd done he was scared sober and immediately scaled the catwalk with suicidal intentions. It took half an hour's pleading to coax him back to the ground, which saved his life, but made no difference to the ruined show. And that very night Derek insisted :

'You're wasting your time and your talent, baby. There's only one way out : you must go overseas as soon as possible.'

I argued with him, mainly because it still sounded too far-fetched to believe. But it began to brood inside me.

It was some time before I had the courage to discuss it with Dulpert, afraid that he would regard it as a form of escape. But when I eventually did confide in him, one evening when he found me with the *I Ching* and started questioning me, he reacted very calmly : 'Surely it's for you to decide, Joseph. If you really believe in your future in theatre, you've got to go, I suppose. What else can you do?'

All right, I decided, as soon as I'd completed my drama course I would go. Derek was prepared to help me. He knew all the right people in London.

Then it all happened much faster than I'd anticipated.

First there was Sharpeville, that March.

We heard about it in the street, Dulpert and I, late that afternoon, on our way back after a rehearsal in the Little Theatre. The first rumours were so extravagant that we refused to believe a word. All we knew was that *something* had happened, that a number of people had been shot by the police, that something had begun to erupt.

In District Six the streets overflowed with people, but it was different from other days, a solemn silence hanging over everything. In a small junk shop where a crowd had gathered round a radio, we elbowed our way inside to listen to the news in the dusky interior. There were all sorts of wares hanging from the ceiling : bicycle wheels, rolls of wire, brass, harnesses and saddles, guitars, chewing tobacco, enema sets; on the floor stood open bags, half filled with samp and flour and brown sugar and dried fruit. We stood there like members of a sect at a service, while the radio went on talking and talking, mentioning numbers, sixty-something dead, more than double the number wounded. Comments and declarations by police chiefs and spokesmen of the Government. Nobody in the shop said a word. But it was the beginning of the strangest week I'd ever known in our part of the city. There was a combination of a fair-like and funeral atmosphere in the air. Shops which had never before been closed, not even on Sundays, stood barred and shuttered; others stayed open over time, and the barber shops were filled with clients until ten o'clock at night, if not later. Occasionally two or three police vans would come driving down a street, painfully slowly, silently watched by bunches of sullen people. Sometimes there were sirens. Urchins with police whistles ran amok. Radios were kept on full-blast until closing time at night. Everybody was on the streets, even the sick were carried down on their mattresses as if they were expecting the Second Coming. Gran'ma Grace went up and down in the district, like Jonah in Nineveh, to prepare the world for the terrors of the Last Judgement. Even Dulpert, not easily ruffled, went about repeating, 'It's coming. It's coming. It's coming.'

Within a day, within two days, it no longer was a report from Johannesburg but a living reality all around us. Cordons of soldiers and volunteers ringed Langa and Nyanga and all the other black townships in the Peninsula; and when a baby was shot dead in his mother's arms at a road block, it stirred up a dark hum of protest in our District, like a hive suddenly getting the smell of smoke. Suddenly the streets were filled with strangers in civilian clothes, all of them heavily built, all of them White, and long processions of police vans came streaming past with ominous warning.

We were just waiting for something. Nobody dared to formulate it. It was just something. But the vagueness made it no less terrifying.

And Gran'ma Grace went her way prophesying: 'The end is nigh. Come, yea come, Lawd Jissis.'

And then something did happen.

From the slopes of Devil's Peak, along the winding course of De Waal Road, we saw the huge black procession approaching like a black wave, down towards the city, towards Parliament, those thousands, with the subdued roar of a wave, with the deep silence of a wave.

'It's coming,' said Dulpert.

The Cape was deadly silent all that day, but a silence of secret life, not of death. The procession came down slowly and the city was silent, as if the Black Southeaster was moving through the streets in slow motion. The Cape was terrified that day. It was silent and terrified, caught in a soundless convulsion. And then all of us merged with the procession, all of us with our outspoken or mute expectations. Even cripples on crutches. Even a blind man.

The news spread: the leaders would form a deputation to the Government, everything would be arranged, we must disperse. In the middle of a final act, on the verge of the climax, the curtain came down.

'It's a mistake,' Dulpert said, pale with anger. 'My God, they're making a mistake.'

Everything that had been building up through those tumultuous days, was dispersed with us.

'You know what's going to happen?' asked Dulpert. 'It's just a trick to play for time. Do you think the Government is going to pay any attention to our men? They'd sooner banish the lot of them to Robben Island. We've had our chance – and now it's gone. They'll all be taken away from us. It's all been in vain.'

And when his prohecy came true and the Cape slowly uncoiled from its convulsions, yielding once again to the persuasive warmth of the autumn days, Dulpert became unbearably depressed.

Several times Gran'ma Grace nagged him, 'Why you eating yo' head like this?'

Something irrevocably changed him, that March. He became brooding and bitter, and would spend hours huddled over his books without doing a thing. Before the end of April, one morning as I was preparing to go to a lecture, he casually announced:

'I need another free period, Joseph. It's no longer working out here.'

With dull fear in the pit of my stomach I asked: 'What are you going to do then?'

'I'm leaving.'

'Where to?'

'Don't know yet.'

'When?'

'Today.'

'But you can't go away like this . . .'

'Of course I can. I need it.'

'Can't you stay on for a few more days?' I couldn't find any reason to justify it, but I didn't want to let him go.

'You'd better keep the old trunk,' he said. 'It'll just be in my way. And you can have the *I Ching*. You may need it.'

'But, Dulpert . . .'

He took my hand. 'Well, see you, then.'

'When?'

'Sometime. I'll come and look you up with my White wife.'

'I want to go with you!'

'Don't be silly. Now hurry up, or you'll be late for your lecture.'

I never saw him again.

145

Dulpert's departure disrupted my whole existence, much as I tried to keep going. Although he'd given Gran'ma Grace a month's notice money she insisted on rearranging our rooms without delay so that a new boarder could move in next door. Two days later I had another neighbour, a Turkish Cypriot with a moustache like Stalin, formerly a sailor but now of uncertain occupation, presumably a drug pusher, judging by the zombies who turned up on his doorstep at all hours. At night I was kept awake by his snoring, and whenever he had no visitors during the daytime he would sit on his bed humming monotonously in a high-pitched voice, like an emasculated bee.

It broke down my concentration and increased my own restlessness: I also wanted to get away. I began to feel claustrophobic about the Drama School, and my own group could no longer hold my undivided attention.

For a while I found precarious new stability with Sheila, a primary school teacher from Observatory, whom I'd met through her sister, a member of my group. Sheila was attractive, a gentle sort of attractiveness, and in some ways reminded me of my mother – perhaps the smell of soap, or the smoothness of her arms and legs, something about her laugh.

For a long time a strange reticence kept me from her: she was obviously not a girl for a night or a week, but at the same time I felt too unstable emotionally to offer her any more than just that. The mere fact that she attracted me and that I daily became more conscious of it, troubled me. It was as if she, coming so soon after Dulpert's departure, exposed a dangerous breach in my defence, revealing the extent to which I still relied on others rather than on myself.

I didn't *want* to feel driven to her. But it was futile, of course. A month after I'd met her, all my logical defences had crumbled. Even as I was entering her for the first time I thought, almost sadly: *It's such a pity.*

In the small hours, lying in my arms and stroking my body with her fingertips, the first gesture of possessiveness, she whispered: 'I was scared of you. Now I love you.'

I remembered Dulpert's words, one day: 'Joseph, the moment a woman tells you that she loves you it's time to clear out. Unless you're prepared to be completely possessed by her. And if ever you feel like telling a woman that you love her, then get away before you actually say it. Unless you're prepared to take the responsibility for a whole life beside your own.'

146

In the dark I asked her : 'Why were you scared?'

'I thought you'd hurt me.'

'And now you know I won't?'

'No. I still know it. The only difference is that I don't mind any more.'

'Don't say that, Sheila!'

'You've got your work, and it's important to you.' There was something disarming about her lucidity. Or was that her way of self-defence? 'Promise me you'll tell me if I get in your way, if you want me to go.'

'I won't ever want you to go.'

'You're only human. Me too. And I'm glad it's happened this way.'

'If you're so sure that I'll leave you, why did you allow me to make love to you tonight?'

'Because it's tonight that I love you.' She moved beside me and in the dim light from outside I could see the outline of her cheek and shoulder and her breasts. 'I'm almost scared to say it,' she admitted. 'For I don't want you to think that I'm smothering you.'

'I don't want to smother *you*.'

'Suppose I want to be smothered?'

I thought hopelessly : I'll never understand a woman. Stubbornly I insisted on the seriousness of my feelings, and even convinced myself. For I really needed her then, rest for my restlessness, protection for my loneliness. It was a time when I still thought loneliness could be dissolved in someone else, the sweet delusion of youth.

And we were happy together, that little while. There was a humble and attentive quality about her love – nothing grovelling, nothing sentimental at all : it was simply that she fulfilled herself by caring for me and ministering to my needs. There was something pure about it, like the smell of her soap. And if I think back to it now, I can rediscover with much compassion the beautiful and innocent arrogance that form of love from a woman evokes in a man. To buy me delicacies from her small earnings, or a new jacket for the August cold; to arrange my collar before we went to theatre, or to sew on my buttons; to bring us a hand-embroidered sheet for the bed, or flowers for the window-sill; to sit quietly in a chair, reading while I was working; to put her body at my disposal without reserve or compromise – such was the nature of her love. I was too young to really value its depth; and I fell into the easy mistake of taking it for granted. And through her utter unselfishness she bound me more inescapably than either she or I could realise.

147

At the end of August Derek burst into my room one evening, announcing: 'You've got an audition next week. The moment of truth has come. Praise the Lord and pack your cases: I think you're going overseas.'

'What on earth has got into you now?'

He was deadly serious: 'You've heard of Geoffrey Barnes of the Old Vic touring the country, haven't you?'

'Of course. But what about him?'

'He's arranging auditions for budding young geniuses like yourself. There are three British Council grants at stake. Geoff is a darling and he's mad about me – and I told him about you.'

'But I can't be ready in a week!'

'Pull yourself together, baby, we're starting tonight.'

Day and night, he worked with me, until, weak and trembling, I walked out on the bare stage of the Little Theatre the following Wednesday. After the audition I felt convinced that it had been the worst hour I'd ever spent on stage in my life. When Sheila and I sat down to the special meal she'd prepared for that evening, opening the bottle of champagne she'd bought, I interrupted her toast and said: 'Let's just drink because we're together. For the grant is down the drain.'

Three weeks later the letter arrived.

Under different circumstances I would have waited until the end of the year to finish my course first. But suddenly it seemed like the answer to all my restlessness. My old impulsiveness overruled all logical arguments and before I fully realised what was happening I was at the airport, surrounded by the members of my group, a handful of student friends, Derek, Gran'ma Grace in a brand-new dress and purple hat with a pocket Bible as a parting gift, the moustached boarder who urgently tried to talk me into delivering a small package to a stranger wearing a red carnation in his buttonhole at Heathrow Airport; and, of course, Sheila.

'I'll come back,' I whispered during the last confused moments, suddenly frightened and moved. 'I promise.'

She shook her head.

'I promise you, Sheila!'

'I told you to go, dammit!' she answered with unexpected vehemence. 'My God, it isn't your fault that I love you!'

VI

Gnawing uncertainty often darkened to near-despair those first few weeks in London. The city was filthy, and gloomy, and wet; after District Six I found it apathetic, often openly hostile. Derek had recommended me to Peter and Janet Sweetman, two of his English friends willing to put me up temporarily in their spacious but melancholy flat in Ovington Gardens, off the Brompton Road. During the first few days they dutifully 'showed me around', increasing my bewilderment: it was too much to take in, I would never find my way around, I didn't want to be there.

Peter was attached to the BBC, Janet painted; and their conflicting temperaments resulted in daily upheavals which usually raged on until the little old gentleman upstairs started hammering on his floor with a blunt object. Peter set great store by correctness and precision, while Janet couldn't care less and left brushes, tubes of paint, clothing and soiled towels trailing all the way from the hall to the outsize bathroom. Meals were seldom ready on time and more often than not she forgot to do the shopping, so that we had to dash off to the nearest pub for a bite. They were actually very much in love and their fights always ended in spectacular reconciliations; still, the sound and fury of it all was highly embarrassing to the stranger within their gates.

In the beginning I tried to avoid the eruptions by slipping out and going for endless walks; in this way, during my very first week, I discovered the Victoria and Albert Museum where I began to spend most of my free time. When the weather was too bad for a stroll, I took refuge in a hot bath. But this return to the surrogate of the womb brought a whole complex of new problems in its wake – comic in retrospect but certainly not at the time. Janet namely had the unnerving habit of entering without knocking whenever I was in the bath (the door had no key), wandering past the aspidistras in their ornate Victorian stands or casually sitting down on the toilet to obey whatever call of Nature came to her, talking non-stop all the time, while I lay half-submerged feeling the water grow cold over me.

The first time it happened she nearly scared me out of my wits; and even after she'd made a habit of it I could never really get used to it. I was exposed too unfairly – not only to her but to the enormous gulf between us.

Janet had a singular sort of beauty : a very white, very soft skin and delicate bones, with enormous, intense eyes, almost too large for her small face surrounded by hair cropped boyishly short. At first I thought that in her absent-minded way she never even realised that I was naked in the bath; but after a few days she one morning brought her sketching pad with her and started drawing me while she was sitting on the toilet – and from the result it was obvious that her seemingly vague eyes had minutely observed every detail of my body. So I tried to persuade myself that she simply regarded me as an interesting object for drawing, like a dish of fruit or an architectural construction. I deliberately willed myself into the role of object, because that was the only way in which I could handle the situation.

It helped me to react more naturally; and when her conversation went on for an impossibly long time one morning I finally stood up in the bath, reached for the towel from the rail and began to dry myself.

'Don't move,' she said quickly and flicked over a page in her pad. Her hand was moving in rapid, rough strokes across the white surface. Then she lowered the pad for a second, the pencil still in her raised hand.

'You've got a beautiful body,' she said.

I felt a tautness in my throat and hurriedly stepped out, turning my back to her and rubbing myself vigorously with the towel.

'No, don't turn away, I haven't finished yet!'

I went on drying myself, keeping my back to her, embarrassed by my erection.

She didn't say anything. I heard the sound of another page being turned over, then draped the towel round my waist and went out without looking at her again. In my room I put on warm clothes, with my new London overcoat on top, and went down to the streets. An hour later the wretched weather, like many other times, drove me back to the V & A.

That was the first day I discovered the large room with replicas of Michelangelo's sculptures. And I must admit that not even the confrontation with the original works in Florence, years later, could move me so deeply as that first discovery. Perhaps it was the sheer unexpectedness of the Michelangelo collection that morning, after all the rooms with Chinese lacquer, and furniture, and delicate German woodcuts : I came through the door and looked up to the high glass ceiling, suddenly surrounded by the most powerful sculptures I'd ever seen. Immediately in front of me was the David, in all the overpowering self-assertion of his youth, relaxed and yet ready for action in every muscle, arrogant and pure, with a disconcerting innocence about the arms and shoulders and torso and the smooth, restful sex. It wasn't so much a discovery of Michelangelo as of the beauty of a body.

And I thought: *This is how she looked at me, this is how she saw me – she White and I Brown: she woman and I man.*

Three days later I had to attend an audition for RADA. I'd already been awarded my grant, but still had to be accepted by one of the theatre schools. And with great trepidation I went up the tube escalator at Holborn station that Monday afternoon and walked to the uninspiring YMCA building. The day before I'd taken five or six trips to Holborn to make quite sure that I would find my way; and I arrived more than an hour early, having made ample provision for the possibility of power failures, tube accidents, traffic jams or some other form of *vis major*.

There was a group of other candidates assembled in the large room to which a ratty Cockney janitor had motioned me. One or two of them smiled wanly, but most of them either ignored me or glared at me with intense hostility. Suddenly the scene was familiar to me: I was back in the classroom where we'd been preparing for *The Tempest*. The memory broke the worst tension. I sat down in a corner, opened my books and went through the work I'd prepared for the audition: prose and poetry, classical and modern passages, Richard's 'I have been studying how I may compare . . .' and a Treplev monologue from *The Seagull*. I closed my eyes and tried to recall what Derek had told me when he'd put me through my paces before my departure; and then I was called, with three others, from the waiting room.

We had to wait in the bleak corridor while the first girl was inside. With my back to the others I stood at the window looking out, trying to forget about what lay ahead by concentrating on the drab scene outside. I was the second to be called in. The audition room was cavernous and bare. Behind a long table a row 'of strangers sat waiting, at least six of them, including two middle-aged women. I breathed in deeply and started with *Richard II*. The judges sat unearthly still. A familiar detachment which Brecht, no doubt, would have appreciated, returned to me: I was aware of them and me, and of how out of place Shakespeare was in those surroundings, in that room with the musty green curtains and the worn-out carpet and the row of cheap glass ashtrays on the table. 'You bastards,' I thought, 'I'll show you.'

I doubt whether my performance was really impressive. How on earth could I have any conception of Richard's variety, of Shakespeare's subtle rhythms and hidden meanings? My technique was still so erratic. But I had faith, burning like a fire in my brain : and then that detachment which lent me self-control. Outside, the enormous city went its way, people were murdered and born, fruit and jewellery and plastic rain-coats and virginity were bought and sold and given away, planes arrived from all the continents and left for the four corners of the earth : and there in the drab room I did my bit of Shakespeare and my bit of Chek-hov and politely took my leave and returned to the corridor; and some time later I was called to a small office at the far end of it, where a consumptive middle-aged man mumbled unintelliglble instructions and thrust a handful of forms and brochures into my hand.

Two weeks later I plunged into the work which was to dominate my existence during the next few years. Gower Street became the axis of my world : the lectures, the rhythmic and vocal exercises, the impro-visations, the group work and individual work, the rehearsals and pro-ductions of RADA determined the meaning of my life – all the rest was ephemeral and peripheral. All impressions and impulses from the outside world were referred to that centre to be interpreted, evaluated and made manageable.

Not that it was always pleasant. I know such groups differ from year to year, but ours was a difficult one. In Cape Town there had been a sense of co-operation in our class : if someone got stuck in a practical exam, there were always friends at hand to help him out; each derived pleasure from the achievements of the rest. But not in our group in RADA. There were a few extremely talented students among us, but each one was concerned exclusively with his own progress. In some class productions it created a form of electricity yielding remarkable results; others were very nearly wrecked by it.

I soon changed digs. Janet contributed to it, I suppose, although it had never been the idea that I'd permanently stay with her and Peter. Her visits to the bathroom formed only part of a complicated situation. She was making unreasonable demands on my time, even after I'd started working at RADA, by expecting me to pose for her whenever she felt like it, or to do the household shopping while she was painting.

And then her dressing habits created singular embarrassments and guilt feelings for me : in the overheated flat she usually wore nothing but a short loose paint-smudged tunic; wandering through the flat, or even going to the front door when the bell went, the tunic would be mostly unbuttoned. She might have been blissfully unaware of this exposure of her unusually small breasts with elongated brownish nipples, the provocative bulge of her belly with the deep indent of her navel, and her luxuriant pubic patch : but I was not. What would the visitors have thought of it, what would Peter have thought? My name might be Joseph but I had no intention of getting involved in a Potiphar scene! At night it plagued me with dreams of lust and violence; in the daytime I caught myself wandering through the flat with the sole aim of seeing her again and again – not because I really desired her at all, but merely to unnerve and tease and provoke myself. It was like Hermien on her Bain's Kloof rock, only more attainable, and therefore more dangerous.

I'm ashamed to recall it all, but I owe it to myself to be honest, even when it concerns reactions which today seem to me silly, exaggerated, adolescent or – indeed – prudish. Whether Janet was 'available' I don't know : it was never really the issue at all. What matters is the mere fact that I could start thinking of such a possibility. And I just didn't know how to deal with it. I was a stranger in their country, a guest in their house, I was in a position of trust and dependence, and I was Coloured. In all possible respects I was unequipped for such a situation. And my instinctive reaction was flight.

It was more difficult to find lodging than I'd expected. The answers from most landladies advertising rooms ranged from a curt : 'We don't want any Blacks around', to a condescending and hypocritical : 'Of course, *I* don't mind, but the neighbours . . .' I began to spend all my spare time trudging through the likely districts, following up leads supplied by co-students or newspaper vendors. It was fruitless every time, but at least I got to know London in the process.

More than a month after I'd first set out on my systematic exploration of the city (Peter, who never worked regular hours, had come home at eleven that morning when we were in the lounge together – I reading on the sofa, Janet moving about with a vacuum cleaner, wearing only an old blue shirt barely covering her hips, leaving her seductive lower half exposed) I first discovered the shabby district of S.E.1 behind Waterloo Station. I'd been to the Old Vic before, of course, but at night it looked quite different from the scene in merciless daylight. I couldn't

153

believe that a city could change so rapidly: a mere few hundred yards from the monumental complex of the Royal Festival Hall lay this maze of streets and alleys where one felt scared to risk it alone even in broad daylight.

I bought some fruit on the market in Lower Marsh, at the same time enquiring, more from habit than anything else, about lodgings in the neighbourhood. The thin, mousy little woman fluttered her eyelids and said she had a sister-in-law who had a friend who might know some-one . . . And when she shut up her stall half an hour later, she took me with her to the sister-in-law, who introduced me to the friend, and before the end of the day I'd rented a minuscule room in an ugly black building in The Cut, with a view over chimney-pots, roof-tops and tiny courtyards strung with washing and teeming with innumerable cats.

For a year that little room was my fortress. The light bulb on the staircase had a habit of disappearing overnight; there were two broken panes in the window on the landing outside my room which were never repaired; and the whole building was redolent with more than two centuries' cooking and human excrement. But once I'd put my shilling in the slot and drawn the single curtain in front of my window, I felt at home.

Actually it was a strange year, a monotonous year with little or no relief. I didn't know a soul in London apart from a handful of colleagues, and my contact with them was limited to Drama School classes or the occasional pint in the pub. There simply was no place for serious friend-ships or relationships in my overworked existence. Most of my time was taken by RADA and reading. I read even more voraciously than during that first year in Cape Town, and not just drama but every-thing I could lay my hands on, with little or no discrimination. All of Dostoyevsky and Camus; studies on the Renaissance, biographies, art history, anthropological accounts of ancient civilisations, Toynbee, the letters of Van Gogh; I spent nights on end reading Bertrand Russell; in the end I always returned to Camus. Whatever money I had left after paying for food and rent (in the course of that year I lost fifteen pounds in weight), I spent on shows. I would return four or five times to plays I liked, to find out what made them tick. Occasionally I felt obliged to visit Peter and Janet who would take me out into the coun-try with them – excursions to Windsor or Henley or Brighton, and one unforgettable weekend to Stratford. For the rest I continued to explore London on foot. And every time I returned to my 'own' district, to the street market bursting out of its seams on Sundays, offering for sale anything the human mind could conceive of; I came to know the market women and the bakers and butchers, and often I got something for free in exchange for carrying or fetching; the two middle-aged, alcoholic prostitutes from the building next to mine offered me a 'special tariff' as an inhabitant of their district, an offer I felt obliged to refuse as tactfully as I could.

With Mrs Blake, the furtive little mouse who'd sold me fruit on that first day, I struck up a warm friendship. In her eyes I was the 'pore luv' struggling to stay alive far from home and hearth, with the result that I was always sure of discount or even of some free fruit on days when I had no money for food; sometimes she 'hired' me to help her in the stall, in exchange for a crumpled pound note which I didn't really deserve and she could hardly afford.

For a couple of months I was employed as a billsticker on Tube stations at night to help stave off hunger and cold. It remains one of my most vivid London memories: those familiar station scenes suddenly dehumanised in the near-dark, a lugubrious hollow echoing with the clanging of the glue bucket as I moved from one spot to another. During those nightly hours of subterranean seclusion I could give my thought free rein to explore or dissect a play or a character while my hands worked on independently, plastering the walls with ads for coming films, Guinness, cigarettes, the *Evening Standard* and typing pools, or with the colourful photographs of naked and half-naked girls, all of them blonde, all of them lithe, promoting the sales of bra's, panties, stockings, bikinis or radios. Perhaps my imagination is of a kind which draws inspiration from the macabre: when I really feel in an exuberant mood, I usually sing Handel's Funeral March at the top of my voice. (Not that that has happened much lately.)

Another solution for the hunger problem was the parties regularly organised by other students. I didn't go very often; but in exchange for a filled stomach I would occasionally venture from my solitary existence to share their conversations and hilarity. It usually came as a relief when, late at night, I crossed the Thames and returned to my own dark district.

At one of these parties, early in my second academic year, I met Beverley. Even this sounds too pretentious. I hadn't eaten all day and since no meal was served before the party had got well under way, I was abnormally affected by the first few drinks. In fact, it was one of the few occasions in my life when I got hopelessly drunk. When I woke up the next morning with a blinding headache, I found myself in a strange bed in a strange room, with a strange girl in a kimono in front of me.

It is all too easy to equate women with 'experience'. I can remember a young actor in our group, Will Grogan, who kept a complete catalogue of all the women he'd made love to: name, address, measurements, particulars of appearance, positions(s) preferred, reactions during inter-course. They were filed according to physical characteristics, with cross-references to an index of nationalities ranging from Afghan to Yemen (by the time I left RADA Zulu was still missing). And so Will Grogan was 'a man of experience'. But all he could contribute to any conversa-tion was a list of characteristics of female physiology, which in any case fell short of the research by Masters and Johnson. Hence my scepticism. And yet I must admit that each of the few women of importance in my life did, in fact, represent for me something of a 'stage of insight'. And, if it is true, as it seems to me, that my life found its final meaning in Jessica, it is imperative that I painstakingly recall those others who had made her possible.

And so: Beverley.

'What am I doing here?' I mumbled dumbly when I woke up in her bed that morning and saw her standing in front of me, tall and blonde, with the light from the window behind her forming a blinding halo round her head.

'I brought you something to drink.' With a small laugh she sat down on the bed and patiently, as if I were a sick child, coaxed me into swal-lowing some sort of infusion.

'What is it?' I asked.

'Don't talk so much. You're tired. Sleep.' She forced me back on the pillows. I shut my aching eyes and drifted back into sleep. It must have been hours later before I surfaced again. She was still wearing her kimono, curled up on the foot end of the bed surrounded by news-papers – loose pages of the *Sunday Times* and the *Observer* scattered all over the bed. I've never come across another person who could read a newspaper like that, as if a hurricane had raged through it.

'Oh, you're awake,' she said when I sat up. 'Feeling better?'

'Much, thanks. But I still don't understand . . .'

'You'll want something to eat first.' Before I could stop her she'd gone out, the blue kimono sweeping round her long legs. The food must have been waiting in the oven, for in less than five minutes she was back with the most substantial meal I'd seen in months.

'What time is it?' I asked.

'Four o'clock.'

I started gulping down the food and it was several minutes before I asked again : 'How did I get here?'

'I brought you.'

'But . . .'

'You were a bit . . . unsteady last night.' She smiled, shaking back her blonde hair with a small gesture of her head. 'You asked me to take you home, but when we got in my car you couldn't tell me how to get there and after driving round in circles for an hour I thought I'd better bring you back here.'

'I'm terribly sorry.'

'Why?' Another smile. 'I had a room. I slept on the sofa in the lounge.'

'Yes, but . . .'

'If you get up we can go for a stroll on the Heath. You need some fresh air.'

I threw off the bedclothes to get up. Only then I discovered that I was naked. Hastily I drew up a corner of the sheet and looked at her in surprise.

'You couldn't sleep with all your things on.' She got up and brought me my clothes in a neat bundle; they'd obviously been ironed. 'The bathroom is through there.' Then she took the tray back to the kitchen.

A quarter of an hour later we left Belsize Park in her small Austin and drove to Hampstead Heath. I was impressed by her driving. Through the heavy Sunday-afternoon traffic she deftly picked her way without a moment's hesitation.

The afternoon was already sinking by the time we reached the Heath and began to walk across the gently billowing grass; the voices of children frolicking among the trees with their dogs had the thin, distant quality of dusk. The leaves were yellowing with the first intimation of autumn. All awareness of the city began to ebb away; S.E.1 seemed scarcely real. Leisurely, lazily, through trees and across clearings; at last we sat down on the grass, plunging into conversation like bathers seeking relief in a cool pond after a hot day, both of us eager to catch up with all the years we'd lost by not knowing each other.

I told her of my year in London and my work with RADA, of Peter and Janet; and further back, of District Six and Gran'ma Grace and Dulpert, of life on the farm, and of my mother, of Willem, even of Hermien. And then Beverley spoke, while the light wind played with her long hair and her skirt.

Her father was an industrialist, a self-made man, hyperconscious of his new status and overfastidious about her having 'nothing but the best'. At school she'd more or less passively allowed him to have his way; but she'd refused to go to Oxford, preferring London University and the School of Oriental and African Studies. Between her father and herself, I soon discovered, there existed the sort of tension which can only develop between two people who love one another very deeply but who are too similar temperamentally, too stubborn above all, to make any concessions.

The previous year he'd given her the expensive flat in Belsize Park as a twenty-first birthday gift. She couldn't stand the place and had threatened, on several occasions, to abandon it; at the same time she could never really go so far as to do it, because she knew it would hurt him too much. And so she'd acquiesced, having followed her own will in so many other respects in the choice of friends, vacations, studies and her general way of life.

She smiled a little sadly: 'I don't always understand myself,' she admitted. 'Don't you think it's perverse to want to turn one's back on everything one has? I don't want to be poor and miserable, I'm not equipped for it. On the other hand . . .' She lifted her head and looked straight at me with her almost violet eyes: 'If I try to talk to him about his parents, who were working class, he seems to close a door between us as if he really doesn't know what I'm talking about. Whereas all I want to do is to keep that door open.'

'Is it quite impossible?'

'No. But the most difficult thing is to remain honest about it. Honest to oneself, I mean. To do something because you sincerely believe in it and not only because it rejects someone else's values. Even that can become confusing: would my convictions have been the same if they hadn't been a rejection of his, a rebellion against his?'

'Aren't you trying to raise imaginary problems now? It's all so theoretical.'

'It's not theoretical! One pays for it. With one's own body.'

It was silent for a long time. Then I said: 'Tell me?'

Once again her eyes urgently examined me. 'Perhaps you'll understand,' she said. 'I was eighteen, just after I'd finished with that deb
factory masquerading as a Public School. I was still new, and curious
about the world, and perhaps a bit embarrassed because in comparison
to most of my friends I was still so inexperienced. I mean about men
and everything.' A pause, while we sat watching a flock of swallows
flying south through the glowing sky, heading for home. 'I was alone
at home that afternoon. My parents were on holiday, on the Riviera
I think, with a group of friends. Then the man knocked, a mechanic
from one of my father's factories. He was quite young still, under
thirty. I can't remember all the details of what he told me, but it boiled
down to some misunderstanding or other, as a result of which he'd lost
his job. He wanted to see my father; he was still wearing his dirty overalls. I told him my father was away on holiday but he wouldn't believe
me. "It's just because I'm poor," he said. "You bloody rich are all the
same." I desperately tried to convince him, but he just smirked. So in
the end I asked him in for coffee, to convince him that I was speaking
the truth.' She turned her long legs under her. 'We started talking. He
went on and on about my father and his factories and the whole system.
I thought I'd just let him get it all off his chest. But gradually I became
more aware of him – I mean, of him as a man, as he was sitting there . . .
there was something about him, his anger, his strong hands and the way
he moved them, and he was very handsome in a way – it made me feel
out of breath. It was the first time I'd ever reacted to a man like that,
a sort of wildness that came over me. I tried to keep calm at first, but
the more he ranted against my father, the filthier the names he called
him . . . it was a terrible, incredible wave of something, of lust, rising
up in me, I couldn't control it – and him with his dirty overalls and all.
It was dark in the lounge by then, and that also made it easier. And
then . . .' She looked down at her hands. 'We made love. In my room.
He was almost brutal, he must have hated me terribly, and he hurt me.
But I wanted to get hurt. And when he'd finished I looked up at him
and said: "You'd better hurry, I'm expecting my father back any moment now." It scared the shit out of him. He jumped up and got into his
clothes, fumbling and stumbling all over the place, it was so ludicrous,
it was so humiliating, and when he left I despised him.'

'Miss Julie,' I said quietly before I could help it.

Beverley shook her head fiercely. 'I'm not a character from a play:
I'm *me*!'

'I didn't mean it like that.' With the knuckles of my fingers I barely touched her cheek. She stiffened, then slowly relaxed again.

'Was that all?' I asked. 'Just that once?'

'No, it wasn't. I got involved a few more times. Not often, though. Sometimes I think it's a way of finding out whether I'm immune from hurt : and if it doesn't work, I try again. So I tried a few times. Did I try, or was I tried?' A pause. 'But there was only one who ever really mattered to me. Tony. He was in my class, a brilliant bloke. Came from Wolverhampton – have you ever been there? His mother was a widow and they were very poor. He had only his grant. And something of a grudge against the world. When we made love . . .' She shut her eyes for a moment. 'Sometimes he would stop just before I came and say : "You can finish it off yourself : why do you try to use me?" He brought me to the brink of a nervous breakdown. I loved him, but he wouldn't believe it. He said I was confusing love with charity, with missionary feelings. Do you think it's possible?'

'All I think is that you're much too suspicious about your own motives. Where does all this introspection lead to?'

'But I want to know why it's happening to me!'

'Couldn't Tony help you at all?'

'Tony's dead.'

The sun was setting now. The last people were wandering back under the trees.

'He committed suicide. Everybody said he would have done it anyway, sooner or later. But what use was it to me? I should have been able to help him. I know I should. But I was so tired by then . . .'

'Was it long ago?'

'Six months.'

We sat still for a while. Then I asked : 'And now?'

She shook her head.

Dull fear rose up in me. I wanted to protect her vulnerability. After all those months of loneliness, I was greedy for her. But I was frightened. How could I have the temerity to force myself into her life? What would become of me? What would become of her?

'Come on,' I said, and I helped her get up. 'I suppose we must get back.'

'I suppose so.'

The sky was bleeding itself to death over the smoky park and the distant, low sound of the city.

'This time I'll be able to show you the way.'

'Oh, you mean back to your place?'

'Yes. Sooner or later I'll have to . . .'

'Of course.'

In almost painful silence we drove back. At the turn-off to Belsize Park she stopped and asked: 'Shall we have something to eat first?'

'We may as well. It's still early.'

I sat on the table in the tiled kitchen while she made us food. *Beverley*, I thought with a mixture of sadness and revolt, fear and desire: *Yesterday I didn't even know you existed; today I'm here; and tomorrow?*

After the meal I helped her to wash up. Then she went to the bathroom while I browsed through her records and took out Mozart's Flute and Harp Concerto. It used to be Dulpert's favourite. When she came back, she sat down on the thick carpet in front of my chair to listen, leaning back against my knee with her blonde hair. I looked down over the lines of her hair and forehead and the slight bulge of her breasts in the thick sweater she'd put on, feeling the warmth of desire spreading through me. At the beginning of the Andantino I moved my hand to her shoulder. I could feel her muscles stiffen. Neither of us moved. The record came to an end, but she remained sitting. After a while I got up. There was something like anguish in her eyes when she looked up at me. I avoided her eyes and put on another record.

As I turned back from the last record, hours later, I said: 'I don't want you to take me home and drive back on your own this time of the night. Just show me the way to the Tube.'

'It's too late for the Tube.'

My throat muscles were tense. She got up.

'You see?' she said. 'I'll have to drive back on my own.'

'Unless I stayed here.'

'Yes. Unless you stayed.'

It was as if we'd both held back to the last, as if we had to wait for that final train to leave in order to be exposed to the inevitable. Yet, now that it had happened, we were suddenly shy of each other.

After a while she said: 'Will you make us some tea? I'm going to have a bath.'

When she returned half an hour later, wrapped in her blue kimono, she stopped in the door, and hesitated, and said: 'Joseph, when we talked about staying, I didn't mean . . .'

I came to her. 'Are you frightened?'

She nodded.

'Don't be.'

'Aren't you?'

It came so unexpectedly that I had no answer ready. I looked down. Then back into her eyes. 'Yes. I think I'm much more frightened than you.'

And then it was she, with a brave little smile, who said: 'Don't be.'

She came past me to the large bed where my day had begun, and started unfastening the buttons of her kimono with her back to me – it took a long time – then shook it off with a shrug of her shoulders and turned round to face me.

'You're so lovely. You're so white.'

Only her love hair, a small furry cloud, was dark.

I came to her. She didn't look at me. Her hands were trembling as she undid my buttons.

'Don't be afraid.' Once again. For my own sake, or hers?

Covered by the blankets, sheltered, I held her against me, caressing her to exorcise our fear and kindle her desire: and when she was ready to receive me, I entered her. It was no deathless ecstasy. We were one of the thousands of couples in London that night making love.

In the dark she asked: 'Are you very disappointed in me?'

'Why on earth do you ask that?'

'You expected more of me.'

With the palm of my open left hand I brushed over the sensitive tips of her nipples and felt them reacting. 'There's no one else I want to be with. Do you believe me?'

'Yes.' After a while she whispered: 'But you'll have to be patient with me. You must teach me. So that I can come with you.'

She lay awake for a long time. I know, for I was awake too. It wasn't only her fear that separated us, but everything in myself I still had to overcome. We were both seeking liberation: not from each other, but through each other. We meant it so profoundly. And when deep in the night I put my hand between her legs and gently brought her back to life, both of us believed it implicitly.

162

Less than a fortnight later I left S.E.1 and moved into the large white Victorian flat in Belsize Park. It was she who insisted, of course. She acted with the decisiveness of someone used to having her way: it didn't take me long to discover, in her, those qualities which presumably had helped her father to reach the top. I was sad to leave my old quarters. Not only because the neighbourhood itself had fascinated me, but because, by moving, I had to give up something of that very independence which was so important to Beverley. But I was too much in love, and after a year's abstinence too famished, to oppose her. Perhaps there would have been more hope for us if I hadn't let her have her way so readily right in the beginning.

I paid my landlady two weeks' rent in advance. Beverley wanted to settle the account herself, but I wouldn't allow that. She helped me clear out my wretched room. All my possessions barely filled her small car, and I felt sad and exposed as we piled the last odds and ends on the back seat. It was a rainy day and the streets were black and glistening like tarnished silver.

For one last time we went up to the little room to make sure we'd taken everything. She went to the window, looking through the tear streaks of rain to the roof-tops and chimney-pots outside; the sour smell of poverty lay with a heavy wetness on the buildings all around us. I came to her from behind and pushed my hands under her arms, placing them on her small breasts naked under the large sweater. Suddenly she turned round, raising her open mouth to kiss me with wild passion I'd never noticed in her before.

'I want you, Joseph,' she panted.

The little room was stripped completely bare, with a few dark patches on the walls where I'd removed my theatre posters; one wardrobe door stood open, revealing the empty shelves covered with newspaper; the cardboard box under the table was filled with crumpled paper, used toothpaste tubes, empty food tins; all the bedclothes had been removed, leaving the striped mattress vulgarly exposed on the narrow iron bed.

I kicked the door shut. She was feverish. With eager fingers we tore at each other's buttons. It was cold, but that wasn't the reason why we didn't undress completely – we were simply in too much of a hurry. I forced down her jeans and panties and she kicked with small jerky movements to get them out of the way, draped round one of her ankles. She moved her hands in under my shirt and her nails started clawing into my back as I rammed into her with primitive fury, all sensations intensified by the contrast between our thickly clad chests and arms and our nakedness from the waist down. I was intensely conscious of her fragrance and her beautiful hair on the shabby mattress; conscious of her smoothness, her youth, her womanness, so white and lovely and luxurious, a complete anomaly in my miserable little room. But this was my domain, and I was master here, here my body could force and govern hers in every movement, every moan.

It was the most excrutiatingly wonderful moment of our entire relationship when, on that cheap mattress in that bare room, she reached her orgasm simultaneously with my own, breaking through to the agony of pure pleasure. Far away, close to me, I heard her sob and cry and call out: 'Oh God! Oh God! Oh God!'

Whenever I shut my eyes in an orgasm I always see patterns of colour: green is good, blue is better, red is wonderful; but the absolute extremity of sensation is black, and that happens very rarely because it is almost unbearable, a complete abandon to nothingness, an affirmation of death. And on that afternoon it was black. When at last it ebbed away, the last warm seed throbbing quietly out of me and deep into her, it was like a return from heaven, purgatory and hell, all at the same time. With closed eyes she lay under me, tears under her long lashes, making small sucking sounds against my throat with her open lips while I drew my fingers through her hair and kissed her forehead, feeling the small drops of perspiration turn icy cold on my buttocks and thighs.

It felt like hours before she opened her eyes and whispered: 'What happened?'

'You went with me, all the way.'

'Yes. I was with you all the time. Yes. And now you're wholly mine.'

It was strange, when we got up, how self-conscious we were. As if what had happened had been too much to believe; as if, after that, a body seemed too ordinary, too specific. In silence we went downstairs to her car outside. I sat waiting while she brushed her hair. And still without speaking we crossed the river and drove northward through the late, wet streets, through Camden Town, to my new quarters in Beverley's domain.

Why is it so important to me to write down this particular episode in such detail? Is it to conjure up a bit of passion in this depressing cell and comfort me in my womanless seclusion; my long enforced abstinence? Surely not. For I don't need sex any more: it's a dimension I have transcended. Or is that the very reason? – *because* I have transcended it, I must discover why it used to be of such importance to me before, to find in that moment of most intimate sharing and togetherness the seeds both of our defeat and of what came afterwards, long afterwards, with Jessica.

Beverley, Beverley. I remember so much, and so well.

Beverley in jeans and a large loose navy-blue sweater, her hair in two thin plaits, and reading glasses on her nose, writing an essay surrounded by stacks of books and magazines and papers, grumbling impatiently if I come up behind her to kiss the nape of her neck. Beverley held back by numerous hands as she tries to break through a ban-the-bomb demonstration in Trafalgar Square to get at the police. Beverley naked on her belly on the bed, reading aloud with choking voice from Yeats's *Easter 1916*. Beverley soaking wet on the threshold with yet another stray cat she's found somewhere. Beverley reading the newspaper in the bath, until the pages get soggy in the water and she calls me to help her remove small slithers of paper from all over her body. Beverley encouraging me on days of uncertainty or depression: 'You must go on, Joseph. I believe in you, don't you realise?'

And also, inevitably, Beverley coming to bed in a long white nightdress, innocent as a novice, saying: 'I didn't put in foam tonight. I want you to make me a baby, Joseph.'

In the beginning it was a game only. But soon it involved the whole significance of our relationship. She wanted us to get married. She wanted to bear my child. And why not? There were many days I wanted to go home from the RADA and take her in my arms and say: 'Come, let's go to the Registry Office straight away.' Or when I woke up at night, listening to her breathing quietly beside me, the urge was so strong to roll her over and say: 'Yes. We'll get married tomorrow.' But the body seems to contain a truth of its own which I couldn't deny or avoid. Something withheld me: a small, intense fear that she wanted to get married and bear my babies only to confirm, through me, her rebellion against her father. It was an unreasonable and degrading suspicion – but it was *there*. And added to it was the doubt about myself: whether my love for her had become a way of both rediscovering the innocence of Hermien and to avenge her fall from grace. And unless I could get beyond all these uncertainties, unless I could say the decisive Yes from my whole self, I dared not say the one word which would irrevocably have changed everything for us both.

In small, bitter ways the destructive undercurrents of our relationship began to assert themselves. I would lie in bed waiting for her to come to sleep; and while she was brushing her hair, or putting cream on her face, sometimes while she was applying contraceptive foam, she would begin to talk quite casually about her previous lovers, preferably Tony; a joke he'd made, something he'd said, an odd or endearing little habit; and I would retaliate by telling her, with as straight a face, about Ursula, or Fatima, or Sheila. We knew each other so well, we knew so exactly how to wound most effectively. Futile efforts to set us free from one another, to deny the meaning of the bond between us. Perhaps that remains the most terrible of all discoveries: to know that you are completely dependent on another, that someone else has become so indispensable to you that the centre of gravity of your world is no longer seated in yourself but in him, in her.

And so the problem developed new aspects: if I didn't want to marry her, should I stay with her at all? She wanted me to; I did, But wouldn't it degenerate into a form of parasitism, emotional whoring? Hadn't it become necessary for us to separate for the very reason that we were beginning to need each other too much?

There were weeks of tension and arguing and fighting. Sometimes everything became so absurd that it seemed as if we were both going mad. But through all the upheavals we slowly, in the course of many months, broke through to a form of serenity I have very rarely experienced in my life: a mutual acceptance of the inevitable (equally inevitable as the beginning of it all, one Sunday night with Mozart playing), something which I can only, inadequately and tentatively, describe as a form of respect for one another, because each *allowed* the other to be free.

We parted.

Sometimes I yearned to return, if only to be with her for an hour, reading together, sleeping together. It would be easy: picking up a telephone, getting into a bus or Tube train, knocking on a door, saying the simple words: *I longed for you, I've come back*. But then it would all start again, and sometime we'd again reach the same point, and make the same choice, and cause the same suffering. And the least we owed one another was not to let that happen. So we persisted, even on the few occasions when we couldn't avoid meeting socially. Until, in the end, we transcended even that, although it took a year or more. And later a young Pakistani student leader moved in with her and I could meet them at parties without a pang of jealousy.

I never entered into another relationship which contained a possibility of security. There were women, but never for long : a couple of months, a few weeks, a night or two. The longest was with a girl from Trinidad, Monica, who strongly reminded me of Sheila. There was a German Ingrid, a French Michèle, and even a temperamental half-Russian dancer Murka : most of them actresses or stage hands working with me. But it was all very insignificant. Sweet and touching at times, but insignificant. I'd passed the point of no return. For without fully knowing it at the time, and certainly without deliberately intending it, the break with Beverley had implied a decisive choice. I'd chosen against permanence and security, against those more peaceful and intimate forms of happiness derived from sharing : what I'd chosen was the theatre, here tonight and gone tomorrow, this month Ibsen, next month Molière – or nothing. What I'd chosen was uncertainty and unfulfilment, insecurity, change; what I'd chosen was possibility rather than certainty, hope rather than consummation; and wandering rather than any chance of arriving at a destination.

VII

I moved to Hackney; and I must admit that I often longed for the comfort and convenience of Belsize Park. It's easy to despise luxury while it's yours, I often thought cynically : just as it's easy to regard poverty as a virtue when you're not suffering yourself, or to commend martyrdom while you're safely protected against the thousand natural shocks.

For a few months I lived in a garret in Hackney, near Victoria Park, but I was soon driven out by the concerted efforts of my landlady, an army of bedbugs, and the breweries in the neighbourhood. Normally I couldn't care a damn about the breweries but whenever the fermentation reached a certain stage and the wind changed to south, it became unbearable; the bedbugs I could stand, but my landlady destroyed all my peace of mind by carrying on an endless row because I had the 'bluddy cheek' to demolish the pests against my walls instead of throwing them out of the window 'like decent folk'. And so I packed up and moved a little way to the north – still in Hackney, in an unillustrious and mostly unilluminated street bearing the pretentious name of Navarino Road. Approaching from Islington, the buildings gradually sink lower and become more grey, surrounded by tatty gardens festooned with washing and resounding with children; occasionally a bit of bad Edwardian architecture, but mostly the monstrous and monotonous vulgarities of the '30s and the cheap yellowish facebrick façades of shortly-after-the-war. That was Navarino Road: and yet I spent my happiest years in London there.

I kept my small flat in spite of the interruptions of Continental holidays or country tours. It was always there to return to, small and dark, even at the height of summer: a tiny hall, one bedroom, a lounge, and a kitchen containing a chipped enamel basin in which I was supposed to wash my dishes, my clothes, and myself. Outside on the landing was a toilet with an unlockable door and a whimsical cistern, serving the whole building. The gas meter was chronically out of order as a result of daily raids by the neighbour's seven children. In summer it was an overheated oven, my flat being on the third floor, directly under the flat roof; in winter one shivered of cold. The neighbour I referred to was an unemployed alcoholic who spent his weekends in a drunken fit, beating all the members of his family including his wife, and committing incest with all four of his daughters, the youngest of whom, at the time of my arrival, was ten years old. In addition to all this it was difficult to reach the area from the city, with no Tube station in the vicinity and the nearest buses down at Dalston Junction. And yet I stayed on. There was something about Hackney and its inhabitants which touched me from the very first week of my stay, when I fainted in the street after going without food for a few days.

The butcher in front of whose shop it had happened took me up to his flat to revive me with a cup of tea, and when I left he gave me a few pounds of meat as a present. There was a sense of brotherhood and helpfulness in the district which deeply touched me. Any shop was prepared to give one credit without asking any questions or insisting on security; if you fell ill the neighbours would turn up with food and home remedies; even my alcoholic neighbour would readily have given half his drinking money to help a friend in need. The community spirit was partly fostered by the general antagonism against 'the city', so remote from us, and so foreign; and partly by the fact that it was a predominantly Black neighbourhood, mostly West Indian, although the

Whites were accepted as readily in our midst as they had been in Cape Town's District Six. Our communal deprivation made all the differences irrelevant.

The first year I spent there was an unending struggle just to survive materially, but there was ample compensation in the warmth and generosity of friends. A significant group of these friends were South Africans. Most of them, ironically enough, I'd met through Beverley: by that time I'd grown so far away from the country that it had been relegated to a coincidence in my life. It would never even have occurred to me to return any more: the theatre was all that mattered to me, and that was naturally identified with Britain and Europe. But as a result of her studies and her interests Beverley had a large group of South African friends, and she'd brought me back to them, initially much against my will. And long after we'd broken up they played a role in my life.

Most of them were expatriates, some of them refugees, others living in voluntary exile. There were Whites and Coloureds and Blacks among them — advocates, doctors, writers, lecturers, sociologists, priests, a microcosm maintaining, in a strange way, a form of apartheid with respect to the world around them, conditioned by the very system they'd tried to escape. If I had to return to them today . . . Yes: today I would have reacted differently. I think I should now be able to understand what used to surprise or irritate me then. But in writing it down I must be true to my impression of the time. And when I recall them the way I saw them then — Simon Hlabeni, Chuck Nkosana and Stanley Ngobo, Henry Arendse, Joe Cohen, Barbara Grant and all the others — I discover a strangely negative quality about them, something they had in common with some Jews, or with some of the Greeks who'd fled after the Colonels' coup: a quality difficult to define, a suggestion of something hollow about them, a vacuum, like an electric car, not driven by a battery inside but remote-controlled from the outside. Simon and Chuck and Stanley, Henry, Joe and Barbara: their control centre was not the intellect or will or emotion, but South Africa.

Without exception they had traumatic histories. Chuck had at one stage been detained for a year without trial, and during one interrogation he'd been shot in the stomach (in the newspapers it was reported that he'd been wounded 'trying to escape'); Joe had been 'banned', with the result that he'd had to give up his practice as an advocate; Barbara had spent ninety days in the hands of the Security Police before being released without any charges, with a broken leg and internal injuries;

et cetera. Each story was upsetting in its own right, a sickening revelation. But after I'd heard it ten times or more, I began to feel irritable. There was an essential denial about it, as strong as that in the Rosmers of *Rosmersholm*. I realised, I could *see*, that some of them belonged to the élite of the South African intellect and creativity : but it was as if each in his own way had been maimed so terribly by his own experience that he was no longer interested in anything but that. They were like a group of veterans who had nothing but their missing eyes and amputated legs and warped hands to boast of and to subsist on.

It is bad enough if something like that happens to one person, but one might still be able to find an explanation for it. But if it expands to a hundred, to an important section from an entire generation of people, it becomes a dark circle of hell. And I think I was afraid of what they represented : afraid, because it appealed to the accumulated suffering of my own history from which, God knows, I wanted to be liberated. I didn't *want* to be drawn into their fate; I didn't want to get involved in their 'cause'.

During the long time I knew them, I often saw new ones arrive, inspired by youthful enthusiasm, full of revolutionary ideas, alive with profound and sincere convictions – and I noticed how, years later, they would still be saying the same words, making the same gestures, uttering the same promises, but then with the stubborn insistence of dogma, no longer with the passion of original inspiration, the schemes they'd conceived having ceased being a means to an end and become a sacred end in their own right.

On the other hand, of course, they could, and did, accuse me of shirking my responsibilities, avoiding the real issues, ignoring realities – including that southern morsel which nurtured them – and of using the theatre as an escape and a form of denial. 'You're acting so you needn't have to live!' said Henry Arendse, a young Coloured. And when I tried to justify myself by referring to Brecht and Camus and the entire *théatre engagé* Chuck Nkosana was immediately on the attack: 'Any third-rate speech by a bloody crank at Hyde Park Corner has more social influence than the best Brecht or God knows who else you can perform on the stage!'

Sometimes I got angry, mostly I was saddened, and occasionally, when one of them through word or gesture reminded me of Dulpert, I was deeply disturbed, far beyond words, in a gutsy way which I would have preferred not to admit to myself. And the person responsible for this reaction, more than any of the others, was Simon Hlabeni.

The others remained something of a closely knit group to me, a collection of ideas and attitudes, 'the South Africans' : but Simon was different. Perhaps I felt less exposed in his company because his circumstances were so different from theirs. Simon was a poet and he hadn't left South Africa for political reasons at all, but simply to satisfy an urge to see the world. Before leaving he'd been a taxi-driver in Durban, studying at night until he'd obtained his BA. After saving for several years he finally had enough money for a single ticket to England, but he was desperately unhappy from the beginning. He simply couldn't stand the climate; and for the English, especially the men, he had a profound contempt. ('They're like bloody snails – got no bones in them and always hiding under the leaves. They don't know the sun, man, and they don't know a thing of women either. No wonder their women are so bitchy and randy.' Adding with a flicker in his eyes : 'When *I* fuck a woman, she stays fucked.')

All he had wanted to do was to earn enough money as soon as possible to afford the return journey to South Africa. He kept on writing poetry, but exclusively in Zulu. About a year after his arrival, when he'd finally saved enough to buy his ticket, he met Bridget in the Army and Navy Stores ('God knows what I was looking for in that stupid place, but I found a wife'), and a few months later they were married. She was an attractive, slightly built, very pale Scots girl with large green eyes and strikingly beautiful red hair; and eight years later, when I first met them, they were still doting on each other. Their one dream had been to have children, but after two miscarriages they were forced to give up the idea. That made them even more dependent on each other. That, and – of course – the fact that, with a White wife, Simon could no longer go back to his country.

Over the years I saw him pining away. He was already middle-aged by the time I met him, but he was still an impressive man, more than six feet tall, with the chest and shoulders of a gladiator; but slowly his shoulders began to sag and he became more bony through his clothes; he took to drinking heavily, and after a few years his reflexes were shaky, his hands trembling. Alcohol and the climate combined to aggravate the gout in his left foot, and so he would drink more to forget about the pain, which would make the pain worse.

Encouraged by Bridget, he'd begun to translate his poems into English, which she would then revise and prepare for publication. In the beginning it was pure lyrical poetry, mostly *vers libre* form with subtle rhythms and subdued but compelling imagery in a vein reminiscent of Césaire Aimée. But gradually it became more violent, and more morbid, more apocalyptic. Several reputable magazines published his work, and on one occasion the TLS even carried an article on Simon. That was the only outlet he had for his suffering, words choking in his throat like blood.

She kept them alive with her secretarial work. But to him, with the ancient pride of Chaka in his blood, that was the final humiliation. And that was how he was drawn into politics. I don't know exactly what his function in the ANC was when I met him – I suppose it's a barometer of my interest in politics at the time! – but he was one of the leaders, and at rallies, including mass meetings in Trafalgar Square, he used to impress the audience with his calm dignity, and with the deep, rich voice which, without training, he could use better than many actors with whom I've worked. I can't remember a single occasion when it sounded as if he was 'making a speech' : every phrase carried the immediacy and deep conviction of a man prepared to commit himself completely.

As the pain inside him grew more consuming, his public appearances became more rare, but all the more unforgettable for that reason. Only a few of us knew how readily he would have exchanged all that for the simple joy of sitting back home in the sun again, writing verses in Zulu which would never be published.

I met him at a party in Stepney to which Beverley had taken me : that was still the time of Belsize Park. There were several other South Africans, Black and White, including a young Afrikaner journalist who'd just arrived in London on his first trip overseas : an intelligent bloke, Hennie Cilliers, but very young and absolute in his convictions, with the exaggerated self-confidence of a young dog, the sort of young man who can't find questions for all his answers.

I noticed that he and Simon spent considerable time talking together in one corner; and because I knew Simon's political convictions and affiliations, it surprised me. Chatting to someone else at a window near them, I overheard part of their conversation. It had nothing to do with politics at all. They were exchanging memories and anecdotes, obviously with great pleasure : *D'you remember . . . ? D'you remember . . . ? When were you in Johannesburg last . . . ? D'you know X . . . ? D'you know Y . . . ?* It wasn't all just small talk. There was genuine enthusiasm in their conversation, an eagerness which struck me in the midst of all the other polite cocktail chats. What specifically impressed me, which young Cilliers probably never realised himself, was something about Simon's attitude which I can only describe as fatherly, as if he deliberately tried to be protective and patient towards his young White son.

Later in the evening, after most of the people had left, it was my turn to talk to Simon. I mentioned Cilliers. 'I can't understand how you could be so patient with him,' I complained. 'He's such an impudent puppy.'

'Give him time,' Simon said with a smile. 'He's very young. Let him have his way for a while – sooner or later he'll discover that he also belongs to Africa.' Adding, without warning, with the barest narrowing of his eyes : 'Just like you.'

'I can't see that Africa has anything to do with it,' I hedged.

'For how long have you been here now?'

'Almost two years.'

'Some take longer than others.'

'I'm definitely never going back,' I insisted stubbornly.

Simon wasn't convinced. 'I suppose I'm sentimental,' he said, disarmingly gentle. 'But as I see it a man is like a plant : if he hasn't got his own piece of earth to grow in, he just withers and dies. You know that thing about plants – what do you call it? – positively heliotropic, or something : growing towards the sun. Well, we're positively something else : we've got to grow towards the south.' And suddenly, looking over my shoulder to Beverley in another group, he asked : 'Are you two going to get married?'

'I . . . I don't think so.'

He put his hand on my shoulder : 'Joseph, if you do marry her, my God, then you'd better be good to each other. For then you won't have anything but each other left.' He went away to refill his glass, but stopped halfway and came back to me first : 'And even if you don't get married, you'd still better be good to each other. Else you won't be able to go on.'

After that evening Beverley and I fairly regularly visited him and Bridget. They had quite a large flat in Highbury Hill, but it was in the basement of an old building which the sun never reached. Why didn't they move to a better place? I often ask them. Simon would answer : 'It's my way of doing penance : it keeps me humble. You know, like

173

some monks who tie knotted cords round their bodies or flagellate themselves.' His attitude was flippant, but I thought I discovered a hidden seriousness underneath. And there was, indeed, something about him which reminded one of St Ignatius and others like him, even though, like several other truly devout people I've come across, Simon had no time at all for religion.

After the break with Beverley I continued to see Simon and Bridget – more often, in fact, than before. Perhaps it was the only significant friendship of my London years. Even friendship is a tricky word: my affection for him was deep and sincere, and I think he felt the same about me, and yet, until the very end there was an aloof, enigmatic quality about him which kept a certain distance between us. That was why I was so shattered by that particular night which was to have such a decisive influence on what happened afterwards.

It was during my eighth year in Britain, just after I'd joined the Royal Shakespeare Company and while we were rehearsing *The Merchant of Venice*, in which I played Morocco. Actually it is ironical that Simon should have come to me that night, because there was a link between him and my interpretation of the role.

The customary approach to Morocco's character I found too facile, too obvious, too 'White': I didn't want to turn him into yet another arrogant black potentate who chooses the golden casket because it is the most precious of the three: I didn't want him to 'get what he deserves' when Portia sends him away with her haughty 'Gentle riddance . . . Let all of thy complexion choose me so.' I suppose I wanted, among other things, to prove to my friends that the theatre needn't be as irrelevant as they used to insist. Morocco would be a man of our time, and Portia's words an accusation against every audience willing to endorse her 'Gentle riddance'.

The choice of the golden casket had to become something completely opposite to a reflection on Morocco's avarice: it should be done in such a way as to reveal that the real fault lay with Portia and her whole anti-Jewish, anti-Black world. He should choose gold because he could associate only the most precious of metals with the woman he loved: and if she proved to be anything less than that, he would turn away majestically, a parallel to the great outcast Shylock, impressive in his dignity to the very end. And all of that had to be prepared from my very opening words:

Mislike me not for my complexion,
The shadowed livery of the burnish'd sun . . .

At RADA we'd often been warned against the dangers of impersonation, and so I didn't want to model my role on anyone, least of all on the obvious example of Olivier's towering Othello a few years before. All I needed was a point of departure. And where could I find a better inspiration for my Morocco than Simon?

That's why I found it so ironical that he should visit me just while I was working on the part. Ironical, too, because on that night he was anything but the Simon I used to know and who'd inspired my interpretation.

I had locked myself up in my flat to work on the great passage in the second act. It was cold, it was mid-February, and the tender buds of the horse-chestnuts in front of my window had been blackened by late snow; but inside it was snug and warm, for by that time I was earning enough to furnish my flat and instal heating and acquire a modicum of comfort.

Is't like that lead contains her? 'Twere damnation
To think so base a thought

and then there was a knock on my door, and when I opened he stood there, Simon, bottle in hand, one foot swathed in thick woollen socks, his heavy army overcoat soaking wet, and scattered snowflakes on his large sagging shoulders.

'May I come in?'

'Of course, Simon.'

He staggered over the threshold and had to steady himself against the door-frame for a moment; his left leg was dragging behind him.

'Can I give you a hand?'

He shook himself free. 'Fuck off!' he said, shuffling unsteadily towards the light and warmth inside. The wine splashed inside the open green bottle he held in his hand, and spilled on his sleeve. He shook off the drops on my shaggy white carpet.

'What's up with your leg, Simon?'

'Gout. None of your business anyway.'

I'd never seen him so aggressive and felt quite unnerved, for it was like standing opposite a total stranger who'd accidentally assumed the appearance of Simon Hlabeni.

'Warm in here,' he said. 'Nice aesthetic way of life.'

'Let me help you with your overcoat.'

'Let go!' Once again he shook off my hand, with the violent movement of a wet dog shaking itself dry, and started fumbling with his buttons. The wine bottle dropped to the floor, leaving a growing red stain on my carpet. I clenched my teeth. But Simon's dull eyes were watching me so intently that I daren't make a move. Finally he looked down, smiled at the bottle, and gave it a kick with his bandaged foot. 'You can have it,' he said. 'Too late for Christmas, but you can have it.'

As I bent down to pick up the nearly empty bottle, he wrestled off his overcoat and threw it down on the divan; without it, he was shockingly thin, all the more obvious because of his huge frame.

'What are you doing?' he asked, collapsing on the overcoat.

'I'm working on my role for the Royal Shakespeare.'

'And what's your role for the Royal Shakespeare?'

'Morocco.'

'Morocco.' He made a vague gesture. 'Well, bottoms up to Morocco.'

'Haven't you had enough yet, Simon?' I asked cautiously.

'Let's drink, I say! Let's drink to Morocco for the Royal Shakespeare Company, Proprietary Limited. *Are* they Proprietary Limited?'

Deliberately ignoring the question, I busied myself at the drinks cabinet.

'Well,' he said as he took his glass. 'To Morocco then.' But as he raised his hand, he stopped: 'Who the hell is Morocco anyway?'

'In *The Merchant of Venice*.'

'Of course,' he said. 'In *The Merchant of Venice*. Here you are in the centre of London – just off-centre, anyway – drinking to Morocco in *The Merchant of Venice* while all around you the world is falling to pieces. Have you no sense of decency?'

'What's the matter with you tonight, Simon?' I asked, worried and angry and lost. 'There's something seriously wrong.'

'Of course there's something wrong. Right here.' Emphatically, with unrestrained glee, he slowly turned over his glass of wine on my Spanish bedspread.

'Look what you're doing!' I said sharply.

'I'm looking bloody well what I'm doing. I'm fucking up your lovely

176

flat. And d'you want to know why?' He tried to get up, grimacing as he moved his gouty foot, and fell back on the divan. 'What are you doing in London anyway?' he asked, and I couldn't make out whether he was pursuing his offensive or changing the subject.

'I'm acting. You know that very well.'

'Why don't you go home?'

'This is my home.'

He jumped up, succeeding this time, and before I could stop him he stumbled and half-fell on top of me. I saw him pull back his arm; then his fist thudded against my ear. As I tried to get out from under him, the chair toppled over with us. I got up, panting, and picked the chair up again. He remained sitting on the floor where he'd spilled the wine.

'My God, Joseph,' he mumbled, slightly more sober than before. 'You must go back, man. You've got nothing to do here. Leave it to people like me to stay here. You understand?'

'No,' I said coolly, determined not to anger him again, but as determined not to let him have his way. 'No, Simon, I don't understand you at all. I'm happy here, my work is here, my life is here.'

'Ha!' The short laugh broke from deep inside his guts. But he didn't say anything.

'Can I help you up?' I offered.

'Nobody can help me.' Morosely he remained sitting, his head in his hands. After a while he said dully: 'Give me something to drink.'

'You're not going to spill it again?'

'Give me something to drink.'

I filled his glass and handed it to him. Sitting on the stained white carpet he emptied the glass in his mouth, wiped his lips with his sleeve and for a long time sat studying the empty glass.

'Have you ever thought . . .' he suddenly said, still looking at the glass. 'There are so many ways of committing suicide. You can slash your wrists. You can hang yourself. You can drown yourself. You can buy a gun. But d'you know what's the surest way of all?' He raised his eyes to me and gazed at me for such a long time that I thought he'd lost the train of his thoughts. But then he repeated: 'D'you know what's the surest way of committing suicide? You just go on living. That's all. That finishes you off.' He shook out the last few drops from the glass on the carpet and said: 'Give me some more. And why don't you help me up? Do you always receive your guests on the floor?'

Strange: it was as if the wine sobered him up instead of making him more drunk. After that glass, installed on the divan, he began to fumble in his overcoat.

'What are you looking for?'

'Nothing. I just brought something I'd like you to . . .' He tugged impatiently at the pockets of the overcoat. 'Something you must . . . ! Got it.' It was a small seven-inch record.

'Put it on.'

I took it from him and glanced at the title. It was a cheap South African record, pennywhistle *kwela* music from the townships.

'Put it on,' Simon urged impatiently. 'Put it on.'

I opened the record player, wiped the record and lowered the needle. The thin sounds came tumbling through the room. Simon sat motionless until it was finished.

'Play it again,' he ordered.

'Other side?'

'No, same side.'

I moved the needle back to the beginning. He listened in silence.

'Play it again,' he said when the needle reached the end.

'You're sentimental, Simon,' I scolded him.

'Play.'

I obeyed to please him. Once again he sat motionless, with an air of detachment, as if he wasn't even conscious of the music, impassive, unfathomable.

And after the third time, so help me God, he said again : 'Play.'

By this time I no longer tried to argue. I allowed myself to be drawn into the spell of the silly ritual, convincing myself that I was doing it only to keep him happy, because one shouldn't frustrate a drunk, but against my own will I got caught in the strange fascination of the music, almost curious to find out how long it could go on like that.

I can no longer remember how many times the record was played : later I no longer even waited for Simon's instructions. Only vaguely I was wondering how a scene like that would work in the style of Beckett or Pinter, how many times one would dare to repeat it onstage.

And then Simon began to dance. Somewhere in the course of the music he began to dance. One can hardly call it dancing, for his painful foot brought something heavy and clumsy into his movements : all he did was to get up from the bed and go to the middle of the floor and start gyrating slowly, round and round, staying in one place, like a sea bamboo attached to a deep bed and swaying, swaying in the motion of the current. There was something grotesque about it, the contrast between the nostalgic exuberance of the cheap backstreet music and the tortured dance of the huge, thin, black man on the floor : it wasn't liberation but pure suffering, the barest, most exposed, most inhuman suffering I'd ever seen. I couldn't take my eyes off him. It would have been sacrilege not to look just as it was sacrilege to look. I don't know, it was all too paradoxical, too terrible.

His eyes were tightly shut, his face distorted in impossible concentration, as if his whole face, his whole body tried to withdraw into itself, behind those eyes, into a black pith of searing silent pain; and from under his closed eyelids the tears broke out and ran down over his cheeks while he went on dancing; running into his collar, breaking from his closed eyelids. He uttered no sound, he didn't sob or even breathe deeply – it was only the tears running down his face, from under his closed eyelids, while he went on dancing in one place, shrinking down to the floor and then growing taller and taller again, like a black candle flame shrinking and growing and burning down, and the tears running down his face.

The record had been silent for a long time, only the needle was still scratching with a harsh, grey sound along the final groove, before his movement slowly began to tremble back to immobility, his eyes still closed, the tears still on his face.

I think if one of the disciples had followed Jesus into the depths of Gethsemane he would have felt the way I felt that night. And when I could not bear it any more, I turned away from him, and lifted the arm off the turntable, switched it off, and remained standing like that, with my back to him, aware of my hand shaking on the arm of the turntable. After some time I heard him move, heard the bed creaking as he sat down, but I still couldn't turn round. Then the bed creaked again and he came shuffling across the floor, and put his hand on my shoulder, and said, too loudly :

'Don't cry, man. Tomorrow we're going home. Tomorrow we're going home.'

I turned round and said : 'You must stay here tonight, Simon.'

'Of course not. I'm going back.'

'Your place is too far away.'

'I know my place is too far away. I'm only going back to Highbury Hill. Don't worry about me. Come, let's have a last one to Morocco.'

He seemed to be playing cat and mouse with me: I could no longer distinguish between lucidity and raving in his drunken talk. He absolutely refused to stay over, so I had no choice but to escort him home. How could I let him go into those dark streets all by himself in that state? But it was hell. It was too late for buses, and he didn't want me to call a taxi (I even had the luxury of a telephone by then), so we had to walk: left in Graham Road, and on and on, Dalston Lane and Ball's Pond Road and St Paul's Road, to Highbury – and him dragging his gouty foot. Every now and then we had to stop for a while; sometimes, from pure stubbornness, he would refuse to budge, trying to persuade me to go back:

'Why don't you leave me alone? Why don't you go back to your electric heater and your Spanish rug and your woollen carpet and your Royal Shakespeare? I can manage.'

Sometimes he broke into long tirades in Zulu, only interrupted when some late wanderer passed by, in order to shout at him:

'Fuck you!'

When I tried to calm him down or remonstrate with him, he would shut me up bluntly: 'Why can't I say it? The world has a great need for somebody to shout "Fuck you!" at it.'

Then he would fall silent again and shuffle on beside me, silently and painfully, because one had to keep on moving so as not to freeze in the night's black snow; but after a hundred yards or so he would begin to walk more slowly, and stop under a streetlamp and blow out a cloud of breath, mumbling drunkenly:

'If I were a man I would have spoken with the tongues of angels. D'you know the tongues of angels?'

'No. Come on, Simon.'

'Of course you don't. All you can speak nowadays is the tongue of the English.'

'Come on, Simon, please. Bridget is waiting for you.'

'*Bridget* waiting for me?' He burst out laughing, grabbing the lamppost so that he wouldn't fall, an unearthly sight in his enormous overcoat.

'Come on, Simon.'

And then we turned left into Highbury Hill and reached his dark building, stumbled down the dirty, broken staircase to the door of the basement flat where he struggled with his keys; and at last we were inside.

'Here we are,' I said. 'Thank God. Where's Bridget?'

He was turning on lights as far as he went, from room to room.

'Don't wake her,' I pleaded. 'Please be reasonable, Simon.'

'Reasonable?' He swung round with flaming eyes and grabbed my lapels with his large bony hands. 'Reasonable? Come, I'll show you.'

I tried to resist, but he was amazingly strong and forced me to the bedroom with him. He turned on the light.

'No, Simon.'

'Yes!' he shouted, thrusting me through the door.

The bed was unmade, but there was no sign of Bridget.

Still uncomprehending, I asked: 'Has she gone out to look for you?'

'She's gone to look for *something*. Not for me.'

My face went numb. 'When did she leave?'

'This morning. Leaving a letter, just like a story from *Woman's Own*.'

'But . . .'

'Oh, go to hell!' he burst out.

'I'll stay with you tonight.'

'I don't want you here.'

When I tried to take his arm, he shook me off with such a violent jerk that he lost his balance and fell down, hitting the edge of the door with an eyebrow. When he sat up, dazed, a thin line of blood began to trickle down his cheek-bone.

I squatted down to help him.

'Leave me alone,' he said.

'But you're bleeding, Simon.'

'It isn't blood,' he said with a deliberate, theatrical air. 'It's red tears.'

I got up dumbly, went down the passage to the kitchen, then had an inspiration and made some coffee. At first he refused it, still sitting on the floor where he'd fallen, but eventually he took the cup and drank the hot, strong stuff. It seemed to have some effect on him, for after a while he said quite calmly:

'You'd better go home now, Joseph. I'll manage.'

'But how . . . ? I mean . . .'

'Sooner or later I'll have to face it, won't I?' The vehemence subsided and in an almost fatherly tone he said: 'It's late. You must go home.' With deeper, more painful significance, he repeated: 'You must go home.'

'Can't I get you into bed?'

'No. I'm fine like this. You need some sleep, you've got to work to-morrow.' And, as I reached the front door: 'I hope the Prince of Morocco is a great success.'

In as much as any change can be associated with a specific incident I suppose that night with Simon marked the turning point. But the only reason why it could influence me so deeply was that at that stage some other secret and subconscious progress had already developed far enough for me to become aware of it. Because it was so secret it is more difficult to retrace.

After completing my course with RADA I was offered a role in a Haymarket production. It was only a small part, the Son in Pirandello's *Six Characters*, but it was a beginning. Immediately after that I accepted an offer to join a repertory company. It was no easy decision, for I would have preferred to stay in London, fearing the obscurity of the provinces. At the same time I wanted to get as much stage experience as possible. For nearly three years I toured with the company, playing some fifteen or sixteen parts altogether, an incredible mixture including more or less the whole spectrum from the classics to drawing-room comedy. In many respects it was nerve-racking, an endless series of third-rate hotels, bad English food, unpredictable audiences, infighting and backbiting in the company, tatty dressing-rooms, hopeless heating. But it was an education I wouldn't have missed for anything; and by living as cheaply as possible I managed, for the first time in my life, to have some extra money.

There were other advantages connected with touring: while my colleagues were drinking or fornicating in their rooms I wandered through the streets of Birmingham or Manchester or Liverpool observing people; I continued my reading; I visited the provincial museums. In the Tate the work of the Pre-Raphaelites had already fascinated me: now I could indulge myself. I never left Manchester without visiting the City Art Galleries to look at Millais's *Autumn Leaves*: it never failed to intrigue me how he'd managed to move so precariously close to the edge of sentimentality without ever sacrificing his dignity. I can still recall every detail of it: the beauty of those four young girls, two already with a hint of womanhood in body and eyes, contrasted so romantically, but with such restraint, with the pile of leaves, premonition of death. This was the true innocence of the world before the Fall, before Raphael; but at the same time it was contemporary, real, and uncompromising. This painting alone was ample compensation for all the frustrations of a long tour.

But gradually the old restlessness emerged again. This was not the theatre I'd been waiting for all my life. With very real fear I began to realise that I was still caught up in the long process of waiting for something, sometime. I could so easily spend a lifetime travelling with the company, presenting one box office success after the other, until, finally, I'd also be flung on the inevitable pile of leaves with nothing to show for it all. And everything in me revolted against that.

Like Dulpert, years ago, I suddenly discovered that I, too, was in need of a 'free period'. And unruffled by the anger and consternation of my bosses I resigned at the end of the tour we were on, left the group, and went to Europe.

For a few months travelling became an end in itself – Holland, Belgium, France, Italy. Then I developed a more systematic approach. I spent some time in Germany, mainly to attend all possible performances of the Berliner Ensemble; in Paris I spent a semester studying mime with Lecoq and sitting in on Barrault's rehearsals. And then I followed the sun down to Spain.

Soon after my arrival in Madrid I heard about the Festival of Pamplona and went there without wasting any time. My first experience of a corrida left me sick and disgusted; but within three days I was an *aficionado*. I think I acquired a deeper insight into theatre in the course of ten days of bullfighting than on all my repertory tours. It was pure spectacle, theatre at its most primitive and elemental, it had the precision of ballet and all the extravagance of a circus: it forced me back to the sources of tragedy. I bought myself a Spanish dictionary and a *Teach Yourself*, and after the Festival withdrew into a cheap *pensión* in a back street of Salamanca, reading myself into a stupor on the *Don Quixote*, Calderon, Lorca, and Unamuno: not in search of Spain, but of myself.

The outcome of it all was a still inexplicable but growing discontent, a discovery that I desperately had to break through to a form and an experience of vital meaning in the theatre. Acting as such was not enough. I had to discover, on the stage, an hour of truth as liberating as the matador's in a corrida; it had to become a projection, a focal point, of the blind thought and feeling of an entire society. It had to break down all the conventional barriers: something like Brook's *US* which

I'd seen in London and which had been one of the most shocking and exhilarating experiences of my life. But it also had to be less hysterically experimental than the Living Theatre I'd seen in Amsterdam. But how? I spent whole nights wrestling with it. One should really return to a medieval existence and travel from town to town with troubadours and jugglers, acting on the dusty market squares . . . With that in mind I read every available article on the *Barraca* group with which, only a few decades before, Lorca had performed on the paseos and plazas of the smallest Spanish villages, presenting plays to the hungry crowds assembled to buy and eat without money, yea wine and milk.

But what could *I* do? And how?

Every time I ended up against the same questions. For the moment there seemed to be no solution. But the discontent and passion and restlessness remained dormant in my guts, so that I would be ready to respond to Simon's challenge later.

There were other moments, outside the theatre, which contributed to this slow growth of my revolt. In Amsterdam I met Annamaria at an exhibition of paintings in the Kiezersgracht. It was an intolerable confusion. The paintings weren't bad, but the gallery was hopelessly small for the crowd milling past in a merry-go-round of flesh and flashy clothes. In the throng I passed the same tall, dark girl several times; and the third or fourth time I saw to it that we both ended up in the same corner. In the crowd of predominantly fashionable socialites she was blatantly different in her faded blue denim jacket and jeans, the fly held together by a few safety pins stuck in more or less at random. Her hair was short and black and curly, surrounding an elfish face with dark eyes; but what particularly fascinated me was her dirty hands, long nervous fingers with bitten nails, smudged with paint. Even her left cheek had a streak of blue paint on it.

We talked for a while. She told me that her name was Annamaria; that her mother was Dutch, her father an Argentinian who'd disappeared from their lives at a very early stage, that she was an artist herself. But the crowded gallery was too oppressive for proper conversation, and when I caught her looking anxiously towards the door I impulsively suggested :

'Let's get out of here.'

'Please.'

I opened up a passage through the throng, followed by her; we went down the steep Dutch staircase to the damp air outside and started walking, oblivious of time. From the Central Station we approached the prostitute quarter, heralded by the enormous neon sign: *Jesus calls you*, and worked our way back towards the Amstel. Opposite the Mint Tower she said: 'Would you like to have coffee with me? I live on a river boat. Near the Westermarkt.'

It was a strange homecoming in the boat moored to the quay below the market place: everything was dark when we came there, but when she opened the hatch the hold was dimly lit by a lantern hanging down low from the ceiling. And everywhere in the warm, dusky interior cats were moving about, at least a dozen of them, black, grey, brindled, ginger, and Siamese. The first thing Annamaria did was to take raw meat from a cupboard and distribute it in the hold; and from all sides half invisible cats came sneaking closer to grab bits and return to the darkest corners where they began to eat noisily, filling the entire gloomy interior with their animal presence. It was like a return to primitive origins; the almost imperceptible swaying of the boat on the black water, marked by the slow rhythm of the lantern on its chain, was in itself a blind and comforting form of life: in that dusk we were like Jonah in the belly of the fish.

'I'm going to make coffee,' she said.

I caught her wrist and held her back: 'Later.'

She looked at me, and I pulled her closer and kissed her. We, too, were like animals that night, beautiful animals. On one end of the hold, stretching across the full width of the boat, was a sort of platform, at least eight feet high: one had to climb up a rope ladder; and the whole platform was covered with the blankets of her bed, woolly blankets like animal hides; and there, in the slow motion of the boat, we made love all night long, against the background of innumerable cats purring and growling.

I stayed with her for ten days, practically without ever emerging into daylight: it was complete withdrawal.

She showed me her paintings – large canvases, two square metres at least, which she first covered with boiling tar and subsequently painted gold or silver before the actual painting could begin, the patterns determined by the contours of the congealed tar. Her work had a strongly Byzantine quality – like stained-glass images of saints and angels and demons – although Annamaria herself was blasphemously antireligious.

We talked a lot. They were never easy conversations: Annamaria

185

refused to take easy answers, and she had the sharp, uncompromising intellect of a Jesuit.

Often a conversation would start in a deceptively ordinary way : one night she asked me my age. Twenty-eight, I said, which was her own age too. Was I afraid of getting old? she asked.

'No,' I said. 'I think the decade from thirty to forty is the prime of one's life : you still have all the energy you had at twenty, but in addition you've acquired a bit of wisdom.

'It depends on what you mean by "wisdom".'

'I suppose it's the faculty of living in the fullest consciousness of what you're doing, and being able to accept responsibility for it at the same time.'

She pulled a face. 'I think wisdom is, quite simply, the ability to condition yourself.'

'In that case even Pavlov's dogs would qualify as wise. Surely a human being is more than that.'

'How do you mean "more"?'

'One can interpret things. You do more than live; you can also find meaning in it.'

She went on relentlessly : 'What do you call "meaning"?'

'That quality which makes something more than the sum of its parts.'

She sniffed in disdain. 'You're romantic. It's no use looking for meaning where there isn't any. I won't be surprised if you even believed in the supernatural.'

'No, not the supernatural,' I said. 'But certainly in something I'd call a sense of the miraculous.'

'A person on the lookout for miracles all too often stumbles over the stones of reality.'

It was my turn to ask : 'What do you regard as "reality"?'

'This!' – she waved her arm to include the whole interior of the boat. 'Boards, paintings, cats, a rope ladder, blankets.' Then she put her paint-smudged hand on my penis – we were both naked on the high bed – and waited for a while until she could feel it stirring in her palm; and with a mocking laugh she said : 'This is real. Not abstractions like "faith" or "hope" or "charity". Not the past, for that's gone. Not the future, for that doesn't last. But this, here, now.'

'That forms your reality. But I've got mine. Everybody creates his own.'

'Balls. One never creates realities, only illusions. Because you lack the courage to face it as it is.'

'I don't think it's all that easy, Annamaria!' I protested. 'I can study a thing from all sides and examine all its parts, and still not know it. And so, in *my* reality, I've got to leave room for many possibilities.'

'And suppose those possibilities negate each other and turn into paradoxes?'

'Perhaps that's part of the wisdom we were talking about: to learn to live with one's paradoxes.'

'Crap. Paradoxes are evasions of reality. The entire scientific development of our century has been a clearing up of paradoxes. Reality is facts, not possibilities. Some of them may not be known yet, but that makes no difference to the fact that they exist.'

'All right,' I said, perhaps to avoid the argument. 'Then I'll content myself with your facts.' And in the warm, fertile darkness I reopened her legs. Half lightly, half seriously, I whispered:

> *'But O alas! so long, so farre*
> *Our bodies why do wee forbeare?*
> *They are ours, though they are not wee ...'*

She stiffened. 'What's that?'

'Donne. Don't you know it?'

'Joseph,' she said almost viciously. 'Don't you ever quote anything to me again.'

'Don't you like poetry?'

'Poetry is fine to write or read. But don't use it as a substitute for what we've got.'

'Why a substitute?'

'Because other people's words make it impossible for you to think or feel yourself. I want to know it's you I've got inside me, not some goddamned Donne or somebody. Stop acting, Joseph, Jesus! And fuck me!'

The river boat was a libido from which, after ten days, I returned to the world outside, like Jonah spewed back to Nineveh. That morning, bending over, naked, to put on her thick woollen socks, surrounded by cats, she announced: 'It's time for you to go, I'm beginning to paint again today.' For months afterwards I treasured the visual memory of those days: the gentle swinging of the low lantern marking the patient rhythm of the boat, the dark womb of that interior with its warm odour of linseed oil and tar, of cats, of man and woman; and a girl, smudged with paint, with short black curls, white and passionate against my body. But I knew it was more than a vivid memory, and that with my return to the world a germ of thought had escaped from the subconscious, like a bubble from the seabed. Something about my way of life had irrevocably been exposed by Annamaria: something second-hand, an aesthetic game watched against the back wall of a cave, remote from the world. And once I'd become conscious of it, it implied the beginning of a process of return to the world and the sun outside.

A very slow process, of course, and nurtured by the theatre which remained the essential dimension of my existence. And as it happened my return to London meant a first real breakthrough. I was given the part of Archibald in a production of *The Blacks*. The play drew raves and changed my life overnight: contracts were beginning to come in, it was no longer necessary to turn up hat-in-hand at auditions. The title role in Büchner's *Danton's Death*; Treplev in *The Seagull*; the fool Clarin in an ultra-modern production of Calderon's *Life is a Dream*; I was Jean in *Miss Julie* and Sagredo in *Galileo*; and then I was offered the full-time contract with the Royal Shakespeare, opening with *The Merchant of Venice*.

The crisis came very suddenly, in a most bizarre manner and quite unexpectedly, at a time when there seemed to be absolutely no need or reason for it.

Feeling flaked after a particularly difficult day of rehearsals I went to bed very early. When I woke up – it must have been about two or three in the morning – there were deafening rolls of thunder and an unearthly flickering of lights. Still befuddled with sleep, scared stiff, I half-fell out of my bed, stumbled to the window and opened the curtains. Outside, everything was ablaze with fire while the city rumbled as if the Last Judgement was upon us. Bewildered, lost among the debris of my dreams, my first blind thought was: *It's war! It's a nuclear bomb!*

Still holding on to the curtain I began to mumble aloud: quite incoherently, something like: 'I want to get out. It's your war, not mine. Why must I be caught in it?'

Only after a long time I discovered that it was only a thunderstorm, and rather shamefacedly crept back to bed. But I couldn't sleep again, and the next day I knew that something decisive had indeed happened inside me. What I'd discovered in my sleepy stupor, was only too disturbingly true: I *was* a stranger in London. After nine years I was still a stranger. The city and its people existed apart from me. They didn't need me, they could get on without me; and if I kept on clinging to them, it was an imposition. Whether they allowed me to do so, whether they might even offer me their hospitality, was beside the point. I was not necessary, I was dispensable, I was even a parasite.

For the first time I discovered a coherence in what had been happening to me over the years: the break with Beverley, the frustrations in the repertory company, the shock of the corrida, Annamaria, Simon's shattering visit. And for the first time I could really see my sojourn in London and my attachment to my work the way it must have appeared from the outside, through Simon's eyes or Annamaria's. However sincerely I might have meant it, in London the theatre had become a form of escape, of dilettantism, an evasion of problems, in exactly the same way as that in which I'd avoided Annamaria's questions by opening her legs: here I could collect beautiful furniture, and books, and records, an actor in the heart of a society old and sophisticated and vain enough to permit itself the luxury of artists.

In the heart of such a society the theatre could never become what I demanded of it. No, that wasn't true. The theatre as such might be able to become it: the problem was in myself — it was I who could not play a significant role in any society but my own.

I stubbornly refused to accept Simon's terminology; but in the final analysis he was the catalyst who'd brought about my decision. He could never return home, not even now that he'd lost Bridget, since by now he'd been compromised by his political past. But I could still go back, for my own sake and partly perhaps for his. If I really believed in the sort of theatre Brook and the corrida represented, I had to return to establish it in the heart of the one society to which I was committed by the accident of my birth. I had believed for so long that I'd liberated myself from my country that it came as a terrible shock to discover that I could not, in fact, survive without it.

It wasn't even a decision: it was the inevitable result of a process which had started that first day in the flat in Ovington Gardens when Janet had come to talk to me while I was lying in the bath.

I had thought I could escape. Now I had to return to pick up the link with my prehistory again. The years on the farm had been a prologue to the Cape, and the Cape a prologue to London, and my years in

London a prologue to – what? That was what I had to find out; and more than that : on the basis of everything which had already happened, I had to create a future for myself.

I was thirty years old. Young enough to have faith and to work; but old enough to be tired of a continuing process of preparation which never reached fulfilment.

And so I went back.

Home.

Four

I

There was something private about my return, something I wanted to keep between the Cape and myself; like returning to a lost love after many years without knowing whether you will recover anything of the old closeness, or even whether she's got married in the meantime. And so I didn't write to anybody about my plans for coming back.

My things were cleared very rapidly by Customs; but just as I was moving away from the official's counter, he suddenly called:

'Hey, you!'

I looked round. It was obvious that he was referring to me.

'Those books you got there: let's have a look at them.'

Vexed by his tone I returned to show him the pile of books I was carrying under my arm: a couple of plays, the poems of St John of the Cross, Camus's *Carnets*, and the large Phaidon edition of Michelangelo's sculpture.

With open suspicion completely incomprehensible to me the official in his stark white safari suit started paging through the books and moving them aside. Then his hand descended on the Michelangelo: a pale, freckled hand with bristly red hair between the knuckles. He opened the book, drew in his breath, and exhaled with a sharp: 'Ah!'

'What's the matter?' I asked.

'What's the matter?' Breathing deeply, he was flipping through the pages. 'You can't bring this book into the country.'

'Why not?' I asked, flabbergasted.

He quickly came round the counter, the book in a firm grip under his arm. 'Come along,' he said. 'It's a serious offence to smuggle dirty pictures into the country.'

'But it's Michelangelo!'

'Doesn't matter who it is. Come along. Hurry up.' His knees appeared obscene between the long white stockings and the flapping white shorts.

Speechless I followed him to a partititioned corner of the vast Customs hall. Two of the walls were made of wire netting. He sat down inside, like a Rhode Island Red in a coop, scratching among pens, forms, carbon sheets and empty paper-clip tins.

'Full names?'

'Joseph Malan.'

'Malan?' He looked up accusingly. 'That's a White name.'

I was getting angry. 'Is there anything wrong with it?'

'Listen,' he said, half rising from his seat, 'I won't take no bladdy cheek from your sort, hey? You come into the country with pornography and then you try to throw your weight around!'

'I'd like to know . . .'

'You answer when I ask you a question, and for the rest you just shaddap, you hear?' He glowered at me for a minute before he shifted his pale eyes back to the form he was filling in, and sat down again. 'Address?'

I gave him the only address I could think of on the spur of the moment: Gran'ma Grace's, up in District Six. He wrote it down.

'May I have a receipt for the book?' I asked after he'd finally signed his name.

'A receipt?' he asked aggressively. 'D'you think I've got time for . . .'

On that moment a singular *deus ex machina* made his appearance: a dishevelled creature with unkempt hair and a large red-veined nose, wearing a press camera round his scrawny neck.

'Mister Malan!' he exclaimed. 'I knew it was you. I checked with the agency, so I knew you were on board. You can't give me the slip so easily!' And before I could recover from my amazement the camera flashed.

'What are you doing here?' the Customs official asked in a rage.

'Press,' said the shabby stranger, plucking a card from his pocket. 'You finished? Can I take over our celebrity?'

'Celebrity?' asked the Rhode Island Red.

'This gentleman has just confiscated a book of Michelangelo,' I explained to the journalist.

'Priceless!' said the little runt. 'Oh priceless! Can I have a photo of the two of you with the book in the foreground?'

'Get out!' shouted the official. 'Both of you!' When we reached the door of the coop, he added, obviously for my benefit:

'You'll hear from us again! – probably from the Attorney General.'

'You'll hear from us again!' retorted my companion. 'Just read your paper on Sunday!' Grabbing my arm he eagerly pushed me on ahead of him. 'Now come and tell me all about it. I won't keep you long.' He thrust a sweaty hand into mine. 'I'm Davey Sachs. Everybody knows me.'

In a corner of the large hall we sat down on some crates and with great excitement he began to set and check his tape-recorder ('One, two, three, fuck, what the hell's the matter now? one, two three, oh Jesus Christ, one two three'). Ten minutes later everything was ready. 'OK?' he asked panting and perspiring. 'You're a showman, so you won't be put off by the mike. Where'll we start? That shit business with the Customs people? What was the book they confiscated?'

'Michelangelo.'

'Christ, can you imagine it?' A pause. 'How do you spell it?'

Patiently I spelled out the name. Then he insisted on hearing the whole story from the beginning, and only when he was quite sure that there was no drop of melodrama left to be squeezed from it, he started on my years abroad.

'You never acted with Olivier?'

'No.'

'Pity. Anyway, one can stretch a point. You *saw* him act?'

'Of course.'

'Fine, that's all I need. Now tell me . . .'

It was nearly an hour before we'd finished. He started ordering porters left and right to take my luggage to his car.

'I won't be a minute,' I said, and walked off. Not because I needed it, but because I could do with a few minutes' silence. Automatically I went in the direction in which most of the other men around had gone in the past hour. But just before I could enter, somebody touched my arm from behind. I looked around. A cheerful young man was smiling at me, making a warning gesture with his finger and pointing to the notice above the door which said :

HERE – GENTS

SLEGS BLANKES – WHITES ONLY

Then he came past me, and the door swung shut behind him, with the smell of disinfectant and stale fish characteristic of such places all over the world.

Blindly I returned to where Davey Sachs and his army of helpers were transporting my earthly possessions to an ancient, battered Volkswagen. I wasn't conscious of the throng around us. A car, driving off with screeching tyres, nearly ran me over. I felt a dryness in my throat, and my limbs were numb.

God, I thought. *I'm home.*

That Sunday there was a long, embarrassing report in Davey's newspaper. It was obvious that he'd been working overtime to cover the story as comprehensively as possible, for the report contained a fantastic synopsis of my entire biography, culminating in the confrontation with the Customs officer, and framed by comments from several other people. Of the officer himself there was only the laconic remark: 'I didn't know Malan was an educated man, I thought he was just an ordinary Coloured.' A minister described the incident in a few well-chosen clichés as an unfortunate mistake which had already been rectified and which had been blown up out of all proportion. Some secretary or other asked 'why Malan supplied a fictitious address if he had a clean conscience?'

I deposited my luggage in the box-room at the railway station. Davey must have noticed my surprise about the new building, for he touched my shoulder confidentially: 'You no longer know the old joint, hey? Prosperity, Joseph, that's what it is. Can I call you Joseph? Call me Davey. Prosperity, yes. Who was it that said: "God has tried to ruin us with droughts and locusts and rinderpest and Communism; and when everything failed, He sent his worst plague: prosperity"?' He giggled. 'And now you're back, hey? Good. Things need a bit of a shake-up, man. But let me tell you, man to man . . . Christ, I don't want to stick my nose in, but I don't know what you've come back for. Don't say I didn't warn you.'

At last I managed to shake him off. For a while after his car had disappeared into the traffic I remained standing on the pavement before I began to walk on. Upstreet, then left to the Parade.

The enormous old herb-seller was still sitting in her usual place; but the rest . . . the square seemed to have shrunk. It had grown ugly, most of it taken up by hundreds of parked cars. It was like a play which had been running for several seasons and which one went to see again after a long absence, with a different cast: so that, with nagging discomfort, one tried to discover why one had liked it in the first place, and what had gone wrong in the meantime.

Still I refused stubbornly to accept that it had really changed, ascribing my impression to unreliable memory. It would still be all right. It would soon be all right. The Cape would become itself again.

Leaving the Parade behind, I went down Darling Street. On the outskirts of District Six I bought a greasy packet of fish and chips : not only to appease my hunger, but also to postpone my arrival, now that I was so close. On a low window-sill outside a small junk shop I sat down to eat. In the street in front of me was a crowd of urchins playing dice; I relished their razor-sharp voices.

'Hey, ghwaan, don' sail my ship, men!'

'Throwing tight-arse are you?'

'How you get?'

'Get yourself. I warn you.'

'You wan' to put up?'

They were on the point of starting a fight when one of the others, glancing in my direction, warned them : 'Hey, thet lightie's throwing pig's eyes. Cloak it!'

In a flash all the dice and the small pile of cents had disappeared. So as not to upset them any more, I crumpled my empty packet and began to move on.

'Lookit thet jecket, en' then he's eating chips!' a piercing voice commented. 'It's a salt.'

Their suspicion stabbed my conscience. I would have liked to turn back to explain to them : but how could I convince them? – they wouldn't want to be nuggeted with me. At the same time their talking and their game had brought a sense of warmth back to me, a glow of recognition and rediscovery. And with more confidence I went uphill to where I wanted to be, Gran'ma Grace's house on Oxford Place. As I went higher, the district grew more silent and sordid : several of the houses were empty, windows and doors barred and boarded up; many had been demolished, bulldozers were roaring in the open spaces, and the outline of the buildings looked like a mouth in which some teeth were missing and others badly filled.

Gran'ma Grace's house also stood vacant, the broken windows haphazardly covered up with cardboard and plywood, and part of the charming old Victorian wrought-iron railing missing. Although I could see that it was useless, I went up the broken steps and knocked on the front door. The sound echoed through the hollow house. Aimless and con-fused I turned back and lit a cigarette, leaning against one of the stoep pillars.

Suddenly all hell seemed to break loose in one of the neighbouring houses: children's voices screaming and crying, mingled with women's half-hysterical voices and the grumpy bass of a man. Then it broke out on the stoep outside. A greyish old man in a checked shirt and flapping corduroy pants with gaping, buttonless flies, emerged from the house surrounded by five or six small girls sobbing and screaming together. He was cursing and yelling at them, trying to beat them off with flaying windmill arms, but they kept clinging to him; in the doorway behind them appeared two fat women, both of them shouting at the top of their voices. When the noisy procession was halfway across the square I went down Gran'ma Grace's steps to offer some help in case there'd been a death in the family.

As soon as the old man noticed me he came straight towards me, still surrounded by the frantic children. The noise was so great that for the first few minutes it was impossible to make out anything they were try-ing to say: the children were wailing and hopping round me in a frenzy, as if they were on the point of wetting themselves. Then, at last, one of the bigger ones thrust a mousetrap into my hands with a weakly strug-gling, bleeding, squeaking mouse caught under the wire frame.

'You all go to hell!' the little old man shouted. 'I won' touch it. I won't!'

'Kill it!' the girls pleaded, sobbing. 'Kill it! Help it! Please kill it!' And they started tugging and tearing at my clothes and grabbing my arms.

Slightly bewildered I put the trap on the ground, raised my right heel over the bleeding grey head of the struggling rodent, and stepped on it. A terrible scream went up. Under my foot I could feel the fragile bones crunching and felt my stomach contract. Turning away brusquely I began to walk off, dragging my right foot on the cobblestones – *Not all the perfumes of Arabia* . . . – but the old man caught up with me and took my hand. The children, at last calmed down, picked up the dead mouse in the trap and carried it back home, still racked by dry sobs.

'Sorry fo' de shitty mess,' the old man lisped with a toothless mouth. 'I jus' can't put my foot onne thing like det, en' I tole the chilluns, but dey don't lis'n. I got to much rust fo' such things en' I'm too near my God awreddy. So thenk you fo' helping us out.' His watery eyes looked at me with great curiosity. 'You very dressed up fo' our kotter?'

'I've come to see Gran'ma Grace,' I explained quietly. 'She used to live up here.'

'I know mos.' His eyes became more openly inquisitive. 'But Gran'ma Grace was dug in a long time ago, didn' you know?'

'I've been away. I used to rent a room in her house.'

'But then I mus' know you, men!' He examined me meticulously. 'Well now! isn't you Joseph?'

'Yes. But I don't seem to remember . . .'

'I lived over dere all de years. Don' you remem'er Oom Sassie then? It's only my teeth what I lost, praise de Lawd; de heart is still strong.'

Now it came back to me: the jovial old neighbour who'd spent his days on the stoep in the sun, and drawing such pleasure from pestering Gran'ma Grace on Saturday mornings on her way back from the Church of the Seraphs and Cherubs.

To please him, I went back with him for a cup of coffee. The two fat women with their worn-out slippers were still waiting on the stoep, one of them Oom Sassie's daughter, the other a friend. And while they were preparing coffee we went upstairs to the stoep where his chair still stood, worn out after so many years.

'You said Gran'ma Grace died a long time ago?'

'Long ag, jis – lemme see – three years this coming Chris'mus. Jus' befo' Chris'mus it was, en' jus' in time too.'

'In time?'

'So's she couldn' see what dey done to us here. Ay, ay.'

A few tears trickled effortlessly from his eyes. 'En' lookit olly years we been living here in peace. No, I say it's time de Lawd come en' take me away too, dere's no place left fo' a man who's got a brown skin.'

I still didn't quite grasp what he was aiming at.

'You mean you don' know what's heppen' here?' he asked in amazement. 'All Distric' Six gone to shit?'

'How do you mean, Oom Sassie? I've been away for so long, I have no idea of what's been happening here.'

He shook his head slowly and, lapsing into senility, began to hum: 'Nearer my God to Thee . . .' until he suddenly became aware of my presence again. 'Gone to shit, I sez. We spitted pepper, but no use. It's tickets with us. Dey turning Distric' Six into a smart place now, fo' de Gov'ment's White boys. We Coloureds getta kick inne arse en' it's out we go.'

197

'Out where?' I asked, shocked.

'Dey building us littul housetjies onne Cape Flets now, dere inne openness, inne wind.'

'Why don't they go there themselves?'

Oom Sassie grinned. 'Nay,' he said. 'Newwe'. Dey too white fo' de wind, men. Is only us what can live dere, us en' de Port Jeckson bushes, you see, oll de weeds of de Lawd.'

He went on talking, uttering his thin dry laugh from time to time, while I sat looking out across the sad little square towards Gran'ma Grace's ruined house sitting on the hillside like the wreck of an old ship. I tried to imagine the place in a few years' time: with imposing white mansions in New-Cape Dutch, Pseudo-Corbusier, and Hottentot-Gothic, business centres and supermarkets, concrete courtyards with playing fountains, and asbestos benches with notices, like epitaphs, saying: BLANKES – WHITES. And I remembered it the way it used to be: Gran'ma Grace's noisy backyard filled with pigeons and children, where at night we rehearsed in the light of the nearest streetlamp. The two front rooms upstairs, divided by a wooden partition. Ursula in her petticoat at the broken mirror, and her provocative hand, her deep singing voice: 'From working too much it'll fall off.' Dulpert moving in with me, and our endless conversations, and our excursions into the district. Hairdressing saloons smelling of meang sticks, coconut oil, buchu and grass. Cavorting children darting in and out between the cars parked haphazardly on the cobble-stoned streets. Fruit-carts, and the fish trumpet. The common urinal for Whites and Coloureds downhill. Misty night scenes. Fatima. Sheila.

Immediately after finishing my coffee and quite rudely, for poor Oom Sassie was still eager for conversation, I said good-bye and left. 'I'll come again,' I tried to reassure him. 'Then we'll talk about everything, about the old days.'

'You promise, Joseph?'

'I promise, Oom Sassie.'

When I arrived downstairs, the children appeared furtively behind me to watch me go away. The youngest announced shrilly: 'We buried him beside de privy!' I stroked her head. And I'd already gone a long way downhill when I suddenly became conscious of the fact that I was still dragging the heel of my right shoe, trying to get rid of whatever might be clinging to it.

Once before I'd walked down the narrow street with such a sense of almost astral alienation. That had been the morning after my first night with Ursula. But then the strangeness had existed because everything had been illuminated by the miraculous, filled with endless potential, the world breaking from its seams and becoming larger than life. Now it was different, now it felt shrunken. The houses around me, the narrow balconies and pillars peeling with paint, the hairdressers and the stalls selling herbs and spices, the noisy children, the fruit-carts, the sun-smeared façades and dusky interiors, everything seemed temporary and false, destructible like the drapes and flats of a play played out: they were only waiting for the stage crew to break down and clear up and sweep out, to clean the dressing-rooms and hang new toilet rolls, to prepare the stage for the next production, for a new set of characters in search of an author.

This world of flimsy cardboard through which I was walking down-hill, which I could touch with my hands and scrutinise with my eyes, suddenly, even while I was moving through it, felt more remote and more unreal than Ovington Gardens, or The Cut, or Belsize Park, or Navarino Road. The people passing me were unreal, more vague than memories.

Everything had become as confused to me as Segismundo's two worlds in the Calderon play: Prince of Poland, brought up in a dungeon, clothed in animal skins, and then suddenly, in his sleep, taken to the palace where he is allowed to rule for a single day before being drugged and taken back to the mountains, and waking up in the dungeon – all he can conclude is that everything has been a dream. Unless the palace was reality and this dungeon is the dream?

Recalling the Calderon, something happened to me which had for so long been characteristic of my reactions: I began to feel more relaxed, more contained, for now I'd found a parallel to my situation, an archetype of myself. And from within the theatre, my only reliable reality, I could begin to redefine my world.

In London I'd played the part of Calderon's fool, Clarín: now I would produce the play myself, it would be the first thing I'd do here, and this time I would be Segismundo. In great excitement I stopped on a street corner to visualise it all: I would turn Segismundo into a Coloured man, banned from the glory of the White court; and we would use exactly the same set for dungeon and palace – a very simple set, perhaps a mere outline indicated with white ropes on black curtains – to

199

insist on the similarity between dream and reality, and to offset them against surrounding night. And then . . . and then . . . and then . . .

I only walked on when I became conscious of passing people regarding me curiously and I realised that, as usual, I'd been talking aloud to myself. I couldn't give a damn. In the spell of the new project I'd already begun to resolve the disillusioning elements of my return.

II

All the telephone booths in the area were broken so that I had to go back to the station to phone Derek de Villiers.

Suppose he wasn't there? Suppose he'd left on a theatre tour? I was aware of panic inside me as I stood there listening to the dialling tone burring in my ear. Suddenly the city seemed inhospitable again : where would I sleep if Derek didn't answer? Gran'ma Grace was dead. There was no hotel I could go to. Back, then, to Oom Sassie and his grandchildren in his house overrun by mice?

But Derek answered after all. And although I offered to take the bus to his flat in Bantry Bay, he insisted on coming to the station to fetch me.

In his green Capri we sped up Strand Street, weaving through the late-afternoon traffic.

'When did you come back?' he asked as we went round the corner at Robb's Motors.

'Early this morning. On the mailship.'

'But good God, why didn't you let me know? What have you been doing all day?'

'I first had to go up to District Six to kill a mouse.'

Derek glanced at me, smiled uncomprehendingly, then looked back at the traffic ahead, hooting angrily at a car braking in front of us, raising two fingers to a driver behind, pulling on a cigarette in the corner of his mouth, from which every now and then a few flakes of grey ash dropped onto his black polo-neck sweater.

In the nine years I'd been away he'd aged more than that time. How old would he be now? Forty? Forty-two? His face had an unhealthy sallowness about it, there were bags under his eyes and a purple network of veins across his nose and cheeks. In his neck the longish hair curled untidily over the high collar flecked with dandruff. The second and third fingers of his left hand bore the brownish yellow stains of excessive smoking; and the black eyes, which used to be as penetrating as Picasso's, had become shallow and stale. It shocked me, for I remembered his nervous vitality so well. He looked like a weary Mephistopheles.

'How are you keeping?' I asked deliberately.

'I feel like an old whore,' said Derek. Then, with a small flicker: 'When you left, I was still fit to play Juliet. But now . . .'

'Lady Macbeth?'

'I lack the passion, darling,' he said. 'I'll settle for one of the weird sisters.'

'What's the matter then?'

'Must have reached my menopause. The flesh is still willing, but the spirit is flagging. I used to feel like this before, but only in between productions. Now it goes on even when I'm onstage. And in the long run it makes one impotent.'

'You're just tired.'

He recklessly swung to the right, crossing in front of approaching traffic, towards an open parking area on the roof of a building rising from the sea below to the level of the road above.

'Of course I'm tired. And I need a new lover. But that makes no real difference.'

'Is it really as bad as all that?'

'No, it's worse. Listen, Joseph.' He opened his door, then leaned back: 'There are only three pastimes in this goddamned country: rugby, immorality, and death-on-the-roads. And in the entr'actes we call elections and transplant the hearts of Coloureds on dying Whites. There's no time left for theatre. You'll soon find out yourself.' He got out. 'How long are you staying?'

'I've come back for good.'

'Don't be bloody mad,' he said from his side of the car. 'You can't possibly be serious about *staying* here.'

'Why not?'

'You've got a macabre sense of humour.' He took one of my suitcases from the boot, staggering under the weight. 'Look, anyone can understand why a prisoner should try to escape from jail. But why in God's name would anyone try to break *into* a jail?'

'If its so unbearable, why have you never tried to get out?' I slammed my door and followed him with another trunk.

'You may well ask!' He led the way to a staircase into the building; a floor lower down he pressed the button of an elevator. And while we were waiting, he continued, with a newly lit cigarette in his hand: 'I should have gone with you. But at that time I still believed I had some sort of a "vocation" here: I thought I could bring a ray of light to Darkest Africa. But all I saw . . . It's like the song: "I joined the Navy to see the world . . ." '

'You can still leave.'

'You think so?' He laughed. 'Who will put up this old whore for a night? No, my darling, I've had it. I've got no desire to become a martyr by starving out in the British cold. I'm much too fond of my creature comforts: so I prefer to stay here and dazzle the barbarians with my talent, eating out my heart and sharing my sorrows with a bottle of VAT 69 or some young innocent thing falling into my claws. Rather bear such ills we have and all that. Here's the lift. *Après vous.*'

The interior of Derek's flat came as a surprise after the faceless facebrick façade which already appeared old-fashioned, barely a decade after it had been built. The pictures on his walls were modern – reproductions of an early Picasso, a Klee, a Marini; also a few original local works, the most striking of which was a strong and sensual charcoal study of a male torso – but the furniture was Victorian: a chaiselongue, two grandfather armchairs, an oval rosewood dining-table and bustle-back chairs; even a bell-jar with exquisite feather-flowers. In his bedroom was a fourposter, fully draped, and a tall mahogany cheval mirror; the single bed in the spare room had painted medallions incorporated in the wrought-iron patterns at head and foot.

'It's charming, it's very cosy,' I said when we came back to the lounge and he poured us some whisky.

'Up yours,' he said. 'Oh yes, it's charming. But it's no use.' He flopped down in an armchair. From a dark corner a large Persian cat appeared, jumped on his lap, and began to purr, watching me through half-closed agate eyes. Outside the sunset was glittering on the sea, casting trembling patterns on the walls. An occasional wave sent sheets of spray over the rocks immediately below the window.

Derek kept the whisky bottle next to his chair and refilled his glass long before mine was half gone. We both pretended to be relaxed in the long silence, but I could guess that he was as uncomfortable as I. For what did we have in common? Many years ago he'd helped me with my group of amateurs, and got me the grant, and sent me overseas. But what did I really know about him? I'd never even crossed his threshold before. And now, all of a sudden, I was back, and he was the only person who could offer me a place to sleep.

After a time he began to enquire about London, and I told him of the plays I'd been in and the people I'd worked with. At regular intervals he refilled his glass, and I wondered whether he was really listening. His eyes were half-closed, like his cat's.

Halfway through my talking he interrupted me : 'And now you're back,' he said. 'That's what I can't understand.'

'There were a few minutes this morning when I couldn't understand it either,' I said, and told him about my arrival. 'But when I came down from District Six I had an inspiration about the first play I'd like to do here. Calderon's *Life is a Dream*. And now I know I've done the right thing.'

Life is a Dream. He lit a cigarette and shot the match through the open window. 'And where, and with whom, are you going to do it?'

'I want to get a group together as soon as possible. Like the old one, but much better, more professional. And then . . .'

'My God!' He got up, carrying the cat under his arm, and closed the window to shut out the cool breeze of early winter. 'You've still got stars in your eyes, it seems. I'd hoped the years abroad would get you over it. Have you got money?'

'A bit. Not much.'

'Darling, buy yourself a ticket back to London tomorrow. You've forgotten what it looks like here.'

'I know what I want to do.'

'Joseph,' he sighed. 'Why don't you go to my bedroom and take off your pants and go down on all fours in front of the mirror? – then you can have a good look at your own arsehole. Why go through so much toil and trouble if the end result is going to be the same?'

'What's made you so cynical?' I asked.

'Why shouldn't I be cynical? It safeguards one's last bit of dignity. And God knows, I don't want you to get involved in something which will land you where I've got. And worse. For let's face it, I've still got a few things on my side.'

'Like what?'

'Like the colour of my skin.'

'I grew up here myself,' I said. 'I know very well what to expect.'

203

'How long have you been away? – eight, nine years? That can make one hell of a difference.' He put the cat down on the Afghan carpet and went to his bedroom door. 'We'll talk again, later. I must get my things together, I'm working tonight.'

'What?'

'We're playing Strindberg for the thirty-one people who were interested enough to book.'

'I'll go with you,' I said with a smile. 'Then, at least, you can count on thirty-two.'

'We're doing it in the Hofmeyr,' he said.

'Does it matter? Strindberg remains Strindberg and you're you.'

'I mean : you can't go with me, Joseph,' he said slowly and emphatically. 'You see, we pick our thirty-one culture vultures very carefully. And you haven't got a white wedding garment.'

It was cold on the black rocks below Derek's flat building, but it was a pure, honest form of cold. The tide was going out and carefully feeling my way with my bare feet I could walk far across the slippery jagged formations towards the whiteness of the foam beyond. Perhaps it was a good thing, I tried to rationalise, that I had to stay behind : it gave me time to review the long day behind me.

I sat down on a wet rock, abandoning myself, like a drowning man to the waves, to what had happened : the ridiculous squabble with the Customs official and the vulgar interview with Davey Sachs; Gran'ma Grace's empty house and Oom Sassie's thin voice telling me about District Six; the messy business with the mouse; Derek's cynicism.

There had been one refrain echoing through the day :

Don't say I didn't warn you.

You mean you don' know what's heppen' here?

Darling, buy yourself a ticket back to London tomorrow. You've forgotten what it looks like here.

Even if it were true, why should it affect my future? Was that sufficient reason to run back, tail between the legs, before giving the country and myself a chance? I'd come to work in the theatre, to get something going among my people – to fulfil an urge within myself, but also to give to them what I knew they were yearning for. That was all. Surely the country wouldn't refuse me that? My God, they couldn't shut the door in my face, it was my own place. I had the seed and blood of many generations in me : Huguenot and Malay and Hottentot,

Xhosa and Irish and Boer, White, Brown, Black, everything. Made in South Africa, not for export.

Like a cold, sick seagull on a rock I sat there thinking, remembering. The tiny flicker of a flame which we'd been keeping alive through the centuries . . . I didn't know what talent the slave girl Leah had had apart from her virginity, nor what spark the first Malans had brought with them from the dark mountainsides of the Luberon or the Cévennes in the Midi; what had my forefather Adam possessed apart from the sob of violence, the poetry of murder? And yet there must have been something in them, filtered through all the generations after them: a slave singing little songs to amuse his master, and preaching to his brothers; a musician, cursed by God, playing by the wayside; a woman of sorrows humming cradle songs; an Abraham publishing anonymous rhymes in a pioneer newspaper; David committing arson with his art; and my father Jacob, fool of the death-camp. Now it was my turn, with my exits and my entrances.

For their sake I couldn't just turn back and flee: *that* was the illogical passion which kept me here. That, and the old stubbornness which refused to be mastered.

I would stay on. After all, that was the only thing I *could* do. Free will was an overestimated concept.

My watch had stopped and I didn't know what time it was when I finally got up, shivering, and went back to the flat.

'Is that you, Joseph?' Derek called as soon as I opened the door. 'Get yourself a glass and come and sit with me.'

He was having a bath, the whisky bottle on the ledge beside his head, a large bubble-glass in his hand. The bottle, which he'd opened for us that afternoon, was half empty.

The first sip sent shivers down my spine.

'God, you're numb with cold,' he said. 'And soaked. Where have you been?'

'Down at the sea.' I sat down on a small French boudoir stool.

'I thought you'd run away,' said Derek. His black eyes were studying me intently. 'Not that I would have blamed you, mind.'

'I found the air singularly stimulating for thought.'

'I hope you've decided something sensible.'

'Yes. I'm staying.'

He emptied his glass, poured some more, and took another mouthful before he spoke again: 'Exactly *what* do you hope to do here?'

'Start my own theatre.'

'Right. So where do you find a building, where do you get money?'

'I don't need a building. What I've got in mind, is something like Lorca's *Barraca*. To tour the Western Province in a wagon or something, performing wherever we stop. We won't need much.'

'Do you think they'll leave you in peace?'

'Who are "they"?'

'Principalities, powers, rulers of the darkness.'

'Why won't they leave me in peace? I've *come* in peace.'

'Like Christ our Lord,' said Derek, drinking deeply. He changed his position in the bath. Against the foamy surface I could see the movement of his prick, a limp water lily on a dark leaf. It affected me strangely, as if it confirmed something vulnerable in him denied by his cynicism.

'And you want to tackle it all alone?'

'I'll get a group together.'

'That's not what I meant. Even with a group . . . In the end one remains alone, baby. Have you got guts for it?'

'I didn't return all that impulsively, Derek!'

'I know. Perhaps that's what frightens me.' He put his glass on the edge of the bath to refill it, but opening the bottle his arm jerked and it was shattered on the tiled floor. 'Fuck!' he said. 'Another. Don gave me a dozen of the bloody things and look what happens. Anyway, that's about all I've got left of him. Never get attached to things, sweetie. Oh, well!' He put the bottle to his mouth and took a swig.

'Who's Don?'

He shrugged, and the water eddied across his chest and belly and prick.

'Do you think one ever gets used to loneliness?' he asked without warning.

'I'm still hoping that one can be self-sufficient.'

'We all try. And all the time it's bloody balls.' He stood up and began to soap himself. Grinning: 'If only one could do without them.'

'Without what?'

'Balls.'

'There's more at stake than a couple of balls,' I said.

'It's only because you're still fond of abstractions. I try to content myself with small, concrete, round facts. It isn't always pleasant. But it keeps you sane, darling. Sanity *über-umlaut alles*.' He rinsed off the soap and began to dry himself with a large white towel. 'Do you know when I first realised I was on the way down? When I discovered that my taste in sex was growing younger every year. Don was nineteen. One of these days I'll be a dirty old man, all set for the sordid suicide in the Gents'. For God's sake, let us sit upon the ground and tell sad stories of the death of kings!' He put on his maroon dressing gown, tying the golden cord with an elaborate bow. For a moment he lay his hand on my shoulder where I was still sitting on the low boudoir stool – a small, tentative, enquiring gesture, barely a touch. Then he brusquely turned away, picked up the bottle and went out. The floor was still littered with broken glass.

'Why are you so negative?' I insisted when we reached the lounge and I sat down opposite him.

'I'm not.'

'That's exactly what I mean!'

He scrutinised me for a moment before he got up to get a new glass. And then, pouring with his back to me, he unexpectedly said, in such a way that I couldn't make out whether he was trying to answer my question or change the subject:

'I don't know how you managed it, baby, but after all these years you're still a virgin. And this is no fucking world for virgins.'

'You're underestimating me.'

'I'm not referring to whatever beds you may have slept in over the years,' he said angrily. 'I'm talking about something quite different. And perhaps that's what I'm envying about you, and I can't stand it: because make no mistake, I'm a bastard.'

'What has happened to you these nine years, Derek?'

'Nothing,' he said. 'Absolutely nothing. I've just got tired, that's all. It's like the old story of the bloke who bought a sow because he wanted to get a pig farm going. But she wouldn't litter, and so he went to ask for advice from his neighbour. You'd better take her to a boar first, the neighbour said. So he put the sow in a wheelbarrow and pushed her to the nearest farm, and paid a rand, and brought her back. Next morning: no pigs. So it's back in the wheelbarrow and pushed her ten miles to the champion pig of the district, paid ten rand, and came back, convinced that his troubles were over. Next morning he went to the sty at daybreak. Still no litter – but the sow sat waiting in the wheelbarrow.' He crossed the room as if it were a stage and turned back: 'I'm like that old sow, see? And I get into my bloody wheelbarrow, not because I like it, but because there's nothing else I can do.'

'Sounds like Beckett.'

'No. Tonight Derek de Villiers holds copyright. I've drunk too much, I know, and now you've got to listen to my sob stories. But it includes a little bit of veritas. It was I who sent you abroad, Joseph. I'm also responsible in a way for what's happening to you.'

'It was I who chose to go,' I reminded him. 'You're talking as if you're reviewing a melodrama. What's wrong with my coming back? What's wrong with you?'

'Everything's wrong with both of us,' said Derek. 'Can't you see? Ten years ago, or however long ago it was, I believed just like you're doing now. I wanted to show our people what theatre meant, I thought I'd convert them. Worse than any third-rate faith healer. And what happened? I'm still playing for the same small herd of culture cows. Jesus . . . !' He came closer. 'Do you know how many people still come to my dressing-room at night to ask me what sort of work I "really" do?'

I couldn't help laughing, but he wasn't amused.

When he spoke again, I was suddenly reminded of Dulpert: 'I'll tell you what I find the worst of all, Joseph. Eleven o'clock at night I come from the theatre in the fucking cold to find a couple of thin kids with Käthe Kollwitz eyes, begging on the corner. And then I begin to ask myself: aren't those culture cows right after all? Shouldn't I go out and look for a "real" job? I'm a luxury here, nobody really needs me. That's what I find so degrading and demoralising.'

'That's exactly why I left London,' I said. 'I have just as little time for a theatre that's a mere sickness of the bourgeoisie. But that's why I've come back. I don't want to have anything to do with the establishment: I want to get in touch with *people*. My own people.'

'Joseph.' For a moment all mockery had gone from his eyes. 'Don't you remember what Joseph's brothers did to him?'

'My circumstances are different.'

'The Old Testament is still very much in power here,' he said. The mockery returned: 'All you need is a squire.'

'What do you mean?'

'Every Don Quixote needs a squire.' With an effort he got up from the armchair and approached to within a few inches of me, his eyes blazing: 'But you know what you'll get for all your trouble, don't you? — a blow from the windmill.'

And·then I got up too and said, rather melodramatically it seems to me now: 'At least give me a chance to try. Give me a chance to believe.'

For seconds on end we looked at each other, from very close. Then he put out his hand again, after a long time, the way he'd done earlier that night, but now with more confidence, more deliberately; he took my hand, and looked at it, like a fortune-teller, like Gran'ma Grace years ago. Then he raised it to his mouth and brushed his lips against it.

'Fuck off and go to bed,' he said roughly, dropping my hand. 'And flights of angels sing thee to thy rest. Don't let me contaminate you. If there's anything you think I can do to help you, you must tell me. I'll try. Now go to bed.'

III

I often thought about the circus during those first weeks: the circus Willem and Thys and Hermien and I had gone to in the days when everything had still been true. Now, after my return, I felt like the day I'd gone back to the Cape on the truck loaded with boxes and remained behind on the Parade. 'One day I'll run away to the circus and never come back,' I'd told Willem. And now I'd indeed gone in search of my circus, and returned: now I had to start from scratch, but how?

I had to find lodgings, I had to make arrangements, I had to get a group together, I had to sort myself out.

Lodgings was the most urgent. A few of Derek's neighbours had begun to suspect something and we noticed that the caretaker was watching our coming and going. He was a retired civil servant with grey hair cropped close to his skull, and a sunken mouth, a pious man, and most concerned – he one day confided in Derek – about the reputation of 'his' block of flats. What would happen if people started talking?

On the far side of the mountain, in Kenilworth, I found a small flat, just off Rosemead Avenue, one of the few districts where White and Brown still lived together. I suppose 'flat' is too dignified a word for the few rooms in Mrs Geustyn's dilapidated house in the hideous style of the '30s, painted blue and pink and lemon: but like my little box in Hackney it was mine, it was home.

I had my own entrance on the side of the house, from a narrow lane humming with bees, smelling of wisteria and honeysuckle in the daytime, and at night of the contents of the chamber pot regularly emptied through her bedroom window by Mrs Geustyn's invalid mother. My front door led straight into a small lounge, with my bedroom to the left, and another room, which I converted into a kitchen, to the right; on the back stoep I even had a bathroom.

After I'd whitewashed the interior – the Geustyns' weren't sure whether they should feel pleased or affronted – it began to look more cosy. Curtains, a few small carpets, my paintings and prints (Van Gogh, Degas, and a small *Titus* by Rembrandt), theatre posters, bookshelves of bricks and boards – and suddenly I was at home. Just as in London I began to pick up stuff in junk shops and slowly cluttered up the flat; a small dining-table of yellow-wood and stinkwood on which I spent a week to rid it of old layers of paint and dirt; a brass standing lamp; a broken cupboard which Jerry eventually repaired for me, an old-fashioned washstand with Victorian basin, ewer and chamber pot. And a brass bedstead, like my mother's long ago and really much too large for the bedroom, but I couldn't resist it: I picked it up when one of our theatre tours took us to Wupperthal, where the people had been using it as a stand for drying fruit. But that was much later, just before Jessica came.

In the beginning I had strong reservations about Mrs Geustyn, for she constantly visited me, using the inner door connecting my lounge with their passage, subjecting me to a long review of the endless catalogue of complaints she and her eighty-year-old mother were jointly and severally suffering from. I never saw the old lady. The only signs of her existence were inexplicable shuffling sounds at night, and occasional mumbling, and then of course the ceremonial libations from her chamber pot into the narrow passage beside the house. After I'd acquired my cupboard and shoved it in front of the inner door, Mrs Geustyn's visits were severely curtailed and as she gradually subsided into a greater variety of illnesses and complaints she finally stopped coming altogether.

Her husband, Oom Appie, spent most of his time 'on the road' selling funeral policies. Weekends when he was at home, he regularly sounded me out on the possibility of my buying a policy ('One newwe' knows what c'n happen, Joseph, God is a God of su'prises'), trying to encourage me by telling me about his five children who'd all been 'set aside' before their tenth birthday. One had been run over by a car, one had fallen off the roof when his mother sent him up to fetch a pumpkin; one had died when the doctor's aspirin didn't cure his diphtheria; another when the doctor's aspirin didn't cure his pneumonia; and the last one had given up before he'd started, stillborn with three loops of his cord round his neck.

After Sunday dinner Oom Appie regularly left for the Woltemade graveyard with a bunch of flowers for his best clients; and he never returned until nightfall, as drunk as a lord. The arrival of my cupboard also caused a decrease in Oom Appie's visits, especially after a few unfortunate incidents in the passage below his mother-in-law's window. And so, in the end, the cupboard was responsible for the fact that my coming and going to and from Jessica went largely unnoticed.

More and more urgently she is returning in my memories, more and more urgently she wants to be written. The time is approaching. Jessica at night, Jessica in the rain . . .

But not yet. Later.

It was raining when I first arrived at the Geustyn's and the roof was leaking. It rained all that winter, an old-fashioned Cape rain which lasted for weeks and left large dark patches on my newly painted walls. It was raining when I took the train to town in the morning. It was raining when I hurried through the Gardens to the Library, or up the incline to Oom Sassie's house with a woollen rug for the old man or sweets for the children. It was raining when I went to the Little Theatre in search of recruits for my group. It was always raining.

Among the final year Drama students there was only one Coloured boy, Renier Arendse, very young of course, but with a beautiful, agile way of moving like a lean black cat, and a suprisingly rich voice for his thin body. His eyes were cat's eyes, too, strange amber eyes, cool and fierce at the same time, with a suggestion of smouldering fire behind them. His enthusiasm was still largely undefined, it might still flare up in any direction, which was why he appealed to me. However, knowing that he'd already started hunting for grants to go overseas, I didn't want to exert any pressure on him. But as soon as he'd heard of my plans for a group, he impulsively decided to abandon all his other arrangements.

One evening he turned up at my place in the rain – I don't even know how he'd got hold of my address – and without bothering to take off his plastic raincoat, he announced :

'I want to work with you.'

'You must first go to England to study, Renier.'

'Fuck England. I only wanted to go because . . . well, what else could I do? But now you're here, and I think I know what you've come back for.' He looked at me intently, as if he was exposing something inside me of which I wasn't aware myself.

I deliberately tested his self-confidence: 'I'd like to audition you, Renier. But you realise it's not going to be a soft job. I'm not interested in a group of amateurs: I need people who can keep up a hell of a pace and remain absolutely loyal.'

Keeping his amber eyes unwaveringly on me, he said: 'That's why I'm here.'

'I'll let you know when you can come for an audition.'

'I'm ready whenever you need me.'

His eyes were unchanged, but there was a slight smile on his lips when he shook my hand and went back through the rain. And I was left behind with the curious feeling that it hadn't been so much I who'd wanted to test him as he who'd been testing me.

I provisionally rounded up two more recruits. One of them was Barney Salmon, my colleague at Drama School years before, now a teacher, and a baritone with the Eoan opera group: it wasn't easy to convince him, for he'd already grown accustomed to regular habits. But once I'd persuaded him to risk it, he shook off the crust of security and habit and became enthusiastic in a very youthful way. And it was he who brought me my second recruit. Frikkie Mantoor was a few years younger than myself but he'd been at Drama School for two years and he was an outstanding guitar player, a member of an orchestra who spent their weekends travelling all over the Peninsula to perform at weddings and christenings, dances and funerals. During the week he was a store clerk for a publishing firm in town. Frikkie was of slight build, with bandy legs and enormous ears, a born clown with music in his fingertips and an invincible *joie de vivre*.

And so there were four of us: Renier and Barney and Frikkie and myself. But then it became more difficult to find others. The two or three graduates from the Drama School whom I approached were either married or had parents or other relations to look after, and I couldn't take anyone dependent on a regular income or tied to a regular routine. Whoever wanted to join me, had to be prepared to forsake father and mother and give up security, running the very real risk of getting nothing in return.

But I knew I would get them sooner or later. Perhaps as soon as the winter rains ceased and spring approached. In the meantime I started selecting and adapting plays for the future. In the beginning more or less everything would have to be rewritten to make it suitable for us. Calderon kept me busy for a long time, followed by *Romeo and Juliet*, on rainy evenings under my leaking roof: a story of the Cape, with Coloured fishermen and the Coon Carnival, with *skollies* and street fights and guitar serenades in front of colourful façades in the District Six of yesteryear. Even Molière's Sganarelle could learn to speak the Cape dialect. There was so much to do; and behind each completed play so many others stood waiting: wild, satirical fantasies based on Aristophanes or Plautus, with music and dancing, and the Coloured Hamlet I'd been dreaming about for so long.

It was my decision to visit Willem which suddenly made me aware of it: previously, on the farm and in Cape Town and abroad, my life had been following a more or less straight line like any chronicle; but now, since my return, it was changing into a spiral, returning to all my previous moments: now I was beginning to live on my own myths.

I saw his photograph in a newspaper, accompanying a report on extensions to the large group of companies of which he was managing director. I studied it for a long time. Willem had been so deeply woven into the texture of my childhood memories: now he was an industrialist, one of the Afrikaner economists regularly featured in profile articles in the weekend newspapers. And suddenly it had become imperative for us to meet again.

My call was filtered through several secretaries before I was finally put through to him.

'Viviers speaking.'

'Willem, it's Joseph.'

'Joseph . . . ?' A moment's pause, in which he presumably tried to fit the name to the surname the secretaries had mentioned. 'But of course! I read about you in the paper.'

'I read about *you*. I'd like to come and see you.'

'What for?'

I was put out by his tone, but tried to explain: 'Just to look you up. But I'd like to discuss some business as well. Perhaps I could come round to your house?'

'Oh. Unfortunately . . . My wife hasn't been too well lately. Rather come to my office. I'm off to New York tomorrow, but I'll be back next

Tuesday. If you don't mind, I can put you through to my private secretary to make an appointment.'

It was raining again, or still, when a fortnight later, just before twelve, I stepped out of the lift on the fourteenth floor of the huge new building on the foreshore. A receptionist in the front office accompanied me down the corridor to a secretary who led me deeper into the heart of the emporium, to a large waiting-room furnished with futuristic Swiss and American tables and chairs on a carpet which absorbed all sound. Almost inaudible flute music insinuated itself through hidden speakers; on the walls were paintings by South African artists; a low glass table carried magazines in four languages: *Paris Match*, *Stern*, *Time* and *Panorama*. And from this room Willem himself escorted me into the holy of holies, five minutes later. His enormous office had two glass walls, two layers of plate glass completely isolating us from the city and the rain outside. With a gentle hissing sound an air conditioner kept the temperature inside pleasantly constant. Everything in the office was of leather, chromium and tinted glass.

'Sit down.' In his fashionable Italian suit he led the way to the opposite end of the room, motioned me to a deep round chair and offered me a cigarette. 'Well! After all these years.'

We were silent for a while. Then I said, deliberately: 'So you didn't become a farmer after all: you kept the promise you made that night on the mountain.'

'What did I promise?'

'You said: "I'm going to see the world and get rich!" '

'You have an extraordinary memory.'

'That's what I make my living on. And I said; that same night: "I'm also going to see the world. And everybody will know me and say: That's Joseph Malan." '

'You've nearly succeeded. After the rumpus in the papers about your return.' He shook the ashes from his cigarette. 'I must admit, I don't know whether that was such a wise move on your part. You antagonised many people who might have supported you.'

'I didn't ask for publicity. The journalist cornered me and then distorted everything I said. I'm sure you've also been a victim of the papers from time to time.'

He crossed his legs. 'You need a PRO,' he said lightly.

We fell quiet again, he in his Italian suit, I in my London outfit, in those expensive chairs with the chromium legs, surrounded by paintings and panels and pot-plants with dark waxy leaves, in this capsule isolated from the city. I felt an urge to get up and take his shoulders and say: *My God, Willem, it's me. We've grown older, our circumstances have changed, but it's still us.* Or had this gulf between us always existed as a possibility? That day at the circus when he and Thys and Hermien had gone in together while I had to go round to the back with my ticket crumpled in my sticky hand: had it already been destined for us then?

They'd taken Sagrys into the shed and beaten him, and he'd gone on screaming and screaming; and on the other side of the house Hermien, hysterical, had sobbed: 'D'you hear that? D'you hear? Don't try to run away, Joseph!'

'I heard that you were hoping to launch a sort of Coloured theatre,' said Willem with polite interest. 'How is it coming on?'

'Very slowly. But surely.' I got up. 'I'm sorry I've come to waste your time, Willem. I think I'd better go.'

'But you've just . . .' He got up too, obviously surprised by my impulsive move. 'I thought you were coming to discuss business?'

'Yes.' I breathed in evenly to control my voice. 'I've read a lot about your group of companies lately. I noticed that you're spending considerable amounts promoting the arts, so I thought I could approach you for some sort of subsidy for our group. For the sake of "good relations".'

'We can still . . .'

'I didn't mean to beg,' I said. 'I know I tend to react emotionally, but I thought I could come to you as the friend I used to know. I can approach other companies on a purely business level. But I don't want any gestures of goodwill towards the Coloured cause from you. I refuse to face another *Robinson Crusoe*.'

'What on earth has *Robinson Crusoe* got to do with it?' he asked, amazed.

'Your father gave me an education after catching me behind the dam with the book I'd stolen from you.'

'I can't remember.'

'No. To you it was nothing. To me it meant – more or less everything.'

I was already holding the knob of the padded door in my hand when he said behind me: 'Don't go so soon, Joseph.'

I stood still, overcome by weariness.

'Please sit down again.'

I turned round and looked in his eyes, bluish green under the neatly combed hair. 'Are you sure there's anything we can discuss without being merely polite?'

'Sit down,' he said quietly.

He remained standing against one of the glass walls, opaque with weeping rain outside. 'Haven't had a winter like this for years,' he said, lighting a cigarette. 'If we have a good summer after this, Thys will have a record grape harvest.'

'Is he still on the farm?'

Yes, he's in charge now. Father died five years ago. Mother is living with Hermien.'

'She married?'

'Yes, a Robertson farmer.' He hesitated. 'Things haven't worked out so well for her.'

'How come?'

'She was engaged to a chap from Transvaal, who left her in the lurch. With a baby. Afterwards she married the farmer, but they're not very happy.'

'Hermien was the Virgin Mary,' I said automatically, more to myself than to him.

'What do you mean?'

'Christmas Eve, when we were children, don't you remember? You were Joseph. Which created quite an ontological problem for myself: how could Willem be Joseph if Joseph was Joseph?'

He laughed and sat down opposite me again. 'I can still remember how you used to let us work on all those plays you made up.'

'Wearing your mother's washing from the line.'

'And all the red and yellow finches we caught.'

'Remember,' I suddenly said, 'the day the foreman's wife . . .' Something of the shock and shame returned.

He grinned. 'My God, can you imagine?'

A discreet bell rang on the desk. Willem got up and pressed the intercom button.

'You asked me to remind you of your lunch appointment, sir.'

'Miss Henderson . . .' He looked round at me. 'Please phone Dr Roux and tell him I'll be busy over lunch.' He came back to me.

'Thank you, Willem,' I said, looking him in the eyes.

'It's nothing.'

'Perhaps we can go out for a meal,' I suggested.

He stiffened. I immediately realised my *faux pas*.

'I'll have something sent up to us,' he quickly said. This time he didn't use the intercom but went through to the adjoining office. I remained behind, guarded by leather and chromium, carpets, curtains and double windows.

He seemed completely at ease when he returned after a while, but he didn't sit down again.

'I can imagine what it must be like for you,' he said. 'Having to get used to everything.'

I just looked at him.

'I don't know whether it's much of a consolation,' he said. 'But I can assure you that there are many of us who feel strongly about it.'

'Strongly enough to change anything?' I asked.

He looked through the window, pulling at his cigarette. 'Things are changing,' he said. 'In ten years time you won't recognise the country.'

'I already don't recognise it.'

'You're bitter!' he said.

'I'm trying not to be. I'm trying to go on believing. Why else do you think I have come back?'

'It's changing,' he repeated. 'We're right in the bottleneck now. From here, things can only improve.'

'Are you sure?'

'You must realise it can't happen overnight. In a country with so many groups, so many standards . . . People must be prepared for it first. If they'd all been like you, there wouldn't have been a problem.'

He seemed to expect an answer. When it didn't come, he went on: 'I can see for myself what's happening around us, Joseph. And sometimes it makes me shudder. I don't shut up about it, either. But on the other hand you must try to be reasonable and at least give the Government some credit for what has already been done to raise standards of living . . .'

'I didn't attack you, Willem,' I interrupted him. My hand holding the cigarette was trembling. 'So why are you trying to defend yourself?'

I could see him struggling. Then he suddenly stamped out his cigarette and faced me squarely: 'All I'm trying to do is ask you to remain reasonable. Even though I realise that it's almost impossible.'

'Suppose everything around me is unreasonable?'

'Then it's even more necessary to keep calm. We're living on the slope of a volcano, Joseph. I know that as well as you. All we can hope to do is to try not to go mad.'

217

For a moment everything was open between us. Then there was a movement at the door and a Coloured girl in black uniform, wearing a silly little cap like a Christmas hat, brought in a large tray with cups and sandwiches.

'Thanks, Doris,' said Willem. 'You can put it on the table over there.'

Just before she left, she glanced at me. It was only for a moment, her eyes on mine, mine on hers, no gesture, no word.

Then she turned back to Willem and asked: 'Anything else, Master?'

'That'll be all, thank you, Doris.'

The padded door swung soundlessly shut.

'Nice girl,' I said.

He looked up very quickly. There was a hint of colour in his cheeks. Then he came to the table.

'Tea?'

'Thanks.'

He arranged the cups on the saucers.

'Our volcano used to be a mountain,' I said quietly. 'A very beautiful mountain. Where did the change begin then? It must have started somewhere, such things don't happen by themselves.'

'Do you prefer weak or strong?'

'Willem,' I said. 'That night we fell asleep in one another's arms things were different.'

'We were children,' he said. 'As one is drawn into one's society one inevitably becomes part of its patterns.'

'Even if those patterns are evil?'

'Are you sure they're irremediably evil?' he asked, pouring tea. 'There's room for an urge like self-preservation. If not, what would become of minorities?'

'Self-preservation at the cost of others?'

'No. Surely the ideal is to create breathing space for all. Sugar?'

'Two.'

'It's only a transitional stage,' he insisted.

'And the ends justify the means?'

'You know what the policy is aiming at!'

'I know what the policy *is*. I experience it physically, from day to day. Don't try to act as PRO for the Government, Willem: I want to now what *you* are thinking.'

He poured saccharin tablets into his cup and began to stir the tea.

'Why are you trying to hide?' I asked mercilessly. 'Who are you, Willem? What have you become?'

He stood still for a very long time, the teaspoon motionless in his hand. 'Sometimes I wonder . . .' He looked up, his eyes more naked than before. 'There's one form of fate you must never underestimate, Joseph. The one experienced by people like me : I can see what's happening; through the colour of my skin I'm identified with those who allow it to happen, yet I can't do anything to stop it.'

'Are you sure you can't do anything? In your position?'

'I can help to postpone the explosion. I can try to make life more bearable for the people working for me. Wages, working conditions, prospects . . .'

'Do you really believe in that?' I asked.

'I have to,' he said softly. And then : 'Just as you've got to believe in what you are trying to do. In a way, perhaps, both of us are avoiding the larger issues. But in a way we both help to make life a trifle more liveable. If we could no longer believe in that . . .'

For a moment we stood very close together. We could have touched each other.

Then he turned away and gestured towards a photograph on his desk : 'I have a wife. I've two children. For their sakes I've got to ensure that the change which lies ahead happens peacefully.' He came back to pick up his cup. 'Let's forget about politics : it's not pleasant for either of us. Have a sandwich.'

'No, thanks. I'm not really hungry.'

'Tell me about your group and your plans.' We were back on more formal territory.

'I've only started. Must go to Johannesburg first. It's not easy to find the right people. And of course, I can't offer them much more than faith, hope and charity.'

'How much money do you need?' he asked pointblank.

'Enough to keep a group of eight or nine persons going,' I said. 'Under ideal circumstances we should require at least five or six months' working together before we can go into production. And then we'll need transport, a kombi or something. Once we've started, it should be easier because we won't have many running expenses.'

He was making calculations on the back of his cigarette box.

'Give me a couple of weeks,' he said after a while. 'I'll discuss it with my board.'

IV

Beyond Hex River the green and rain disappeared; from Laingsburg emptiness expanded around us, the stony hills and ridges prehistoric against the white sky, the grey tarred road an anomaly, an anachronism. The interior was a wholly new discovery: to me travelling implied the billowing hills and overgrown hedges of England; Holland's grey and green, cobblestones and cows; German industrial cities, castles, forests and valleys; French panoramas, ochre churches in ochre villages; and the gradual whitening towards the south, Spanish plains fanning open to all sides. There was something similar between Spain and this interior, the same vastness, the same light: but the Karroo was more ancient and cruel, lacking the gentle welcome of mottled white and red villages on the hills, donkeys, olives, guitars. Here, perhaps, a row of sienna-coloured mud huts, square as a child's playblocks, bare red earth, chickens scratching beside the skeleton of an old car, naked children with bulging bellies and pencil-sharp pricks; then a thin line of people walking along the road with bundles or cardboard suitcases on their heads; a tattered man on a bicycle, with a plastic orange on an aerial, a home-made tin banjo, a pair of shoes tied to the carrier. Occasionally a car rushing past at enormous speed, throwing out orange peels or crumpled paper, growing small, disappearing in the distance. And then, once again, the veld and the absolute silence of space. Even if there were wind, I once thought, one wouldn't hear it on these plains, for there was nothing it could blow against. Elegiac emptiness. It was hard, and bitter, to be human in such a land of stone and desolation with the whirlwinds whirling on in silence. In this Africa three hundred years of civilisation had hardly left a scar: man hadn't yet achieved a hold on it.

The villages, far apart, were identical dusty beads on the grey string of the road. Most garages offered conveniences marked Whites only, so Derek occasionally stopped in the veld, in a sandy ditch or under scraggy trees, to open a can of beer, to eat a sandwich, or to pee.

Accompanying him to Johannesburg had partly been brought about by Davey Sachs. How he'd managed to unearth my address in Kenilworth, I don't know, but shortly before my visit to Willem he'd turned up on my doorstep one Friday night, wet and windblown, smelling like a damp chicken; he left a row of mud tracks across my floor, sat down before I could invite him to, and took out his tape-recorder from under his jacket.

'Nice joint you got here,' he said. 'Listen, how about another story? It's time we did a follow-up. When do you get cracking?'

'I'm still trying to find actors.'

'I'll get them for you. How many do you need?'

'About five more.'

'Girls?'

'A couple.'

'I'll put it in. They're all dying to be actresses in this country.' He was fidgeting with his tape-recorder, but in the end he had to give up and take out a ball-point pen and a greasy notebook. 'Haven't you got any booze? I'm as cold as hell.'

I poured him a stiff tot and hopefully put the bottle away again : but he stayed on until he finished the last drop at nearly two in the morning.

Once I teased him : 'But, Davey, it's Friday. Didn't your Sabbath start at sunset?'

'So what?' He grinned. 'I'm a detribalised Jew, man. We've all got the same trouble, haven't we? Screwed for life.' And then, without any logical transition : 'Why don't you go up to Jo'burg to look for people? That's where the real talent lies. *King Kong* and all that.'

'But I want Coloureds, Davey. Africans need passes.'

'Well? Don't you think there are Coloureds in Jo'burg? They've got the bladdy United Nations there, man. Just give it a try.'

'You think it's worth while?'

' 'Course. And I've got just the contact you need. Harry Tsabalala on *The Star*. Fabulous chap, and he'll fix you up, I can guarantee that.'

A day or so later I heard about Derek's intended trip – he'd signed a contract with the Performing Arts Council in Pretoria – and immediately made up my mind. And now we were on our way, after I'd placated Mrs Geustyn with a month's rent in advance and Derek had made elaborate arrangements for his cat. For long distances we drove without talking, and I abandoned myself to the sensation of the vast country which was mine and which I hardly knew. Sometimes we had short snatches of conversation, relaxed and unhurried, about the Chekhov he was going to do in the Transvaal, about the progress of my adaptations, about the *commedia dell' arte* in whose footsteps I was eager to follow – Arlequino and Pantalone, Sganarelle, Scaramouche, the whole motley gallery.

'All clowns,' he once mocked, 'Are you going to act or have a circus?'

'What's the use of a society without a circus?' I asked, half flippantly, half seriously. 'What would Lear have been without his Fool, or Hamlet without Rosencrantz and Guildenstern? You see, I'm trying to stick to the role Sartre had assigned to the *bâtard* : for him bastard and clown were equivalent!'

'I should have thought you'd prefer to be Hamlet rather than one of his fools.'

'Don't you realise that Hamlet himself is a kind of court jester? — the only one who, under his mask of flippancy and buffoonery and vulgarity, dares to speak the truth.'

'A truth rejected by all because they regard him as mad. It's all right for him to talk, he's innocuous.'

'They may reject him superficially, but not in their conscience,' I replied. 'I know you've become a heathen, but I'm still a believer : "The play's the thing wherein I'll catch the conscience of the king!"'

In a sense our conversations, our theorising, our aesthetic abstractions, were out of place speeding across those plains where everything was so elemental and concrete : stone and dust, harsh shrubs, an old man with an ostrich feather in his hat and a *trompie* droning in his gnarled hands cupped before his mouth. And after some time we gave up talking altogether and just sped on, doomed to awareness of the landscape.

Harry Tsabalala was expecting me in his newspaper office, after a telex from Davey Sachs. Derek dropped me outside and immediately drove on to Pretoria; both of us felt a bit groggy after spending the previous night in the car. It was the beginning of two of the most hectic weeks of my life.

Harry, large and thickset, for some reason older than I'd expected him to be, at least fifty, his eyes bloodshot behind his glasses : Harry talking, gesticulating, laughing. I'd never heard a man laugh as he could, a volcano erupting in his enormous stomach. In a shebeen one night : 'Why shan't I laugh? D'you want me to cry?' That first night he made me so hopelessly drunk in 'his' shebeen that by late the next afternoon I still thought I was going to die. 'My God, Harry!' I pleaded, 'never take me back there. That hellish concoction nearly burnt my insides up.'

'That's exactly why we going there,' he said, hitting me enthusiastically between the shoulders. 'It's the only way one can keep going, man. You Cape boytjies are softies. But we'll get you right, don't worry.'

I had to travel on the Soweto train with him every day; much later I discovered that he possessed a car, but deliberately refused to let me off with an easy initiation. Good God, those train journeys at five in the morning, five-thirty in the afternoon! We swarmed down the station steps like cockroaches, tumbled into the coaches in a stench of perspiration, tobacco and stale beer; then pulled off with a jerk, accelerate, speed on insanely, swaying round the bends, in a whirlpool of infernal noise: the roar and rattling of the train, deafening conversations, bursts of singing; afternoon papers, tins of curdled milk, food parcels, brief-cases, shopping bags, nagging children.

'This bloody thing is going to crash, Harry!' I called out the first time we travelled on it, completely terrified.

'Of course!' he laughed. 'That's why we're riding on it. Johannesburg roulette. Saves one the trouble of suicide and keeps the population explosion in check.'

Milling, thrusting, cursing, laughing, complaining, swarms of people at the last stop, a wave surging across the platform, past the control gates; and then Soweto.

Soweto with its phalanxes of identical houses, row upon row like the crosses of Delville Wood, with bare patches of bleeding red earth in between, erosion ditches, water taps, the stench of bad sanitation and the thousand gallons of *skokiaan* emptied by the police during last night's raid; groups of teenagers in smart clothes or in rags, yelling at the passing women, occasionally grabbing one; children playing noisily with stones and wheels and broken dolls, children fighting, children pissing in the street. Cars parked beside houses and tatty gardens: enormous black American monsters from ten years ago, old wrecks with wide-open doors like chickens nestling in the sun, shiny new models; bicycles, box-carts, tyres.

'Look at those houses,' said Harry. 'Look at them: I can just imagine standing out there in front of them one day and shouting: ' ''Ten-shun! Forrard maaaaarch! Left, right, left, right!' ' – and I swear the whole army will come marching across the plains, up to Jo'ies. Jiss, I can see them coming through Booysens, down Paul Sauer, over the bridge, right into Houghton.'

Music from open doors, Lourenço Marques and Radio Bantu; and records : some *kwela*, lots of rock, remnants of Matshikiza, snatches of Makeba; God, and Beethoven! And a woman's choir of deep earth-voices from the slithery, soapy mess of an open-air washing-place. A man with a mouth-organ on a doorstep, a tin guitar; and one wizened and half-blind old man in the watery sun, with a length of wood across his knees, stroking imaginary strings.

Streetlamps protected by wire-mesh; a white goat; women breast-feeding their babies in front of their houses; a child beaten barbarously with a leather thong; and far away, far but visible, a barbed wire fence to hedge it all in, to stop the march of those regiments of houses.

The muddy mess of early mornings, half past four, five o'clock, six, when the people go to work in the rain : the sound of thousands of feet, the low hum of voices, a single piercing cry, Harry's booming laugh, children crying.

Children crying at night, everywhere, never completely stopping; sudden outbursts of sounds, shouts, silence – the low, ominous drone of police vans passing in the streets, patrols on prescribed hours, *two o'clock and all's hell*, the sudden barking of dogs, a voice shouting or pleading, steel doors clanging, gears gnashing – silence, with the moaning of a child or of children, and the sensual sounds of a woman, nearby, in the physical warmth of the house. In Annamaria's boat the darkness had been just so alive with sound and movement, but that was caused by cats, and this by people in the innumerable identical houses.

I didn't spend all my nights in the same house – naturally not, for I was an illegal visitor and daren't raise suspicion. But they were all variations of the same pattern and there were never fewer than ten people spending the night with me, often twenty; once, after a late-night party, as many as thirty-four. Sometimes there were murders in the street; sometimes one could hear the gangs passing; sometimes there was singing; and always the police were near; everywhere I was accompanied by the laugh of Harry Tsabalala.

'What else can you expect? There's more than a million of us here, man, and we've got nothing to keep us busy : but we're not doing too badly, d'you think? We fuck and murder and dance and die : never a dull moment. What more could you want? In this place you need a *man's* guts and a *man's* balls to survive, else you just disappear along the way.'

Dances breaking out spontaneously in small lounges, in dingy she-beens blue with the bittersweet smoke of grass : women with rocking buttocks and bobbing breasts, old dresses of German chintz, minis, cat-suits, Afro wigs, slim bodies gleaming in the light, ebony and mahogany; the glitter of teeth, the flashing white of an eye, the strident music: then the sudden low wave: 'They're coming!' And the night breeze cold on your face as you blindly follow Harry into the night, stumbling over wires and bicycles and rubbish, falling flat in a back-yard and lying motionless until the barking of the dogs subsides and the blue lights on the police vans disappear into the night.

'But how does one survive here, Harry?'

And he with his glass of hell-brewed beer: 'We who've seen the people loaded on the trucks in Sophiatown, we who've seen them walk to work from Alexandra during the bus strikes, we who've seen the dead children carted away from Sharpeville – do you think there's anything that can still shock *us*?' He emptied his glass in one long gulp, and looked at me with his ageless eyes, droplets of foam clinging to his upper lip; and putting his hand on my wrist, he said: 'I died in Sharpeville, man. It may take another ten years before they bury me, but that's where I died. They shot my wife there, didn't you know? She'd seen the crowd, she went to find out what was going on, she had our son on her hip, he was eighteen months old.'

'What happened to him?'

'He was lucky. She only fell on top of him, on a stone, when the bullet struck her. He's been soft in the head ever since. The old people are looking after him.'

I felt the beer grow thick in my throat.

'That was when I started laughing,' he said, the light shining on his large white teeth. 'And I've never stopped since. You see, the day they take everything away from a man, you're free for the first time in your life. So why shan't I laugh?'

Other nights in lounges with ball-and-claw furniture, linoleum-covered floors, plastic flowers in vases, demijohns of wine and cans of beer: nights of intense conversation, twenty or thirty people crowded on settees and chairs, on window-sills and floor: stories about how the police had been outwitted; how a jailer had been bribed; how to get your lost or stolen passbook replaced for free. But other conversations too – with the graduates working as teaboys in the city, the teachers smuggling spirits to supplement their meagre salaries, the writers whose work could not be published, the doctors and architects whose passports had been refused – conversations about Camus and Fanon, Stokely

Carmichael and Leroi Jones and Eldridge Cleaver; they made me listen to the recording of Mandela's speech, they gave me Bram Fischer's statement from the dock to read. Many of the conversations were identical to those I'd had with the expatriates in London, but there was a difference: Harry and his friends weren't theorising from a distance, they were right in the midst of everything; a single word – *Mayebuye!* – could lead to imprisonment on Robben Island. And they were prepared to take the risk.

On Harry's word they accepted me and gave me food and a place to sleep and shared their near-nothing with me, without asking a question or raising an eyebrow, in a brotherhood which must have resembled that of the early Christians.

Through the whorls and whirlpools of smoke: jokes, witticisms, bitchiness, philosophy.

'My father earned four pounds a month, I get a hundred rand: but he was richer than me, for he didn't know that he was poor.'

'If you hate another, it also poisons your love of yourself.'

'The Law is my Shepherd.'

That was Jerry's remark. Harry introduced me to him, as he'd done to all the others. Jerry Buys.

'It's my mother's surname I took,' he explained airily. 'Hoping she might be a descendant of old Coenraad Buys. Remember him? White Boer in the wild days of the Cape. Took a Black wife and crapped on the law-and-order of his age. Ruled like a king, discovered the meaning of freedom, the first of the pioneers. That's my claim to fame, thanks to my ma – who'd never even heard of him.'

'And your father?'

'Never heard his name. White policeman who'd taken my ma for a ride. You know mos the old story, hey, Capey?' His Afrikaans was as perfect as his English – he had an Honours degree from Cambridge – but often he would deliberately lapse into Cape slang. And it was with conscious irony that he called me 'Capey', for he was as much a Capetonian as myself, and much darker too: 'It's my father's colour I inherited,' he explained. 'You see, my mother was Coloured, but her skin was nearly white; and my father a White, but nearly black in looks. By rights I should have been speckled.'

Jerry had much of Harry's brand of humour, as well as his cynicism, only Jerry's had a lighter touch; compared to Harry's guffaw, his reactions were more subdued – deceptively so, for he could keep his slight smile even when he was seething inside. But that I discovered later: during those two chaotic weeks in Johannesburg the most obvious difference between them seemed to lie in the fact that Jerry hadn't died in Sharpeville.

The night I met him I sat watching him as he danced in the small lounge where we'd all assembled. He was improvising endless variations on the patterns of the others, twisting and contorting his body with effortless ease. Harry sat beside me, his eyes slightly dazed, a grass *zoll* in his hand.

'That man knows how to move,' I remarked.

'Of course,' said Harry. 'That's why I brought him here tonight. He's your man all right.'

'But will he be interested?'

'Ask him.'

'What's his job?'

'Teacher in Cape Town. He only comes up here during vacs to make some extra money.'

'How?'

'None of my business.'

'Is he married?'

'Jerry married? Don't be silly. He's too sorry for all the women who'll have to do without him if he got married.'

His companion that night was a particularly attractive Zulu girl, Noni, not the sort of girl one would have expected after Harry's description of Jerry: she was quiet and reserved, extremely intelligent, a nurse who'd just returned to the country after following an advanced diploma course in London.

Inevitably our conversation turned to England when Harry arranged for Jerry and Noni to join us an hour or so later.

She hadn't liked England at all. 'I was sick most of the time. Not a real illness, just sick without the sun.'

'And now you've recovered?'

'No,' she answered, to my surprise. 'Now I'm sicker than before. Because now I've seen what I never used to know.'

'Why don't you go back?'

'Why don't *you* go back?' she asked without hesitation.

'I . . .'

'Me too.'

We were quiet for some time.

227

'And I used to be happy!' Noni suddenly said.

Jerry, quickly: 'Happiness, my dolly, is a function of blindness. Once you've eaten of the Tree of Knowledge...'

'It gives you cat's eyes,' she said. 'So you can see in the dark.'

'Just as well,' he replied. 'One's got to see in the dark. One's got to learn to know the night. Else you stumble and break your neck. Now, at least, you can go on walking.'

'How far must one go on?' asked Noni.

'Doesn't matter, just keep going. We're all driven on by something inside us. The Tree of Knowledge is the Tree of Despair. It gives you adrenalin.'

'An overdose can be lethal.'

'Not of this sort of energy,' Jerry countered. 'Rather too much than too little. Because if you've got too little, you're heading straight for suicide.'

'If you want to keep on, you need something to believe in,' I said, almost mechanically.

'Faith is as blind as happiness,' said Jerry. 'You've got to liberate yourself from both. So that your despair can be absolutely pure. It's not the light in the distance that keeps you going but the fire in your breast.'

'You need more *skokiaan*,' said Harry loudly. 'Then you've got fire all over, not only in your breast.'

'Look at this old Bacchus,' said Jerry. 'He thinks he's the only one who can swig. But I can easily drink him under the table.'

And then a drinking contest started which went on till daybreak, when both were lying lights-out on the floor and had to be taken to bed by the rest of us.

After that first night we spent much time together, but Jerry consistently refused to give me a straight answer whenever I invited him to join our group. I don't think he was trying to avoid a decision: a choice had simply not yet become relevant to him. And perhaps he wanted to make sure about me first.

The two of us, and often the three of us, explored the city from one end to the other. Early mornings when the streets began to fill up. The station when a train from the Transkei or Lesotho pulled in, loaded with hundreds of recruits for the mines, swathed in colourful blankets, half-loaves clutched under the arm, white eyeballs showing:

gloomy battalions from whose midst an occasional too-loud laugh would break. The dances on the mine dumps to please the tourists, like circus animals performing, eager for the final shower of cents: *Thank you, Boss! Nkosi! Dankie Baas!* Lunchtime in the streets, the Whites streaming to cafés and restaurants, the Blacks squatting on the pavement with bread and Coca-Cola. The roar of drills and cranes and bulldozers in the vacant lots among exhilarating skyscrapers. Shudderings of the earth, hidden rumblings of dynamite exploding in subterranean tunnels. *Dogs and Natives not Allowed* above the entrances of large new blocks of flats. 'Yes, tsotsi?' from the friendly shop assistant. Blobs and daubs of colour in the groups on the Zoo Lake Lawns, crowd scenes by Renoir. White babies in prams pushed by Black nannies. Police vans passing with dark figures behind wire-mesh, like monkeys in a cage. The brown panelling of a courtroom on a Monday morning when the hundreds of pass-offenders were brought in: two minutes per case, *Guilty, your Worship, guilty your Worship, guilty.*

Harry saw to it that I spent much of my time in court: not only because he had to do so himself in search of 'stories' for his paper, but mainly, I think, because he regarded the court as an operation ward where I could get acquainted with the anatomy of the city. Immorality cases in which bull-necked constables smirkingly gave evidence about what they'd seen through the half-drawn curtains of servants' rooms. Violence. Three young White miners raping a pregnant Black woman repeatedly before throwing her from their moving car, resulting in a miscarriage. 'You have acted like animals,' said the Judge. 'Two years' imprisonment each.' A nineteen-year-old Black gardener raping the daughter of his employer. For him the death sentence: 'Our White women must be protected.' A young Black boy accused of stealing a loaf of bread from a café: 'I was hungry, Baas, the pollies they take my mother away.' Eight strokes with a cane. The farmer and his two sons beating a labourer with a length of hose, afterwards tying him up in a bag suspended from a rafter in the servants' toilet, resulting in death from suffocation and internal haemorrhage. Two hundred rand fine, collected by their neighbours packing the courtroom. The messenger from Soweto who'd spent the night with his wife in her room in the yard of a Randburg home: 'But she's my *wife*, your Worship!' Six months' imprisonment. 'Our White suburbs must be kept clean at night.' During five or six days in court I saw, at close quarters, the heart and liver and lungs, the guts and veins and sex and glands of the city, of my country. I staggered out sick and trembling, and finally refused to go back. And yet, I don't think Jerry and Harry had done it to shock me: they'd seriously wanted to show me 'their city'.

They showed me another city too, both friendlier and stranger than the other. On evenings when Harry had to work late we didn't go out to Soweto but went to an office block not far from his paper. When we were early enough, we could go up in the lift (there were two: *Whites*; and *Goods and Non-whites*); else we had to climb the stairs up the sixteen or seventeen floors to the tiny cage sitting on the roof, like a pimple, where the Zulu nightwatchman lived. There was something unearthly about those nights in the dark beside Dhombe's drum of smouldering coals: Dhombe in his bulky khaki overcoat, with grizzly wool on his cheeks and round his ears; Harry short and heavy-built like a Japanese prize-fighter; Jerry thin and tough; and I.

I couldn't fathom the old man. He gave the impression of living in one world only: the green hills of his country, the round huts, the large fertile women, everything he'd left as a young *umfaan* and to which he would certainly return soon, oh soon; for him, Sensangakona and Chaka were still real; and when he opened his grey-striped bag of wildcat skin, and shook out his smelly *dolos*-bones to read our fortunes, there was something about it which penetrated through all my sophisticated cynicism to make me shudder.

'Tell the stranger who he is, where he comes from, where he's going.'

The bones and weird little objects clicked on the asphalt roof; for a long time he sat studying them, mumbling and drooling.

'He's a man of darkness. But he's afraid of the dark.' A grunt. 'He don't *know* the dark yet. I can see him come a long way, a very long way, from the other side of the morning star.' He glanced up and in the glow of the coals I could see his eyes burning on mine. 'I see people stamping their feet on you.'

'Why are they stamping?'

'They ask you stones, you give them bread.'

'You mean the other way round!'

'They ask you stones, you give them bread,' he repeated irritably, looking up again. 'How far can you throw a piece of bread?'

'Not very far.'

'No,' he said. 'Not very far.' Then unexpectedly: 'You have the woman?'

'No.'

'I see the woman. I see him.'

'What do I give her?' I asked lightly. 'Bread or stone?'

'You give him the night,' he said laconically, mumbling something, a curse perhaps, scraping his bits and pieces together and throwing them back into the skin bag. Far from us, in the direction of Brixton, I could see the illuminated head of the radio tower, and many floors below us cars came humming past, lights glared in shop windows, sirens wailed, the rhythms of jazz orchestras in exclusive clubs thumped on, and in the night cafés of immigrants the juke-boxes made animal sounds.

To me his throwing of the *dolosse* was part of his whole anachronistic world. And yet, Harry assured me, he lived close to the heartbeat of the city: often he could tell you exactly at which jeweller's shop, in which executive homestead in Houghton, in which club in Hillbrow there would be a burglary that night, where a car would be stolen, which bank's armoured truck would be hijacked the next day. But if one tried to interrogate him, he would just smile vaguely and shake his grey head, empty his tin mug and take up his baton with a sigh, to go on one of his hourly inspection rounds, returning to help us settle for the night beside his faintly glowing coals.

Jerry accompanied me through the city in search of traces of my history. He took me to the posh White suburb where Sophiatown had been – 'That's what District Six is going to look like,' he said – with no sign of a hovel in which, half a century before, an old blind man and a young boy might have lived; and he took me to Kazerne, where my grandfather was supposed to have died under the stones of the strikers – but all one could see was a panorama of glittering parked cars against the concrete mass of bridges and the station complex.

Jerry didn't share my gloom about the fruitless search: 'What do you want to find proof for?'

'I want to know!'

'You know already.'

'What I know is completely subjective.'

'So what? Do you want to find proof of your existence in other people's lives? You're so fond of quoting Sartre' – referring to a long discussion we'd had the previous night – 'but you don't remember that he also said: you cease to be a bastard the moment you stop regarding yourself as a bastard?'

'Yes, Professor,' I answered. 'But there's a hell of a difference between philosophy and reality.'

'Bugger philosophy!' Jerry said angrily. 'Do you think I don't know what I'm talking about?' He stopped on the pavement; the cars of the peak hour came streaming past from one set of lights to the next, like a flood bursting through one dam wall after another. 'I have a sister,' he said. 'It's always been just the two of us and I used to love her immensely. A beautiful girl, she still is. But she was like you : ashamed of being Coloured. She simply couldn't come to terms with it. Because her skin was so light, you see. And she finally persuaded my mother to send her to a White school. She didn't want to know us any longer. Don't ask me how she managed it – it's not so very difficult, really – but in the end she married a White man in a top Government post.' He paused. 'There's a hell of a lot of our people thinking the way she does. But I spit on it!' He raised his hand against the late afternoon sun. 'There,' he said. 'It's black. It's mine. And I swear to God : I don't want to be different. Black, brown, it's the colour of the earth, Capey, it's the colour of a tree-trunk, it's life. White is maggots, it's bird shit, it's pus, it's rot. And the sooner you discover that, the sooner you will become human.'

Something about Jerry remained an enigma to me : I still had the impression that he was watching me and weighing me all the time. And it was only on the long road back to Cape Town that something was finally resolved.

He'd invited me to go back with him, a full week before his school was due to reopen. 'One never knows,' he'd said cryptically, and soon I discovered what he'd meant by it. The car was the almost unrecognisable wreck of a Volkswagen which he'd bought as scrap after an accident. One of his numerous esoteric friends 'borrowed' a pick-up van from the garage he worked for and towed the carcass to Soweto where ten or fifteen helpers turned up to hammer and bend and weld the chassis back into shape; from obscure sources a windscreen and windows, wipers, tyres and a battery were contributed, while Jerry bought a second-hand engine. For hours on end, including at least two full nights, he struggled patiently to make the car roadworthy again. To me it seemed nothing less than a miracle. Just to get a sound from the thing, I thought, would be a major achievement. But with almost loving care Jerry worked on until, one morning, the jalopy began to move; and before nightfall it was capable of doing sixty.

Afterwards, once again aided by friends, he registered the car outside Johannesburg, in Edenvale or Alberton somewhere; explaining, when I enquired about it :

'Capey, it's plain murder for a Black man to drive a car with a Jo'burg registration : with a TJ on your bumper you won't reach the other end of the Free State.'

But even without that Cain's mark we certainly had no prosperous journey : or rather, that was what *I* thought; for Jerry, clearly experienced in this form of travelling, remained unruffled throughout.

To start with, there were seven of us in the Volkswagen, because Jerry simply couldn't say no to anyone hitching a ride; and of the seven only he and I were going to Cape Town – the others had to be deposited in towns all over the country. We set out for Cape Town by first driving straight north to Pietersburg where the first passenger had to be delivered; from there we drove to Harrismith and to Newcastle in Natal; then back to Bloemfontein, Aliwal North, and the snow-capped mountains of Barkly East; through the Transkei to Umtata, and into the Eastern Cape, Graaff-Reinet; coastwards to George, then back to the Little Karoo until, via Worcester and a final detour to Malmesbury, we reached Cape Town. That we managed to do all that in a week was in itself the most remarkable feature of our journey. And on the way we never really had fewer passengers, for wherever we stopped to let one off, new strangers would turn up and beg for a lift. Once or twice the number dropped to four; the maximum, but that, admittedly, included a baby in arms, was nine.

In addition, we were often delayed. Jerry couldn't pass a broken-down car without stopping to help. After the seventh time I stopped counting. Almost without exception the stranded cars were huge antediluvian monsters like Harry's, and the occupants Black. Then Jerry would cheerfully crawl in under the car or bend over the open bonnet to locate and repair whatever fault there was; on other occasions he used a length of hose specially taken along for the purpose to suck petrol from our car and fill the tank of a stranded driver. When he couldn't help, which didn't happen very often, he would give a passenger from the broken-down vehicle a lift to the nearest garage.

Only once we came upon a stranded car with White occupants : a tyre had burst, and the old man and his wife had no conception of how to set about changing a wheel. As helpful as always, Jerry stopped, jacked up their car and removed the useless wheel. But the spare turned out to be flat too. Jerry left most of our passengers behind while he and I drove, taking the old couple's wheels the twenty-four miles to Graaff-Reinet. There we had both of them repaired, paid for the job, and drove back. Three-quarters of an hour later the two helpless old people were ready to go on. Our passengers were bundled back in the Volkswagen, but as Jerry was preparing to drive off the old gentleman hurried over to us.

'I just want to say thanks, boy,' he said to Jerry. 'And here's something for your trouble.'

He pressed a fifty-cent piece into Jerry's hand.

'Thanks, Oubaas,' said Jerry without turning a hair. He put the money in his pocket; and in Graaff-Reinet he bought ice-cream for us all.

We were delayed in other ways too. The first time it happened we hadn't even reached our first stop, Pietersburg. We were blithely driving along when a provincial traffic officer passed us, pulling his car off the road a few hundred yards ahead and motioning to us to stop. Before the car had come to a complete standstill he'd already wrenched Jerry's door open.

'Where's your licence?' he demanded.

' 'Afternoon, Chief,' said Jerry cheerfully. 'Here you are, my Baas.' He took out his driving licence.

The officer studied it carefully. 'Where's the car's papers?' he asked.

'The Baas must just say the word, I'll oblige. There, the whole lot of them in the Baas's hand.'

'What about the passengers? You're not licensed as a taxi.'

'No, Chief, but they not paying anyway. Is all free, just friends and family like.'

'This thing isn't roadworthy.'

'Tested yesterday, my Baas. Look.' He produced the roadworthy certificate. But the officer insisted on testing the car himself, so we all had to get out and allow him to thoroughly inspect the vehicle. After half an hour I was seething, but Jerry still didn't turn a hair and stood waiting without a hint of irritation. When at last we were allowed to drive on again, he rubbed his hands together and bowed :

'Thanks, my Baas tog, the Lord will bless and protect you.'

'Fuck off !' said the officer.

When we turned a hundred yards away, Jerry quietly said : 'And the same to you, my Baas,' spitting through the open window.

Then he turned to me to ask, still in his Cape accent: 'How you like that, hey? What you think of my performance?' And he smiled, but his eyes didn't change: there was something dark and cool in them, a dark which glowed, a burning coolness.

'My God, Jerry, do you think it's funny?'

'Of course it's funny. Didn't you notice how that little shit fell for my act?'

'But what about you?'

'It doesn't touch me at all. I knew what was going on, I was in control.'

'I swear the bastard can't even write his own name properly. And then he dared humiliate you!'

'Newwe'!' said Jerry. 'He humiliated the role I was acting, not me. I wasn't there.' He winked. 'In fact, I enjoyed it.'

When it happened the second time, on the godforsaken stretch of road between Reddersburg and Smithfield in the Free State, Jerry played the coon to perfection:

'Ay, my Crown, jiss! Lookit de poo' ole *gamatjie* from de Cape en' hef mercy upon us! Here's my papers, my big Baas, I's a law-abiding cit'zen, inne fear of de Law enne Lawd.' And at the end he rounded off his performance with a wild reel and a obsequious bow.

'The Free Staters like *gamats* from the Cape,' he said afterwards. 'So I had to give him value for his money.'

'It's not necessary to call them "Baas" and "my Crown" whenever you open your mouth!' I objected angrily.

Jerry laughed. 'Capey, there's a hell of a difference between that bloke's idea of what "Crown" means and mine.'

'What does it mean to you?'

'The crowning glory of my arse.'

When it happened the third time it required all Jerry's ingenuity and virtuosity to calm the aggressive officer – one of those who hit first and ask for the papers afterwards. But even from that dilemma Jerry saved his own skin and ours.

This time I came close to losing my temper. Jerry probably noticed that I couldn't be convinced by mockery any longer, and for the first time he spoke with deadly seriousness:

'Listen, Capey. There was a time when I regarded this sort of thing as part of one great moral mess in the country. But morality's got nothing to do with it: it's plain politics. And I can play the game too.'

'It depends on what you mean by "politics".'

'Precisely what it means all over the world. Politics knows only two basic methods: the first is cheating, the other violence.' He was quiet for a while before he added, looking straight ahead: 'And I'm prepared for both.'

'Do you realise what you're saying, Jerry?'

His eyes on me, dark, sardonic, calm: 'Don't worry, Capey. I know.'

Near George another man in blue uniform jumped out of his car as we approached and put up his hand. I was driving. As I stepped on the brake to pull off the road, Jerry quietly said:

'Over to you, Capey.'

I drew in my breath as the official came walking up to my window.

'Good afternoon, sir,' I said.

'Get out when you speak to me!'

For a moment I didn't move. His face was dancing in front of my eyes. Then I became aware of Jerry's quiet presence beside me, and I drew another deep breath. It was as if a smile was forming deep inside me, and suddenly, in a very strange way, as I got out, I felt free.

' 'Scuse, my Baas, my big Maaste',' I said, bowing deeply. 'I didn't want to offend, I jus' wan'ed to greet my crowning glory with respec' mos.'

We all had to get out and open our luggage. He removed the trunks from the roof-carrier and scattered the contents on the ground. 'Where's the dagga?' he asked. 'Hey? Where's the dagga?' When he couldn't find anything, he subjected the car to every conceivable test and ticketed us because a small corner from a figure on the number plate had chipped off. Then he got into his car and left us.

We repacked the trunks and stacked them on the roof, took up position in a row at the side of the road to pee, and went back to the car.

As we got in, Jerry said: 'Now you know, hey, Capey? Here's my hand.' And when I took his hand, he smiled: 'I think we'll get on together. OK, I'll join your company.'

V

My group was complete. There were five men apart from myself: Jerry, Frikkie Mantoor with the musical hands, young Renier Arendse with the cat's eyes, my old classmate Barney Salmon; and then Doors Kamfer, who'd turned up in response to one of Davey Sachs's newspaper reports. Doors was a remarkable person, in his early thirties when he joined us, over six feet tall, with the physique of a Greek statue. He'd never had any formal education, but we were constantly amazed by the vast store of general knowledge he'd accumulated through the years to satisfy his greed for learning. He'd grown up as an orphan, going out on the boats of Lappies Bay until he'd become one of the fishermen. Finding it boring in the long run he'd first joined the crew of a whaler, on which he'd earned more during one season than he'd ever seen together in his life, and then he'd gone overseas as a deckhand on a cargo ship. For a few seasons he'd played professional rugby for a Midland club, followed by several years as the Strong Man of a circus which regularly toured the Continent.

I hesitated to appoint him, uncertain about how long he'd stay with us before yielding to his wanderlust again, but my fears proved groundless. Doors was loyalty itself, and his solidness and earthy sense of humour helped us through many a bleak day. In the beginning he was very clumsy and unpolished, of course, but he possessed the sort of natural talent which hit one like fire or water; and like a medieval troupe of troubadours we could often rely on his circus acts when our own performances didn't draw enough spectators.

There were also two girls in the group. Antjie Jonker was a teacher, with just enough drama training to give shape and direction to her innate spontaneity and eloquence. She was thirty, rather plump, flamboyant by nature, ready-made for character parts – for nobody could call her attractive, although Jerry assured me she was outstanding in bed (he never missed anything coming his way). On our tours she became an indispensable mother-figure.

A greater difference than that between her and the second girl, Lucy Hartman, was difficult to conceive: Lucy had just turned twenty-one, a tall girl, slim, and devastatingly beautiful, the sort of Mediterranean beauty one would expect on the Spanish coast. It was, naturally, Jerry who'd recruited her.

'Has she any talent?' I asked him.

He kissed his fingertips. 'Try her out yourself, Capey. If a girl can perform in bed, she's ready for the stage. I tell you, she's a natural.'

My own experience, later, was that her performance in bed was much more consummate than on the stage: still, she was good enough, and she was enthusiastic and prepared to stick it out with us – although she probably regarded acting more as a means to an end.

For five months, until the end of December, we worked flat out to forge one dynamic group from eight vastly different individuals, starting with the most basic exercises, with fencing, rhythmic work, mime, improvisation, breath and muscle control, until we'd sufficiently liberated body and voice to become expressive instruments.

And I was happy. If it was true, as Jerry had said, that happiness was a function of blindness, well, then I was blind too, and I'm not ashamed to admit it. For those were the last months of blindness I ever knew.

By the end of November we began to work with more concentration on specific plays for our repertoire. Our opening play, as I'd decided long before, was to be the Calderon. In addition we rehearsed an adaptation of *Le médécin malgré lui* : there remained even less of Molière than of Calderon, but it didn't upset me at all – it was necessary for the *biblia pauperum* we wanted our theatre to be. So we tried to change it into what it might have been if the actors of the *commedia dell'arte* had lived in Cape Town, today, and if they'd been Coloured like us : an exuberant musical with sharp but playful comments on the political scene.

On January 3rd, after the boisterous Coon Carnival of Second New Year's Day, we opened with *Life is a Dream* in the Luxurama. The house was packed, partly as a result of the sensational stories Davey Sachs had splashed in his paper. I suffered from the worst attack of stage-fright I'd ever experienced in my life; we were all so nervous that during the first few minutes we were worse than amateurs. But as we slowly warmed up the auditorium became charged with electricity. By the time the unconscious Segismundo woke up in the palace discovering that his chains and skins had changed overnight into the robes of a prince, we had the whole audience with us. And when, shortly afterwards, he threw an impudent lackey through the window, there was spontaneous encouragement : 'That's right! Chuck 'im out! Kill the bastard!' It almost caused pandemonium when King Basilio ordered the return of the prince to his dungeon.

When Segismundo woke up the second time, once more chained and miserable, there followed a bit of dialogue Calderon would not have recognised :

'Was it a dream?' the prince asked his keeper Clotaldo. 'But you were there too, I saw you. And now I'm back, look at my chains. But why aren't you chained too?'

'I'm White,' replied Clotaldo.

238

'Your day will come,' said Segismundo.

As these words were spoken the entire audience rose up, all those hundreds of people, shouting like one man :

'Yeeeeeeeesssss!'

And only after they'd calmed down again were we able to continue, delirious, shocked, ecstatic. I had trouble controlling my voice in the final monologue : *We are so strange in this world that life itself is like a dream. The rich man dreams his riches, the poor man his rags and tatters. Each man dreams what he is, and none can understand it* . . .

The theatre was deadly quiet after the final curtain. For ten seconds, for twenty, for half a minute there was no sound or movement. But when the applause started it was like the sea breaking through a dyke. After the last curtain-call we began to dance onstage, embracing and kissing each other, laughing, sobbing.

For the first time I could *see* why I had to come back. My blind faith had been rewarded. It hadn't been illusion, it hadn't been in vain.

Yes, I thought, Artaud was right : the theatre really was something like the Black Death, a plague raging in darkness, a delirium, a terrible and contagious thing born from a dark and ancient urge, nurtured by a black sun, as inescapable as freedom.

And attached, says Artaud, to the inexplicable sexual power latent in the oldest myths . . . . : was that why I slept with Lucy that night? Slept?! We were wide awake through every ecstatic moment, close to each other, on each other, inside each other, naked and slippery and smooth, barely conscious of Mrs Geustyn's mother coughing in her room next door; and only with the breaking of the day did we fall asleep, drunken and dazed, our hands between each other's thighs, our bodies sticky, our mouths sated with each other's taste.

And later that morning, just before Lucy left, Oom Appie defied his mother-in-law's chamber pot to visit me and impress upon me the need of a funeral policy.

From the deepest tides of the subconscious the dream returned to me last night, of me and Jessica on the beach beside the pool where we ritually cleanse our bodies; and of the fleet of green ice-cream trucks approaching over the dunes like tanks coming over the hills of a conquered land : and once again I saw her taken away by them, but they stared back at me with terrifying eyes and I discovered that I was naked. Folding my hands over my sex I stopped and looked at them driving away and dissappearing; and then I was on a height far above the sea, like the promontory of Dover reached by Gloucester and Poor Tom, both of them tattered and the old man blind: and still I was naked as I'd been when Jessica had been with me, and on the edge of the white precipice I saw Dulpert standing. He was waving to me, come on, waving, come on, and I started running, but before I could reach him he'd jumped and disappeared into the sea, and I woke up with an erection painful in its stiffness: but why? for there hadn't been any desire in the dream, only anguish: unless one carries anguish with one like white sperm to fertilise destructive nothingness.

For eight nights we performed in the Luxurama, offering our two plays alternately; and there wasn't a single seat open all week. We could have played for double that time, but the theatre had been booked by others and we had to go off into the Western Province, in the brand new kombi which Willem's companies had given us together with a year's subsidy.

In ever-widening ellipses we toured the more accessible parts of the Boland, two nights in every town: in school halls or church halls, many of them prefab; on squares and clearings, weekends in locations; once on a rugby field; often on a commonage behind a row of labourers' houses; and if it couldn't take place in the afternoon – which was usually the case on weekdays – then everybody came with oil lamps and lanterns to light the acting area. There was no fixed admission fee. Instead, we had a collection afterwards, often earning more butts and buttons than cents. But they fed us well, providing us with fruit and grapes in summer, the eggs of stray chickens, often a scraggy little rooster, once even a suckling pig which Doors slaughtered and Jerry cooked, basted from one of the countless bottles of farm-wine which also came our way.

As soon as the kombi stopped somewhere in a cloud of dust, the entire community would converge on us to gape at the actors and help us unload. Sometimes a special permit was required for a performance, but Willem's name was a magic password. And when the hour struck, everybody would be present, some on *riempie* benches or rickety bentwood chairs or even half-decayed Victorian easy chairs distributed among the farmhands by a previous generation of nouveaux riches more interested in acquiring the latest 'Swedish' furniture; but most of them seated on the ground, on bags or blankets: children grey with dust, staring at us with enormous eyes like field-mice, wailing or restive babies soothed with a nipple, teenagers in the latest fashions; older people – labourers and a sprinkling of others 'used to better things'; and even the very old, half-deaf and half-blind and half-senile. There were some who asked whether we represented a sect, others who thought we were either a circus or a political party. But whatever the circumstances or the motivation, the wholehearted audience-participation and wild enthusiasm were the same everywhere.

It was taxing. Not even my rep. years in England had prepared me for such exhaustion. For we seldom knew, once we'd proceeded beyond a certain distance of the Cape, where we would sleep that night, or if we would sleep at all, and where we would perform, and what we would get out of it: fortunately money was the least of our worries, having the safeguard of our subsidy, and the nest-egg of our earnings from the Luxurama.

After three months we returned to Cape Town for another week in the Luxurama, followed by a fortnight in the Little Theatre, under the auspices of the University. At the same time we started rehearsing our next productions: an *Antigone* collage and a wild farce based on Aristophanes' *The Poet and the Women.*

In a way the second tour was easier than the first, because we were better prepared for conditions. But it was also more exhausting. With winter coming on, the weather deteriorated, and it was seldom possible to perform outdoors. In future, I decided, we would stay put during the winter months: a time to rest, a time to experiment, a time for review and consolidation.

But something else happened which was more unnerving and disrupting than physical discomfort and fatigue. It was announced on the radio one night: in a series of raids all over the country the Security Police had detained scores of people for interrogation. Among the names listed in the next day's paper was that of Harry Tsabalala. And two days later Harry Tsabalala was reported dead. 'Of natural causes in his cell,' said the paper.

Jerry immediately wanted to go up to Johannesburg but I restrained him.

'There's nothing you can do there now. And he's left nobody you could help.'

'I want to go and find out what happened. I must know.'

'How will you find out?'

'These things always leak out somewhere.'

'And suppose it leaks out: what can you do about it? What more can you do there than here? Be reasonable!'

'Doesn't it mean anything to you, Capey?'

I could feel my voice trembling in my throat: 'You know me better than that, Jerry!'

He hesitated, then put a hand on my shoulder. 'Sorry, Capey.' After a while, with more composure: 'But there must be something one can do. We can't just go on as if nothing has happened.'

'We won't do the farce tonight,' I said. 'We'll do our *Antigone* again: and we'll do it in such a way that they'll know what it means to say No.'

He looked at me for a long time, before he nodded slowly and turned away; perhaps he didn't want me to see his tears. Or had he noticed mine?

Harry was dead. Part of my own experience had become disjointed through his death. It had been Harry who'd initiated me into my country, he who'd started laughing at Sharpeville and never stopped since. *Of natural causes in his cell.*

That night Jerry came back to me.

'Right,' he said. 'Now we've done our *Antigone*. So what? Is that enough? Aren't we playing a little game, Capey? All round us the world is dying, and we go on acting *Antigone*. Why do we act *Antigone*?'

'Because it's the surest way I know of waking people up.'

'Do you think they're asleep?'

'I want to show them. So that they'll know what is happening to them.'

'And suppose they take it to heart: what then? Will you show them the way from there?'

'In such terrible moments no one can show others the way, Jerry. If we can manage to open a few eyes through what we're doing, then each can decide on his own course of action from there, assuming responsibility for himself.'

'No!' His voice was like a whiplash. 'Capey, if you wake up a woman at night and get into her, you can't withdraw halfway and tell her to finish it off by herself: then you've got to take her all the way.'

'We're not talking about women now, Jerry.'

'What's the difference? You want to open people's eyes – and then stand aside. But let me tell you: in this time, in this country, nobody has the right to stand aside.'

'I'm not standing aside. Why do you think I have come back? Everybody must choose his own area of commitment, and the theatre's mine.'

'But you're more than just an actor,' he said softly. 'You're also a human being. Don't ever forget that.'

That was the watershed in the experiences of our group. To convince Jerry of my sincerity I abandoned the *Romeo and Juliet* project I'd already lined up for our next production, and chose something of more immediate relevance, based on Peter Weiss's *Mockinpott*. It was amazing to discover what new shades of meaning could be brought to light in our context in that devastating comedy about the meek little man who fulfils his obligations towards wife, work and country for a lifetime and then, suddenly, lands in jail. Finally released, and wearing the wrong shoes on his feet, he stumbles through the world trying to find his place again; when everything else fails, he turns to Heaven – to discover that God Himself is merely a capitalist trying to keep His vast concern profitable.

That was the first time we opened in the Little Theatre. Perhaps it was a mistake, for two days later there was a letter in an Afrikaans newspaper complaining about 'blasphemy'; the same afternoon a telegram arrived from the Publications Control Board to stop the play.

After a week of urgent negotiations we were allowed to go on, provided all references to God were cut and the rest more or less emasculated.

Jerry wanted to abandon it straight away, but I persuaded him to go on: once we were on tour, we could start 'working' on it again. He accepted reluctantly. But on the third night of our tour, in an apple shed outside Grabouw, two plainclothes detectives approached us from the audience during the interval, informed us that we'd deviated from the 'approved text', and stopped the performance.

Without asking for the customary collection we carried our things back to the kombi.

'Well, Capey?' asked Jerry.

I looked at him. There was nothing aggressive in his eyes, he even seemed sympathetic, but I knew that a decisive moment had arrived.

'Now we go back to Cape Town,' I said as calmly as I could. 'And tomorrow we start again. If that's the way they want it, fine. We can fight back. They won't silence us.'

I hadn't reckoned with another immediate result of the incident. In some obscure way the story reached the next morning's paper, and when the Publications Control Board reacted by placing a total ban on our version of the play, a press war erupted. The following Sunday Davey Sachs, with the best of intentions, asked the question : 'What is the prominent industrialist, Willem Viviers, going to do about this petty persecution of a group subsidised by him?'

And the prominent industrialist, Willem Viviers, reacted immediately, although in a way different from that anticipated by David Sachs. I received an urgent message that he wanted to see me without delay. The moment I entered his sumptuous office it was clear that he wasn't feeling very comfortable.

He offered me a cigarette and began to talk about the weather, and the farm, and international politics, and rising prices, until I interrupted him :

'I presume it's our theatre group you wanted to discuss?'

He stubbed out his cigarette. 'Yes. Quite a furore, isn't it?'

'Does it upset you?'

'Doesn't it upset *you*?' he asked quickly.

'Of course. On the other hand it's encouraging : it suggests that people are still concerned about what is said in the theatre in this country. As long as that is the case, there's some sense in what I'm trying to do.'

'But to deliberately provoke confrontations . . .' He shook his head. 'That's very unwise.'

'Who provoked it? Who tried to find blasphemy in *Mockinpott*?'

'You know how people feel about these things.'

'You can hear more blasphemy from most pulpits in the country every Sunday than you'll find in *Mockinpott*,' I said. 'What happened was that people didn't like the politics in the play but they were afraid of saying so openly. The additions and alterations we made in Grabouw had nothing to do with religion at all. They were only looking for a pretext to get at us.'

'Now they've got me too.'

'What are you trying to say, Willem?'

He looked down at his hands; his cufflinks were small lumps of gold. 'You must understand my position,' he said. 'I'm not free to do what I want : I must always think in terms of my companies. We're in the money business, our field is economics, not politics. And the sort of thing which has happened now can influence us adversely.'

'So?'

'There are people on my board who are in favour of discontinuing your subsidy.'

'If that's your decision . . .' I got up.

'Wait, Joseph.' He also rose. 'I persuaded them to give you another chance. We have shown that we have confidence in your undertaking and I think we also have some responsibility towards you. If you can give me a written guarantee that you will avoid contentious matters in future, I am prepared to guarantee your subsidy indefinitely.'

'What is your definition of "contentious matters"?'

'Things which tend to cause offence.'

'To whom?'

He didn't answer.

'To the establishment?'

'Why are you so rebellious, Joseph?'

I turned to the door. 'You can keep your subsidy,' I said. 'We'll manage. I'd rather die of hunger than live on that sort of money.'

'Joseph,' he said.

I looked back.

'There's one thing I want to ask of you. Please don't confuse my companies with myself.'

Abandoning my first adaptation of *Romeo and Juliet*, Jerry and I prepared a new one within three days. All we kept of the original was the outline of the plot. Our Romeo, Renier, was a Coloured boy; our Juliet, Lucy, was White.

It was remarkable what a difference the withdrawal of the subsidy made to our existence. Thanks to our earlier successes we still had a fair balance in the bank, so it had no immediate material effect : but the mere knowledge of being on our own created a new sense of unity and purpose in the group. Now we had to prove, through the simple fact of persevering, that we couldn't be silenced or suffocated from outside : and with that our theatre immediately became more than a 'cultural activity'. Whatever we were to present in future – even drawing-room comedy if necessary! – would be interpreted as a form of defiance, a proof of our validity as opposed to 'theirs'. The result was that even in Jerry a new enthusiasm caught fire which inspired the whole group.

'Don't worry, Capey,' he said at one stage, later that year. 'Just tell me if you need money, I'll get it for us.'

And once he did go to Johannesburg for three weeks, returning with nearly a thousand rand which he deposited into our account.

'Where did you get it?' I asked, amazed.

'Ask no questions ... !' he replied.

But there was another change in our lives caused by the withdrawal of Willem's support: suddenly we were no longer protected game, suddenly everyone was free to join the hunt on us. In eight or nine places, where, previously, we'd rented halls without any problem, we now found that they'd been 'booked' anonymously; farmers who'd lent us their sheds now needed the space for more urgent activities; municipalities who'd readily allowed us to perform in their areas now demanded permits or set up impossible requirements. The Provincial Administration, who had allowed us exemption from entertainment tax without a moment's hesitation, now reversed their decision. At all possible and impossible hours, often in the middle of a performance, obscure officials would turn up to check our 'books' or control our tickets, or demand figures and statements we'd never heard about.

Nor did the police leave us in peace. We could no longer go on a journey without being stopped to have the kombi searched, our costumes examined, our texts confiscated. On several occasions performances had to start late or be cancelled altogether because the police would turn up a minute before starting time to check on a hundred different regulations we were supposed to adhere to.

Early in the new year Natal University invited us to present a season of *Romeo and Juliet* in Durban and environment. The first performances, presented by the University itself, took place before mixed audiences so that special arrangements had to be made for them to qualify as 'private' shows, by invitation only. In spite of all the precautions the police turned up five minutes before the opening curtain on the first night, delaying the performance for more than half an hour in order to control the list of invitations; even then they refused to let us proceed unless they were allowed to attend the show themselves. This was done. But directly after the final curtain these same policemen came round to the dressing-rooms to arrest us all because we had allowed them into the auditorium without the prescribed invitation! The University authorities intercepted to prevent our spending the night in custody; and two days later the case was summarily thrown out by a magistrate. But the new furore created by the incident did nothing to make our lives more easy. ('So you're the chaps who always look for trouble, hey?')

But we went on. And we retained a sense of purpose and direction. Relations within the group were cordial and sound. Renier tended to become emotional, Frikkie would occasionally sink into a depression, but we had no serious problems. My only personal worry was Lucy. We still made love occasionally, but it never developed into a definite relationship – a night of passion, an alleviation of physical tensions, a bit of tenderness, that was all. But she wasn't so easily satisfied. In practice, however, it was resolved because she would then go to cry on Jerry's shoulder, and he would take her to bed and comfort her.

There were an endless series of girls on our tours whom he 'comforted' in his way. 'It's good to know that people need one,' he excused himself with a smile.

'Don't you ever get enough?' I asked him.

'Well,' he said. 'I know I can't fuck every woman in the world. But I can at least make a serious effort.'

I, too, would occasionally pick up a girl and share a night's compassion or lust with her, and then move on, ever onward on the elliptical road which had no end but which possessed its own dark significance. I accepted it like that, unable to think of any other way of living.

After our Natal tour we started rehearsing the *Hamlet* which had been dormant inside me for so many years. From the first day there was something special about it; it might well become our best production ever.

We often invited guests to final rehearsals – friends, acquaintances, students – in order to try out the effect of key scenes on them. At one of the last *Hamlet* rehearsals a friend of Jerry's, a lecturer in English at UCT, brought a guest with him: a large angular man with an impressive manner, greying at the temples, with clear grey eyes; he was wearing a very stylish suit which yet appeared untidy on his large frame; and when he was introduced to me I was struck by the hairy backs of his hands.

'Richard Cole,' Jerry's friend introduced him. 'I suppose you've heard of him?' When I hesitated, he added: 'The writer.'

'Of course.' I smiled apologetically. 'You must forgive me: I've not yet read any of your books.'

He grinned: 'That's nothing unusual. I'm listed, so nothing I write may be read over here.'

Something, the barest suggestion that he regarded it as an achievement, made me feel uneasy about him. Yet his eyes were very frank and clear – almost innocuous, I thought – so that I couldn't help liking him. And after the rehearsal he stayed behind for a last short conversation.

At first he only took my hand. Then he said: 'Thank you. You've showed me a *Hamlet* tonight which made me realise how disturbingly modern Shakespeare can be.'

I couldn't make out whether he really meant it, or whether, as a writer, he was only trying to formulate it as deftly as he could.

'Do you realise how much you're risking?' he asked.

I shrugged.

'If you ever land in trouble,' he said, 'please remember: there are many of us who'll back you up.'

The next day there was a small parcel waiting for me in our rehearsal room, a gift from Richard, a copy of his latest novel, inscribed:

To Joseph Malan, fellow fighter. Sincerely, Richard.

Inside was a cutting from the TLS with a very flattering review of the book.

Two days later we opened in the Luxurama and then left on a new tour; in early April we returned for our customary short season in the Little Theatre. On opening night there was a card with good wishes from Richard, inviting the whole group to a party in Oranjezicht the next evening, in the house of friends of his.

And then Dulpert died.

VI

It is impossible to believe that the only reason for our living should lie in a torment that seems to us unjust and inexplicable – Pirandello.

When I'd played the role of the Son in *Six Characters in Search of an Author* in London, I'd first been deeply disappointed: what could one do with a part which kept one onstage through most of the three acts but contained less than five minutes' dialogue? But in the course of working on it I'd found it more and more challenging.

The Director and his group of actors rehearsing on the bare stage, and interrupted by the six Characters, fugitives from the imagination of a writer who has abandoned them – the Father and Mother estranged –

the Stepdaughter encountered in a brothel years afterwards and only recognised when his wife turns up at the crucial moment – the family reunited under the brooding eyes of the eldest Son who loathes˙the stepfamily – the absurd catastrophe of the little girl drowning and her brother committing suicide on the crossing of imagination and reality – the comic and shocking way in which the Director interprets their lives, falsifying everything.

To the Father and the Stepdaughter the stage offers an opportunity of justifying their existence; the Mother's animal grief has some significance too, that of Heidegger's 'unreal being'; and even the two children uncomprehendingly drawn into the action fulfil a function of the victims of the others' egocentricism . . . But what about the Son, what about me?

His only function is to deny everything that happens, a constant No. He has something of the pathos one finds in the brother of the Prodigal Son : the one who remained loyal, who never demanded anything, who never squandered anything – and who didn't even get a fattened calf in the end. What can one do with so much negativity?

And yet : what else can the Son do except say No to the sordid Italian melodrama in which they want to involve him? To say Yes to that sort of martyrdom would be a Yes to all meaninglessness. And he can't do that. Deep in the heart of his rejection of the others' story there must be a terrible conviction of *meaning* in the world : for, only if he believes in the possibility of meaning can he demand the right to reject meaninglessness and madness.

But now his tragedy resides in this, that he forms one of the group of six characters only by virtue of the very fact that he does share their history! He isn't 'human', he isn't even an 'actor' capable of choosing his roles : he is nothing but a character from the mind of a writer who, like God, has turned his back on his creation. His only *raison d'être* is precisely that melodrama he wished to deny : if it hadn't been for that, he wouldn't even have existed. And so he turns against himself.

It becomes even worse. Those six characters, including the Son who belongs to them although he doesn't want to, are so involved in their unfinished 'story' that none of them realises that they have all become part of a different play altogether : that bitter comedy which is born out of their interaction with the Director and his troupe, and which is taking place before the audience. In that way, through his very silence, he becomes a catalyst of the final catastrophe, the death of the children.

Through the years the Son has remained a nagging shadow in my mind : he who has been doomed to futility because he is involved in a play of which he doesn't want to form part; he who persistently closes his eyes to the real play into which he has been thrust.

Had I closed my eyes? Then the worst of all would be the fact that all the time I'd been thinking that, my eyes had been open. It was like dreaming of being awake : and only when one woke up afterwards one realised that it had been a dream. Unless everything was part of a dream like Segismundo's. Or unless there really was an endless series of circles through which one had to break, one after the other, layer upon layer, discovering every time that the previous waking state had been nothing but another station of that long dark sleep.

Perhaps there were those, saints, who one day reached a final awakening. But for that one would have to believe in God : and I couldn't do that any more than the Son could believe in the existence of his Writer.

VII

Dulpert was dead. Jerry brought me the paper that morning, trembling. He wasn't even aware of the fact that I'd known Dulpert. For him it was only another one; yet another one.

' "Natural causes" again . . . ?' I asked with numb lips.

He flung the paper down on my bed. 'No. This time, for a change, it was suicide. Hanged himself in his cell in Durban where the SB had been interrogating him.'

'Then you can't have the name right,' I said. 'If it's suicide it can't be Dulpert Naidoo.'

'Did you know him then?' Jerry asked, stunned.

'Yes, I knew him.'

Yes, I knew you. You turned up at Gran'ma Grace's, in the room where the randy Ursula had lived, and you had an enormous black tin trunk with you which we couldn't open; in the end we threw it from the balcony and woke up the whole neighbourhood, but it was no use; and later pale vegetable shoots began to sprout from it. And you told me what to read, from Marx to Gandhi, and back to the *Kama Sutra*. Then Jim borrowed the book to prepare himself for his marriage, and broke his leg; and when he committed suicide, you took me with you to the morgue in Salt River. There was a capsized cart, remember, and bananas and apples littered the street. One corpse had a ticket tied to his toe. And on our way back you spoke more urgently and seriously than I'd ever heard you speak before.

You taught me to love music, and introduced me to the terminology of the Mahatma : to *ahimsa* and *satyagraha.*

You came to see the plays I was involved in, but one night when a Coloured woman had been humiliated in the street and you'd given all your money to a beggar, you didn't turn up.

You went to the Parade with me to buy a love bed, and sometimes you would sit on it, cross-legged, and hum : 'Om. Om. Om . . .'

You were a friend to me, you were my brother, and now you're dead; and I love you.

I don't know where you've been all these years : perhaps the newspapers will reveal more about it later. But wherever you've been, you shared everything we did together : now you are dead and that half of our memories which you carried has disappeared. Now there will always be something missing from my life : that of myself which I gave you.

The Lord gave and the Lord hath taken away. But for that I cannot bless his name.

In the small blue Austin I'd bought second-hand just before our *Hamlet* tour, and which Jerry had fixed up for me, I drove away from home that morning, up to the Rhodes Memorial. From there I walked further up the mountain, into the silence of the pine trees, to where the landscape of sea and city lay very far and very exposed below me.

I didn't want to see that landscape of sea and city. I didn't want to be there, I didn't want to stay there.

I thought : *How can one go on living in a country in which one no longer believes?*

I thought : *How can one go on living in a world in which one no longer believes?*

And I wondered : *Why is it that love should be akin to despair?*

I'd been back for eighteen months now, longer than that, nearly two years. We'd learned to work together, we'd been successful in many ways. And then the tide had turned against us and it had become more difficult – to go on, and to believe. But we had to go on. And it was a peculiar satisfaction just to know that we hadn't allowed ourselves to be silenced.

But what did it all come to in the end? What had I achieved? Was that what I'd come back for? Was that the function I'd wanted to fulfil? Was that enough? Was that all?

I was tired. For the first time since the day I'd returned on the white steamer, I realised how tired I was, a weariness which had sunk deep into the bones. I tried to recall everything that had happened since that distant day: the banality of my quarrel with the Customs official, the *Whites Only*, the theatres I had to stay away from, Willem's gesture; I thought of my brutal initiation into Johannesburg, of Soweto and the courtroom and the old man on the tall building, and our epic journey back. *Yes, my Baas. Yes, my Crown.*

I searched further back through time, groping for impulses in my childhood: first discoveries: a Nativity play, a circus; a runaway boy beaten until I'd got sick and vomited; a day in Bain's Kloof and a young girl on a rock; a foreman's wife in a privy. I recalled the winter mornings and the slave bell tolling in the dark, and my mother's restlessness on Sunday afternoons, my mother choking on her dry brown bread.

Now I was tired. Now I was alone.

I thought: *I can't go on.*

And then I thought: *No, I can still go on.*

Dulpert had said: One can always go on, one never reaches one's own limit. Dulpert had said: If you remain true to your own nature . . .

Subdued, I went back to my small car.

After the performance that night we went to the party in Oranjezicht. I withdrew into a corner with my glass, morose, defensive against the world.

But later in the evening Richard came to me and said: 'I'd like to introduce you to somebody.'

There was a girl with him. I stood up.

Her hand was cool and firm in mine.

I heard him say: 'Joseph, this is Jessica Thomson.'

Five

Finished, it's finished, nearly finished, says Clov, it must be nearly finished. Grain upon grain, one by one, and one day, suddenly, there's a heap, a little heap, the impossible heap. Soon afterwards blind Hamm will ask: What time is it? And Clov will answer: The same as usual. Outside it will remain dusk, an evening which never draws closer and never recedes, a lasting purgatory. For there are such forms of darkness, I know them well.

I cannot recall the months of imprisonment preceding the trial without interpreting it through *Endgame*: the *Endgame* I'd been working on last, and which we never produced. I know what Annamaria would have said of it: that I'm trying to transform even this last darkness into theatre – she and her purring feline animals in the dark swaying boat accompany me like a conscience – and yet that was what kept me going: that I could experience it as theatre, however macabre, and however final; endgame indeed. For if I had to repeat it in the terms important to Advocate Joubert I would sink. In that night the only remaining facts were the spasms and struggles of the self. It was a form of death, the undiscover'd country, which I cannot, now, narrate in my own words. Moments, yes, but in a fluid, without cause or effect. I know there was a beginning, I remember it well, I think: and there was a sort of end. But in between?

In between was pain. That was dangerous. Not because of its destructiveness or the irrational reactions it called forth, but because pain, pure pain, only pain existed.

But that came slowly, not immediately.

In the charge office the young sergeant with the crewcut read my brief statement back to me and made me sign it, then closed his file and said: 'And then you people want the vote! A little thing happens, and all the civilisation is stripped off, you're just barbarians again.' With his

253

large blunt hands he stroked down the sides of his uniform and turned to the two constables who'd brought me from Bain's Kloof. 'Take him to the cells,' he said. 'I'm coming.'

It was dark already. I remember the sudden ringing of church bells as we walked over the gravel in the courtyard to the white row of cells, sounds shaken loose in the damp air like a flock of pigeons. Of course, it was Easter, the Lord hath truly risen, it was time for the evening service.

The cell was empty. The two constables stood with their backs to me waiting for the sergeant to arrive, then stepped aside to let him enter, and slowly turned round to face me. He was carrying a rubber baton. His face was quite neutral. Naïvely, I hadn't the slightest idea of his intentions before the baton struck me in the face and I heard the crunching sound in my nose. The suddenness and violence of the pain sent me down on my knees. The two constables picked me up from behind. Through red and black pain I shook my head and opened my eyes. The next blow caught me on the right side of my head. The men behind me kept me standing and brought me back for the third. I don't know how long it went on. There was blood in my mouth, in my nose, and ears, I couldn't see any more.

When they let me go, I dropped to the concrete floor.

'Get up,' ordered the sergeant from far off. 'Get up, Hotnot. I'll teach you to mess around with White women.'

I tried to get up, but my legs were useless.

'Get up!' he repeated.

I tried again. Without warning he kicked me in my stomach. I fell forward and began to vomit on the floor and on his heavy boots.

'Pig,' he said. 'Look what you've done. Clean it up.'

With my left hand I tried to reach the boot, but he kicked it away.

'Eat it,' he ordered. 'Every drop of it.'

They hit me across the back while I was licking up the vomit from his boots, through blood and broken teeth. At last it was done, but that was not the end. *Oh no, there is not the end; the end is death and madness.* And there was daylight in the high barred window by the time my eyes got used to a distorted world again.

Someone, I didn't notice who it was, brought me food, a tin plate and a mug, but I couldn't take in anything. I don't know when they came for the things again. The first I knew was when hands grabbed my arms and ankles and carried me outside, the sun was white in my eyes, and I

254

was swung through the air – and landed on metal; a door was barred, and my floor began to shake and rumble. It took a long time before I discovered that I was in a police van, for there was wire-mesh between me and the light.

I tried to get up and finally succeeded. With my fingers caught in the mesh I dumbly sat there staring out at the world shuddering past, vineyards and oak trees, blue mountain ranges in the distance. Like a child learning a lesson I fumbled with thoughts until they began to flow more readily again.

At times I had to lean my head against the mesh to overcome the spells of dizziness. But through the pain a small hard satisfaction took shape. An awareness, without either pride or humility, of: now it's come, now it's happening, yes, and I can endure it. Before the moment arrives one never knows how you'll react to it, whether you'll prove a coward after all. Heroism, no, it wasn't a case of that. All that mattered was: to be able to endure. Now I was inside it, now it was taking its course, and I was *there*. It wasn't like those other times when I could withdraw to a level of detached objectivity. I was present.

The pain never left me. But on the previous afternoon, the Sunday, when I'd come down from Bain's Kloof to the farm where I'd surrendered, I'd exposed myself to whatever might lie ahead, like Jessica's grooved pebble. Not passively. But ready, prepared. And it went farther back than Bain's Kloof. With my head against the mesh I tried to trace it. It went back, at least, to that decision, long ago, to return from London to Cape Town.

Was it Nietzsche who'd said, and where could I have read it, had it been with Dulpert? – that that which doesn't kill me, makes me stronger?

I wasn't dead yet. I was in the back of a van once again on my way to Cape Town. On my way.

It would kill me later, I knew that; that was why I'd given myself up to them. I *wanted* death. But at that moment I was still alive, and I was content. There was, however absurdly, a sort of dignity about knowing: I'm still here, I haven't given up. Without rod or staff to comfort me in the dark valley, I was still going on. Do you see that, Lord? Even against You.

Nearer the Cape the world became more open and empty, a wide inhospitable plain where the wind stirred up dust. It was as if one needed that openness before tumbling into the city: as if all remnants of a previous existence had to be stripped from one, everything reduced to elementary facts of earth and sky, wind and stubborn shreds of vegetation. It wasn't a return to Cape Town like many other times in the past, for what awaited me was not the city, but prison, a cell, a courtroom, and the final certainty of a sentence. My new Cape, this last cape, had nothing in common with the city in which Jessica and I had loved and been together, nothing with Jerry or the Geustyns or Richard or Dulpert or Gran'ma Grace. So I was grateful for the emptiness, for its sobering and purifying influence.

The suburbs unfolded on either side. The shanties and shacks of Windermere, the world of Father Mark : flocks of children, specks of colour moving beyond the high barbed-wire fences fluttering with countless rags and torn bits of paper, pathetically exuberant like the restive festoons of a beggar. Then the Cape broke over us. We stopped in a courtyard. Arms dragged me out. On uncertain legs I was marched into a building escorted by two uniforms. What had to happen would start happening very soon now.

In an office someone told my escorts : 'Take him up to the Security Branch, they're waiting for him.'

The second office I recognised from the previous time; but passively. I couldn't understand why that was happening – it had been a plain murder, nothing to do with the SB – but even that wasn't very important.

That was the beginning.

What's happening, asks Hamm in anguish, what's happening? And Clov answers calmly : Something is taking its course.

'We know each other, don't we?' says the man in the brown jacket. 'You've changed a bit since I saw you last, but we know each other, all right. And if I'm not mistaken, I told you last time you mustn't cry if you got hurt someday, remember?'

'I'm not crying.'

He laughs. 'Oh, but give us some time. We haven't started yet.'

The cell is like a shaft, the walls are so high and close together. They're painted a dark grey, and through the paint, deep into the plaster, names and initials and dates have been engraved, obscenities and *Jesus Saves*. My hair-mattress and my grey blanket with three off-white stripes lie spread out on the floor, below the unreachable window. The bulb is protected by wire netting. In the corner opposite my bed is an open pail which they allow me to empty some mornings. Lounge, dining-room, bedroom, bathroom, all mod. cons., and these same thoughts people this little world. How many years ago did I play Richard II in a class production? And I never got round to *Endgame* in the end. I must exercise my memory, I must arrange my days and set aside hours to rehearse all my old roles. To keep going. We mustn't get mad, Willem said. You can put it on the table over there, thank you, Doris.

The little window is too high to see anything outside, except the difference between day and night. They've confiscated my watch and removed my shoelaces. I suppose one can cut one's wrists with a watch glass or hang oneself on a shoelace. That must be what Dulpert did.

When they're not with me, a gloomy Coloured man brings me food three times a day. A rubbery grey mess and bitter black coffee in the morning. In the afternoon, samp and a curious, bluish, coagulated mass which can be anything; occasionally a bit of rancid bacon. In the evening a monk's meal of brown bread and coffee. By his one oblation of himself once offered, world without end, to the contrary notwithstanding.

'Today you're going to talk,' says the man with the long white hands, wiping his fingers as if they're sticky.

'I've already made a full statement.'

'You haven't said anything yet, my boytjie.'

'I killed her. Isn't that enough?'

'I can't care a fuck whether you did it or how you did it. I want to know *why*.'

'It's personal.'

He casually moves his cigarette very close to my face. My eyes are fascinated by the glowing tip.

'Think before you answer,' he says softly.

'What else is there to tell?'

'We know more than you think.'

I shake my head.

'We know that whore. We were watching her for a long time.'

'Because she didn't agree with what was going on here?'

He grins. 'We know her type. Common little Liberalist opening her legs to every new idea.'

I bite on my teeth. 'She's dead. There's no point in insulting her now.'

'We know her. We know all about her trip through Africa.'

'What do you want me to tell you then?'

'Clear up a few things. About her and your friends.'

'I don't understand.'

'Chap's tight,' he remarks to one of his colleagues, sitting on the table in the bare room. 'He needs some help.' He pulls at his cigarette, blows the smoke out lazily, then returns to me. 'It started with Dulpert Naidoo,' he says.

'You asked me all about him last time.'

'But we weren't very happy with your answers. Don't you think it's remarkable coincidence that Richard Cole should also enter into the picture? And Harry Tsabalala. You seem to like the company of such people.'

I look up. The thin smile is still on his mouth. 'You see?' he asked. 'We keep our eyes open. And what about your so-called theatre group?'

'There's nothing you can bring in against us. We openly . . .'

'I'm not interested in what you did openly. I want to find out what was happening behind that little façade.'

'There was nothing behind it.'

'Listen, man,' he says, 'you're still green in our hands. But you realise we can keep you here for a hundred and eighty days without upsetting anybody. And then another hundred and eighty. Until we've heard the lot.'

'But there isn't anything!'

He walks round the table and returns leisurely. 'In the end we're going to get out of you exactly what we want,' he says. 'So why not make a clean breast of it straight away? You'll save all of us a lot of unpleasantness.'

'There's nothing more I can say.'

'We want to know what you and Richard Cole and Jessica Thomson and your actors were involved in and why it suddenly became so important for her to be removed.'

'You're looking for a cloak-and-dagger story. There's nothing of the sort.'

With his head he motions towards the walls around us, the soft sound-proof asbestos tiles. 'You know this room, don't you? You've been here before.'

I nod.

'Right. We're waiting, Joseph.'

I shake my head.

He stays silent for a long time before he says: 'It's your last chance.'

'I've told you everything I know.'   •

When they pull a transparent plastic bag over one's head there's a strange sensation of relationships in space. For a moment the world is still clear, as always. Then it feels as if you're sucking it in towards you. You try to breathe in the room, you try to grab it, but someone's holding your hands. Then everything becomes double, and turns inside out, and disappears. After it's happened a few times you're no longer sure about which world you belong to. Perhaps you're dead and only the brain is still glowing on for a while; and the questions echoing around you seem to belong to a world you've already shed. But usually the pain comes back, a boot in your belly, a baton across your kidneys, the edge of a hand striking the nape of your neck: and as a result of the pain you can reorient yourself, knowing that at least you're not dead yet. Which is disappointing.

There is another sensation : when they tie your arms round your legs in a squatting position and cover your head with a bag and pass a broomstick under your knees to suspend you upside down. Sometimes it grows very quiet, for minutes or hours on end, only the sound of the blood in your head, until it feels as if it's going to burst. And then there's a voice calling at you through the noise in your ears, and the questions start again, until the pressure on your eardrums becomes too great to make out anything. But you're always brought back to the questions. Sometimes they never leave you at all and when they're not asking questions you can feel their hands tearing at your clothes. You're very exposed in that position, of course, every blow smarts, and they vary them skilfully : the thick, blunt batons which bruise your bones and the thin canes shattering the nerve-ends. It's even worse when they burn you while you're suspended like that, stubbing out their cigarettes on the insides of your thighs or the skin of your scrotum. There's an awareness of weightlessness, as if you're shooting through space like a falling star. Sometimes you can hear your own voice strung from your guts, endlessly and monotonously, like Sagrys's in the shed.

It's a very tall man with a swinging cloak who forces her down into the hay, the rough stalks prickling her thighs, his hands bruising her tiny breasts; and after he's left she discovers the rix dollar in her hand, but the Baas becomes suspicious and has her led out to the yard where they tear off her clothes and the boys take turns with the long whip, laughing with too-loud voices.

'Tell us about Father Mark,' the voices say. 'Tell us about Jerry Buys and Renier Arendse. Tell us what brought Jessica Thomson to this country.'

259

And there's the panic which strikes one when they hold you on the floor and press a length of wood down on your throat to strangle you, slowly, they're not in a hurry, slowly, until you're choking and sobbing; or, if you're lucky, until you pass out. The mouse must have felt like that the day I killed it for Oom Sassie's grandchildren. Only it was faster and it died, and they buried it beside the privy.

Perhaps the indignity is the worst of all. Worse than the pain. But that's only in the beginning, until they've destroyed every vestige of dignity. That must have been the way some saints destroyed their pride, St Simon Stylites with his stinking wounds on his pillar, St John of the Cross in his cell. The active phase of purification, says St John, is followed by the passive phase of fulfilment. And to attain full knowledge of the 'dark night of the soul' both processes must be experienced. To purge and empty and break you down. Only after you've transcended the body and its demands, its need of pleasure and of pain, its love and lust, its fears, its senses, its weight, are you ready to start loving anew; blindly in the dark, warmly, and in silence.

Break down, break down. But how far can it go? Where does the body reach its limit?

The dark grey cell is my home, but transient and penetrable; its obscenities and *Jesus Saves* are inscriptions in the waiting room of a railway station. My body, strange to my own hands and eyes, is one gaping wound. I tend it like a wound, with love, but without getting too attached to it.

Winter is early and bad this year, and it's cold at night, much too cold for my single threadbare blanket. Sometimes I ask the gloomy man who brings my food to let me have another, but he never says anything and never brings anything either. All he's ever confided to me, suddenly one morning, is the news:

'Western Province won yesterday, 12—6.'

Bravo, Province, I think after he's gone, warming my hands round the mug. It's good to know there's still someone winning somewhere in the world.

It's monotonous to be beaten all the time, but one doesn't get used to it either. The difficult part is to keep standing afterwards. Not only for hours, but for days and nights, sometimes with bricks in your hands. They don't bring you any food and you're not allowed to move. Your body, unable to be controlled by orders, fulfils its excretory functions where you stand. Your cheeks grow stubbly, your hands tend to tremble, your pants are messy, your breath is fetid; and if you fall, the heavy boots are there to help you up.

They bring me a sheet of paper and say : 'Sign.'

I try to read through it, but cannot grasp the words. So I ask one of them to read to me, trying my best to concentrate on what he's saying. When he's through, he looks at me, and I bend forward and burst out laughing.

'Are you mad?' they say, pulling me upright. 'What's the matter with you?'

'I don't know,' I say, wiping off the tears.

'Sign here,' they say, forcing the pen into my hand. 'That's all we want.'

'I won't,' I say.

They turn my arm up against my back.

'Sign,' they say.

'No.'

Something snaps and black splinters pierce my brain. Now the arm is useless, I'm like a crow with a broken wing.

One ought to maintain a daily programme of exercises to stay fit, to keep one's mind in order. It helps one to sleep more easily at night as well. But my body has given up. On the stage I used to be able to control every muscle, every nerve, now too many of them are torn or strained or numb.

'Why are you making it so difficult for yourself?' they ask with deep sympathy. 'Do you think *we* enjoy doing it? It's a job like any other.'

I begin to cry because they're so friendly.

'Sit down,' they say. 'Have some coffee. Take your time, no need to hurry.'

The tears run into my cup. I drop the saucer, but they assure me it doesn't matter, the State will pay, it's a trifle.

'We know you're innocent, Joseph,' says the friendly middle-aged man. 'We've found out everything. About the money you got from abroad. And how Harry Tsabalala and Jerry Buys tried to use you. And when it didn't work out they arranged with Jessica Thomson to help them, to draw you into their net. You still refused. And then they forced you too far . . . Just sign here, Joseph, then we'll use you as State Witness.'

'It's all lies.'

'I know you find it difficult to believe that you were exploited by your own friends, even by the woman you loved. But we've rounded them all up. And last night Richard Cole broke down and told us everything.'

'He couldn't.'

'You needn't try to protect anyone, Joseph. We know everything.'

'If you know everything, why don't you leave me alone?'

'We want you to co-operate so that the real culprits can be punished.'

'It's all lies, you don't know anything. There's nothing you can know. There's nothing.'

'Richard Cole has spoken, Joseph!'

'I don't think he has. And if he said what you're saying now, he lied.'

'That girl used you, Joseph. She spent a lot of time in Tanzania with the Chipembere crowd, she was with Frelimo in Moçambique. And all the time you thought she loved you, she was using you in a deliberate and callous and completely unscrupulous manner.'

Things haven't worked out so well for Hermien, he says. A chap from the Transvaal, and she was left in the lurch with a baby. They're living in the Robertson district, they're not very happy.

'Come with us,' they say, leading me to a small room I haven't seen before. The only furniture inside is a tall bed, like a hospital bed, I suppose they want me to have a baby. When they take a Coloured to hospital it's jus' to die, says my mother. They order me to strip, beating me with a rubber baton when my lame hand fumbles with the buttons. Get on the bed, they say. There's a rubber sheet on it, sprinkled with water. They jerk my useless arm up to the head-post to tie it up : strange, I didn't think it still had any feeling left. Then the second wrist. And my ankles down below. I lie waiting. They open the lid of a small black box and attach a copper wire to each little toe. It's difficult to move my head, but it seems as if someone is cranking a handle. Like an old-fashioned gramophone, His Master's Voice. Sudden stalagmites of pain pierce upwards through my legs and my body jerks uncontrollably.

'Are you going to sign?'

'No.'

They lift the electrodes to my earlobes. Splitting through my head my gramophone voice screams into darkness.

He lies spreadeagled among the horses and when the animals are suddenly, violently hit on the rumps they tear him apart, galloping off to the four corners. The labourers are allowed to have the meat for burial.

There's a long desolate strip of beach protected by high rocks on either side and the dunes inland, and hand in hand we wander to a pool formed by the high tide, warm and still beneath the sky. Our bodies are covered by sand. I begin to wash her, her shoulders, and small round breasts, her hips and belly and legs, and kneeling before her with my arms round her, my tongue discovers the sea inside her. 'I'll wash you too,' she says, cleansing me the way women wash a corpse. But I have no sex, the small crabs must have nibbled it off. 'I'll bury you,' she says, and helps me to lie down, spreading out my arms and legs and covering me with sand. The small crabs devour my eyes, and as they scurry back to the water's edge I look through their protruding stick-eyes and see her kneeling beside the cross she'd planted between my legs.

Hamm, blind Hamm, spreads his handkerchief in front of him and says: We're getting on. You weep, and weep, for nothing, so as not to laugh, and little by little . . . you begin to grieve. If I can hold my peace, and sit quiet, it will be all over with sound, and motion, all over and done with. I'll have called my father and I'll have called my . . . my son. Ah let's get it over!

In between there are long silences, which are often worse. Days, it may even be weeks, when I see no one except my surly jailer. They don't let me out to stretch my legs, at most I'm allowed down the red-brick passage to empty my pail some mornings. The silence brings no peace, for although they're not with me I know they can return at any moment, and in their absence they're really more terrifyingly present than when they're interrogating or torturing me. There's a small peephole in the door and although one can never hear anything in the passage outside I know they spy on me, which falsifies all movements, changing them into theatrical gestures in front of a mirror, like Pirandello's. It's good to think of Pirandello, it's good to think of anybody, to keep the thought processes going.

With brushes and glue buckets one goes down the immobile escalator to the empty platforms below, plastering the new posters to the walls, the naked and half-naked girls advertising bras and panties and stockings, the agencies, Guinness, Benson & Hedges. One introduces those signs of the exterior world into this subterranean darkness as if they're really relevant: read the *Evening Standard* and don't be vague, say Haig, and dream your dreams in your Maidenform Bra. It's important. On either side the open black tunnels glare like the empty sockets of a skull. If only I knew when they're coming back. If only I knew what's still going to happen. If only I knew when it's going to end. At the entrance to the prostitute quarter there's a large neon sign announcing: *Jesus Calls You*, and beyond that, in the silent lapping water of the Amstel, lies her river boat below the Westermarkt, swaying on the slow tides. Her nails are bitten, her hands always smudged with paint, under the clothes her body is very white, and in the darkness around us the cats are fighting and devouring their meat. Out of the belly of hell cried I, and thou heardest not my voice, she's a heathen but her paintings are like stained-glass images of saints and angels. If only I knew when they're coming back.

My only future is a negation. Therefore, to say that one can't live without some form of expectation, is a distortion and an abstraction. The needle of my compass indicates exclusively the past. I dare not be untrue to that, I must assume full responsibility for it. I don't believe in the future, says Annamaria, for it doesn't last. The only lasting things are the past and this moment. I'm connected to all the humiliations and failures of my ancestors. That is the sum of my morality.

But it's difficult. Everything is threatened and tested. Oom Koot's teeth are washed away by the sea and to wreak vengeance on God he drinks himself into a stupor on Communion wine: but how can one get drunk from blood?

With the Jewish trader he travels through the Eastern Cape singing his songs to the people and reciting his poetry; and taking the slaves and Hottentots aside he teaches them the obscure wisdom of liberty, equality and fraternity. He preaches to his wife Sbongile and their child: and if they don't pay attention, he addresses the flies and tells them that they are born free. Nothing can silence him, except, at last, death.

There aren't flies left in the cold, but I find enough fleas and bedbugs in the thin folds of my blanket to subject to discussions on Kant and Camus and long monologues on the theatre, on the most effective approach to Morocco and Segismundo, a project for *Endgame*, and the essential difference between Othello and Iago. I crush them between my nails and recite long passages from my past roles to their dead bodies. They are my only audience, they and the invisible eyes behind the peephole in my door. If only I knew when they're coming back.

'Tell us about the money,' they say. 'Those large amounts paid into your account from abroad.'

'Is it illegal to get money from abroad?'

'We want to know where it came from.'

'It's all in the books.'

'Suppose we tell you it came from the ANC?'

'That's not true.'

'Do you mean to say we're lying?'

'Yes.'

'Bring the black box, Sergeant. He's been sitting too long. Put one wire on his tongue, perhaps it'll teach him to speak.

One grows weary. Blind, he wanders through the world in search of his child. Everywhere he finds rumours of her, but he can't find her. Until weariness takes over and he lies down in Bain's Kloof, too tired to go on living. What does it matter, he asks : the night is the same everywhere. But the night isn't the same everywhere, it was different with Jessica on the mountain, it was different in the theatre, it was different on her balcony, and one's tongue is so sensitive, it's like eating the pain, swallowing it, as if you'll never be without it again.

My body has become thin, I can count my ribs, and my arm is useless. I don't think I'll recognise my face if I see it again. All those hours in the bath with her, and look at the dirt covering me, the stench of Job is in my nostrils and I can taste it on my bitter palate.

You've got such a beautiful body, she says. Don't move. Her charcoal pencil grates on the stiff paper. I turn to the wall, rubbing myself dry with the towel, angry and embarrassed about my erection. And if you come in through the door, suddenly the David is standing there, overpowering, one arm tense, the other relaxed, his face so beautifully arrogant, and below his young belly the sex quiescent on the large full balls. He can still have children. With Giacometti's figures it's different, they're thin and wind-blown cypresses, tortured saints, mere shadows, figures like Beckett's, Vladimir and Estragon, or old Nagg and Nell in their dustbins, or Clov.

'You're filthy,' they say. 'Go and wash yourself properly.'

From all the extremities of the body the fierce cold creeps into my blood, deeper to the small remaining pith of life. I try to keep moving to stimulate the circulation, but my legs are too frozen to move.

'Dance for us,' they order.

Strange that a body so numb with cold should still be so sensitive, but the sjambok burns through it all, cutting into the skin, and the blood crawls out, trembling and surprised, dissolving in the water. On my shoulders and back and kidneys and buttocks and legs, and then the front, my belly, my sex and thighs.

'Sing,' they say. 'One always sings under a shower.'

265

The blood comes singing from my body, forming small puddles round my feet. Come and drink it, Oom Koot, don't be afraid, it won't make you drunk.

'Come on, man,' they say. 'Sing for us, dance for us.'

God, I'm tired, she says, gimme that rest where I newwe' got to open my two eyes again on de hungriness en' de soreness of a new day, gimme, Lawd, that sleep what got no end.

What do I give her? I ask mockingly. Bread or stone? But cursing over his *dolosse* beside the drum with coals he spits it back at me: You give him night.

It should be possible to commit suicide. Just go on living, says Simon, that's the surest way of all. It's simply a matter of waiting for the right moment, when they're not on their guard, or not too close. If you can get past them, you can jump through the window, glass and all. With a bit of luck you'll fall to your death outside. Else you can tear your blanket into strips and hang yourself from the bars of the window, provided, of course, you can reach so high. For hours I contemplate and examine the possibilities, working out the finest details. But I never try to put it into action of course. Just go on living, says Simon.

It's not because I'm too tired or my body too weak, one can get past that. It's simply that I have no right to. I've had a chance, and in complete lucidity I decided to give myself up to them. If I die, which will happen sooner or later, it must be *they* who perform the deed. That's all I have left, else I would deny everything which has happened so far. Everything. And one cannot suffer all this and then give up. It may be Camus speaking again, but then in my own voice. With all my silence I'll pit myself against them to the end. That is all which still makes sense: to continue saying No to them, so that they can perform it. They have their part to play, I mine; and neither may be unfaithful to that.

What fascinated me from the beginning in Pamplona was that the bull had no chance. Sometimes, of course, the matador gets killed and often he's gored: but it makes no difference, existentially, to the fate of the bull. And yet, with the outcome a foregone conclusion, and without any possibility of escaping, he plays the game to the end. I suppose the difference may lie in the fact that he doesn't know it, while I do. But I think, judging from the best corridas I can recall, that the bull certainly knows. And his beauty lies in the fact that he doesn't try to avoid anything, that on the last moment he lowers his head for the sword, serene in the face of the inevitable, yet without defeat.

You will kill me. Not because you're so clever or so powerful or violent. Not even because I'm so tired. But because I have decided it, because I will it so. Because that is the only role this life and this country has assigned to me, and because I have accepted it. I shall say Yes to death. He is my brother. Through generations and centuries he has been born into me. But to *you* – to you I shall never cease saying No.

'Wash yourself properly,' they say. 'Come on, pick up your feet. Higher. Faster. Dance for us.'

He dances. Standing in the middle of the floor, his eyes tightly shut and his face distorted with concentration, he dances, gyrating slowly, without moving from that one spot, the large, thin, black man : he doesn't sob or pant, but the tears are running slowly from under his closed eyelids, until long after the record has stopped playing. Don't cry, man, he says. Tomorrow we're going home.

Until it's no longer cold but languidly warm; until I'm no longer standing, but lying down, with her in my arm. Quiet, quiet, you're keeping me awake, says Hamm wearily. Talk softer. If I could sleep I might make love. I'd go into the woods. My eyes would see . . . the sky, the earth. I'd run, run, they wouldn't catch me.

My clothes lie on the floor in a small dirty bundle, I lie on my mattress in a bundle. They've covered me with the blanket, but I'm still wet under it. It may be perspiration. I can't make out whether I'm warm or cold, there's no difference any longer. I feel drowsy, sleepy. But I mustn't. I must get up and put on my clothes. I mustn't make it easier for them. Of natural causes in my cell.

These are my clothes, this is my mattress, this is my cell. I know them. I love them.

What are you doing here, Ma? I ask her.

How d'you mean? We living here. It's our place.

What makes it our place?

Yo' place is yo' place.

That other Missus said I don' know my place.

The hell, she says.

She sat there, I think. I saw her. She a White woman. And there's no difference, none at all, it's exactly the same, God, and it smells just like a Coloured's.

The cold, returning, becomes worse. It's impossible to sleep at night and my lungs are racked by coughing fits. Sometimes, when I wipe my lips, there's blood on my hand. Perhaps the fever will destroy me. But l don't want it to. I struggle violently against it. I don't want to take it out of their hands. They must decide for themselves how far they are prepared to go. I've made my decision.

Sometimes Dulpert comes to visit me and we have long conversations. I think he's more pleased with me now, I haven't failed him yet; so far I haven't been unworthy of him. If only I can go on. We'll still get that trunk open. If only one knew.

To go on, to endure. It would be so easy just to let go. This doubt is agony. For there's no reason left, it's all blind now. How can I know that I'm not mad? How can I know that it will have meaning in the end? Who will know if something happens to me, who will care? All that matters is what has already happened. And to be loyal to that, even if nobody knows. Even if I myself don't know anymore.

What's he doing? asks Hamm.

Clov raises the lid of Nagg's bin, looks into it, and says: He's crying.

Then he's living, says Hamm.

Somewhere in these cold months it's my birthday. Perhaps it's passed already, perhaps it is today, perhaps it's still ahead. Strange that one should want to maintain this little link with chronology and history. It'll be my thirty-third, and this time we won't go to the circus, my mother is dead. He travels all over the country, missing everything. Magersfontein, Colenso, Spioen Kop, Paardeberg, the lot. But early one morning they shoot him outside Worcester and present him to history, a Cape Rebel. Capey, if you wake up a woman at night and get into her, you can't withdraw halfway and tell her to finish off by herself; then you've got to take her all the way.

If I choose again, now, if I could start right from the beginning again, knowing exactly what was going to happen, would I change it in any way? Would I be wiser, more careful, more suspicious, more 'realistic'? I must be very clear in my mind about it. Suppose I could walk out of here today and start from scratch?

She's sitting on a rock, her pussy and her smill tits wet, untouchable. Mother of God, look at the soft hair shining on the roundness of her arm. She says: If it was good for you, I'm glad. She says: My God, it isn't your fault that I love you! From behind I move my hands under her arms and put them on her breasts naked under the large sweater, and in the small bare room on the stripped mattress, half clothed and half unclothed, we violently make love.

Here's a pebble. Look, it's a little girl.

I shall love her again. It's so obvious, so clear. It's the only pride I have left. No dignity, nothing of significance, nothing important, just this bit of love. Even my rebellion is love. They can take everything away from me, but not this, for this is me. Before, I sometimes was an actor, sometimes lover, sometimes traveller, sometimes this or that. Now they've stripped me until there's nothing else left, only a man, wretched and weak and thin and cold and hungry and full of love. More and more man, more and more nakedly man, with all the rags peeled off. He loves her. They're mere children, but they love one another. With their bruised bodies they escape into the wilderness, in the night she gives birth, death gnaws at them. They try to find safety among the Israelites with their rusty swords, but death finds her there. There is no Last Judgement, and the victory of the Black race remains a dream like Nonkwasi's. But he goes on loving her memory, looking after their child; and even when he's stoned to a pulp at Kazerne, that love remains somewhere and finds its way.

'Come,' they say. 'Now we've had enough of you. Today you're going to talk.'

I shake my head.

'Look at you,' they say. 'Aren't you ashamed of yourself?'

Somebody pushes me from the front, and I fall down.

'Get up, dog.'

There are more of them today than ever before. They're pushing me around, from the one to the other. They pick me up and throw me against the wall, I don't weigh much. They spin me round until I'm dizzy and kick me from the one to the other.

I've long ago lost control of my bladder and my guts. My ankles tend to give way when I walk. My broken wing hangs limply down. One of my ears has gone deaf; I have double vision. In the centre of the floor I lie in a bundle, shivering like a mouse after a cat has played with it for some time.

'Looks as if he's cold,' they say. 'Let's warm him up.'

They form a long row, legs astride, each with a baton or a length of hose or a belt with a buckle.

'Take off your stinking rags,' they say. 'Down on your hands and knees. Move on.'

It's difficult with one useless arm.

'Faster,' they say.

I fall prostrate.

'He's out,' they say. 'Pour water over him.'

It burns my trembling body.

'He's cold again,' they say. 'Warm him properly.'

I say to myself – sometimes, Clov, you must learn to suffer better than that if you want them to weary of punishing you – one day. I say to myself – sometimes, Clov, you must be better than that if you want them to let you go – one day.

They tell me to stand up, but I can't stand. Some of them hold me upright, others come with matches. They lift up my arms and singe my armpits. They open my legs and singe my pubic hair. I want to fall, but they're holding me steady. I lose consciousness, but they revive me with cold water. There is no end to it. Tonight there is no end. It is night, I can see it through the window. Is that what you meant, St John? Then purify me. Liberate me from myself.

'He's cold again,' they say. 'Warm him up.'

'He's warm,' they say. 'Cool him off.'

They insist that there must be a code message in *The Pilgrim's Progress*. The other prisoners stand watching from a distance while his broken body is dragged behind the Commandant's jeep. They murmur rebelliously, but the guards have them covered with their machine-guns. And the jeep drives on, until nothing remains but a bundle of dusty flesh and bones. Something must remain, matter is indestructible.

Will they always just look on like dumb animals? Or will they one day storm the fence? The machine-guns will mow them down. But perhaps three or four will reach the fence and overpower the guards and take their guns. Perhaps one or two will break out and throw open the gates. Perhaps.

I hang crucified in their arms. My breath is a small bleeding animal struggling in my throat.

'Have you had enough?' they ask. 'Say, "Baas", then we'll stop.'

'I won't.'

'Bring the black box,' they say.

'No,' I whisper.

'Say "Baas".'

'No.'

'His toes,' they say. 'Say "Baas".'

'No.'

'His thumbs,' they say. 'Say "Baas".'

'No.'

'His ears,' they say. 'Say "Baas".'

I shake my head.

'His nipples,' they say. 'Say "Baas".'

I move my head.

'His balls,' they say. 'Say "Baas".'

I try to move my head.

And then, suddenly, the David is in front of one, just a replica of course, but unforgettable in its greatness. *Ecce Homo*.

'Take him back to the police,' they say. 'Tell them to go ahead with the murder charge. He won't get away.'

All I'm afraid of, shivering, sobbing, feverish, delirious in my cell, is that they may still find a means for me to get away. For that, I know, I won't be able to endure.

Dulpert is very close, and Jessica. Touching each other.

Don't let me get away.

You cried for night, says Hamm. It falls: now cry in darkness.

Six

I was still confused by the interruption of my thoughts, unable to arm myself with social politeness, and for a while all I could do was to stare at her. She was small, and slight, wearing a mauve vest and faded jeans, with a wide leather belt round the hips. Her hair was darkish blonde, not very long, just touching her shoulders; and then that pair of large dark brown eyes, smouldering but serene. Our host came up to call Richard Cole away from us, and we were left alone.

'I told him not to bring me to you, I could see you didn't want to be bothered.' A brief pause as if she was waiting for me to protest. 'I won't intrude, I'll go away again.'

'No.' I made a vague gesture with my glass. 'Sit down.'

'Why don't you tell me to fuck off if you prefer to be alone?' she asked point-blank, her dark eyes glowing with light. There was nothing uncouth about the way she'd said it, nothing provocative either; and after the broad Cape accent to which my ear had grown accustomed again her warm voice had the gentle singing syllables of British English.

'What did he say your name was?' I asked after a moment.

'I knew you weren't listening. Jessica.'

'I've been wondering for years.'

'What do you mean?'

'I met you in Manchester, long ago.'

'I've never been to Manchester in my life.'

'On a painting by Millais,' I said. '*Autumn Leaves.*'

For a moment she was put out. Then she asked, searchingly: 'Do you like the Pre-Raphaelites?'

'I adore them.'

'But how did you know that I . . .' She frowned pensively. 'Which one on the painting is me?'

'You have something of all of them. I suppose the resemblance with the little one holding the apple is the most obvious, only your hair is darker.'

'I used to call her Little Miss Muffet,' she said. 'All through University I had a print of it on my wall.'

'But I think you take after the redhead,' I added.

'In what way?'

'She's so serene. But I think she can be a bloody little hell-cat too.'

'My own favourite is the oldest girl, the one pouring the leaves on the heap to be burned.'

'I find her disturbing. She's so provocative, a little virgin with a "What are you going to do about it?" air about her. And so sad too. Something ageless. She looks so straight at one.'

'I wish I could see it again,' she said.

'I've a copy at home. I'll show you sometime.'

'Please. And you must also . . .' She stopped.

'What?'

'I'd like to talk to you about your Hamlet tonight. But in the day-time, not now. I'm still too close to it, I still feel too upset. You know, I've been in the country for six months now, but tonight for the first time I discovered what it really was all about.'

'How did you interpret it?'

She spoke absently, as if she hadn't heard my question: 'The dark crown-prince playing the clown, rejected, soothed, cajoled. Until nothing but madness remains.' She looked up. 'But I told you I didn't want to discuss it now. Neither do you, I should imagine.'

'No. In fact I find it almost unbearable to discuss a performance with people. Isn't it ridiculous? If they don't say anything, I'm in a state – I *must* know whether they liked it, whether they understood it: but the moment they do start talking about it, I want to run away. I suppose that's what a slave must have felt like on the market place, long ago: standing naked in his chains surrounded by buyers who examine him, opening his mouth to count his teeth, feeling his biceps, measuring his shoulders, testing his legs, weighing his balls on their hands . . .'

'Your imagination is too vivid.'

'My ancestors were slaves.'

With a quick movement of her head she looked at me.

Deliberately testing her, I said: 'On the farmyard where I grew up we were still awakened every morning by the old slave bell.'

Her reaction was quite spontaneous : 'I had a small blue alarm clock. And a Nanny, who used to divide the day very precisely into hours and half-hours.'

'It sounds oppressive.'

'In some respects, I suppose.' She brightened. 'But she also knew the most wonderful stories, I don't know where she got them from . . . And in the back garden of our estate she cleaned a small summerhouse for me, with a painted board saying *Ivy Manor*. And nobody ever disturbed me when I was playing there. The whole garden was my kingdom, with castles under the elms and the beeches . . .'

She spoke, and I listened; and then I spoke again, and round us the hours of the night went their way : the guests departed, the host and hostess joined us for a late liqueur and then they, too, went to bed – it was that sort of household – and we remained in our corner of the smoke-filled room talking, talking with unquenchable thirst. It was as if, breathless, we daren't stop for a moment because then something would remain unsaid; and we had to talk on, exposing everything which lay eager and waiting within us. I was half-sitting, half-lying on the settee; she sat on the thick carpet, her sandals kicked off, her knees pulled up. Never in my life, not even that afternoon on the Heath with Beverley, have I had such a conversation. It was as if in one night I had to unburden a lifetime's walled-up talking, receiving her life in return. The growing frustration dominating my life since my return to Cape Town, the struggle against despondency and despair, the thousand trivial irritations, the exhaustion of a long tour with *Hamlet*, Dulpert's death – all that weary bewilderment in me wanted to get out, like a herd of cattle trapped in a kraal, dumb with struggling, who'd suddenly found a breach in the wall and now came bursting out. I was tired of containing everything inside me, tired of going on, tired of the tension of holding on to faith in an uncertain future : I wanted to talk and rid myself of everything in order to be purged, so that I could start again, naked and new, like somewhere on a beach, washed clean.

We were barely conscious of the chaos around us : the overfilled ashtrays, the butts on the floor, the empty bottles and cans, the large dishes with wilted lettuces and asparagus, the scattered olives : we went on talking.

She told me of her upper-middle-class parents and her beautifully protected youth, of Oxford where she'd spent three years, and LSE afterwards. And then of her year-long hitch-hiking journey down through Africa, from Ethiopia through Kenya and Tanzania and Malawi; of dingy holes she'd shared with three families and their poultry; of the shells and pottery and weaved fabrics on the market of Dar-es-Salaam; of Zanzibar's palm beaches where she'd collected shells with a young Arab and of the coral reefs at Mtwera where she'd skin-dived in the lukewarm water; of a Sicilian doctor in Kenya whom she'd accompanied, as nurse and secretary, on a clinic tour through the bush, and a German pilot who'd been killed in an accident shortly after showing her Ngorongoro; of farmers on the White Highlands and missionaries on inaccessible outposts; of colonial officials, adventurers, pariahs and alcoholics in Nairobi and Mombasa and Addis Ababa; of a young teacher couple in Blantyre she'd stayed with; of a priest who'd tried to seduce her on Pemba . . . and through all that she'd come unscathed, with that radiant smile and that unassailable serenity.

'But didn't you have problems sometimes?' I insisted.

'Of course, every day. Half the time I was trying to keep drunken or sex-mad men from my body. There was a night when I really thought I'd had it: an army officer in Addis Ababa . . .' She suddenly laughed and looked up at me: 'But have you ever tried to rape a girl in jeans in a sleeping-bag?'

'And it didn't upset you?'

'Upset? At the time, yes. But then it was past. One can't carry something like that with one. I don't think it left any real scar. Not that sort of thing. But there were others . . .' She looked down at the carpet, tracing the outline of her feet, slender feet with irregular toes which fascinated me. Then she resumed, absently: 'There were others. Wherever I stayed for some time. People who meant it seriously. Who wanted to get married. And then, every time I had to pack my things again and go on. That was the most difficult part, especially when I liked them too.'

'What were you scared of then?'

'If one's travelling, every moment is so . . . self-contained. And every person too. You can't tie yourself to a future.'

'But you can't go on travelling all your life.'

'No. One day . . . It's difficult to explain, it sounds pretentious. But you see, I left home so that I could . . . somewhere, somehow, by exposing myself to the world . . . learn to know something about myself. Something not determined or defined by my parents or my class or my education or friends or anything outside. Something exclusively my own. And

I think it would be presumptuous to tie myself to anyone before I've discovered who I am.'

'Does one ever know? Can you ever "be" somebody? Aren't you just . . . *en route* all the time?'

'Perhaps. But even then I must – how can I put it? – keep up with being *en route*. My eyes must be open, I must be aware of what's happening.'

'Has South Africa made any difference?'

'South Africa?' She sat thinking for a while; the night grew old around us. 'I told you I've been here for six months now. But I'm still struggling to get a grip on the country. Richard has helped me a lot, but I am still not sure. People over here are so . . . so preoccupied with things. It comes as quite a shock after the rest of Africa. It's as if, here, they're trying to deny, or at best ignore, that they're part of the continent. And there are small things . . .'

'Like what?'

'Trivial things, I suppose, but nonetheless upsetting. You see, everywhere on my trip I made new friends and went home with them and stayed with them, White or Yellow or Brown or Black. But here . . . They seem to become suspicious if one starts asking questions, as if everybody's suspecting everybody else. And I've had trouble with the police, too, when I tried to visit friends in the townships. All those regulations . . .'

'Are you sorry you came?'

'Of course not. In England life is so theoretical if you belong to a privileged class. Here you're immediately involved in everything, whether you want to or not. And I must get away from protection. I must make myself vulnerable – to everything.'

'That can be dangerous.'

'It is dangerous. Sometimes I even think I must be a little bit mad. But you see, there's such an urge in me to be "free", to be "independent".' I tried to interrupt but she stopped me : 'I know what you're wanting to say. And I'm deeply conscious of it myself : a person who's so obsessed with independence is often merely trying to deny that, in reality, he can't exist without others. And if you are by nature dependent on others and yet deny it, then you're really being untrue to yourself. Which makes it even more impossible to be free.'

'What is the "freedom" you're looking for? To be able to do exactly what you want? Then you can easily become the slave of your own convictions.'

'I know. That's why I'm really fighting on both fronts at the same time. And it's exhausting, Joseph.' With her intense eyes she looks at me: 'I suppose you'll laugh at me: but sometimes I feel so terribly old, as if I'd learnt too much too soon.'

I couldn't help laughing. 'You, old?'

'I know I'm not twenty-five yet. And perhaps it's just an adolescent obsession with me. But often – how can I explain it? – I feel so second-hand. And then it seems to me that the only thing in life which remains worthwhile is innocence.'

Grey daylight was filtering through the window.

I hesitated for a second, then asked directly, with my eyes on her: 'When did you lose your virginity?'

Smiling wryly, without any hesitation, she said: 'That's not what I meant with "innocence" at all.' Somewhere in a passage a clock was striking. 'But it may have some connection. Not with the fact that it happens. But with the way in which it happens.' She leaned with her back against my knees. 'It was in Spain, my first holiday without my parents, one July, after I'd left school. On the Costa Brava, near Port Lligat. The parents of one of my friends had a villa above the village, an enormous castle-like place. We were like a lot of young horses suddenly let loose. We swam in the day and danced at night, and had picnics on the beach, and ran wild. Within a week the villa'd become a sanctuary for all the adventurers and homeless souls on the Costa Brava. Young Spaniards, single Americans, Germans, God knows what else. Like flies catching the smell of those flowers – what do you call them? – they look just like a woman's . . .' She broke off, embarrassed. 'My friends all had bets on their conquests. I felt quite lost and reckless at the same time. All the way through school I'd been so safe and protected, you see. But I wanted desperately to be free, and not to be shamed by my friends.'

'So you did the same?'

'Yes. But with one man only, a young Australian. They all thought he was terribly handsome. To me he looked a bit grotty, and that night he was high too. I actually had to help him. It didn't hurt or anything, it was just – so damned ordinary. Afterwards I lay awake thinking: "Is that what all the fuss is about?" You know the way one feels when you read an ad and order something, but then send it back with a little note: "Please refund my money." Only, I couldn't send this back. It wasn't something I'd got, it was something . . . taken away. I stayed with him till the end of the holidays. It wasn't a matter of "Close your eyes and think of England" – but the earth didn't move either, the way it does for Hemingway's girls. And I kept convincing myself that now I was free, now I was free, now I was free. You know? *"I am smilin'."*

'And afterwards?'

'One's life seems to form a pattern: you may learn, but you never really change. And that's what frightens me. At LSE one of my lecturers . . . it was Easter and he invited me with him. That was lovely. Only those five days, and he was very considerate and gentle. It was as if he'd released something in me. I wanted to cling to him, I felt safe with him. At the same time I knew it couldn't last. Bill was married and although they weren't terribly happy I knew he wouldn't ever get divorced. To him it was a sweet escapade, he was pleased to add another student to his list. And I wanted to help him achieve his aim! I sometimes think I have an urge for the impossible.'

'It may be a way of protecting yourself: then you know beforehand you won't really get caught.'

She laughed quietly. 'Maybe. One is so complicated, really. And yet, if I could really choose, you know, I think: to love someone without reserve, to be loved in return, to be together . . . Someone who doesn't stay with me because he needs something, but because he wants *me*, and I him. And nothing from the outside. But do you think that's possible?'

It was quiet. Outside the light had increased. I got up to look through the window, perturbed and surprised. I, too, had been struggling towards self-containment all my life. When I'd had the choice, with Beverley, I chose aloneness with open eyes. But wasn't Jessica right after all? if one were really honest, how could you deny that you needed someone else, that you sometimes reached a moment where you couldn't go on alone, where you didn't want to?

I turned back to her and stretched out my hands to pull her up from the carpet. She smiled, she was so small in front of me, so warm. We didn't touch each other; we didn't speak. But I felt something in me, an illogical joy, a sense of homecoming.

After a long time, she said: 'The sun is out. I must go home.'

'I'll take you. My car is outside.'

'I prefer to walk. It's so lovely outside.'

'Then I'll walk with you.'

We walked through the early morning streets, up towards Kloof
Nek. At first we still went on talking, but as the sun rose higher we
became silent. The day was like an impostor between us, and it was as
if we'd suddenly become ashamed of looking at each other because
our faces were so naked. Our breathless conversation, the whirlpool
and wonder of the past hours, all that could only have been possible
in the night, because of one's vulnerability in the dark, and the way it
sets one free to be sincere.

Now the day had broken over us; and everything we'd been through
appeared vaguely incredible, part of a different dimension.

In front of the old building high up on the mountainside where she
had her flat, we looked at each other again, briefly, shy, but smiling.

'You must go to sleep now,' she said. 'You've got another performance
tonight and I want it to be just as good as last night's. I'll come again.'

'I'll sleep all day, I promise. You too?'

'Me too. Good-bye, Joseph.'

'Good-bye, Little Miss Muffet.'

II

'To pray on a mountain won't bring Dulpert Naidoo back to life,' Jerry
said fiercely when I invited him to the funeral service on the slopes of
Signal Hill. 'It won't move the Government suddenly to feel remorse
either. So what's the use of it? A mere gesture. You know what I – and
Sartre! – think of gestures!'

'A thousand people gathering for such a purpose makes something
happen, Jerry! They help one another, it gives them a sense of direction
again.'

'They only take a thousand roads back home again.' He was adamant.
'It's past the stage of praying, Capey.'

'What do you want to do then?' I asked, startled.

His lean, dark face was inscrutable, his eyes as mocking as always:
'You do it your way, Capey; I'll do it mine.'

'Do you mean . . . ?' My mouth felt tense. 'You're not leaving the
group, are you?'

. 'No,' he reassured me. 'It suits me very well like this. For the time
being.'

'You must tell me what you've got in mind!' I felt like grabbing his shoulders and shaking him to force a confession out of him; it was so obvious that he was hiding something.

But all he did was to put his hand on my shoulder and keep it there for a second. 'Capey, I like you. God knows why, for you're making me the hell in. But that's the way it is, and therefore I don't want to weigh on your conscience. Go up to your mountain, and pray: leave me down here.'

Perhaps he might have persuaded me to stay too; but it was Jessica who'd suggested, on that second night she'd come to see *Hamlet*, that we all go together in one group. All my actors went, with the exception of Jerry and Renier; and we gave Jessica and Richard and our host from the Oranjezicht party a lift in the kombi. It was just after Easter, the weather was clear and still, early autumn; that April was exceptionally beautiful.

There was a large crowd on Signal Hill that afternoon, even larger than the thousand I'd expected. The service was jointly led by an imam, a rabbi, and four or five representatives of different Christian denominations, all of them English. It suddenly moved me to think how often Dulpert and I might have passed some of those people in the street and that they hadn't even known him then: now they'd all been brought together by his death. Could it really be as futile as Jerry had said? For Dulpert, yes. He was dead. But for us: not the praying, I myself had gone beyond that, but the act of assembling in collective bewilderment, so that each could see his own agony or rebellion or incomprehension answered by that of the others, so that each could transcend his loneliness. We seemed to form part of one enormous wave breaking on the high slope, blind energy which could not be dispersed by itself again.

The service was extremely simple. A short opening. Readings from the Koran and the Bible, with moments of silence for reflection in between; a few prayers said by the priests and repeated by the crowd. Each of us had a sheet of paper with the texts on it.

I can't remember the texts any more, except for a brief passage from a Psalm which I recognised as one of my mother's favourites:

If I say, Let only darkness cover me, and the light about me be night, even the darkness is not dark to thee, the night is bright as the day, for darkness is as light with thee.

It was followed by another silence so that we could ponder the words.

281

A light breeze was moving down the slope, causing the grass to rustle and the women's dresses to stir; I was unnervingly conscious of Jessica beside me, in her light summer dress touched by the mischievous wind, the purple headscarf on her hair: a person, a woman, a girl, near and breathing: turning my head I could see the outline of her cheek and the stubborn chin, her folded arms and a fine dust of shiny hair covering her skin: and beyond her, beyond the whole reality of that afternoon, was Dulpert's death. I tried to grope back to him, but it seemed so impossible, and all I felt was a dull resentment throbbing inside me like thwarted passion.

Then one of the priests stepped forward for the main prayer of intercession, an elderly man, very tall and lean, his shoulders broad but slightly drooping, his grey hair cropped closely, his face deeply tanned yet ascetic:

'Let us pray for those who rule and those ruled.'

I looked down at my sheet of paper.

'For the Prime Minister and his Cabinet,' the priest said slowly and emphatically.

For a brief moment the crowd hesitated, before their voices followed his:

'For the Prime Minister and his Cabinet.'

I didn't pronounce the words. I felt Jessica's eyes on me, but I stared grimly down at my sheet . . . And somewhere, resonant and moved, the voice of the priest went on praying, followed by the multitude of other voices:

'For those who make and administer the laws:
   For those whose duty it is to obey:
   For those pressured by the conflict of duty and desire:
   For those pressured by despair:
   For those pressured by ambition:
   For those pressured by the need to show their authority:
   For those pressured by their desire to rebel against authority:
   For those who fear the future and for those who hate the present:
   For all of us who need thee.'

Followed by Hermien's prayer, like so many years before: *Our Father which art in heaven, deliver us from evil, deliver us from evil.*

It was quiet again. In the harbour far below a horn groaned and a white ship began to sail out into the breakers, accompanied by small pilots. The service was over. We went back to the kombi. Richard and the others were held up by the crowd and for a few minutes Jessica and I were alone again.

'You didn't pray with the rest,' she said.

'Did you?'

'I couldn't either. I wanted to, but I couldn't lie to myself.'

'But wherefore could I not pronounce "Amen"?' I said softly. *'I had most need of blessing, and "Amen" stuck in my throat.'*

'We should have tried.'

'It was unreasonable.'

'Perhaps that's what love means, Joseph. To be able to pray for everybody. Father Mark could do it.'

'Who's Father Mark?'

'The priest who read the prayer.'

'Do you know him then?'

'I sometimes give him a hand – with his church books and so on, small odd jobs. He has a congregation in the poorest district.'

'Are you a believer?' I asked.

'No. But I'm trying. I wish I could. But sometimes it seems to me that faith must be a thing like innocence, something one loses.'

'It's too easy a way out, a shirking of responsibility.'

'That's why I find it so hard. I don't want any ways out. But real faith, like the saints had, St Francis or St John of the Cross . . . I don't think that was easy at all.'

'Do you aspire to be a saint?' I said it flippantly, but it sounded serious.

She asked: 'Do you think it's at all possible for saints to exist?'

She was implying so much more. I looked in her eyes and felt immensely close to her through the question she'd asked; I could have put out my hand and touched her, but I didn't – of course not. I wanted to react to her challenge, to offer her peace from my own lack of peace, I wanted her to know that I understood: but the intensity of her presence was too disconcerting, I was too conscious of us, of her and me standing beside the grey kombi; and all I could answer was: 'I wish I knew.'

III

The road weaving through the pines to Bain's Kloof. She beside me, looking out over the deepening valleys open below us; autumn in the vineyards. The day like a large ripe fruit surrounding us.

When it's time to turn back, she protests: 'Please, not so soon.'

'There's a kloof behind the hotel I'd like to show you. But it's late already.'

'Doesn't matter, you're not performing tonight. You said you had the whole week free. Please take me there.'

Down the silent slope; mountain herbs and buchu shrubs.

Sometimes I lead the way, jumping from rock to rock; sometimes she passes me and goes on ahead, squatting down from time to time to collect bright pebbles from the pools, or watch small fishes or the uncertain progress of a scuttling crab. Nothing escapes her; nothing can hurry her.

(Somewhere here we boys were swimming, and the girls in another pool; and when, exasperated, we clambered over the formation separating the pools they sat down in consternation on the rocks, their wet vests and pants plastered on the stones; Hermien too.)

Upstream, deeper into the mountain, to the pool. The small cave opposite; the amber water glittering in the sun, reflected on the sides of the great boulders.

(Somewhere, here, or farther? And Willem and I went on alone, and in the mist that night we fell asleep in each other's arms.)

'We didn't bring anything with us.'

'To eat?'

'No, I mean: we didn't bring anything from the world down there. It's only us.'

And the water.

Casually stripping, peeling of shirt and jeans and tiny briefs. Her tanned body, small white breasts and a white bikini-pattern across her hips, darkish golden pubic hair on her prominent mound.

Diving in, emerging on separate rocks, then back into the water, the momentary embrace with a panic of drowning; her flight.

'I've brought you another pebble.'

Wet in her hand, white and perfectly round, with a single apricot cleft.

'It's a little girl.'

(Liesa, Hermien.)

'I wish I could be like this pebble, so whole and smooth. I can let it drop, look, it doesn't mind. It has no pride. It is so completely itself.'

'Jessica.'

(Can a body save us from memory?)

'Yes. Come into me.'

And the sleep afterwards in the sound of the water and the cool, sweet notes of birds. Awaking in the early evening, her wide open eyes, gazing at me.

'Do you know, for the first time in years I'm not frightened. But later ...'

'Don't think of that. We're here now.'

'I wish it could always be now.'

Moonlight meekly touching her hair and cheeks, the tip of her nose, her nipples.

Her face between my palms. Her fingers on my wrists. Yes. So easy. Simply to say : 'This is you.'

'This is you.'

Then we turned away from each other and got dressed, followed the long course of the stream, crossing the white rocks, to where the car was still waiting near the hotel.

We didn't speak on the way back. In the glare of the headlights trees stood up on either side of the road, like the gloomy hulks of animals; and occasionally leaves would reflect the light in small brilliant spots, like eyes.

I parked my car two blocks from her flat building. Already the scheming and planning and precautions had started. We walked the last few hundred yards. In her small kitchen the phosphorescent hands of her alarm clock indicated half past four. Soon the day would be with us again.

She went to the bathroom and bedroom. I could hear her moving in the dark : neither of us considered turning on a light. From the balcony I could see the distant row of lights dotting the outline of the bay. It was very quiet. She came out to me wearing her short cotton gown; the buttons were undone. I put my arm round her shoulders. Standing like that, we watched the first signs of light approaching and the city stirring to life, as if we had to see, with our own eyes, how everything which threatened us was slowly being shaped by the relentless light.

Now we were together, and alone in our togetherness.

There weren't really thoughts in me, merely blind submarine stirrings.

Something was taking its course. It would probably lead us some-where. But there was no noticeable movement, only a vague trembling, and endless compassion, as if everything – not just she, not just I – had become more mortal and destructible, more humble, than ever before. All one could do in that immense loneliness was to be kind to one an-other, and to others, and to oneself; and silent; without presuming any-thing, ever, without wishing anything, without the pride of hope or plans or faith, however blind: only – perhaps – this compassion, so utterly vulnerable.

We stood on the balcony watching the sun rise and the early mist drift upwards from the harbour, and the shadows diminish, so that every building was defined more separately; in the flower beds below us the bobtails were scratching for worms; there were doves in the high pines in front of us; in the street the first cars were coming past.

I went to the bathroom. When I came out, she was in bed, her mauve gown lying across the foot end. She looked up at me with a small uncertain smile. I sat down on the edge of the bed and kissed her fore-head; then undressed and moved in beside her, her head in my arms. Her hand began to stroke my cheek, but absently.

After a long time she whispered: 'I'm so scared, Joseph.'

'Don't.' I held her close.

'What's going to happen?'

'Nothing. I love you.'

'But . . .'

I pushed myself up on an elbow: 'Just for this day: let's not talk about it.'

Her large eyes gazed up at me: biting on her lip, she nodded. I re-moved the sheet from us and bent my head over her. I heard her whisper-ing my name, and moved my head down to her waiting wetness; her hands pressed me violently against her, and when I covered her with my body, she began to sob against my shoulder: 'Oh my darling, oh my darling, oh God!'

We were so exhausted that we didn't even pull the sheet to cover us again. She slept, and I lay in a daze, still vaguely conscious of the day-time din outside. After some time she laughed softly in her sleep, and when I lifted my head to look at her, she drowsily opened her eyes and

286

mumbled : 'I dreamed of sparrows farting.' Then she slipped back into sleep. I drew up the sheet over us and fell asleep too, very deeply, for a very long time; and when we woke up, the sun was setting.

Someone was knocking on the door.

Confused, in complete bewilderment, both of us jumped up. My heart was struggling like a panicky finch in a trap.

After a few seconds the knock was repeated.

'Stay here,' Jessica whispered, her voice choking. She put on her short gown and went to the door. I wanted to hold her back, but it was too late. Stumbling out of bed, I grabbed blindly at the bits and pieces of clothing on the floor.

She opened the front door. I heard voices, women's voices, hers saying something about 'headache', about 'next week'; the door was closed again. I sat down on the bed, pressing my head down on my knees to recover from the dizziness. When she came back, she was laughing hysterically. I had to press her close to me to calm her down.

'Two of my friends,' she said after a time.

'I heard them.'

'I'll make us some tea.'

It was as if the intrusion had made us strangers to each other. But only momentarily. While she was making tea in the kitchen I went to the bathroom to run a bath. She poured for us, shook off her flimsy gown and got into the bath with me. In the warm water we slowly relaxed. Dusk was deepening, soon it was dark. Only a street light from outside shed yellowish light through the frosted glass window so that we could distinguish each other. She opposite me, her eyes in shadows, her body a pale presence in the blackness of the water, her nipples two small stains, and between her legs a soft darkness gently straining against my foot. We were back in our familiar domain, and all our confidence returned.

We must have stayed there for two hours or longer. Every now and then I opened the tap to add some more hot water; and later she got out to put a record on her small player in the lounge, Bach's flute sonatas.

At times we talked, sometimes we lay still, or lazily caressed each other. The gentle immersion into love was like learning a new language, learning to spell together : I am, you are, we are . . . Finding new names for old things, conjugating the verbs of love, getting used to a new syntax.

'It feels so safe here,' she said once.

'Were you scared when they knocked?'

'Don't talk about it.' The water lapped over me. 'It was horrible. I don't think I've ever ...'

'I love you.'

'I want to say it to you too. I know it's true. But when we go out of here, when it gets light again, when they scare us again ...'

'The night will always come back.' Pensively, groping for the words, I quoted:

> *'O night more desirable than dawn!*
> *Oh night which joined us*
> *Lover with beloved,*
> *Beloved transformed into lover!'*

'St John of the Cross?' she asked after a brief pause, with something like joy of recognition in her voice.

'Do you know him then?'

'I've been infatuated with him for a long time. Yesterday – no, it's already the day before, now – Father Mark had another long session with me, explaining some of the lines.' She laughed: 'Just look at us: two heathens in the dark – talking about St John!'

'I'm sure he would have approved. Perhaps our darkness is not altogether different from his.'

She was silent. With my foot I gently caressed the half-open fruit of her sex.

'I wish ...' she said after a while, 'I would have loved ... if only you could have been the first with me. So that I could have come to you completely innocent.'

'I want you as you are, denying nothing of your past or mine.'

'My love.'

She moaned softly under my caress, and I moved over to lie on her, entering her, smooth as a fish, in the lukewarm water, and once again we abandoned ourselves to the insatiable urge of our bodies; and when we came, the water swirled over us and splashed on the floor and we burst out laughing; and then she went to turn over the record, and we added more hot water and lay in the warm dark listening to the flute.

At last, much later, we got up and dried each other. There was a sultriness in the air outside and it wasn't necessary to put on clothes. I changed the record and remained sitting on the lounge carpet while she was making food. She didn't put on the light. Of course, she knew the flat well enough not to need light: but the real reason, I knew, was that the kitchen window overlooked the inner passage and she didn't want anyone to know she was home.

In the dim glow of the record-player's green pilot light we had our meal on the floor. After resting all day we weren't sleepy yet. We went out to the balcony where there was a divan, and sat down to look out over the nightscape of the city, the light tracks of the cars, the reflections far below in the bay.

If it had been a week before, we would probably have gone for a walk; now it had changed, now we were aware of the world surrounding us. We were beleaguered on our small balcony. But there was a peculiar beauty even about our fear: out there was the world, and we were here.

She began to talk about my work; we discussed the *Hamlet*; and then she asked: 'What are you going to do next?'

'Camus. *The Just*: do you know it?'

'I saw it once, years ago. Can't remember any particulars. Only the long debate about violence . . .' She reflected for a while and shook her head. 'I remember I couldn't accept it. The play, yes, but not the argument: that violence is justified if you're prepared to pay with your own life . . .'

'Of course it isn't just. But by offering yourself in exchange, at least you're guaranteeing a certain integrity. Then you don't commit murder in cold blood. And once you've done it and paid for it with your own life, like Yanek, you really transcend the ethical and move into the realm of grace.'

'Do you agree with it?'

'I don't think I could ever have Yanek's courage.'

'To kill somebody?'

'That, yes, to start with. I can't even kill a mouse without lying awake for nights! But I suppose in a fit of rage or despair one might still be *driven* to murder. Only, in Yanek's case it was so much more. To be able to decide like him: "The death of this Archduke is necessary for the freedom of the oppressed masses: so I'll kill him: and then I shall allow them to kill me . . ." What he kills, is a concept, a title, an Archduke; but by giving his own life, he really offers a prayer for the soul of the *man* he killed. And he does it in spite of not even being a believer himself!' I closed my eyes to think of the play: the typed words on my playscript, and the way in which they would become flesh and blood onstage. And I went on: 'Do you remember the scene in prison, just before Yanek is executed, when the Archduke's wife visits him? That is the most terrible moment of all – when she offers to obtain a pardon for him, provided he repents. But if he does it, it would be a denial of everything. That is the courage I think I lack.'

A long silence; then she asked: 'What difference is Dulpert's death going to make?' I looked at her. 'Perhaps that's not the right question?' she said. 'I mean: you've done *Hamlet*; and then he died. And now ...'

'Now we are going to charge the Camus with Dulpert's death and with everything that happened. So that even those who ignored or denied it won't be able to avoid it any longer.'

'That's what you did with *Hamlet* too,' she said. 'It shocked me. You turned an intellectual and a dreamer into a terrible force of destruction. I think it made me discover something about you.'

'Did it make you pity me?' I asked quickly.

'Not pity. Fear, perhaps. Yes. Fearing you, and fearing for you.' A pause. 'But you see what I mean ... ? With *Hamlet* you shocked people. With your previous plays too, as far as I can make out. With every one of them. And you're going to do it again with *The Just*. But all these shocks ... I don't know how to put it: but doesn't shocking become a habit, a way of life in itself? Doesn't it blunt one – those who shock as well as those who are shocked ... ?'

'Do you think one ever gets immune from shock in this country?'

'Perhaps it's the very sort of country where one does: simply in order to survive, and not to go mad.'

'But then we must probe deeper every time, following the nerve ends of life as they try to recede and hide themselves.' Something strange was happening as I spoke, as if I was discovering the meaning of my own words while I spoke them. The previous two weeks, dear God, had been so confused that I'd had no time to sit down and sort it out and come to terms with it or with myself: now I had to examine it, for both our sakes. 'When I first heard of Dulpert's death that morning ... I was blind, a form of madness. I could have killed. I think if you'd given me a gun then, I would have been ready to shoot anyone remotely connected with his death. But that same evening I met you. And that changed everything. Perhaps I didn't realise it consciously then: but I know it now.'

'How did it change everything?'

'By having to think about you. By considering everything I do in the light of your presence, your life. And all the lives like yours. Those drawn into the whirlpool. Like the children in the Archduke's coach, the first time, when Yanek refused to throw the bomb. It's not a way of trying to defend or justify what I'm doing, but simply to rediscover the sense of it all.' She waited without moving; I was conscious of her breathing. 'There are those who are driven to violence: perhaps they're indispensable, sometimes. But others are necessary too, to give meaning to violence, if it has to happen. So that it doesn't happen blindly, so that people can know very lucidly why it happens, and purify themselves. That's my work, that is what I can do, perhaps all I can do: to keep people aware. I suppose it's very little. But what would happen without it? Then the whole of history would become one stream of blind, irrational violence. We aren't just animals slaughtering one another. It often looks like it. But our only dignity lies in a revolt which never ceases, against everything which wants to deny that we are more than animals . . .'

'And one day . . . ?' she whispered. 'Do you think we'll ever arrive at a world of peace, a world without violence, a world of dignity?'

'No,' I said. 'For I can't believe in Utopia. It's impossible for this world ever to become wholly good or wholly beautiful. But it can always be made a little better than it is. And if I don't fight to keep that small possibility open, everything will be smothered in blood.'

For a long time we sat on the divan on her high balcony, until even the late-night traffic subsided. Occasionally we still talked; then we were silent again. And at last the night grew cool and I became aware of her naked body shivering against mine, and we went inside and drew the curtains. In the dark kitchen I made us tea, which we drank in bed. And once again, with hands and mouths we explored the miraculous familiarity and strangeness of our bodies, unhurriedly, for many hours, stringing the joy of our orgasms like a rosary on the endless night. In between we briefly fell asleep, then woke each other up again into drowsy and grateful eagerness. In the early dawn we fell into a deeper sleep which lasted longer. Outside, the white day was glaring with uncompromising brilliance when I was finally awakened by her caressing hands. Instinctively my body searched for hers again, but she whispered:

'This time I want to . . .'

And kneeling between my knees she slowly raised me through the last layers of sleep to joy and passion and the farthest limits of bearable ecstasy.

'Now you know,' she said, swallowing my seed, my life, and sinking back into my arms.

We slept again, and woke up again, and began to talk again, that endless breathless conversation which could continue through days and months. She made us breakfast and brought it back to bed; we ate, and lay down again, on our bellies beside each other, and as we talked she absently stroked my shoulders and back and buttocks.

'You're so beautiful,' she said. 'Your brownness, your body. You're so beautiful.'

She turned on her back to compare the whiteness of her small breasts and her hips with me. And said again: 'I love your brownness, it's so beautiful.'

There was something profoundly disturbing about her words. Neither Beverley nor Annamaria nor any other girl abroad had specifically mentioned it, all that mattered was a meeting of male and female bodies. Whenever my colour did matter in my life, it was destructive, the way I'd been becoming conscious of it again since my return: a burden, a colour to suspect or hate: non-white, non-European, a shadow, a reverse, a flipside, a negative of all that mattered. And now, suddenly, she: 'I love your brownness, it's so beautiful.' I looked down at my own body, surprised, as if I was discovering it for the first time.

In the early afternoon, when the building became silent once more after the brief bustle of the lunch hour, we ate and drank each other again, for the last time, abandoned to the osmosis of love; and then got up and dressed, slowly, sad and sore, reluctant; yet so deeply content and replete. She went out to make sure that the coast was clear. We kissed, and made arrangements for later, and then I hurried down the fire escape, as furtively as a burglar, round the building and back to the street. She was watching me from the balcony, but neither of us dared to wave.

When I got into my sun-baked car and went downhill towards De Waal Drive, I thought: Now I know, without presumption or pride, how Jesus must have felt when he came back from the mountain to join his disciples: this sadness and fullness inside, this confidence to start again.

When I stopped in front of the Geustyns' door Jerry was sitting on the edge of the pavement, smoking his pipe.

'My God,' he said. 'At last. Have you been on a voyage of exploration?'

'More or less, yes.' I smiled, Jessica's sea-taste still on my lips. 'Have you been waiting a long time?'

'What a question! The old lady tried her best to shower me with her pisspot, bloody old sow. And the old man, Oom Appie, sold me a funeral policy.' He took an impressive document from inside his shirt and opened it. 'Whereas – whereas – whereas – wherever you look.'

'You didn't buy one of them, Jerry!'

'Why not? The poor old soul told me he spends his weeks on the road, but he's got a stomach complaint – which he explained in gory detail – so he's quietly wasting away at home this week. What else could I do? One never knows. There are people dying these days who never died in their lives before. At least my future's assured now. If not in Heaven, then deep in the earth. Provided I remember to pay the premiums.'

He followed me down the narrow lane beside the house; I unlocked my front door and stood aside to let him enter.

'Didn't you come by car?' I asked.

'No. I thought I'd use our bit of holiday to go up to Jo'burg; now the thing's standing at the roadside, condemned by the cops. Had to hike the rest of the way. Picked up by a little White Liberal, one of Shelley's brand of ineffectual angels.'

'And when did you get back – this morning?'

'Last night.' He smiled, his teeth dazzling white against his lean dark face. 'And what a night!' Kissing his fingertips. 'I came back flaked – you know how it goes in Jo'burg – so I thought I'd catch up on some lost sleep. But then two of my former pupils turned up, both of them loyal fans now that I'm an actor: God, and they've both grown so sexy since I last saw them. We talked for a while, and I gave them some wine, the perfect host and all that, and suddenly it was past midnight. So what could I do? Much too dangerous to let them go home that time of the night, so I invited them to stay. Fortunately I've got a big bed.

'Both of them?'

'Both, Capey. It was like playing the organ, you know: with hands and feet.' He knocked out his pipe in the waste-paper basket and started filling it again. 'But these young things are a drain on one's energy, man. When I'm through with the first, the second is opening up; and when I get off there, number one is just charged up again. Oh Jesus, no, that's why I left so early this morning and took the train out here. Brought you some money.' He pulled a fat envelope from his shirt and non-chalantly threw it on my desk. 'A small thanks-offering from the Jo'burg congregation.'

It was filled with ten-rand notes. Without counting, I asked, worried: 'Where does it all come from, Jerry?'

'Organised a fête.' His black eyes watched me mockingly.

'But I must know. Suppose there's any trouble . . . You know we're living on the brink nowadays. They're just waiting for us to make a wrong step.'

'No cock will open its bloody mouth about this,' he said. 'Take it, and say thank you to Gentle Jesus.'

I kept looking at him, knowing very well that I wouldn't get anything more out of him. After a while I went to the kitchen and turned on the gas to make coffee. He sat down on the kitchen table, smoking.

When I wanted to pour, the milk was sour.

'You'll have to take it black,' I said.

His eyes narrowed. 'You seem to have been away from home for some time too. Oom Appie did say something of the sort.' A smile. 'Have you been on the job too, Capey? I must say you're looking rather bruised.'

I hesitated, but just for a second.

'I've been with Jessica Thomson,' I said as neutrally as possible, stirring my coffee.

'Come again,' he said. He didn't stir.

'You heard me.'

'No, I didn't hear you,' Jerry said, very softly. Then furiously: 'I refuse to hear!'

'I was with Jessica Thomson, Jerry. I think it's my own concern.'

'It's not your concern!' He jumped up, slamming his cup down on the table so viciously that half the coffee spilt over the side. 'Are you fucking mad?' I'd never seen him in such a rage. 'Are you suddenly trying for white or what the hell is wrong with you?'

'I never thought you'd have any moral objections,' I said sarcastically.

'Moral objections my arse!' he answered. 'You can fuck the whole of Cape Town for all I care. That's what a man is made for. But stay away from White shit.'

Clenching my fists I went to him: 'Jerry, if you insult Jessica . . .'

He was breathing deeply. For a moment I thought he was going to hit me. Then his shoulders drooped. 'Don't you understand?' he asked. 'My own bloody sister, everything I've been fighting against all my life. And now you – *you* . . . ! My God, Capey, do you realise what you're doing?'

I bowed my head. How could I say: 'No'? How could I say: 'Yes'?

After a long time, without looking at me, he asked: 'When are you leaving?'

'Leaving?' I asked in amazement.

'Surely you're both going back to England now.' ,

'Most definitely not,' I said. 'I'm not that irresponsible, I'm not running away.'

He looked at me. Suddenly he burst out laughing; it shook me. 'I don't know whether I should be laughing or crying,' he said after some time.

'I love her.'

'Please save me that,' he snapped. And then he asked: 'How old are you?'

'Nearly thirty-two.'

'And you haven't learned yet!' Opening the back door he spat outside. For several minutes he remained with his back to me, his hands clutching the top of the lower door. Then he asked bitingly: 'And does Dulcinea del Toboso know what she's letting herself in for?'

'Of course.'

He swung round. 'In an insane country like this nothing ever happens as a matter of course. If you love her, Capey, you'll put her on the first plane and see to it that she never comes back. You're fucking her up, you're fucking yourself up, you're fucking all of us up.'

'I can't see what "all of us" have got to do with it.'

'You spoke to me about the money I brought: you told me we should be careful.' He sneered. 'How careful are you? How long is it going to take before they catch you? Don't you realise the whole world has got eyes? And then? What about the group? What about everything we've been trying to establish? And then you've got the bloody cheek to talk about "responsibility"!'

Every word scorched into me. I dared not look at him. 'Don't torture me, Jerry,' I pleaded. 'We'll be careful. Nobody will ever know. Not a soul.'

He refused to budge. 'Capey,' he said, 'if you'd come to me, now that it's happened, to tell me that you were prepared to work with *me* . . .' He broke off.

'With you?'

'If you'd come to tell me that now you were prepared to take a gun, a stick of dynamite, anything to help : to *do* something, to *change* something – then I would have understood. But how you can have the nerve to think that everything can go on as before . . .'

'Nothing goes on as before. And the work we're doing together is aimed at change. You know it as well as I do.'

'So you still believe – in "culture"?' He spat out the word.

'Because that's the only guarantee for morality.'

'Do you really think revolutions are moral, Capey?'

'I'm not so naïve. But if the revolution comes . . . the people must be prepared for it. Else we tumble into an abyss.'

'And you want to prepare them by offering them White culture? That's a set of superfluous little ornaments.'

'It's not White culture any more than you and I are White. It's ours. Because we're human.'

'Are we treated like human beings?'

'No. And I know very well that that's the worst of it : that so many are beginning to take it for granted that it should be like this. But you and I must remind them, and keep on reminding them, that they are human. If we didn't do that, no revolution would lead us any-where.'

'I see,' he said. 'You want to set people in motion like Christ, and once you've made them so conscious of their suffering that they want to revolt, you try to force the swords back into their scabbards, saying : "Oh no, that's not what I meant at all." ' He pushed the back door shut. '*That* is immoral, Capey. And all it will lead to, is that they'll crucify you. My God! Don't you think we've had enough martyrs already? Weren't Harry and Dulpert enough for you? How many more? On how many bleeding corpses do you want us to step before the earth opens and swallows us?'

'I never said culture alone could save the world, Jerry,' I reminded him when he fell silent. 'I said: if we can't make sure that something human is guaranteed, no revolution can lead us anywhere. I didn't exclude either. There are those who are prepared to "do or die". But there are others too, as indispensable, who've got to "reason why".'

'If I understood you correctly,' he said with his small quiet smile, 'Dulpert also belonged to those who tried to reason why. That didn't prevent his death. You believed in a gentleman's war, Capey. But in this country we fight dirty.'

V

Now night falls more gently than before. Evening is much like autumn, that other humble season of transition. It's not its beginning or end which is important, only its duration, its secret growth. Is that the reason why St John of the Cross had such compassion, such profound knowledge of the evening?

I have more than enough time to reflect on St John. Especially at night, when the prison grows silent. Not that it's noisy in the daytime, not much; but in the evening it is as if everything is emptied of sound like irrigation water oozing into mud. I haven't a clear idea of the prison's topography, for which I'm grateful, for now I can arrange it to suit me, any way I could plan a production. Concentric circles, like Dante's, expanding away from me. I'm close to the centre – not right in the centre, of course, for that is reserved for the gallows: there must always be some scope to progress in grace. And my progress is inward, towards that dark centre.

Sometimes I act my own parts again. Sometimes I just sit. Everything is becoming very tranquil, quite different from my imprisonment before the trial. Then I lived in constant anticipation and fear of their return, and panicked in uncertainty. Now I accept that death is waiting for me and I needn't worry about when it will come. Everything is so still at night when I'm writing.

Sometimes I wonder what would have become of the world without the books written in prison. Villon's wonderful testaments. Bunyan's pilgrimage. *Don Quixote*. St John of the Cross – that small brown Spaniard whom I feel I understand so well. It didn't surprise me at all to hear that most of the *Cantico Espiritual* was written in prison where, isolated from the all-too-blinding Spanish sun, he could probe that darkness which he held so dear.

We often read it together, in her flat or mine, and that night on the mountain. We used to take turns. I would read :

> *Let us rejoice, Beloved,*
> *Let us go to see ourselves in your beauty,*
> *On the mountain or the hill,*
> *Where flows the pure water;*
> *Let us enter more deeply into the thicket.*

And then we would look up St John's exegesis in on of the three brown books Father Mark had lent us. I obviously can't recall all of it now, but I do remember his emphasis on the mystical union of the Soul and the Spouse, and with what moving clarity he explained it all, line by line. *Let us rejoice* means this; and *Beloved* means that . . . And I remember his explanation of the line about the hill and the mountain because Jessica was so moved by it. *To the mountain:* the full knowledge of the morning, the revealed truth of God, face to face, too overwhelming for mortal man to endure; *to the hill;* the knowledge that comes in the darkness of the evening, of God in his creatures and works and wondrous ordinances – a form of knowledge grasped not with the intellect or the mind, but obscurely, intimately, intuitively, through a glass darkly, the way a lover knows his loved one in the night.

After looking it up and discussing it and going back to the poem itself, Jessica would read further :

> *And then forth to lofty*
> *Caverns of rock we shall go,*
> *Well hidden,*
> *And there we shall enter*
> *And taste the new wine of the pomegranates.*

Then I again :

> *There you will show me*
> *That which my soul yearned for,*
> *And then you will give me,*
> *There, you, my life,*
> *That which you gave me before.*

298

I remember the joy with which she would answer, each word reborn from herself :

> *The breathing of the air,*
> *The sweet song of the nightingale,*
> *The wood and its beauty*
> *In the serene night,*
> *With a flame which consumes and gives no pain.*

And then, to conclude, I :

> *For no one saw it,*
> *Neither did Evil appear;*
> *And the siege was lifted,*
> *And the horsemen*
> *Came down at the sight of the waters.*

That was what moved us most deeply : that sublime serenity, the still waters which persuade even the cavalry to descend from their horses. *Y la caballeria a vista de las aguas descendia.* Through all my nights it sings through me. *A vista de las aguas descendia.* For in the throng of our days we knew so little of that peace : moments, stolen hours, few days and fewer nights, each of them perhaps the last, each surrounded by anguish, and fear, steadily growing worse, steadily growing more impossible.

And yet we were so glad, especially in those early days, just for that; to know that we could cautiously return to it when the world became too confused for us. Even if we had to play a game in front of others, so that no one would guess the truth from glimpse or gesture.

We'd arranged to meet 'by coincidence' at a party the next weekend and the moment, when it arrived, was beautiful and not without fun, in spite of my dread beforehand. Of all the people there, only she and I knew about it; and by keeping it secret, it became even more preciously ours.

Richard was also there, in his latest suit and with his great lion's mane, bitter and depressed and less self-confident than I'd seen him before. He'd been planning to go overseas soon in connection with the filming of one of his books; until the very last moment everything had been in the balance, his passport having been withhdrawn two years before. In spite of applying for a new one three months in advance he hadn't been able to get anything out of the Department until the very morning of the party, when he was notified that it had been refused. It cast a deep gloom on the evening, since it had specially been arranged as a farewell party.

Richard felt that he should now apply for an exit permit to leave the country permanently. What sense was there in a writer living here if his books couldn't be read in the country and if he remained isolated from the rest of the world?

But I tried to dissuade him. 'Don't be in a hurry. An exit permit is too final. I've seen too many people pine away overseas through longing and frustration.' I told him about Simon.'

To my surprise he said : 'I know Simon.'

That made me more relaxed in my attitude towards him ; my suspicions began to recede.

He remained adamant : 'Overseas, at least I'll be free to travel and to work as I wish.'

'I've tried it,' I said. 'And after nine years I had to come back to start again. One can't survive in a vacuum.'

'Perhaps it was easier for you.'

'Easier?' I felt like laughing.

He looked embarrassed. 'I mean : you've still got something here you can feel attached to. But what about me? Day after day I'm forced to fight for my very survival as a pacifist.'

'Where did your war begin?'

'Long ago, while I was still at University. From my first books the fight was on. But they left me in peace until about three years ago when I was in the Transkei to collect material for a novel. While I was there, a White family was murdered on a farm, a ghastly business. There was a hint of political motives. And then the police moved in.' We stood in a circle listening to Richard, including those who knew the story; he was an excellent narrator. 'It was imperative for them to find the murderers. But the way in which they set about it . . .' He stopped and briefly closed his eyes in a rather studied gesture, obviously aware of his impression on his listeners. Then he continued : 'They systematically moved from village to village rounding up all the males from twelve years old and upwards. Old men of eighty were thrown from helicopters, dangling by their ankles on thick ropes; mere children brutally beaten

300

to extract admissions of guilt. I heard about it and took several of them to a lawyer to obtain affidavits. Before I'd been working on it for two days I was arrested: Ninety Days. After a month they let me out without a charge. But in my absence all the affidavits and collected material had "disappeared". I was listed as a Communist and had my passport withdrawn.' He smiled slightly. 'The first novel I wrote after that was based on the incident. But now it's banned here.' He looked at me: 'You read it, didn't you? – I gave you a copy.'

I was silent for a moment. Yes, I'd read it. It was technically brilliant, but the anger in it was too narrow, too screwed-up, it never broke loose from the self.

'I think I can understand it better after what you've told me,' I said. 'It's a strong novel, I found it impressive. But you were too obviously trying to prove something, to justify something. I think your material was richer than the book that came out of it.'

He smiled wryly: 'You don't believe in sweetening the pill, do you?'

'You asked me what I thought about it, not what I felt I ought to think. And I can assure you: if you stay here, you're probably going to write a better book than that one day. But if you go . . .' I shrugged. 'Anyway, it's for you to decide.'

I don't know whether I contributed to his decision – it would be the supreme irony! – but for the time being he didn't apply for an exit permit.

He still had to go to Johannesburg, however, to confer with the local representatives of the film company; and so he decided to use the opportunity to start his research for a new novel. Jessica and I took him to the airport in my car.

When his flight was announced, he took my hand: 'Joseph, we must see more of each other when I get back.'

'I'll be around.'

He said good-bye to me and kissed Jessica.

'Poor old Richard,' she said when we got into my car again.

'Why do you say that?'

'He's such a terribly lonely person, always hiding behind that façade of affluent self-confidence.'

'You seem to know him well,' I said, watching her intently.

She glanced at me, shrugging. 'He's helped me a lot since I came to Cape Town. It was he who introduced me to most of the people I've met here.'

'Including me.'

She laughed. 'Yes. Including you.'

Above us the Boeing made a wide smoky circle through the sky before streaking on to the North.

'He isn't married, is he?' I asked.

'No. Poor soul.'

'Why "poor soul"? You make him sound like a little boy – he must be past fifty.'

'He is something of a little boy. Haven't you discovered how much more vulnerable men can be than women? He was married twice. His first wife went off with his best friend – a vulgar business, like any story from a Sunday paper. And then he married again, I think it was about five years ago, while he was still Senior Lecturer at UCT. She was one of his students, thirty years younger than him.'

'And then she went off with his second-best friend?'

She ignored my sarcasm. 'They had a baby, but before he was two years old she fell in love with a bloke younger than herself. I don't know all the details, only that Richard followed them all over the country begging her to return, but she treated him like a dog. She kept on milking him for money, but refused to have anything else to do with him. She didn't even want the child. In the end he realised it was hopeless and started drinking. One afternoon while he was stone drunk the little boy got drowned in the neighbours' swimming pool. Richard had to spend several months in an institution. After that he pulled himself together but there's a wilderness behind his impressive looks. And the tension about the passport over the last few months has driven him back to the bottle.'

'Come,' I said, more disturbed than I cared to admit. 'Let's go for a drive before we go home.'

We drove in the direction of Caledon. But on the lower slopes of Sir Lowry's Pass the road was blocked by an accident. There were two cars wrecked on the side of the road, with bleeding bodies scattered over asphalt and grass. An ambulance came wailing from the distance.

Jessica grasped my arm. 'Let's go back,' she whispered in great agitation. 'Please don't wait, the ambulance is already on its way, there's no point in staying.' She was white with shock. After a while she asked: 'May I have a cigarette?'

I handed her the packet. She clumsily lit one. Her hands trembling. It took a long time before she spoke again.

'Do you think they were dead?'

'I can't see how anyone could have got out of that alive.'

'Did you see the people crowding round them . . . ?' She pulled in the smoke, choking slightly. 'I can't look at people hurt in an accident. They're so exposed to all those eyes, it's so undignified. Surely a person is more than a joint of meat in a butchery.'

We didn't speak again. After a few minutes I removed one hand from the wheel and put it on her leg, trying, through that frail gesture, to recover something, and hold on to something of the agonisingly little we had against the world.

VI

A month later we set off on our new tour. Now that we no longer had the subsidy we couldn't lay off during the winter vacation, as I'd planned.

Jessica and I had to rely on letters: the entire journey became a pilgrimage from one *poste restante* to the next. Occasionally I could phone her. From the larger towns, with direct dialling, it was easy, but from the small country villages it was hell: half an hour or an hour in small filthy booths waiting for a whimsical exchange to put you through, count your coins, and then – presumably – listen in while you tried to recognise and follow the indistinct, strange, bodiless voice on the other side of a crackling line: futility measured in small doses of three minutes each.

The Just was not a success. We'd discovered that during our very first week in Cape Town. What we needed was a forceful, clear statement, conquering the audience with its sheer visual energy. Our audiences found the subtle dialectics of Camus much too abstruse. Under different circumstances we might have been able to shrug it off and carry on, but what with our financial worries and the bad weather it affected us more than was necessary. The tempers grew short: only the large, loyal Doors refused to be upset by anything.

With Lucy I had an unfortunate quarrel one night when, in her old sultry way, she tried to seduce me. My nerves were frayed; and while I would have succumbed without much resistance on previous journeys now I just told her to fuck off.

'Seems I'm not good enough for you any more,' she said viciously. 'Brown bread trying to be white, or what?'

I was shocked numb. She couldn't possibly have been aware of anything; but it felt as if an enormous fist had grasped my heart and was squeezing the life out of it. In the background I noticed Jerry's mocking eyes. He didn't say anything; but later I saw him go off with her. He would comfort her, as much for my sake as for his own. But even that couldn't neutralise my shock.

In such conditions it was difficult enough to keep one's cool through the daily quota of irritation caused by permits, 'routine examinations' and cryptic regulations – but in the long run one does become conditioned, learning to stay one move ahead, and if that had been the sum of our troubles we would have pulled through like before. But then a more serious blow hit me.

It was in the Cold Bokkeveld, on a particularly freezing day, and on our way to the missionary hall where we were due to perform we all took swigs from Jerry's brandy bottle to counter the cold. Near the hall we were stopped by a police constable; Jerry was driving. As usual, the man wanted to see our 'papers'. He kept us standing outside in the cold for fully half an hour while he leasurely searched the kombi. Discovering the half-empty bottle in the cubbyhole, he exclaimed with obvious satisfaction :

'Aha! Driving under the influence, hey?'

'That's a bloody lie,' Renier snapped.

'And cheeky too!' the constable said. 'You come with me, my boy.' When we protested in a chorus he threatened to have the whole group arrested for obstruction of the law.

'OK,' said Jerry with his thin smile. 'Then we all go back with you.'

'Don't be ridiculous, Jerry!' I said, feeling the stirrings of a migraine behind my eyes. I tried my best to reason with the policeman and explained the situation to him, but he refused to listen. Then I lost my temper : 'I demand that a District Surgeon test his blood immediately.'

'Are you trying to tell me what to do?'

I jumped into the kombi. 'All right. Then I'm going to fetch a lawyer.'

Before I could slam the door shut he'd grabbed my arm and pulled me out of my seat. The next moment he was covering us with his large service revolver. 'Now you all come with me!' he ordered.

Bundled into the back of the police van we were driven to the station and locked up for the night – the two women in one cell, we six men in

304

another. Our cell already had two occupants, one of them fast asleep in a corner, the other squatting against the wall, morosely staring out in front of him, the front of his shirt spattered with blood.

I was furious. But while I was still standing in a helpless rage in front of the locked door, Jerry burst out laughing behind me. 'Don't worry, Capey. Just think, tonight we won't have any trouble finding a place to sleep. The State's putting us up for free.'

'And what about our performance?'

'Gone to hell. But we can perform anywhere, can't we? What's wrong with this place?'

Doors was the first one to join in the fun. Then Frikkie caught the spirit; and less than an hour after we'd been locked up, our performance was under way. Accompanied by Frikkie on an imaginary guitar we began to sing, gradually elaborating on it with mime, improvising variations on the evening's incident, taking turns to play the part of the constable; anticipating the next day's court case, we invented the most far-fetched and fantastic scenes. The performance acquired an added dimension through the attitude of the two members of our audience: the morose squatter who, it transpired, had landed there after a knife attack, stared at us sulkily, occasionally muttering what sounded like curses; the other, who'd raped a little girl, slept through the opening part of our concert, then woke up and watched us with curious detachment as if we were part of his dream. We tried to involve them in our acting, more or less like in Dürrenmatt's *Breakdown*, and that was how we discovered the charges against them. The knife-man was in no mood for fun and games, but the rapist began to show interest and ended up by joining in with a raw and robust energy almost frightening in its exuberance. If the two girls from our group had been present he would probably have ended up by giving a live demonstration of his crime.

Early the next morning a burly Coloured guard in a khaki overcoat brought us bread and porridge and coffee; and by nine o'clock all of us, reunited with Lucy and Antjie, were taken to court in a van. Waiting for the magistrate to appear, we listened spellbound to our constable's version of the previous night's incident which he described to the court sergeant. He had such a vivid imagination, especially in his account of the violence we'd used to resist arrest, that he would have fitted in perfectly with our impromptu concert.

The magistrate entered. Our group – with the exception of Renier, who had to appear separately on the charge of drunken driving – were the first to be called: rather unfairly, Jerry thought, since the rapist and the knifeman could have claimed some priority. We filled the box from end to end. When we were asked to plead, I informed the magistrate that we'd been prevented from consulting a lawyer and were not prepared to go on without legal help. After a brief consultation with the Prosecutor we were taken back to the police station.

For just over an hour we were kept waiting in the charge office before an officer made his appearance. Without looking at us, he read out our names from a file and announced:

'Case withdrawn. You may go.'

Back to the courtroom less pleasant news awaited us. Renier had been found guilty and sentenced to six months' imprisonment or a fine of two hundred rand. Noticing our incredulous stares, the Coloured sergeant shrugged and explained confidentially:

'It's because the cheppie pleaded not guilty. Our juts don't like that.'

It took some time to locate a lawyer, and it was past three o'clock that afternoon before he'd managed to get Renier out on bail and arrange for an appeal.

Back in the kombi a final shock awaited us, for while it had been standing open and unprotected overnight, somebody had stripped it of all our possessions.

On our way to the next town Jerry and I began to talk. 'You know,' I said, 'the sort of concert we improvised last night will have much more punch than *The Just*. It's time we made up our own play from the things happening to us. Something mad, and funny, and shocking, and irrational, it doesn't matter. As long as it's our own, as long as people will recognise it.'

'That's the stuff, Capey!'

It was the birth of *SA!* Using Brook's *US* as a starting point – I'd told Jerry all about it – we constructed, in the form of action theatre, a play round Dulpert: what had happened, or might have happened, to him, embroidered with variations, fugues and fantasies, clothed and shaped by music. I think Artaud would have approved. It was vivid and crude and direct, bombarding the senses and the conscience, throbbing with wild beauty, changing, in an instant, from a bloody scream to a howl of laughter. All of us worked together on it. In the beginning we simply discussed the idea and its possibilities as we drove on in our kombi; within a week we'd progressed far enough to begin working on specific scenes. Soon we were rehearsing full-time, whenever we found a convenient venue : even outdoors in the thin, watery sun.

With our evening performances it went from bad to worse, aggravated by the loss of our baggage. The small audiences braving the bitter cold evenings hardly brought in any money, while our expenses increased daily. When Antjie caught 'flu and had to spend three days in a delirious state in the back of the kombi, we decided not to go on with an already hopeless undertaking; and barely a month after our departure we were back in Cape Town.

Back with Jessica. She seemed smaller than I'd remembered her, and still smaller when in our rare, precious hours together I could peel off her layers of clothing to hold her against me. Everything had to happen so circumspectly : in the daytime I never ventured near her building; in the evenings, only after a telephone call had confirmed, with esoteric code messages, that she had no visitors with her – and even then I always left the car several blocks from her building, and took up position in the dark street under the pine-trees until she signalled from her balcony. In spite of all the elaborate precautions fear never left us. One single neighbour accidentally glancing through a window of an evening could destroy everything. And yet there was profound happiness just in being together, talking, reading, listening to music, making love. Outside it was cold; inside it was cosy and warm. In the winter months she lost her tan and slowly grew whiter, with the characteristic delicate, smooth skin of an English girl; and against her nakedness my brown seemed browner than before. 'Now you must be brown for both of us,' she said, stroking my back. The work on *SA!* went on without interruption. The flop of the last tour and the experience of our night in prison appeared to have strengthened us from inside. With new determination and dedication we worked on our play, adding to it, cutting, changing. A month was too short, even six weeks were too short. By the end of August, when the days began to mellow, we were still working tirelessly, redefining our approaches, rearranging scenes, reshaping the whole.

If only the money would last. We had a small amount left from our previous tours, but to sustain eight people for two months, compensating them, in addition, for the loss of their possessions on tour, dug deeply into our resources.

For a week Jerry disappeared to Johannesburg again, returning with a few hundred rand. It still intrigued and worried me, but I couldn't get anything out of him. It was becoming more and more evident that he was involved in something besides our theatre: often, when I went to visit him at his lodgings in Athlone, he wasn't at home; if I enquired about it later, he would laugh it off. Many of those nights he might have spent with women. But not all.

His money helped us through a few more weeks until, in mid-September, we were finally ready to open in the Luxurama. It came just a day after Renier's appeal had been heard in the Supreme Court: we'd managed to acquire a brilliant young Jewish advocate for him, and after only a couple of hours the judge overruled both conviction and sentence, with some scathing remarks about the action of the police and the findings of the magistrate. Coming at that moment, the verdict added a touch of delirious joy to the enthusiasm already engendered by so many weeks of rehearsals.

Small wonder that on opening night *SA!* exploded like a load of dynamite in the midst of the audience. Towards the end it became almost unbearable, the variations on our Dulpert story leading to more and more violent confrontations between the authorities and a group of demonstrators: every time the rebel leader is arrested, and tortured, and killed, leading to new protest, and to new martyrs; this goes on until a deadly silence remains, lasting an agonising eternity, a silence out of which, almost inaudible at first, the national anthem rises while a group of folk dancers in white masks begin to dance on the bodies of the martyrs. The audience went berserk. There were moments when we feared that they might storm the stage: but their fury was not directed at us, they were with us all the way. At the end nobody was seated any more. They didn't applaud, they screamed; and some were sobbing as they stood there screaming.

We couldn't speak. From the dressing-rooms we went to Jerry's place in Athlone. There the tension broke. Half-hysterically we began to celebrate.

It was past three when I left. I phoned Jessica from a public box and went to her, and fell asleep in her arms like an exhausted child.

The English papers, who'd sent Coloured reporters to our opening night, reported it under banner headlines. The failure of our tour was forgotten. Suddenly we were News – not only for Davey Sachs, but for everybody.

But when we arrived at the theatre on the third night there were two policemen waiting in my dressing-room. They greeted me politely.

'Mr Malan?' the senior officer asked, handing me a sheet of paper. 'Will you please tell your actors to go home? The performance has been cancelled.'

I gaped at him.

Someone, he explained calmly, had lodged a complaint and until the Publications Control Board had come to a decision we were not allowed to continue. Would we be so kind as to leave the building immediately?

After a wide detour through the streets of the neighbourhood we returned to watch from a distance.

At half past seven the first spectators arrived, completely unsuspecting, confronted by the two officers on the steps who asked them to go home. An argument developed; more and more people arrived, pushing and jostling to get closer. They seemed surprised, stunned, flabbergasted. Curious passers-by thronged closer to find out what was going on. Soon the whole area was crowded with excited people.

Suddenly police vans made their appearance from all sides; five of them, ten, twenty. A whole commando of constables using their batons opened up a gangway through the crowd and formed a cordon in front of the theatre.

Loudspeakers ordered the crowd to disperse.

In a flash the mood of the milling people changed, amazement giving way to anger. There were shouts and protests, and a surge of movement towards the building.

And then there were dogs, too; no one knew where they'd come from so suddenly. Screams, children crying, men cursing noisily. By then it was quite dark and no one really knew which way to go. There was a milling movement in the crowd, aimlessly, panicky, while the dogs barked and tugged at their leashes.

Once again the loudspeakers bleated out a warning. Then the first tear-gas grenades exploded. On all sides press cameras were flashing. The dogs went mad. The night became one confused turmoil of sound and movement, as the crowds dispersed to all sides to get away from the suffocating clouds of gas.

Gradually it grew silent as the last noise ebbed away into the side-streets. Only a few vans remained behind to guard the building: we watched them from a distance, our throats and eyes burning.

There had been several arrests, the newspapers reported afterwards, and a couple of people had been injured, but only one of them seriously : a three-year-old girl mangled by a police dog. It caused a wave of indignation throughout the Peninsula, with the result that the police chief felt obliged to make an official statement. Enquiries had revealed, he announced, that the child's parents had deliberately tried to provoke an incident by thrusting her into the dog's mouth.

A week later *SA!* was officially banned by the Publications Control Board on the evidence of a makeshift text we'd been ordered to submit.

We could appeal against the ban, of course. But where would we find money to afford a court case? The young advocate who'd handled Renier's case offered to help us at a nominal fee. Even so, the amount would run into thousands and we had almost nothing. We'd counted on the play to keep us going through the next months. Jerry immediately left for Johannesburg again, but for the first time he returned openly pessimistic : he might be able to raise five hundred, he said, or even a thousand, but definitely no more.

And yet we couldn't leave it at that. Everything, our very existence, was at stake.

The day we formally lodged our appeal at the Supreme Court we still had no idea of whether we would have enough money to proceed.

'What about a prayer meeting, Capey?' said Jerry. 'You like to go up to Signal Hill, don't you? I think we can do with a bit of faith.' Perhaps there was more than mere mockery in his words. I tried to keep it from Jessica, but it didn't take her long to discover that something was worrying me. To shrug it off would upset her unnecessarily, and so I had to tell her about the financial problem.

She was surprised and hurt. 'Why didn't you come to me immediately, Joseph?'

'We had so little time together, I didn't want to burden you with something from outside.'

'But you know very well I can help you.'

'No. It doesn't concern you, I don't want to drag you into it.'

She was upset. 'All my life I've wanted to be necessary to someone,' she said. 'I've spoken to you about it so often. I left England because there was nothing I could feel committed to, I ran away from all the money in the bank suffocating me. You have no right to keep me out of this, Joseph!'

'Do you remember the day I went to show you the farmyard where I'd grown up?' I asked. 'You wanted to buy the children sweets – but you didn't want to distribute alms.'

Her cheeks were glowing with indignation: 'Do you think it's alms I want to give you? Don't you understand . . . ?'

'And don't *you* understand that I dare not accept it? Not from you?'

'Not even if you love me?'

'Because I love you.'

'When you started your group, you were prepared to accept a subsidy from your friend Willem – from the heart of the establishment.' She sounded bitter. 'How can you refuse me?'

'It was a business transaction.'

'Why can't this be a business transaction too? What difference would it make to you and me?'

'I'm frightened. Can't you see?'

'Because you don't trust me enough?'

'Because whatever happens I can't face the idea of being "obliged" to you. The way I was forced to feel about Frans Viviers after he paid for my father's death by sending me to school.'

Quietly, almost inaudibly, she whispered: 'Is that what you think of me?'

My world was tottering around me. I didn't want to go on arguing. I didn't want to be petty or selfish or bitter or frightened. But how else could I react?

She tried again, more restrained: 'And if I don't help you? What will become of your group?'

'We'll get money somewhere . . .'

'But if you don't? Don't you owe something to the members of your group?'

'Don't,' I pleaded. 'Oh God, my darling, don't.'

'I love you. Don't you understand that?'

'Don't.'

Two weeks later she handed me the deposit slip of the money she'd transferred. It had been done anonymously, even Jerry didn't know where it came from. And when he asked me point-blank, I said: 'I've stopped asking you about your Johannesburg money, Jerry.'

He didn't say anything more about it. But I think he guessed all right

And even if he didn't, *I* knew. And I so desperately wanted to keep her free from the world outside, untouched by my history, virginally mine. One learns so slowly and so stumblingly.

VII

Antjie Jonker was the first of the group to come to me, about a week after the commotion at the theatre. As I opened my front door it was immediately obvious that something serious had gone wrong. She used to be so carefree, she'd mothered us so warmly on all our trips, but on that night she was edgy and ill-at-ease. And while she avoided my eyes and kept up a stream of uncomfortable and irrelevant conversation I tried to guess her problem: an unwanted pregnancy, financial straits, illness in her family? When she finally came out with it I was caught completely unprepared.

'Joseph, it's a hard thing what I got to say tonight. Please don' get me wrong.'

'What's the matter, Antjie?'

'When we started working together, you said it wasn't going to be easy. And it wasn' neither, but in a way it was nice. But these last times . . .' She fidgeted with a piece of thread on her knee. 'Look, I know the police been buggering us around fo' a long time now, but that didn' bother me. It's jus' a cat-and-mouse business and, after all, we use' to that. Renier's thing was a bit of a shock, but OK, I could take that. But now . . .' She fell silent, flustered.

Steeling myself, I asked: 'Now it's become too much for you?'

'It's this last thing what happened, Joseph. The people what got hurt, that little girl bited by the dog . . . It got on my heart. It's getting bad now.'

'Are you scared?'

For a moment something of her usual fire returned: 'Scared my arse!' she said. 'But now there's mos other people in it too.'

'Suppose we win the court case?'

'They'll always find new ways to fock us up. We can't win against them. It'll just get worser and worser, and I don' want to have blood on my hands inne end. I'm a decent person.'

Strange how that was to become a refrain sounding through the following months: *I'm a decent person . . . I'm a decent person . . .*

Forgive us our decency as we forgive them that trespass against us.

Antjie left. I called the group together to break the news.

Doors Kamfer asked: 'But has the djentoe gone blerry mad now?' Jerry was whistling a tune through his teeth. The others sat staring down at their hands.

'We'll get someone to replace her as soon as possible,' I said. 'We can't sit around idle, we're losing more money by the day. I'll have our next play ready in a few days now. It's based on Frisch's *Andorra.*'

'Is it going to make trouble again?' Barney Salomon asked. The others looked up.

'I don't foresee any trouble.'

'We can't go tame now,' Renier said quickly. 'They won't get us on our knees so easily.'

'But we can't go on cheeking them all the time, either!' said Lucy.

The atmosphere was loaded.

I looked at them. 'All right,' I said. 'It seems the time has come for us to decide exactly where we stand.'

Very quickly, before any of the others could say a word, Jerry answered: 'Don't worry, Capey, we're right behind you.' And adopting the pose of a politician he mocked: 'If it's blood and sweat and tears you want, never before could one man count on so many for so much!' It developed into a full-scale oration which soon had the whole group in stitches, and we rounded it off with a lusty rendering of 'Onward, Christian soldiers'.

After the others had left he dropped his jovial mask:

'Capey, in a time like this it's murder to ask them where they stand. It just confuses them. Give them work to do and keep them busy, that's all you need.'

'You're a demagogue, Jerry.'

'All's fair in love et cetera.'

And during the following weeks it was mainly his zeal and inspiration which kept us going, aided by the challenge of the two new plays we'd started rehearsing – *Andorra*, and a satire based on *Tartuffe*, with a White Liberal in the role of Molière's hero. It was also Jerry who found a replacement for Antjie: Gladys Bonthuys, as plump as her predecessor, slightly older, coarse and exuberant by nature, with a voice like a fish trumpet; she loved the bottle but was a hard worker. There wasn't enough time to polish her rough edges, but at that stage going on was more important than finesse.

On the night before we opened with *Tartuffe* the next move was made against us.

After the dress rehearsal I went to the nearest telephone box to phone Jessica, as usual.

'How are Miss Muffet's curds and whey?'

That was part of the code we'd developed to camouflage our conversations – a silly little game, but deadly serious too, part of the framework of secrecy surrounding our love : for not even a telephone could be trusted.

'There came a big spider.'

So she had visitors. Disappointed, because I was eager to discuss the dress rehearsal and the prospects for opening night with her, I went home. It must have been shortly after four o'clock in the morning when I was awakened by an urgent and continuous knocking on my door. For a while I was too scared to move. The knocking went on.

Still befuddled with sleep, I put on my dressing gown and opened the door. There were four or five men on the step.

'Security Police,' one of them announced. 'We have a warrant to search your flat.' He flashed a document in front of my eyes, but I was too amazed to focus.

'I hope you're not going to be stroppy,' the man in front said, with a note of warning in his voice.

'Of course not.' I was fully awake now. 'I don't know what you're looking for, but do come in.'

When I stood aside, they trooped in : not only the group waiting on the doorstep, but a dozen or more others who must have been waiting in the lane. Suddenly the whole flat was filled with strangers. One of them ordered me to sit down at my table, and stood beside me while the others ransacked drawers and bookshelves and cupboards in the lounge, the bedroom and even the kitchen. Every book and theatre programme and sheet of paper was examined and thrown on the floor. Drawers were emptied on the carpet. In the beginning I felt indignant; then I withdrew into detachment, watching with wonder and even amusement how the entire flat was turned into a chaotic battlefield.

Halfway through their feverish activity the front door was opened and a pathetic figure appeared on the threshold : Oom Appie in striped pyjamas at least four sizes too large for him, his eyes stunned like those of a hare trapped in a searchlight; in his confusion he'd forgotten to put in his dentures, and his mouth sat under his nose like an old prune.

'What'se mette' now?' he asked.

'It's all right, Oom Appie,' I assured him. 'You can go back to bed. They're just visitors who turned up rather unexpectedly.'

He kept gawking at them for a while before he left, shaking his head. There was a slushing sound in the lane outside, followed by a violent curse from Oom Appie, and the dry, contented chuckle of his mother-in-law; then everything was quiet.

It was dawn before the police began to file out of the door again. By that time even the sheets and blankets from my bed had been thrown on the heap of books on the floor.

The leader of the group picked up a small bundle of books he'd set aside and said politely: 'Will you come with us, please?'

'May I ask what the trouble is?'

'Just a routine investigation.'

They allowed me to dress; five minutes later I was in the back of a car, flanked by two of them, on my way to town. At Caledon Square they escorted me upstairs to a reception room, an ordinary civil service office with a notice board covered by papers and cuttings, a counter, a couple of tables with bundles of files, solid brown chairs. I was invited to take a seat. Outside in the passage a group of people came past. I looked up and saw Jerry and Renier, surrounded by six or seven strangers; it was the merest glimpse, but in a singular way it reassured me.

'I'd like to . . .' I began.

'Shut up!' one of my escorts barked. They were no longer the polite visitors of a few minutes before.

Someone filled in forms and made notes in a ledger-like book. They confiscated my watch and my belt, and made sure that my shoes had no laces.

'You'll get them back when you leave,' one of them said. '*If* you leave again.'

It was such a childish form of intimidation, such bad acting; even so, I could feel my guts contract. How could I really be sure that they were only trying to frighten me? They were backed by their entire formidable framework of laws and regulations: not even a court of justice could intervene in their affairs. And yet the situation was so grotesque that I couldn't take it seriously; something inside me remained a spectator, one of the *Six Characters*. Or perhaps – a new idea struck me and for a moment I wondered what they would say if I were to announce:

315

'You've made a mistake, gentlemen. I'm not Joseph Malan. My name is Joseph K.'

I was taken to a small office at the end of the passage, similar to the one in the old YMCA building in London. It was bare except for a single table and two chairs. On one of these I was allowed to sit down; on the other, between me and window, sat my guard – a middle-aged, rather shabby five-o'clock-in-the-pub sort of man. The door was shut behind us. A few times I tried to strike up a conversation with my companion, but he ignored me. The yellowish tint of his eyeballs indicated a liver complaint. I took in everything, noting details for future use; even the bluebottle buzzing against the window was important, and the brown paper stuck to the table-top with drawing pins. Hell can be so bourgeois.

After an hour or so they brought me breakfast on a tray; some of the coffee had been spilt in the saucer. Much later lunch was served, not a bad meal at all. There was a restaurant slip on the tray and I automatically put a hand in my pocket for money.

'Don't worry,' said my guard, his Andy Capp butt stuck to his lower lip. 'It's on the house.'

When they came for the tray a new guard arrived to replace him. He was younger, strongly built, with the appearance of a rugby forward. Like the first one he paid no attention to me at all; once when I said something he merely grunted: 'Sharrap,' absorbed in the colourful comic he was reading.

Much later in the afternoon two men came for me and took me back through the passage to a room next to the reception office. It was bare too, containing only a large table in the middle of the floor, with four men seated on chairs behind it. This time I wasn't allowed to sit, but ordered to stand in front of them under the glaring bare bulb from the ceiling.

One of the men at the table looked up and announced matter-of factly: 'This room is soundproof.'

They kept me standing for a long time before someone finally began to question me about the pile of books brought from my flat. They were particularly interested in the *I Ching*.

'Where'd you get this Chinese book?'
'I've had it for years.'
'What do you do with it?'
'I consult the oracles.'

316

My interrogator paged through it for some time, studying the hexagrams.

'Ever been to China?' he suddenly asked.

'No.'

'Why are you interested in Chinese books then?'

'I'm interested in all kinds of books.'

'Are you a Communist?'

'No.'

'What was that book doing on your shelf then?'

'I have two Bibles on my shelf as well. That doesn't make me a Christian.'

One of the four got up and slowly came round the table to me. 'Cheeky, are you?' he said. 'An accident can happen very quickly. And no one will ever know about it. Do you understand?'

'I'm prepared to answer whatever questions you want to put to me.' I tried my best to remain calm. 'But please remember : I have a performance starting at eight.'

He smiled lazily and went back to his chair.

One of the others started a new series of questions – wide spirals constantly returning to the same key points: the *I Ching*, my sojourn abroad, the activities of my group, the biographies of my actors.

Outside the afternoon slowly deepened into dusk and darkness. It was becoming clear to me that they had no intention of letting me go in time for the performance. Had that been their purpose from the outset? If that was the case, they'd probably allow me to go as soon as they were sure that the performance had been wrecked. Deep, desperate resentment grew inside me. But I suppressed it. I wouldn't give them the satisfaction of showing that they'd upset me. And the very expectation of release was reassuring : at least it made it probable that intimidation had been their sole motive.

But I was shaken when, after yet another round of questions on the *I Ching*, one of my inquisitors leaned forward – a colossus of a man with the neck and shoulders of an Afrikaner ox – and suddenly asked :

'What do you know about Dulpert Naidoo?'

For a moment I didn't know what to say. Then I replied : 'We were friends years ago.'

'Are you very sure it was long ago?'

'More than ten years. Before I went overseas.'

317

'You lived together in Oxford Terrace.'

'If you already know it, why ask me?'

'Are you trying to deny it?'

'Of course not. I've nothing to hide.'

'You were particularly close friends.'

'Yes. I'm not ashamed to admit it.'

'And you agreed with his opinions?'

'With most of them, especially on music and religion.'

'And politics?'

'We often argued.'

'You got this Chinese book from him.'

'Yes. But it's not a political book.'

'It's Chinese.'

'Yes.'

'When did you last see Naidoo?'

'I told you : before I went overseas.'

'You kept on corresponding with each other.'

'No.'

'Don't lie to me!'

'I never heard from him again.'

'How do you explain that we found several of your letters in his room before he was arrested?'

I looked straight into his eyes.. 'It's impossible.'

'Do you want to make out that I'm a liar?'

'All I said was that you couldn't have found such letters because there have never been any.'

He kept on nagging and insisting, in narrowing spirals, trying to anger me, trying to flatter me, trying to catch me off guard. Then, as suddenly as he'd broached the subject, he dropped it.

'For how long are you planning to go on with your acting business?'

'As long as I can.'

'You realise it's a dangerous game?'

'It's not a game, it's my life.'

'You're trying to incite people.'

'I'm trying to produce theatre which has something to say.'

'We're watching you, Joseph. You're heading for trouble. And don't cry when you get hurt.'

Suddenly it was all over. I was taken back to the first office where my watch and belt were returned to me; they gave me a receipt for the books they'd confiscated, and escorted me to a waiting car on the square. It was ten o'clock.

'You needn't take me home,' I said. 'You can drop me at the theatre.'

'There's a prescribed procedure.'

Fifteen minutes later I was back in the incredible chaos of my flat. I didn't know where or how to start clearing up the mess; I didn't know whether I should laugh or cry. Behind all the frustration and anger and bitter comedy lay the one thing of immediate importance: our opening night had been wrecked.

Had there been another crowd waiting in vain? Had there been police, and vans, and dogs? Even if there hadn't been a disturbance, how could we expect any more public support in future? Would we ever be allowed to use the theatre again? My God, I thought: they wouldn't supress us even if we had to resort to guerilla theatre on street corners. It was the only weapon we possessed; we had to use it.

Like Job among the ashes I sat down on my mound of books and clothes in the middle of the floor to survey the scene. There was a knock. I started. But before I could get up the door was opened and the Geustyns entered. Oom Appie in his Sunday suit, his wife in a dotted church dress with a floral hat covering the curlers in her hair.

Elbowing him in the ribs, she said: 'C'mon, speak up.'

Oom Appie bathed his false teeth in saliva. 'Joseph,' he said meekly.

'Not Joseph,' his wife interrupted sharply. 'You call him Mister Malan straight, jus' like that. Tell him to get out when the sun rise.'

'Joseph, Mister Malan,' Oom Appie said with a pained expression on his face. 'The Missus en' I was talking about things.'

'Tell him our name is gone to shit. Pollies all hours of de day enne night. Tell him.'

'It's about de pollies, Joseph,' said Oom Appie.

'Tell him we're decent folk, we don' wan' to be nuggeted with tremps en' crimminuls.'

Oom Appie suddenly lost his temper: 'Why don't you tell him yourself?'

'We're Chrishuns,' said Mrs Geustyn, partly to him, partly to me. 'We live inne respec' of de law en' we don't trubble nobory. Alle years it's decent people what boarded with us. En' look what's heppen' now.' She gave him another shove, sending his lower teeth halfway out of his mouth. 'C'mon, tell de men, Appie, demmit! Tell him befo' he rape me '

I found all the others assembled at Jerry's place, drinking the wine we'd bought to celebrate the opening of *Andorra*.

'Bravo!' shouted Jerry when he let me in. 'The last of the lost sheep.'

'Have you been back long?'

'They released us in two and threes from nine o'clock or so. Lucy and Gladys came first.'

'And the theatre?'

'The people were refunded and went home. There were no police. I saw the manager.'

Doors Kamfer, tall as a cedar and still smiling, poured me a drink. I gulped it down and went to refill my glass. When I turned back, I became aware of the unnatural silence in which they stood watching me.

'Well, Capey?' asked Jerry after a moment.

'We're opening tomorrow night, that's all. We're not giving up.'

I let my eyes wander over the faces I knew so well. Jerry, dark and lean, with a challenging air about him, even in the attitude of his hips as he stood there; Frikkie Mantoor, with his bashful boyish face and large ears; Renier, light-skinned, with his angry young eyes; the corpulent Barney, reminiscent of the Mr Toad of my childhood, with protruding eyes and shiny curly hair and sensual mouth; Doors with his Viking body, broad cheekbones, eyes far apart, his mouth large and vulnerable; and the two women – Gladys, plump, with vast bosom and posterior, Lucy tall and slim, brooding, with long smooth hair and provocative mouth. My group, my people.

'Are you with me?' I asked after some time.

'Why do you ask, Capey?'

'We started together,' said Doors, putting a huge arm round my shoulders, 'and we'll go on together.'

'Renier?'

'I'm here, don't worry. We'll show the bloody swine.'

'Barney?'

He averted his eyes for a moment before facing me: 'It's not that I'm not with you, Joseph. But I think after what's happened tonight it's time we seriously considered our chances.'

'Is true,' Frikkie blurted out, quite unexpectedly. 'One can't fart against thunder.'

I felt my throat muscles stiffen. 'You can't leave us,' I said softly. 'Not now.'

320

'It's now or never,' said Barney.

'Are you scared?' Jerry demanded aggressively.

'I'm not scared. But my life still means something to me. One's got to think of the future too, I'm not getting any younger.'

'You're not much older than I am, Barney!' I said.

'Perhaps it's different for you.'

'How different?' I asked angrily.

'For you the theatre is the only thing that matters. Not for me. I've got to settle down sometime. In the beginning I thought . . . oh, it doesn't matter. What I'm thinking *now* is that we're getting nowhere. I started off as a singer. I think it's better for me to go back to the Eoan people – while there's still time.'

'D'you really mean to say you want to skulk off like a bloody mongrel?' asked Jerry.

Barney looked past him, at me: 'Joseph, God knows I don't want to leave you in the lurch. But it's been a hell of a day. Those chaps aren't going to play games with us, they're serious. We can't win.'

'Do you fight only when you know you're going to win?' I asked.

'Don't make it more difficult for me, Joseph.'

The words burst from me: 'But my God, Barney! We've got to open tomorrow night!'

'For how long are they going to allow us to go on? Two nights, three nights, a month? Then we're back where we started. I can't go on like this. A man gets tired.'

'We're all tired.' I was pleading openly now. 'Don't rush into anything. Let's all go to bed and have some sleep first. Tomorrow everything will look different.'

'It won' ewwe' look diff'runt again, Joseph,' said Frikkie, with more determination than I'd expected of him. All the time I'd been arguing with Barney, he'd kept in the background, but now he was facing me squarely.

'You too, Frikkie?' I asked. 'I don't believe it.'

There were tears in his eyes. 'Don' bogger me up, Joseph.'

'Coward!'

'Yes, I am,' he said. 'I'm scared. They going to hurt us if we go on.'

'Can't you see they were only trying to scare us? There's nothing they can really do to us.'

'There's nothing that they can't do.' He wiped his eyes with a buttonless sleeve. 'I'm scared, I tell you. I'm shit-scared. En' I'm not scared to admit it.' He turned round blindly and went through the door. In one quick movement Jerry flung it shut behind him, stopping Barney who was on the point of following Frikkie.

'You stay right here!' he ordered. 'I'll *moer* you.'

'Let him go, Jerry,' I said, my voice strange in my ears. 'Everyone's got to make it out with his own conscience.'

He looked at me. After a long pause he stepped aside. Barney opened the door.

'Joseph . . . ?' He looked at me.

I shook my head.

He went out. The door remained open. Outside a scavenging dog was nosing in a crumpled newspaper.

'Anyone else?' I asked after Barney's footsteps had died away.

They didn't move.

'It's yes or no,' I said. 'You're either for me or against me. I don't want any in-betweens.'

Lucy made a half-hearted move towards the door.

'Stay here!' Jerry barked.

She stopped, looking at me.

'Are you staying or going?' I asked listlessly.

She began to cry. 'I'll stay. But God knows . . .'

'Gladys?' I asked.

'I hev'n' even ected fo' you yet,' she said. 'En' jus' look at it. I got to look after my brudder's children. It's not that I don' want to . . .'

After she'd left, Jerry closed the door.

'Ten little nigger boys,' he said through clenched teeth. 'OK, Capey, what's your orders?'

'We'll be onstage tomorrow night,' I said. 'Even if we have to offer them an impromptu programme of sketches, mime and music.'

'When do we start rehearsing?' asked Renier.

VIII

A few times Jessica took me with her to Father Mark. We usually found him in his whitewashed office filled with books, in the school building on the windy plains of Windermere. Apparently it had been in ruins before his arrival, but during the five years he'd spent there he'd rebuilt the long low building with the help of his pupils, adding a new roof, and whitewashing it so that it acquired an almost Spanish look. There were no trees apart from a thin lane of Port Jacksons serving as a windbreak for the few struggling flowerbeds he tended with such infinite care and patience. It didn't seem as if anything would ever grow there, but Father Mark never stopped digging and hoeing, watering and raking, setting up windbreaks, picking up litter blown there by the wind, exterminating pests. Actually, he was a Jesuit in the severest scholastic tradition, with a doctorate from the Sorbonne; and according to Jessica there were few evenings when he didn't continue reading and studying until well past midnight.

His appearance had made an immediate impression on me, on that day of Dulpert's memorial service: the tall figure, the severe, lean, tanned face with aquiline nose and deep grooves round the mouth, the short grey hair: an impression of confidence, conviction and great inner strength. That was why I was taken aback, meeting him at his school for the first time, to discover how much older and more exhausted he looked than I'd expected.

He wasn't there when we arrived, so Jessica showed me round the school and the small white church nearby. Inside it was sober, with pews of upainted pinewood, a neat rectangular altar with wax candles, a cheap painted plaster statue of the Virgin. It was quite different from the church of my youth, of course, yet it brought back the past with an unexpectedly violent shock: the winged preacher on the high pulpit, the organ trembling through the pews, by his one oblation of himself once given: to the contrary notwithstanding: Our Father which art in heaven, repeated after Hermien's chanting voice, and Noah on the back stoep on that Sunday afternoon of dazzling sun patches and deep shadows.

I felt sudden panic: I wanted to get out, back to the sun. Jessica didn't understand the near-nausea I felt; perhaps I couldn't explain it myself – there was only, deep inside me, the half-remembered words: *How terrible to give unto God what belongs to man.*

'Father Mark isn't here,' I said, agitated. 'Let's go home.'

But before we'd reached the car he arrived in his, even more battered and shaky than my own, and stopped in front of the school. He hadn't noticed us and for some time he remained sitting behind the wheel, slumped, with hanging head. At last he got out and went up the few steps.

'Father Mark,' said Jessica.

He turned round, screwing up his eyes against the sun. 'Oh, Jessica!' He stretched out his arms, embracing her for a moment when she reached the stoep.

'I've brought someone with me, Father.'

He seemed to stiffen slightly, as if he resented my intrusion. But then he put out his hand with a smile and said: 'Of course. This must be Joseph. I'm very happy to meet you.'

He took us to his office.

'Something to drink?' he asked.

Slightly put out, I looked round. Father Mark smiled, removed a few hefty theological volumes from the nearest shelf and took out a bottle. There were glasses in one of the drawers of his desk.

'It's good whisky,' he said, 'Have it neat.'

He raised his glass. But as soon as we started sipping it, he turned away to the window and remained like that, his forehead resting against the pane, as if he'd completely forgotten about us.

'What's the matter, Father?' Jessica asked.

He shook his head; then said, in a choked voice, without turning back: 'Tired. One gets so utterly tired, my sweet. And one never seems to become immune.'

I wanted to ask something, but she stopped me with a small gesture. After a few minutes Father Mark brought his glass to his mouth and emptied it. Then he turned back to us and sat down on a corner of his overloaded desk.

'I've just been to the hospital,' he said, pouring himself another tot.

'One of your pupils?' asked Jessica.

'Yes. She was.' With great restraint: 'Nellie Burger. Fourteen years old. Left school a month ago. Pregnant. Then approached somebody for "help" and last night there were complications. They called a doctor. Apparently he only gave her some aspirin, without examining her. During the night she grew worse and they phoned the doctor again. He wasn't . . . available.' He moved his open hand across his face. 'This morning they phoned the hospital. She was in a very bad state. But they had no Coloured ambulance available and they said it was against the regulations to send a White ambulance for a Coloured patient. At lunchtime the parents came to me for help. We took her to hospital in my car. But by then it was too late.'

It was quiet in the room with the innumerable books. Outside children were playing football with an empty syrup tin.

324

'One grows so tired of trying to go on,' he said at last. 'But what else can one do but to go on believing, hoping, loving?'

Through the window the late afternoon sun fell on his face. I hadn't seen such utter exhaustion in anyone for a long time; and he seemed so vulnerable in his exhaustion. Somewhere inside me a small angry thought was stirring: this is a weariness which has got hold of us all, for it is a hard land and it shows no mercy.

'How do you manage to go on believing?' I asked.

There was a slight flickering on his lean cheeks. 'Like you, Joseph. I think we're really involved in the same fight.'

'I'm not a believer, Father.'

'There are forms of faith one isn't even conscious of oneself.'

'Now you're trying to find excuses for me.'

'None of us needs excuses!' he said quickly, with something of the force I'd been expecting from him. 'All we need is grace. And none of us can ever have too much of that.'

'Grace?'

'Never to confuse our resistance with hate. To have that love which makes resistance meaningful.'

'I suppose Dulpert would have said the same,' I replied. 'But what does "meaningful resistance" really mean?'

'I'll tell you what it means for me.' He poured me another tot from the whisky bottle, but not for Jessica or himself. 'It's something Stephen Spender once wrote about a visit to a Russian sculptor. They spent hours looking at the sculptures in the studio – Gogol, Mayakovsky, Lenin, Stalin, the lot. And then, hidden away in a back room, the work he'd been working on with his whole heart: an enormous white Christ.'

Almost resentfully I said: 'A pity it had to be white.' He didn't answer; he only looked at me, his grey eyes unfathomable, forcing me to go on: 'You must admit that being White makes it easier for you to believe.'

'No,' he said quietly, without hesitating. 'Judas was White too. So was Hitler. Perhaps there are moments when it may be more difficult for a White to believe, because his faith must overcome all the obstacles of his own whiteness. But suppose we didn't believe, suppose we allowed ourselves to get no further than the skin: what would happen then? That's where my struggles and yours are similar.'

And when we left, he said: 'Do come again. I'll pray for you both.'

We drove back in silence.

'He is so terribly tired,' I said when we got back to the city.

'It's because he's at everybody's disposal. Everybody uses him. And misuses him. They come to him with the most blatant lies, knowing very well he'll never send anyone away. I've often spoken to him about it. But his attitude seems to be: if they cheat him, they're not doing him any harm – only their own conscience.'

'It doesn't sound very practical.'

'No. That's why I'm so concerned about him. He's doing too much.'

'You help him a lot.'

'It's nothing in comparison to what he does for me. He's the only person apart from you whom I can talk to, about anything. If it hadn't been for him . . . just to be able to unburden oneself.'

'About us too?'

She was silent for a few seconds. Then she softly said: 'Yes. About us too.'

'But, Jessica! Don't you realise . . .'

'You've met him yourself. Do you think he'll ever breathe a word to anyone of what one's told him in confidence?'

'No. But it's . . .'

'If I hadn't been able to do that I don't think I could have gone on bearing it.'

I was too upset to speak. It was if she'd momentarily lifted a veil from something I'd never suspected in her before, a landscape of terrifying loneliness.

'And what did he say?' I asked after a long time.

'Exactly what he said this afternoon: "I'll pray for both of you." '

'Do you think it'll help?'

'I suppose it depends on us too.'

The case about *SA!* didn't last long. Anticipating that the nature of our play would make it necessary for the Court to attend a performance, the written text being only a small part of the whole, our advocate had warned us to prepare it for production again. Not that it made much difference. With great trouble Antjie was persuaded to return to us for that one performance, but Frikkie Mantoor was on tour with a musical group and didn't want to jeopardise his new job in any way, while Barney Salmon refused point-blank to have any more to do do with us. Which meant that within a few weeks we had to prepare a couple of raw recruits for a production which wholly depended on the most delicate nuances of interaction between all the members of the group.

The theatre was nearly empty when we appeared onstage that afternoon. The Judge and the members of the Court sat in a small group about eight rows from the front, surrounded by the vast emptiness of the auditorium. Acting in such circumstances resembled the ordeal devised for adulterers in the imperial court of ancient China: in front of the Emperor and his entire household the accused man and woman had to copulate on the floor of the throne-room, guarded by executioners with drawn swords: if they managed to reach a climax, it was interpreted as a proof of innocence; if not, they were immediately beheaded by the waiting guards. In a similar situation my ancestor Moses had impregnated the Xhosa woman, Sbongile, watched by his drunken masters. But my ancestor Moses was a more consummate court jester than I. My performance was sterile.

The next morning the Prosecutors presented his argument, followed by our own Counsel's reply; and the Court was adjourned for a week.

On the morning of the verdict we were all present: Jerry and Doors and Renier and Antjie and Lucy; and separate from us, in the group of White spectators, Jessica.

In a neutral and almost monotonous drone the Judge rejected our appeal, finding that *SA!* might be interpreted as offensive to certain population groups. Costs were awarded against us. It amounted to much more than the money Jessica had given us.

We could still proceed to the Appeal Court in Bloemfontein, of course, but our advocate wasn't optimistic about the prospects. The only result, he warned us, might be that the costs would be doubled.

'But we can't take it lying down!' protested Renier. 'We've got to carry on fighting as far as we can.'

'Let's rather start on something new,' I suggested.

'So that they can ban it again? What are we going to live on?'

'What are we going to live on if we appeal?'

'It's tickets anyway,' said Lucy. 'I can't take it any longer. Sorry, boys. I wan'ed to get out last time but you stopped me. This time it's finish' en' klaar.'

'Let's take a vote,' I suggested desperately.

Renier was the only one who wanted to appeal.

'All right,' he said when the majority went against him. 'Then I'm clearing out too. I thought you had guts. I can use my time better than this.'

'What are you going to do?' I asked.

He looked at me with flaming eyes: 'I had faith in you when we started. I thought you were prepared to fight all the way. Now you're just one of those who make a lot of noise, and then shut up when something happens.'

'You're over-excited, Renier,' I tried to reason with him. 'You're young.'

'And what about you? I thought you were young too. But you're fucking middle-aged already.'

Jerry and Doors and I remained, the three of us.

'Well?' I asked. 'Is this the end?'

'Not a damn!' said Doors. 'We starting again. We'll get new boys. Never say die, man.'

'From scratch . . . ?'

Jerry didn't look at me.

Once again it was Doors who said: 'Ja, from scratch. They think we're weeds but they can't jus' pull us out like that.'

'What can we do?'

'Never mind what. I can do circus tricks if we got to. Anything. Jus' as long as we go on, so people can *see* us going on. We not doing it mos fo' us, man, it's fo' the whole blerry lot what watch us.'

All right. We would start again. He was right: we were no longer doing it for ourselves alone.

After Doors had gone home, Jerry said: 'I can get Lucy back without any problem. It only depends on you.'

'She won't come back, forget it.'

'You want to bet? Capey, you give her one night of the old in-and-out, and she'll be back wagging her arse.'

I shook my head.

'What have you got against her?'

'Nothing. I've slept with her before. But things are different now.'

After a pause: 'Jessica Thomson?'

'You know yourself, why do you ask?'

'But Jesus, Capey! Are you starting a one-man-one-fuck business? You're not quite soft in the head, are you?'

'I'm sorry, Jerry.'

328

'Stuff it.'

'What do you really know about me and Jessica?'

'I don't want to know anything. If you've made up your mind to destroy yourself, it's got nothing to do with me.' Then he suddenly jerked up his head. 'No! That's what's making me so mad: it's *got* a lot to do with me. Do you think I want to see you break your neck? Can't you think for yourself?' He got up and started walking furiously to and fro. 'My God, man! I won't try to stop you if you're feeling itchy. Take anything. But why her? What's she got between her legs that others haven't?'

I hit him. His head jerked up as he staggered against a bookcase. For a moment he thought he was going to come back to attack me. But he only lifted his hand and rubbed his jaw slowly before he said:

'Sorry, Capey. But Jesus! Can't you see what you're doing to me? Can't you see what you're doing to yourself?'

He went home, I remained behind in one of the two small white-washed rooms he'd found for me in the house of Aunt Lallie, an old blind woman, in the Malay Quarter, after the Geustyns had thrown me out.

There was yet another station behind us, I thought. I could see him suffering. Every grain of logic in me agreed with him. And yet I knew of nothing else I could have done. It was not selfishness or sex which kept me with Jessica. But I had only two things left in the world to believe in: Jessica, and the group. In a strange way they were becoming more and more identified with each other. Both were threatened, both were indispensable, both were torture. But without them there was only the abyss.

Strange, the deep need both of us felt in those tumultuous days, to go to the sea, some lonely beach where we could be alone and swim naked and wash ourselves clean of everything. But it never worked out. On the few occasions we did drive to a beach, there were always other people; the only time we were left in peace, near Llandudno, there was a dead dog on the sand, swollen and stiff, legs grotesquely pointed upwards, partly devoured by crabs, and it upset Jessica so badly that we had to leave. The stench was too much even to bury it; and all she did, impulsively, was to tie two sticks together, cross-wise, and plant it in the sand beside the hideous thing. When we tried again, on another occasion, we were driven back by an unexpected thunder shower; another time the car broke down. And gradually we came to accept it as something we were not allowed to have.

Our bit of silence in the heart of the whirlwind – and it was precisely in that time of worrying, anxiety and despair that we spent our most meaningful hours together – we had to find in the city: occasionally in my lodgings, under the blind eyes of Aunt Lallie; but mostly in hers.

Once, one single time, we went up the mountain, a night I remember above all others. We went to Kirstenbosch separately, she by bus, I in my car. From the botanical gardens we strolled up the slope, I in front, she following several hundred yards behind, as if it were coincidence that we were going in the same direction; until we'd gone far enough, safely sheltered by the highest groves.

Through the pine needles the summer breeze was stirring, causing that nearly inaudible hissing sound peculiar to pines, as if it were the earth itself moving through space. On the warm, soft mattress of pine needles we lay down, looking up at the sky, more intensely blue than usual through the high branches. Was it idyllic? Only in as much as a dream can be idyllic if one knows that one's dreaming, or a Nativity play if one realises that Mary is only Hermien, and Joseph only Willem.

In her old, absent, gentle way she caressed my arm and hand with her fingertips.

I laughed: 'It's as if you're reading Braille.'

'I *am* blind.' She looked into my eyes.

'Still?'

'Still. Sometimes, when I touch you like this, I feel I'm beginning to know who you are. But I still don't know who I am.'

'Only when you're touching me?'

'Or you me. It's like you said, like Braille. Touching is important to me, I can't live without it. I first discovered it on my trip through Africa.' She reflected for a while. 'In Ethiopia, or Kenya, or Tanzania: one sits in a bus, with chickens and goats and dried fish, and people chewing sugar-cane; and if the woman next to you gets sleepy, she puts her arm round you and drops her head on your shoulder, and you hold her while she's sleeping. And in Ethiopia, where I stayed with the girl I'd met on the bus, I told you about her: Elizabeth, her father was an army officer and we lived in their quarters in the military camp, three families in one room – she and I shared a single bed, wrapped round one another to stay warm and to keep us from falling off. Now if we'd

330

been two English girls, each would have clung stiffly to her edge of the bed, trying to "maintain her dignity". But Africa taught me how necessary it was to touch people. More than a necessity : a need, a natural thing like eating or sleeping. Ever since I arrived here it's been different, embarrassingly so . . . A man like Richard has a fit if you suddenly touch him. That's also a form of apartheid.'

We talked for hours; then opened the books we'd brought with us and she lay listening while I read to her : the sonnets of Shakespeare, Rilke's elegies, St John of the Cross.

> *Let us rejoice, Beloved,*
> *Let us go to see ourselves in your beauty,*
> *To the mountain or the hill*
> *Where flows the pure water;*
> *Let us enter more deeply into the thicket.*

We went on reading from Father Mark's brown volumes until it was dusk and we could no longer see.

'We must go back,' I said.

'Must we?'

It was silent. Only the pinetrees sighing in the cosmic wind as we drifted through endless space. The sky was deep blue and clear; the night would be warm.

'We can stay here,' I said.

And she answered, from St John : *'The wood and its beauty in the serene night, with a flame which consumes and gives no pain.'*

We spoke a lot about him that night. It was like our first night in the strange house in Oranjezicht when we'd also had so much to say that we never thought of going to bed at all. We didn't exclude the body for a moment, we were as deeply conscious of it as Donne, or St John of the Cross; we sat close together in an embrace lasting all night; but we didn't make love, it wasn't necessary, we'd temporarily transcended the need for it. After the active night of purification when we'd come back from Bain's Kloof, this – was to stay within the framework of St John – the wonderful passive night of fulfilment. That was what we talked about : his *Dark Night of the Soul* when there was no light to distract one's attention and one could penetrate into the heart of love, *O night more lovely than the dawn.*

'It's so easy to have faith when we're together like this,' she said.

331

'When you're gone and I'm alone in the daytime, it all seems so impossible. I never know whether I'll ever see you again. I never know what's going to happen.'

'And then you feel afraid?'

'It's fear, and doubt, and despair, everything. Did you know that I'd already taken out my suitcase once to pack my things and run away?'

'You can't do that, Jessica!' I grabbed her shoulders. Then my grip slowly weakened and I bowed my head.

'It's not because of what you're doing to *me*, it's because of you; I don't want to destroy you. And what else can there be but destruction if they ever caught us?'

'It would be worse for you.'

'For me?' She shook her head against my shoulder. 'Sometimes I feel nothing can ever really happen to me, that I'm untouchable. No, not untouchable; only . . . not involved. How can I explain it? In this country – I can't be Black or Coloured or carry a pass or live in Langa. And it's terrible to remain outside once you've seen what's happening. Not because I'm a foreigner. But because I'm me. And because I don't know myself. Does it sound terribly confused?'

I laughed softly. 'Yes. But one day we'll frighten all the spiders away so that Miss Muffet can have her curds and whey in peace.'

'Perhaps it would be better if a spider really bit her one day. Now she manages to get away every time, and nothing happens to her.'

'One day . . .'

'We shouldn't talk about one day,' she said with sudden vehemence. 'One day doesn't exist for us.'

'What do you mean, Jessica?' I asked in anguish.

'One day it will all be over.'

'Why do you say that?'

Without listening, she went on: 'Perhaps one can only really love a person if one knows there'll be an end. If that end is already part of it all.'

'How can one love in such a negative way?'

'Negative? Perhaps that is the most positive form of love there is. With your blind eyes terribly open.'

'Are mine closed?'

'You're keeping yourself alive by believing in a different world from this one.'

'How can you say that? I know this world, I live it every day.'

'But you don't believe in it.'

'I believe in you.'

'That's what I mean, Joseph. That's what terrifies me. If you become dependent on me . . . While I don't even know myself.'

'*I* know you.'

'How can you ever be sure?'

'Because only when I'm with you I know who I am. These past years I've often thought: among all the parts I've done and am still going to do, there's only one I really want to play, and that happens to be the only one I'll never be allowed to play.'

'What's that?'

'Joseph Malan. Just me. A man. A human being.' I held her against me. 'And you're the only one who's ever made it possible for me.' Even while I was saying it, I knew how unfair it was to her, and how cruel: for through my words I was making her responsible for my life, the one thing she feared – and how could anyone expect that of another, and I of her? Yet, if one really loved, what else could one do but ask precisely that?

That was our night on the mountain. And a week later, at the end of October, Richard returned from Johannesburg.

There was nothing about Jessica which gave me the slightest reason to suspect that anything had changed or become more difficult. She was withdrawn at times, or worried, or depressed, but all that was explicable in the circumstances. In fact, I probably was withdrawn or worried or depressed more often than she ever was – and then it was she who, with her gentle warmth, had to sustain my faith.

Richard was often present when I visited her. Sometimes, when he gave her a paternal kiss or accidentally touched her hand when he took a cup from her, I had to clench my teeth to restrain my possessiveness. Yet, when I thought it over objectively, I realised that my reaction was ridiculous: Richard was fifty-five, he'd reached a stage of unbearable uncertainty about his work and himself: and with her youth and vitality she could help him to regain confidence in himself. That was all, I told myself; that was all.

It was ironical that, in fact, his presence made it easier for me to see her. If I knew that he was with her, I could visit her openly. Of course, we had to go on pretending in his company, revealing neither by gesture nor by word what really existed between us.

Only much later I realised what a macabre comedy we'd been playing.

It was I who suggested that she invite him for dinner that Sunday night. The verdict in our court case had just been given, on the Friday; and I felt a need to be close to her as much as possible. It would be unbearable to wait for midnight or later, as before, to hurry furtively to her flat.

I picked Richard up at his flat at Mouille Point. It never failed to surprise me, not only that he had no car, but that he couldn't even drive. He revealed a strange clumsiness whenever he was confronted by anything practical or mechanical. I can remember thinking on that particular evening, on our way to Kloof Nek: *I'm not surprised that you lost your two wives so easily. If you can't even handle a car, how the hell can you handle a human relationship?*

Richard kissed her lightly when she opened the door; I said: 'Hello, Jessica.'

Drinks in hand, they spent some time with me in the kitchen, while I was preparing the meal (Jessica was such a hopeless cook that I usually took over whenever there was a special occasion), but I soon sent them out. Working by myself, I strained my ears to listen to their conversation in the lounge; and to their silences.

At last I took the food to the table, announcing: 'De Maaste' enne Meddim is served.'

They laughed. For a moment, a fleeting moment, I was the jester in their court. Then Jessica looked at me without Richard noticing it, and through her move the two of us were momentarily united and he subtly excluded.

'How's the new book coming on?' I asked him after pouring the wine.

'I collected an awful lot of stuff in Johannesburg,' he said. 'But I don't know. I've started writing four times now, but I don't seem to be able to get past the first twenty or thirty pages.' Jessica and I looked at him quizzically. He shook his head: 'There's a sort of inner numbness which makes it impossible for me to get down to it. When friends from overseas visit me, they always seem to envy me because of the "challenge" this country offers a writer. But, you know, I'm inclined to believe Toynbee: in some situations the challenge can become too great for effective response.'

'One should never allow it to go so far,' said Jessica.

'I don't think one's got much of a choice.'

'One must. If you can't choose, you aren't human any more.'

334

'Every person has just so much energy and no more,' he insisted. 'In this country so much of it is squandered on other issues that very little remains for creative work. Then one begins to lean more and more on other people.'

'One must be able to be whole and self-sufficient,' she said.

'A year ago I might have agreed with you,' I interrupted. 'But now I'm beginning to think: no man can exist completely on his own. One needs at least *somebody* who believes in one. Utterly alone it becomes impossible.'

She looked at me.

'Perhaps,' Richard volunteered, 'the difference is simply the fact that Joseph and I are men, and you a woman.'

'*Vive la différence*,' I said lightly.

But she couldn't be persuaded so easily. 'That's irrelevant: both of you are inclined to romanticise women. Which is just as bad as degrading them. Your problem is that you're too similar.'

'Our only similarity,' said Richard, 'lies in the form of our commitment.'

I watched his right hand toying with a fork, and the light playing on the coarse hair covering the back of his hand and his wrist protruding from the cuff of his expensive silk shirt. Something in me rebelled against the facility of his comparison.

'How committed are you really, Richard?' I asked, watching him intently.

'All I meant was that both of us chose art, both of us believe in a new world.'

'What does your world look like?' I insisted.

To my amazement he was suddenly so moved that his voice choked: 'A world which won't have any room for me.'

'How can you believe in such a world?' asked Jessica.

'It's the very basis of my belief,' he said. 'For what am I at the moment? I'm White. But I'm revolting against everything White represents in this country, and so my sympathy lies with those who aren't White. It turns me into a sell-out and a traitor, since in our society every person is judged, and damned, by his relation to a particular group. And in the world I want one will be judged solely according to one's loyalty to mankind. I'm sure you'll understand that, Joseph. The world I want is the sort of world your Hamlet believed in – the world of Antigone.'

335

'To have that one would have to be like Antigone all the time,' said Jessica. 'Virginal, in everything. That's why she had to die : only death could guarantee her virginity.'

'Don't underestimate Haemon!' I warned her.

'I'm not talking about a little membrane separating her from the world,' she said passionately. 'I'm talking about, well, something absolute. Innocence. And that she had, because she could still be shocked. We who're living in the world beyond the German horror camps, beyond Algeria and the Congo and Biafra, beyond Vietnam and Bangladesh . . . we're living after the Flood. There's nothing new left. And unless we can return to the first act of faith . . . That's the world I want to believe in. Where everything can be new again.'

'A consummation devoutly to be wish'd,' I said. Then, more seriously : 'You're both trying to exclude yourselves from a new world, you're both thinking in terms of a possible heaven. You're free to, of course. Perhaps I even envy you. But the only world in which I can believe is one which *won't* exclude me – with my brownness and my faults and my defects, with everything that makes me human. And unfortunately that implies a world in which there'll never be an end to struggling.' I got up, gathering the empty plates. 'In any case, we're all talking crap. Does our conversation make any difference to the world and the hell outside? To the hell in us?'

And the real hell, I thought as I took the plates to the kitchen, probably lies in the very words we choose to describe heaven.

Behind all the words, stripped of all the words, all that was important was : she, and I; and he. I stood there wishing him out of the way, longing for her, not for her words but her body which I could eat and drink and change into wine, *to the contrary notwithstanding*.

But Richard remained. Once I felt so desperate that I was on the point of leaving myself, to put an end to the evening's misery. But I didn't move. Rather be with her imperfectly than not at all. For we had no certainty about the morrow. The next day might be much worse.

He kept on talking, talking, enmeshing us in the web of abstractions he could manipulate with such mastery and which I was beginning to find as revolting as the shroud of Lazarus – even though I realised it was his only defence against the world, his alibi against life.

When the clock struck half past eleven I rose impulsively and said : 'Well, it's getting late. Come on, Richard, I'll take you home.'

He was so surprised by the sudden announcement that he was on his feet before he thought of protesting: 'It's – it's not necessary at all, I...'

'No trouble. Come on. Good night, Jessica.'

For a moment I still wasn't sure whether he would really come; then he followed me. I held the door for him to pass; and quickly, behind his back, I whispered to her: 'I'll be back.'

She nodded.

He kept on talking all the way to Mouille Point; I uttered little more than monosyllabic grunts. He invited me to his flat for a drink, but I found some excuse and drove back straight away. In Kloof Nek I parked and locked the car and walked the last few blocks to her building, waiting under the trees until she signalled from the balcony.

We had a bath together; and as we were drying one another there was a knock on the front door.

I know of no other fright in my life so shattering as that I experienced the few times someone knocked while I was with her. The first second of stunned silence, followed by nausea, the feverish grabbing of a towel (*I heard thy voice in the garden, and I was afraid, because I was naked*), the frantic spasms of my heart.

With my bundle of clothes and shoes pressed against me I fled to the balcony where I dressed with numb hands while she went to the front door and called:

'Who's there?'

A man's voice answered. The door was opened. Then I recognised Richard.

'What's the matter?' I heard Jessica ask tensely. 'Have you forgotten something? How did you come?'

'By taxi.' A pause. 'I feel cornered in my flat. All evening I wanted to... What's wrong?'

It was too banal, too melodramatic to believe. All it lacked was for me to come tumbling through the curtain to make it pure Restoration Comedy.

I could hear her trying to control her voice – the balcony door was wide open, only the curtains were drawn – announcing as quietly as possible, with shocking directness:

'Joseph is on the balcony. Shall we go there?'

Without waiting for them I pushed the curtain aside and went to them. The flat was still dark.

He gave a step backwards as if it was he who'd been caught. 'Oh, I didn't . . .'

Jessica put on the light. I was still buttoning my shirt.

'I didn't mean to disturb you.' For a moment I thought he was going to cry. He went back to the door, hesitated, turned round and said, like a well-meaning amateur: 'I left my cigarette lighter here and I couldn't find any matches in the flat, so I . . .'

We all started hunting for the lost lighter, although Jessica probably knew as well as I that he'd put it in his pocket before going home.

'Perhaps you left it in my car,' I suggested. 'I'll go and have a look.'

'No, don't bother. It probably fell in the gutter when I got out, or something.'

'I'll go anyway.'

I walked the four blocks to my car, finished a cigarette and then went back, my hands thrust in my pockets, whistling – not gaily, but the way one whistles in a churchyard. When I entered the flat I could see that she had cried, but I looked past her.

'Can't find it anywhere,' I said. 'Perhaps it'll come out tomorrow.'

'I'm sure it will.' He hurried to the door. 'Well, I'm so sorry I . . . Thanks for the trouble, Joseph. Jessica, I . . .'

'Can I take you home again?' I offered.

'No, no. There'll be taxis close by.'

It wasn't true, of course: but it caused me some bitter satisfaction to say: 'Well, if you're sure . . .'

'Quite sure.'

'I'm on the point of leaving too.'

'No, it'll do me good to walk down the hill.'

'Good-bye, then, Richard.' I took my hand from my pocket. 'Here, use my matches in the meantime. It'll see you through the night.'

He looked at me, his cheeks discolouring; almost snatching the box from my hand, he said: 'Good night.'

I closed the door behind him and turned to her. A few of the buttons down the front of her lilac dressing gown were still undone after rushing from the bathroom.

'Fasten your buttons,' I said quietly.

She looked up.

'Put off the light,' she whispered after a moment.

When I came to her she began to sob. I held her tight, but it didn't really feel like me. That was the worst, that it could be so unemotional.

338

But then, after a long time, I had a curious inspiration. Still holding her against me, instead of trying to comfort her, I said:

'Cry. I want you to cry.'

She sobbed: 'Why?'

'Cry for Little Miss Muffet,' I said.

Grasping me frantically she began to sob more violently.

'Cry for your garden,' I said. 'Cry for your Nanny.' It was as if something completely broke down inside her. I waited for a long time before I went on, with long pauses in between: 'Cry for your parents. Cry for the Australian in the villa of Port Lligat. Cry for your lecturer at LSE. Cry for your trip through Africa. Cry for Father Mark. Cry for the girl who died. Cry for Richard's lost wives. Cry for me.' And at long last: 'Cry for us sitting here tonight.'

It was a strange catharsis for both of us. Afterwards I made tea in the dark kitchen and took it out to her on the balcony. I waited until the cups were empty.

Then I asked: 'Was he here before?'

'You know he often comes here.'

'Does he love you?'

A pause: 'Yes.'

'A long time?'

'He says from the day we met.'

And then the most difficult question of all: 'And you?'

In the dark she turned her dark eyes towards me, saying: 'No. Of course not. I pity him. In many respects I look up to him. But that's all.'

'Why did he come back tonight?'

'To be with me. To ask again.'

'Has he asked before?'

'He asks every time.'

'And what do you say?'

'You know me, Joseph. You know what I'll say.'

'Not yes?'

'How could I be disloyal to you?'

Her simple trust made me lower my head. 'I'm sorry, Little Miss Muffet.'

'No!' she said angrily. 'We mustn't be sorry. That'll degrade it.' She fell silent. After some time she added: 'It's changed already. It's no longer ours only.'

'Father Mark has known for some time.'

339

'He's different. Now ... it belongs to the world.'

'Surely Richard won't talk about it?'

'No, never. But it has changed.'

'I know.'

'Do you understand why I spoke about Antigone tonight?' she asked. 'About virginity, about innocence?'

'I understand it so well, my darling. Not only tonight, but every time you speak about it.'

'And ... now?' she asked.

'Now I suppose Father Mark will have to pray for us again.'

Once again we sat through the dark hours; once again we didn't make love, but it was different from the night on the mountain.

In the early dawn I drove through the empty city back to my small rooms in the Malay Quarter. Richard loved her, I thought. She didn't love him, it was true, but she might still learn to. And if it was possible, even if it would make her unhappy in the end, even if she would leave him later like the others : wasn't it my duty to allow her that freedom? For what could I offer her apart from purgatory and hell? If I loved her, oh God, if I loved her : shouldn't it be a love that set her free from me?

But not to Richard!

Driving through the half-dark streets with dry eyes, I wished that I could say to myself as I'd said to her : Come : I want to cry. Cry for the slave girl Leah and for the murderer Adam. Cry for Moses and his dark wife. Cry for Dlamini/Daniel who was blinded for his love; and for Rachel who cannot be comforted. Cry for Abraham and his beautiful white wife, and for the children David and Katryn. Cry for Jacob and Elise and his *Pilgrim's Progress*. Cry for Sophie in her large brass bed, the Sophie of Sunday afternoons and the Holy Communion. Cry for the note of a piano in the dark and for the slave bell ringing, for *Robinson Crusoe* at the irrigation dam, and a journey on a horse-cart in the rain; cry for Dulpert and Gran'ma Grace, for Ursula, for Fatima's shy breasts and Sheila's love; cry for Beverley; cry for Simon; cry for Harry and for Jerry and for those who left you and for those staying with you. Cry, Joseph, cry for yourself, oh Jesus, cry.

IX

I hadn't seen Derek for a long time. I knew that, in a new spurt of energy stirred up by his enormously successful Chekhov season in the Transvaal, he'd spent a long time overseas. Now he'd just come back and I hardly recognised him when I saw him again.

His flat in Bantry Bay looked like the scene of a shipwreck, strewn with crates and trunks and boxes, with books and clothes, theatre programmes and Victorian bric-a-brac littering the floor.

'It looks as if you've been visited by the SB,' I joked.

'Jesus, baby!' He laughed. 'Have you ever seen such a madhouse in your life? Emigrating at my age!'

'You don't really mean it, do you?'

'Sure I do. I'm going to bugger off. There's nothing like a new beat for an old whore. I thought I was taking a holiday after all these years, but when I opened my eyes I was back on the London stage. God, my darling, and I picked up the most incredibly handsome boy, we've moved into a house in Chelsea, and I got a contract from the Royal Court. Now can you beat that?'

I shook my head. 'When I saw you last time I thought you were a candidate for one of Oom Appie's funeral policies.' I reflected. 'But emigrating? Aren't you going to miss the country?'

'Miss what? Church fêtes and pancakes? Young turds with doctorates and political aspirations? Our culture explosion? You're kidding. You should know by now : for people like you and me it's not a matter of "all the world's a stage" but of "the stage is all the world". All stages are equal, only some are more equal than others, it's just like sex. And now I've found my second breath; life begins at forty and all that. Next thing I'll be on health foods. But before I'm quite decrepit, darling, I'm going to have one last fling, and this is it.' Then, out of the blue, he announced : 'What's more, you're going with me. That's why I brought you here today.'

'How do you mean I'm going with you?'

'Baby, for most of us two years is a hell of a long time. But they still remember you at the Royal Shakespeare. I had a chat with them and they're ready to take you back. Just sign on the dotted line. How long will it take you to pack?'

'Steady, Derek,' I said. 'I haven't said yes yet.'

'Shit, man!' He looked at me with his penetrating eyes; on his cheeks the network of delicate purple veins was more marked than before. 'Do you want me to lick your arse? You're worse than Jesus in the desert.' He came nearer. 'Look, my darling, I was too late for your court case but I read all about it. I've got a hell of a respect for what you've been trying to do. But now they've blocked your way. What else can you do?'

'We've already started recruiting new actors.'

'Don't tell me they're flocking to you like a lot of eager little cunts to a modelling agency.'

'No. But we'll find them. I'm exploring the Cape, Jerry's gone up to Johannesburg.'

'And how long is it going to take you to train them?'

'We can start with a couple of easy little programmes.'

'And is that your new vocation in life? – training young clots for easy little programmes? Fuck it, baby, you owe it to yourself to do something worthwhile. You can't go on mixing with shit.'

'My people aren't shit.'

'O Jesus!' He threw up his arms. 'Don't talk like that, you're sounding like a second-rate Cabinet Minister. What you need, is a proper old-fashioned bout of thinking. Let's face it, man: you've been going down the drain steadily. You've tried the patriotic bit, and it didn't work. Now it's time you start thinking about the theatre again. That's your first and final responsibility.'

I shook my head. 'Don't tempt me, Derek. I can't go away.'

'I'm offering you a contract, baby.'

'I can't.'

'Don't be in such a hurry. You can't miss a chance like this. You've got to face it sometime: there's no future for you in this country any more. Jesus, darling, you've tried, we've all tried: what more could you have done? And look at what I'm offering you.'

'Derek . . .'

'First promise me you'll think it over.'

'All right.' My eyes were burning. My throat felt dry, as if we'd really come a long way through the desert. To think it over, to admit what was only to obvious, to go away with him . . . To take Jessica with me and love each other openly and be together . . . Yes, I did owe it to myself to think again, as he'd said. I did. To stay on here, attacking the same windmill every time . . . ? He was right. I had to think again. With Jessica.

'All right,' I repeated, my throat still parched with thirst. 'I promise you I'll consider it.'

It was very late when I reached her dark flat; as usual, she opened as soon as I knocked, as if she'd been waiting at the door. But in the second the light from outside touched her before she pushed the door shut again, I could see how pale she looked; and almost immediately she said:

'I'd like a cigarette.'

I lit one for her.

'Thanks.' She inhaled. 'I was getting frantic, but I didn't want to go out to buy a new packet, in case you rang.'

'You're smoking a lot these days.'

She shrugged and went to the balcony ahead of me. The night was heavy with the brewing of an invisible storm.

'It's just the tension,' she said after a while.

'Is it really so bad?'

'I don't want it to affect me like this, but . . . Every time there's a knock, even when I know it's you, after you've phoned . . . But what about you? You look so tired, my love.'

'I've been walking all evening. I must make up my mind – and I don't know what to do.'

'About the group?'

'About everything.'

'About us?'

'Why do you ask that?'

'I know it worries you.'

'Does it worry you then?'

'I'm not important: I'm worried about you.'

'You must tell me,' I said urgently. 'I must know what you're thinking.'

'My love, my love, we're just talking past each other all the time.' For a moment she rested her head against my shoulder. 'We're both so frightened.'

'What for?'

'Just frightened. To admit it.'

'To admit what?'

'You know so well.'

343

'I don't know before you've said it. I want you to say it.'

'And I dare not say it. Neither of us dares.'

I suppose I could have decided it on that moment. Was it cowardly not to pronounce the words? Or would it have been cowardice to do so? Everything had become so endlessly complicated.

For a long time we sat on the balcony like two shells washed out by the night tide.

'Derek wants me to go to England,' I said at last.

'Derek?'

'De Villiers. I told you about him. He's just been there for more than a year and now he's back to pack his things. It seems I can get another contract with the RSC.'

'Joseph!' She was overwhelmed. Then, controlling herself, she asked: 'What are you going to do?'

'That's what I've come to ask you.'

'But you're the only one who can decide.'

I lifted her head with my hand and looked at her. 'Little Miss Muffet: will you go with me if I went?'

'Back to England?'

'Will you?'

'And get married?'

'Yes. Above all: to be free to love one another.'

'Will you still want to love me there?'

'Don't you trust me?'

'I trust you, my darling. Your love is the most beautiful thing which has ever happened to me. But once we're there . . . Will you be able to go on loving me? Or will you blame me for taking you away from here? Will you begin to reproach me that it was because of me that you couldn't stay here?'

On that moment I remembered Simon, and the night he'd come to my flat in Hackney: how he'd slowly gone to pieces like a sunflower transplanted to a cold climate; and how it had been impossible for him to come back, even after Bridget had left him. I could go overseas and take Jessica with me, yes: and act, and be happy: and then slowly sink back into a theatre which would insulate me from life like a hothouse; and deep inside me I would remember, inescapably, that I'd run away, that I'd been a coward who'd preferred to live on her; and through the years I would grow more and more bitter of my own poison, and listen to *kwela* music and dance with gouty feet and dream up fantastic re-

344

volutionary plans, and take to drink, and find it more difficult, each morning, to face the day.

But if I stayed : it would mean missing my boat like Dlamini/Daniel. It would mean choosing, open-eyed, a cul-de-sac. The cup was in my hand : I had to drink. Perhaps it would be easier for me than for my forefathers; perhaps I wouldn't be flogged, or drawn and quartered, or stoned, or tortured in a Nazi camp. Still, there were subtler ways, as Simon had said.

'So you're still hesitating?' she asked beside me.

I reacted with unreasonable anger : 'I'm not hesitating! It's you who are trying to complicate the issue. It's you who are afraid I may change in England. Do you remember the first night we talked, and how you said you had a yearning for the impossible? Is that why you love me? – because the impossibility of it all safeguards you and makes it unnecessary to choose?'

'No, Joseph. Now you're being cruel. Are you safe from the impossible then?'

'You don't want to answer.'

'Neither do you.' For a moment I thought she was going to fight back. Then she said softly : 'Neither of us can answer. We simply know too little about ourselves. One tries to be "noble" in love, but perhaps we should rather be humble enough to admit how confused and small we are. Does it matter why we love each other? If that's the only thing we have?'

In my desolation I pressed her against me. Our words had failed us. We tried both to avenge it and compensate for it by falling back on the primitive dialogue of bodies, without compassion or gentleness. On the balcony we wrestled like two possessed, like enemies, like Jacob and the angel at the ford; we wanted to hurt and wound one another, exposing, through the wounds, a deeper and more vulnerable layer; in our violence we tried to exorcise our fears by breaking through to a new tenderness : in that it became a struggle, not against each other, but with one another, together in our loneliness against the unintelligible wilderness around us.

Somewhere in the confusion of the weeks following Derek's departure I went back to Willem's office. It was Davey Sachs who'd turned up gleefully with a letter Willem had addressed to me care of the newspaper. My first reaction had been to throw it away. What could we still have to say to each other? And yet I was prepared to clutch at anything. The very fact that in the end I phoned him to make an appointment was a measure of my despair.

The office was unchanged, but after my long absence it seemed even more sumptuous than before. We talked for a few minutes, and drank tea, and smoked; I was waiting for him to mention the reason for his letter. He did it more directly than I'd expected.

'I've never felt happy about the way in which we parted last time, Joseph.'

'You couldn't have expected anything else in the circumstances, could you?'

'I know. But our friendship goes back farther than that.'

'The first time I spoke about it, you were embarrassed. With reason, I suppose, because most memories tend to be sentimental. And I didn't want to place you under any obligation.'

'I didn't ask you to come here today because I felt an obligation, only a very real need to talk to you.' It sounded just a bit too neatly formulated to convince me. But suddenly he asked : 'I suppose you've heard that I'm getting divorced?'

'No. I'm sorry.'

'You're not sorry and you needn't say so. I'm not sorry myself. It's only – well, a thing like that forces one to have a new look at one's whole life. And lately . . . You know, I can't understand how it's possible for people who grew up together to move in such opposite directions.'

'It's not difficult in a country like this.'

'I'm not talking about politics.'

'I should prefer not to talk about it either. But whether we like it or not, it's politics the moment you and I sit down to talk. For the simple reason that you're White and I'm Coloured.'

'Is it really unavoidable?'

'It happens, and that's all that matters.'

'In the beginning, perhaps. But if one goes beyond that?'

He lit a new cigarette. 'I've followed your career more closely than you may think.'

'The primrose way to everlasting bonfire?'

'I sometimes wonder what I contributed to force you in this direction.'

'Which "direction"?'

'Your particular brand of revolt. The way you seem to be inviting

346

more and more trouble. Your negative way of fighting.'

'If you regard it as negative, Willem, I don't think you understand it at all.'

'What I mean is that you'll get much more done in the long run if you were prepared to be a bit more accommodating towards people, towards the authorities. If, instead of attacking blindly, you were to . . . well, to try and reform things more creatively, from the inside.'

I couldn't help smiling. 'Willem, you and all those like you, in the white suburbs of our White cities : you have no choice but to defend the bourgeoisie. And I have no choice but to attack it.'

'But just attacking, attacking all the time . . . it's not only destructive, but self-destructive. Even a donkey doesn't hit its head twice against the same wall.'

'At least it proves that I'm not a donkey.' But suddenly my passion broke out : 'Do you really think I'm only fighting against walls, and windmills, and sheep? Don't you think I'm also fighting *for* something?'

'It's so vague. What could you be fighting for?'

'Something so simple it sounds ridiculous. I'm fighting for the elementary right to be accepted as a human being. For people to admit that I feel and think and suffer and believe like a human being. You see, if I didn't do that, I, too, might forget that I'm human.'

'Aren't you dramatising things, Joseph?' he asked calmly. 'I'm not for a moment trying to deny that you're in a terrible predicament. But you must be aware of the fact that a very serious debate about the plight of your people is going on among all sections of the White population.'

'That makes it worse!' I said. 'You have the nerve to sit down and talk about us and make plans for us, like a farmer sorting out his chattels for his will. We're only part of the movables.' I got up and looked down at him : 'Willem, how about playing Stanislavsky's game : let's start with the actor's magic *suppose*. Suppose my people were governing this country and decided : from tomorrow White Afrikaners will have political rights in the Orange Free State only. You're all repatriated – but we keep the gold and diamonds for ourselves, of course; and if you set foot outside the Free State, you must carry a pass and keep out of our theatres and schools and restaurants and trains and lavatories and churches : and you're not allowed to have property outside the Free State or to earn as much as we do for the same job . . .'

'Now you're simply reversing an historical process, which falsifies your picture. After all, we're living in an evolving society.'

347

'Are we really so much closer to the apes than you?'

'I'm not talking about the people: I'm talking of an entire social pattern evolving new forms.'

'You're talking about historical processes, Willem! And it doesn't seem to shock you that in the second half of the twentieth century we're still caught in imperialist structures?'

He stubbed out his cigarette. 'I hoped we would be able to find each other, Joseph. I'm still sure we can understand each other.'

'Can you understand what it feels like to come back from the Royal Shakespeare Company and be treated like a tramp or a criminal every day of your life?'

'But you're an exception.'

'My God, Willem! I and my people; every bloody hotnot among us: we're the only people created in this country. We haven't got brothers in Europe like you, or in Africa like the Blacks. All we've got is this country. And what have we got of it? Fuck-all.'

'If only you realised how well I can understand that, Joseph!'

'What are you doing about it? When you were in a position to do something, when you could have stood by us and helped us, you chose to dissociate yourself from us because we'd become an embarrassment to your companies. There's a hell of a lot of goodwill and understanding in this country, Willem – more than enough to fertilise a whole sewage farm.'

He got up too. I expected an outburst, but he quietly walked past me to his desk, and picked up a slip of paper.

'Joseph,' he said, his back towards me, 'the last time I saw you I had to speak to you as a company director because we'd been subsidising you officially. Today it's man to man.' He turned round. 'You must remember : there was a time when we were inseparable.'

'Children always live in a paradise.'

'But one never completely outgrows it.' He held out the piece of paper to me.

I went over and took it. It was a personal cheque for five thousand rand. I could see it tremble between my fingers.

'Do you believe me now? You asked me what I was prepared to do.'

'And in exchange for this?'

'It's yours.'

I reached the door like a somnambulist. Then he said : 'I hope you'll keep it secret. It might be interpreted wrongly.'

I made no theatrical gesture in response. In an illogical way I thought:
for the sake of our childhood I owed it to him to wait until I was outside
the building before I tore up the slip of paper and threw the bits into
the nearest *Keep Your City Clean* bin.

What I remember above all of the end of the year, is the terrible fatigue.
In January we'd opened with our exhausting *Hamlet*: in a way it had
been our climax. From there the rapids carried us down-stream, past
Jessica's arrival – *April is the cruellest month!* – and the winter fiasco
with the Camus, the dead-end of *SA!*, the police raid killing off *Tartuffe* even before opening night, the decisive blow of the court verdict.
The eviction from my flat in the Geustyns' house, the unbearable tension
created by Richard's return from Johannesburg, Derek's offer, the interview with Willem, the disintegration of our group . . . all that happened more or less simultaneously. And still there was no moment of
repose. With Jerry and Doors I had to get our new group going; and
to earn our bread we had to present endless little comic programmes
all over the Peninsula. Often we didn't get home before two in the
morning; and by six or seven the next day I had to be out of bed to
make arrangements, compile programmes, prepare plays, hunt for recruits and lead rehearsals. Blind old Aunt Lallie in whose house I had
my two small rooms, was also demanding in her way: there was shopping I had to see to, a pound of sugar, a small bag of flour, garlic, a
packet of sweets to help her through the dreary days; or else there would
be a leak on the roof to repair, or a loose corner of the kitchen linoleum
to tack down; and her row of red geraniums had to be watered daily.

During the first few weeks after I'd moved in she often came to my
room for a chat, an endless lamentation on the harshness of life and the
cruelty of people: she'd been beautiful in her youth, she assured me,
but a jealous lover had thrown acid into her face and injured her eyes:
ever since, she'd been leading a virtuous life, too scared that in her
blindness she might be saddled with an ugly man who wouldn't do
justice to her 'class'. After a time she seemed to realise that my life was
too busy for these conversations, and apart from the small favours she
still asked and which I couldn't refuse, she left me in peace.

I'd started working on a collage of *Othello*, similar to the *Romeo
and Juliet* we'd done before, but more gloomy, more threatening, more
explosive, approaching Othello as Victor Hugo and Kott had done, as
personification of the night, 'an immense, fatal Night', infatuated with

349

Desdemona, incarnation of dawn and day: and the natural union of these two seasons scandalises the world which, threatened by it and refusing to accept beauty on its own terms, reduces everything to a beast with two backs, to sordidness and infernal darkness. In this context the relationship between Othello and Iago becomes an elemental struggle between morality and intellect, between innocence and an essentially monstrous world. I've always found something elemental and archetypal in *Othello*, enhanced by Olivier's interpretation in London: now, through Kott, I discovered the play's exciting and disturbing links with Artaud – those words which made such an impression on me when I first read them that I can still write them with closed eyes: *All true freedom is dark, and infallibly identified with sexual freedom which is also dark, although we do not know precisely why. And that is why all the great Myths are dark, so that one cannot imagine them save in an atmosphere of carnage, torture, and bloodshed.*

Oh, if we'd still had our original group that *Othello* would have been an unforgettable thing. Jerry and I were still there, we would be Iago and Othello; and Doors Cassio. But we needed Lucy for Desdemona, with her smouldering sensuality which, in the course of the play, would burn out of her original bright chastity like a darkening flame. The girl we used in Lucy's stead, Wendy Claassen, was too loud and vulgar – even in bed, Jerry assured me ('Jesus, Capey, the neighbours asked me this morning whether we'd been slaughtering a pig last night'). The other recruits were equally clumsy. But we had no time to lose. With a frivolous new version of *Don Juan* we tried to break them in for the theatre, in the meantime struggling with our *Othello* rehearsals – for in January at the latest we had to be on the road again.

My only escape from the daily load of duties and crises was Jessica. But even then the escape was not always complete, for she was beginning to suffer from the strain – and also because Richard was often with us, forcing us to play, *à trois*, the game already too demanding for two: to know, and to pretend not to know.

His studied considerateness towards me made it worse. I often thought: God, if only the man would curse me and abuse me, it would make things easier: then, at least, I could have hated him as an equal. But his deliberate kindness, his 'understanding', his exhausting efforts not to offend me, his Anglo-Saxon persistence with the gentleman's game: that made it unbearable.

Changes usually occurred so subtly that they couldn't be recognised as new impulses from day to day: but one was clearly marked, and I recall it with sadness and with nausea.

It happened a few days after my interview with Willem. After a late-night rehearsal I arrived at her flat. She'd already been asleep: the phone awakened her; and she was warm and languid when she opened the door, fragrant with sleep and womanness. She brought me a drink and came to sit opposite me, her legs pulled up as usual, her short gown unbuttoned, so that she was completely exposed to me. In spite of the weariness desire stirred in me. And with the joy of a thirsty man finding a pool in the wilderness I marvelled, as before, at that particular familiar way she had of living with her body. Nothing about it need be covered or withheld; and because we loved one another, everything about her was as naturally and completely at my disposal as at her own. It would never cease to move me.

That was why I found that night so unsettling. For when we went to bed after I'd finished the drink and I took her in my arms, caressing her, tired, with subdued passion, she whispered:

'Do you really want to?'

I tensed. 'Don't you?'

'It's all right if you want to.'

I lay still for a while; then, leaning on an elbow, I tried to read her face in the dark: 'What's the matter, Miss Muffet?'

'Nothing. I'm only tired.'

'You've been tired many other nights. I too. But you've never . . .'

From far away she said: 'I told you it would be all right.'

I took my arm from her. She didn't stir. With weary dullness I lay down, on the edge of the bed, away from her, looking up at the dark ceiling.

'Are you angry at me, Joseph?'

'No. It's only that I don't understand.'

'I didn't think you'd react like this.'

'I didn't think you'd find my caresses irritating.'

'I only wanted you to hold me.'

I didn't answer. That desolation was worse than anything we'd known. The few inches separating us was a chasm.

And then I discovered that she was crying. I leaned over, putting my hand on her shoulder, trying to calm her, but she sobbed uncontrollably.

'What's the matter, my darling?' I pleaded. 'Why don't you tell me?'

'It's nothing.' Her body shook. 'It's nothing. I don't know. I just can't take it any more.'

A small bubble of suspicion rose in me. 'Has Richard been here to-night?'

'Does it matter?'

'Has he been here?'

'Yes. But it's not . . .'

'Did he say something? About us?'

She didn't answer.

'What did he say, Jessica? I want to know.'

'Nothing we didn't know already.'

'What?'

'That I had to think about you. That it was you who would suffer most. That I was being unfair to you.'

'Doesn't he think that I'd be a better judge of that?'

'But you're involved too deeply to see clearly any more. You don't want to see how dangerous it is.'

'What is the danger to us? If that's all we've got to make it worth while living in this hell?'

'It's not all. You have your group. Your work.'

'So he reckons I should concentrate on my work and let him do the bed-warming?'

'No one said a word about that!'

'But you're not blind, are you? You admitted that he loved you. I suppose he'd like to marry you . . .' It came as a shock to myself. After a long silence I asked quietly : 'Was that what he came for? To ask you to marry him?'

She nodded. I felt her head moving against my shoulder.

'And?'

'How can you ask?' There was a sob in her voice : 'I'm not interested.'

'You must admit it'll make everything much easier. You won't have to be afraid any more. You'll be able to appear everywhere in public with him, in the street, in restaurants, in the theatre.'

'Don't, Joseph!'

'Do you mean to tell me that you didn't even consider what he was offering you?'

'I considered it the way you considered Derek's offer.'

'And you're absolutely sure that you don't feel anything for him?'

'You know what I feel for him. I appreciate him very much. I would like to help him – so that he wouldn't be quite so lonely. He's very gentle with me.'

'And very concerned about me.'

'Richard thinks highly of you.'

'Are you taking his side now?'

Furious, I got up. But before I'd reached the bedroom door I stopped and turned back, shocked by the violence of my reaction. What was happening to me? Was I going mad? What destructive force in me was urging me to break down the one thing which still kept me going?

I went back to her. 'Forgive me, Jessica. I don't know what demon has got into me. Oh my God, we must be careful, else it's the abyss. We must keep away from it. We're still together.' Blindly in the dark I pleaded, feeling her hands on my face; she pressed my head against her breasts. I was crying as I did when I was small, with my mother. And she whispered over and over : 'Joseph, Joseph, Joseph.'

Later we fell asleep, still clasped together. And when we woke up the previous night appeared remote and unrecognisable.

'Forgive me, my darling,' I asked again. 'It was all . . . I was so terribly tired. And that business with Willem had upset me more than I realised.'

'What business with Willem?'

I told her about our conversation, and his cheque, and what I'd done with it. She listened very quietly, her head bent.

'You shouldn't have done it,' she said when I'd finished.

'Perhaps not. Perhaps it was the most insane and childish thing I've done in my life.' I looked at her. 'But he was trying to bribe his conscience, Jessica. My God, he was trying to bribe mine.'

'How can you be sure that he didn't mean it sincerely? What else could he have done to prove himself?'

'He'd written out that cheque before I arrived. He wanted to be sure that I'd take it from his hand. And that I would promise to keep it secret.'

'Doesn't it prove his sincerity? He wasn't interested in "gestures".'

'If he really wanted to keep it secret he could have done it anonymously. But he wanted to make sure that I'd know. And that I wouldn't embarrass him.'

'Suppose . . .' Her voice was almost inaudible. 'Suppose I gave you the money you still needed?'

'You've already helped us. That was enough, it was too much.'

'You still owe a lot.'

'We'll pay it off.'

'And if I've already paid it into your account?'

'You would never do such a thing.'

She turned away to her chaotic working table and found a bank slip under stacks of books and papers.

'No, Jessica.'

'I did it anonymously, Joseph.'

'Why do you tell me about it then?'

'Because after what you've told me about Willem . . . you would have guessed. And then you would have despised me.'

There was no blood in my face. I felt sick.

'You must allow me this one thing, Joseph.'

I shook my head.

'Oh my God,' she said in despair. 'I just wanted it to happen, I wanted you to understand . . . But now you've forced me. Don't make me feel soiled, Joseph. Believe me. Please believe me.'

I lowered my head. After a long time I looked up and clutched her to me, concerned about her, concerned about myself, grateful, relieved, confused. And soiled, like her.

Father Mark was watering a bed of nasturtiums when I arrived. After a day's merciless Southeaster on that exposed plain the poor little plants looked tattered and wilted, but nothing could put him off his gardening.

'Sooner or later the sun and wind are going to win,' I said.

'Who do you think won in the end,' he asked with mocking grey eyes : 'The mountain or Sisyphus?'

'I shouldn't expect you to appeal to him,' I said, sincerely surprised. 'Doesn't he belong to the "other side"?'

'I'm not so sure. I've always regarded Camus as one of the great believers of our time. Even though he may not have been conscious of it himself.' Then, with the same gleam in his eyes : 'I know others like him, just as stubborn.'

He handed me a garden fork to help him. Without any strain, like water finding its way through a flowerbed, our conversation went on. It was the first time I'd ever visited him alone and was expecting him to show some surprise or curiosity, but he was quite unruffled, which put me at ease too. We talked about his work and mine, the blazing summer

354

weather, the coming holiday season, about children in his school and members of his congregation.

After we'd finished in the garden and installed ourselves in his office with glasses of his choice whisky, he calmly said :

'I suppose you've come to talk about Jessica.'

'How did you guess?'

'If it had been anything else, you would have thought up enough rational objections not to come.'

'Why should I?'

'I think you're still a bit diffident about priests.'

'I haven't come to you as a priest but because you know Jessica so well.' I looked down into my glass. 'Even that has been difficult enough. I've never believed in burdening others with my problems. One should learn to find solutions on one's own, to suffer alone. But since I met Jessica . . .' I looked back at him. 'And now that I've come after all it feels like a form of betrayal.'

'You shouldn't feel like that. She's often come to me on her own.'

'But this time it's something new. Something worse.'

'You mean about the money?'

'How did you know about it?'

'Jessica was here this morning.' He sipped his whisky, studying the colour of the liquid in his glass. Then he asked :

'Why do you take it so badly?'

'I can't take charity from her.'

'Do you think it's charity?'

'It can easily become charity.'

'Only if you allow it to.'

'I've been helped by other people in my life, and every time it entailed some form of moral slavery.'

'Were they people who loved you unconditionally?'

I didn't answer.

'Doesn't that alter everything?' he insisted quietly. 'Look, I don't want to give you advice, Joseph. I don't think that's what you've come for either. All I can hope to do is to help another person find out what he thinks himself. I'll tell you about Jessica and me.'

Father Mark fell silent. When he looked up again, he said : 'I love her, you see.' Perhaps he noticed some uncertainty in my attitude, for he made a small gesture with his glass and explained : 'Not the way you love her, of course. But not in a cool, charitable way either. It's difficult to explain, but I've often tried to probe it and I'd like to share it with you. Perhaps I should start by saying: if I were younger, and not a priest, I think I would have loved her as a man loves a woman. But that doesn't mean that I regret being either old or a priest! Neither do I mean, and that's even more important, that I feel "safe" as a result of age or priesthood. It's rather a matter of being – shall we say: liberated from something. There is no need for me to "want" or to "have" her, she isn't meant for me. And so it can never occur to me to wish to subject her through giving and taking. In our relationship each remains completely free, because neither is threatened by desire or possessiveness.'

He sat playing with his glass in his hands. As at other times I became aware of the noise of children's voices outside; dogs barking; fowls cackling. The sounds of my childhood.

He resumed: 'Now I've tried to find out: why does this freedom exist between us? It's not simply a matter of excluding the body, for I've never underestimated or despised the body; and I find physical pleasure in being with her, or touching her. So all I ended up with was the exclusion of that element in one which wants to possess something or someone. It turns love into a feudal concept. The body needn't do it, but it tends to – probably because it feels the urge to assert itself in the short time it's conscious of its power. It's such a pity. For the one thing I believe and which Jessica has helped me to rediscover, is this: if you love someone, you want to do more than to give: you also want to have such complete trust in the other that you want to allow him, or her, to give to you. You're not giving because you have to and you're not receiving because you ought to. Giving and receiving become acts of free will. Because neither of you wants anything but that. In fact: in giving and receiving freely even the idea of "I" and "you" is suspended.'

After a while I said: 'Father Mark, but I'm young and I'm not a priest.'

He smiled. 'But that's exactly what I'm trying to say; that it shouldn't make any difference. It's more difficult, but it can't influence the quality of one's love. Do you think Abelard and Heloïse loved one another less after he was castrated?'

'That was different.'

'Was it really? You and Jessica can't ever "have" each other either.' I tried to protest, but he quietly went on: 'It has nothing to do with your being Coloured and her White. Nothing essential. All I mean is:

356

you're human, and so is she, and no human being can "have" another. Perhaps your circumstances even make it easier to grasp. You see, if one looks closely, nothing is left untouched by grace.'

'Do you think it's wrong of me – do you think I'm demanding too much of her – if I loved her?'

'I can't imagine love ever being wrong or too demanding: not if it's love.'

'But if I really loved her and only wanted what was best for her: shouldn't I rather go away and give her peace?'

'Do you think Jessica will ever find peace anywhere?'

'Perhaps not. But if there were such a possibility, don't I owe it to her to set her free from me?'

'Isn't she free with you now?'

I slowly looked up into his eyes. 'We're clinging to each other, Father. We're so frightened . . .' I put my glass down, completely exposed to him: 'I want to tell you the worst. I know it's degrading, but that's the sort of hell I'm living in nowadays: I'm beginning to doubt; I'm beginning to wonder whether she's not staying with me merely because she feels "responsible" for me. If I were a White and she'd grown tired of me, she would have gone away: then we would have been free. Now we are crucified to colour. For if she were to leave me now, she may think that I'll ascribe it to the fact that in our situation, because of my colour, she didn't want to stay with me . . . and so she'd rather torture herself and remain kind to me.'

It was absolutely quiet now, even outside.

'Don't be afraid to tell me that you despise me for it.' I didn't look at him.

'Don't you think I have some experience of hell myself?' He was weighing his simple silver cross in his right palm. 'Why do you doubt her love?'

'Because I'm frightened. Because I'm so terrified that I can't see clearly any more.'

'Because you . . . because you . . .' He smiled again. 'You see? You're still too much in the centre. An "I" which moves in between you and her, so that you can't see properly.'

'Then please help me see again.' I felt empty, squashed dry like a sponge. 'I don't know myself any more. I'm blind.'

'In every relationship one would be able to find the most possessive, narrow, mean motives for one's love. Usually one doesn't do it. Because

357

love is itself a form of faith: I believe that you're staying with me because you want to, and you believe the same of me.'

'That's what I want to believe, Father Mark.'

'It's the only way in which one can honour the other's integrity.'

'You must find it terribly unworthy of me that I lapse into doubting.'

'Do you think I never have doubts?' I looked up quickly and studied his lean, suntanned face in the twilight. 'Do you think I just go on without ever stumbling? Do you think St Theresa or St John of the Cross could ever have attained sainthood without intimately experiencing doubt?'

'Is it selfish of me to want to keep her?'

'In order to keep her you'll first have to possess her.'

Embarrassed, I asked: 'But, Richard . . . ?'

'If Jessica wants to marry Richard, she'll marry him. And if she wants to stay with you, she'll do so. All you can do is to love her. Then you'll be concerned about her. Anything else is less than love.'

Her own reaction, when I went back to her that night was completely unpredictable, and therefore unsettling; moving. After she'd closed the door behind us she shook off the light lilac gown and turned her body sideways so that the dim light from outside fell across her.

'Look,' she said. 'I've shaved it all off. Now it's like a little girl's. Are you glad?'

Glad?

Sad, and passionate, I fought all night against the memory of Hermien, heraldic on her rock.

Sometimes the three of us were together again. And one night when I dropped Richard at his flat in Mouille Point, he said:

'Come in for a drink.'

'Thanks, but I . . .'

'I know you want to go back to Jessica. But . . .'

'I didn't mean . . .' But it was true, and why should I try to deny it?

'You needn't stay long.'

With something cruel and bitter in me I asked directly: 'Are you jealous?'

Richard smiled grimly. 'Of course. But not, as you may think, only because of Jessica. It's because of you too: I never get a chance to talk to you.'

'There's so little we could . . .' But I broke off, almost in sympathy with him, and followed him to his flat in the huge modern building. What struck me, like the few other times I'd been there briefly, was the extraordinary tidiness and precision of everything: the bookshelves, ceiling-high, with the books classified according to subject, the records in alphabetical order; every cushion and modern chair in its place, even the papers on the desk arranged in neat rectangular stacks.

'I envy your orderliness,' I said, in a deliberate effort to unbend. 'It's never like this in my place.'

'Not in Jessica's either, is it?' he laughed. 'I've never seen such a disorderly person.' Then, more wryly: 'But don't let it fool you: this is about the only thing in my life which is orderly.'

While he was pouring drinks I looked through the bookshelves. There was one large section devoted exclusively to erotica, ranging from psychological and philosophical studies of prostitution, lesbianism, voyeurism and related subjects to a vast selection of pornographic books, some of them luxuriously bound in leather.

With a chuckle he brought me my glass, motioning towards the books: 'The noble art of substitution.'

'Does one need substitution?'

'If one's inclined to make a mess of life, yes.' After a while: 'Did you know I was married twice?'

'Jessica told me.'

He studied my face for a while. 'Both of them flops. My fault, I suppose. A writer is a vampire, Joseph. He preys on others. And that's unfair on any woman. There was a time, in England, when I deliberately limited myself to prostitutes. It's so uncomplicated. And strange, what sense of, yes, "loyalty" one finds among them. There was one, a young Scandinavian girl . . .' He sat down on one of his exclusively designed Swiss chairs and tasted his brandy. 'But I suppose the opposite is true too. The worst I ever came across was a girl, quite attractive, young, who kept her transistor radio on while I was there – and all the time I was fucking her she lay listening to a soccer match. The strangest thing of all was – now how do you explain that? – that afterwards I couldn't stay away from her, I kept going back, and every time she listened to the radio. Until, after months, I one night told her to switch off the bloody thing. She did it quite willingly. But do you know I couldn't reach an orgasm that night? And I never went back again.'

'And what about Jessica?' I asked deliberately.

He looked at me, then down again.

359

'Why don't you admit that you hate me?' I asked. 'It'll make every-thing so much easier. For both of us.'

'Perhaps too easy.' Beneath his bushy eyebrows his eyes burnt on me. 'In the Middle Ages, I suppose, we would have fought it out in a duel.'

'Oh no,' I said. 'Remember, a knight could only challenge his peers, not a squire.' And after a pause : 'Of course, no squire would have been so bold as to fall in love with a noble lady either. So there would never have been a problem in the first place.'

'You hate me, don't you?' he asked quietly.

'No,' I said, putting a photographic book back on the shelf. 'It's ludi-crous, isn't it?'

'Yes. All the more so since it was I who introduced you to her.'

'How did you meet her?'

'Friends in Johannesburg gave her my address. When she arrived here she stayed with me for a week.'

I glanced at him, quizzically, suspiciously.

He shook his head. 'Don't worry. You know how untouchable she can be.' He smiled wearily. 'Of course, she's different with you. But when she was here . . . she simply went her own way. In the beginning I thought she'd be like all the other girls I get to help me with typing and correspondence. But she was different. And one night when I . . . All she said was : "No, please don't." And that was that. The next day I found her the flat where she's living now.' He gazed at the ice cubes melting in his empty glass. 'Sometimes she seems to remind me of Browning's Pippa. You know : destined to wander through the world, and waking people with her little song, and going on again as lonely as before.'

'And those she's awakened?'

'They stay awake. They learn to live. But God, life can be so awful.' He got up to pour another brandy and add new ice. 'The worst is, I simply can't get down to writing any more. Before, I used to work methodically. But now . . .'

'Would it have turned out differently if she'd switched off her radio that first night?'

He looked at me for a long time before he twigged, and he blushed. 'I love Jessica,' he said quickly. '*That* is what went wrong. It happened twice before . . . Love is a dangerous thing, Joseph.'

· 'Don't you think I know?'

'Of course you know.' He swallowed some brandy. 'I failed twice.

I thought: perhaps this time . . . But I've already lost Jessica. I know. The worst is: I sometimes get the impression that all three of us have lost. And for which one of us will it be most destructive? I'm getting on: what have I got left? Girls who come round to do my typing and pull down their panties so that they can boast to their friends afterwards? And she, my God: she's trying so desperately to find a corner where she belongs. And you . . .' He drank again. 'One of these days she'll pack her rucksack and move on again, a Pippa with a sad little song, waking others to life, all day long, until it gets dark.'

'It's dark already,' I said.

He didn't hear me, he was drunk; he went on talking: 'And where will she find a place to sleep then? Somewhere in the wilderness, and all alone?'

It must have been in those months that I first had my dream. Of Jessica and me on the beach, and the ice-cream trucks approaching over the dunes, and her running naked to the driver of the leading truck and going away with him, followed by the long convoy; and of Richard and me in the little hut on the beach, and our conversation rambling on through nights and days, until, one morning, she returns and we shut the door to exclude her for ever.

X

Although my bare bulb burns in the daytime too, I'm not really conscious of it then. It's only with the approach of dusk that it starts giving off yellowish light, which informs me that it's getting dark outside, time to start writing. Evening, like dawn (did someone say it, or am I saying it now?) is a crack between two worlds through which one can escape – but whether to hell or heaven I don't know. And it's becoming more difficult these days, constantly more difficult. The end is very close now, everything is so exposed, and words too threadbare to cover all the holes. In the beginning my memories flowed on evenly, elaborate and circumscribed; now they're coming in disturbing flashes.

The *Othello* introduced something of a final movement for us. I sometimes get the impression that my whole life can be summarised in terms of the plays I've acted in: and then I'm not quite sure which of the two worlds is the paradigm of the other.

We had great problems with the play. The new actors simply weren't good enough, however well they meant and however hard we worked. Jerry was outstanding, he was darkness incarnate: and yet even he never really believed in the production. In the beginning I thought he was only being flippant when he asked: 'Capey, don't you think you're cutting it a bit close to the bone this time?' But he became more aggressive as we went on, especially after we were told, less than a fortnight before opening, that as a result of 'an error beyond our control' there had been a double booking for the theatre and that it wouldn't be available after all.

'Now we've had it,' he said. 'That was the only place where we could still make money.'

'We can always come back for a season.'

'I have a hunch that in future we'll always find it booked by others.'

'Do you mean . . . ?'

'What else?'

I didn't answer. It would have been easy finally to admit defeat, and to surrender, and cease trying. I was so exhausted already. But perhaps it was exhaustion which made it impossible for me to stop: it had become such a habit that it was too much of an effort to think of alternatives.

I put my hand on Jerry's shoulder and said: 'Let's get our things ready to go on tour.'

That wasn't the only shock from those days. Less than a week before our departure, coming home from rehearsals one afternoon, I found Jessica was waiting for me in Aunt Lallie's lounge. That was something she very seldom did, and I could see that she was deeply upset.

Even though the old woman was blind I couldn't take Jessica in my arms. I stopped on the doorstep and asked: 'What's happened?'

'It's Father Mark. Oh my God, Joseph . . .' She came to me and grasped my arm. I could see her fighting the tears. But she didn't cry. After a minute she said: 'They're deporting him. He must leave the country before the end of the month.'

'But why?'

'I don't know. Nobody does, not even he. They searched his house and office a week ago and confiscated all the church's books, and this morning two officers called him from his classroom and gave him the deportation order.'

I could only stare at her.

362

'He suspects that they've been watching him for several months,' she said. 'Ever since the day he intervened when they couldn't get a Coloured ambulance for that dying girl. He wrote about it in his church news-letter . . .'

We went to Windermere the next day. When we stopped outside, he came from the small white church carrying a broom. Smiling, he came to us, quite calm. In his presence even Jessica's anxiety subsided.

'Is there nothing you can do about it?' I asked him.

He shook his head; but his eyes were still bright. 'I tried to arrange an interview with the Minister, but his secretary told me he wouldn't be available before February.'

'And you must be out by the end of January?'

'Yes. Fortunately I haven't got much to pack apart from my books. Not all of them either; I'd like to give most of them away. If you two would like to keep St John, I shall be very happy.'

'You don't seem to be taking it very seriously.'

'Don't I?' And then I became aware of the exhausted depths of his eyes, as if someone were looking through them from inside, through ages of suffering. 'It's a test for one . . .' He lowered his head, support-ing himself with his long, straight arms on his desk. 'It goes down to the bone, to the quick.' After a long time he looked up again, not at us, but through the window towards the church and one wing of the school building visible outside. 'I'm sorry – about them. I should have loved . . .' He shook his head. 'But these things don't happen blindly. God will have a reason for it.'

Neither of us could say anything. I felt a desire to go to him and touch him, but I didn't.

'The most difficult of all is not to hate,' he whispered. 'To keep one's heart free from hate. Always.'

That is how I remember him, the way he looked that afternoon, stand-ing against the window with the light on his short cropped grey hair and ascetic face, so old, so exhausted, so unbroken.

I was even more worried about Jessica, because she didn't cry, because she was so tensely quiet. For I knew what she'd been going through these past months and how his faith, so inaccessible to us both, had made it easier for us. Now he was going to leave, now we would be forced back on our own resources, now a last support had been removed; and I didn't know whether we could keep standing.

Those were the circumstances in which, on 18th January, the group set out on our *Othello* tour. I still remember how she clung to me in the dawn of that last day; I remember her anguish.

'I know you've got to go,' she said, her fingers clawing deep into my arms. 'But I'm frightened. Hold me, Joseph I'm sinking, it's like quicksand.'

'I'll come back, Little Miss Muffet.'

'I know. But it's such a long time. And by then Father Mark will have left. What's going to happen?'

From the very first day that had been the death-knell between us: *What's going to happen? What's going to happen?*

In the first light I went away from her through a reeling world. There had been wind all night, but now it died down as if the city itself was holding its breath.

'Why d'you look as if you going to a funeral, man?' asked Charlie Swiegers when we got into the kombi a few hours later. 'Cheer up, tonight we're hitting the jackpot.'

Charlie was one of our most useful new recruits, a musical, quick-silvery bloke, still raw onstage, but bubbling with enthusiasm – perhaps even too much of it, for Jerry'd soon complained that he'd found Charlie too big for his boots. But I welcomed his joviality, all the more so because he was the only new member who'd come to us of his own accord.

But in spite of Charlie's hopes of success the tour was a failure from the start. Were our nerves just more frayed than usual, our defences more frail, or had the police really intensified their psychological war against us? Not a single day passed without our being stopped either on the road or before a performance for a 'routine investigation'. And every time they found something: a small screw missing from the hinge of the rearview-mirror, a handbrake slipping, signs of wear on a tyre, some obscure mechanical fault; and at the performances they regularly discovered an irregularity about tickets or tax stamps, about fire equipment or toilet facilities in the halls where we performed. It was becoming too much for flesh and blood, yet we constantly had to restrain ourselves, knowing very well that they were waiting for the slightest hint of resentment which might be interpreted as interference with the execution of their duties or something worse.

What we couldn't understand was how they managed to keep track of us, for we had no fixed programme. In order to avoid the delays and cancellations of our previous tours and hoping to create some manœuvring space, we'd decided to travel more or less haphazardly from place to place, trying to arrive in the morning so that there would still be time to find a venue and launch a personal advertising campaign in the neighbourhood : in spite of all these precautions, it often happened that the police would be waiting for us at our arrival.

Because the fruit-packing season in the Boland was at its height we had to travel farther inland : and there the unbearable summer heat often exhausted us even before we'd started with the day's business. All of which sapped our energy and our emotional resources. Early on tour tempers began to explode, aggravated by the fact that we weren't, as in the past, a tightly-knit group of friends but an assortment of half-strangers who still had to get used to one another. I'd experienced something similar on some of my early rep. tours in England, but then with a measure of compensation : one's income had been assured; and however depressing many of the country hotels may have been, at least they'd offered a modicum of comfort : a bed, access to a warm bath, an hour in a pub. But not on this tour. We had to take our drink with us, swallowing the lukewarm, distasteful stuff on the road, running the very real risk of being accused of drunken driving or even of smuggling; mealtimes we had to go to the Non-white entrance of some squalid little country café and wait for hours among boxes of empties, discarded vegetables and swarms of flies to be served by fat women with stringy hair and enormous jelly breasts, taking out the bottle of coke and the greasy hamburger or fish-'n'-chips or the unwrapped half-loaf of bread and consume it on the pavement. At night the kombi served as our communal bedroom, parked under a cluster of trees beside the road. On special occasions we were taken in singly or in pairs by people we'd met on previous tours : a missionary, a teacher, a salesman; or else we were invited to share the poverty of postmen, or messengers, or garden 'boys', often spending the night with four or six or ten other people in the same stuffy room.

We encountered a new sort of problem too. In the past we'd never had any trouble with the kombi – it was, in fact, the one reliable and constant factor on our tours – but this time everything went wrong. Before the end of the first week, on the hellish stretch of road beyond Vanrhynsdorp we broke down and all Jerry's ingenuity and experience couldn't get us going again. He and I had to hitch a lift back to the nearest village – and it was five hours before a sympathetic farmer stopped and allowed us to get on the back of his small van. The garage wasn't prepared to send out a mechanic before we'd paid a deposit of twenty rand. It was late afternoon before we all were back in town; and it took another day to discover the cause of the trouble: sugar in the petrol tank.

That was only the beginning. Less than a week later all four wheels were stolen off the kombi during a performance. A few days later my bunch of keys disappeared while we were onstage: and once again it meant a day's delay before a new car key could be supplied. Near Beaufort West, where we stayed with old acquaintances, the bonnet was forced open overnight and every wire and pipe in the engine removed or sawn off.

All these delays were bad enough; the expenses caused by them nearly crippled us. But worst of all was the agonising knowledge of an invisible opponent watching us night and day and planning his moves against us with diabolical finesse. The nervous tension became unbearable. And every day, every night, every hour I was worrying about Jessica back home: what would become of her now that Father Mark had gone?

Early in the third week of our journey one of the two girls in the group, Joyce Vermaak, announced that she couldn't take it any more and was leaving on the spot.

'But you can't!' I protested. 'You signed a contract.'

'You c'n stuff it up yo' arse!' she said. 'You newwe' tole me we was going to have this sort of life.'

I had to clench my fists not to lose my temper completely. 'Joyce, I'll take you to court if you do that!'

'Take a try!'

All my threats and pleading and exorbitant promises were useless.

It was impossible to find a replacement. The only way out was to revise our play so that the other girl, Wendy Claassen, could double Joyce's role. But poor Wendy had been struggling with her own role already, and her doubling proved fatal: nobody in the audience could make out which of the two parts she was acting at any given moment. After a few days we had to cut the second part altogether and retain only Desdemona – a change which unsettled all the other new actors.

And still we went on, I don't know how.

Two days after Joyce had left we had a flat tyre – and when we tried to change it, we discovered that the spare had disappeared overnight.

Night had fallen before we reached the next town, too late to organise a performance; and so another day was lost.

That night, after the others had gone to bed, Jerry took me aside.

'Capey,' he said. 'Today's business has finally convinced me: this series of accidents and obstacles on our way is no bloody coincidence.'

'Of course not. A child can see it's an organised campaign.'

He lowered his voice: 'I mean it's not arranged from outside. We're being sabotaged by somebody in our group.'

'Who would do such a thing?'

'I don't know, Capey. But we're going to get him. And God help him the day I lay my hands on him.'

Jerry and Doors and I tried our best to trace the source of our problems, but in vain. On a few occasions we deliberately didn't tell anyone else in the group where we would be heading the next day – and on those evenings, at least, we were left in peace until the interval. Which confirmed Jerry's suspicions.

Then the turning point came. We were in Gelvardale outside Port Elizabeth when, true to form, the police turned up five minutes before we had to go onstage. This time they were looking for grass. Resigned, we allowed them to search our possessions: after all, one pretext was as flimsy as another. They ransacked the kombi without, of course, finding anything. Then they turned to our baggage. We stood on one side, waiting, smoking.

In a brown cardboard suitcase belonging to Doors they discovered a brown envelope. A single sniff at the contents proved that it was what they'd been looking for. All of us accompanied them to the charge office. When Doors was finally taken away to the cells he looked back at me.

'Joseph, I promise you, man: I never seen that stuff befo'.'

It was a bad night. I don't know about the others, but neither Jerry nor I could sleep a wink.

In the courtroom the next morning, the prosecutor announced that 'certain aspects of the case' still had to be investigated; the trial was postponed for a week, and bail was not allowed.

It was the end of *Othello*, of course. For a week all we could do was to present 'concerts' in the Eastern Cape in order to stay alive. We arranged for a Port Elizabeth advocate to defend Doors. The incident had given a final blow to the shattered nerves of the group and it took every bit of energy Jerry and I could muster just to prevent it from disintegrating altogether.

367

The case was short and simple. The evidence against Doors was overwhelming, although the advocate made as much as he could of the absence of fingerprints on the envelope. All he could manage, and we were deeply grateful for that, was to obtain a suspended sentence. The case had cost us a lot, but at least Doors was back with us and we could resume our tour.

It was the first time since I'd first met Doors that I saw him depressed. Grim and brooding he sat through the days; and when I tried to talk to him, he only muttered through his teeth :

'I'll catch the shit, Joseph. You watch me. I'll catch him.'

When it happened, it caught us completely unprepared.

It was in George. The first half of our performance had gone surprisingly well. But during the interval there was a sudden outburst of noise outside, and when we got there we found Doors attacking Charlie with all the fury of a wounded buffalo. Charlie was a mere boy compared to the enormous Doors, and his face had been beaten to a pulp by the time we came upon the scene. Frantically we tried to hold Doors back, but he shook us off like an Alsatian would get rid of a couple of yapping foxterriers. And when finally Charlie fell to the ground, bleeding and sobbing, Doors started kicking him with sickening, methodic violence – on the head, in the back, in the stomach, wherever his large boots could reach a target.

By that time most of the audience had streamed out to see what was happening, and at last eight or ten of us managed to pull Doors off the moaning bundle of rags on the ground.

'It's him!' Doors panted, pulling and shaking us this way and that. 'It's him. Lemme go, I want to kill him!'

At that moment a police van screeched to a standstill behind us, four or five constables jumped out, accompanied by a dog; and within a few minutes Doors, Charlie and several of the bystanders had been thrown into the back of the van. We followed them in the kombi, but halfway to the police station it gave a few jerks and broke down.

We didn't see Doors again before the next day in court, when we could hardly recognise him from the way his face had been beaten up : Charlie's doing, said the police without turning a hair. Doors himself spoke with such difficulty that it was almost impossible to make out what he was saying, much to the annoyance of the magistrate. All we could make out was that he'd caught Charlie red-handed pouring sand into the petrol tank and that, after Doors had broken his nose and a

368

few teeth, he'd also confessed about planting the dagga in the suitcase.

Charlie, who had to be carried into court and supported by police, denied everything; and although Jerry and I pleaded in mitigation and mentioned the latest breakdown of the kombi which corroborated Doors' statement, it obviously made no difference to the fact of the assault. The magistrate postponed sentence for a week to obtain a report on previous convictions.

Charlie disappeared immediately after the trial. Jerry and I waited for him outside, but nobody saw him leave.

That same evening Wendy packed her bags and left us.

We presented a few more variety concerts, but the income was so meagre that it made very little difference to our plight. Our last hope was Doors.

This time he was given a year's imprisonment without the option of a fine.

There were three of us left. I, and Jerry, and an inexperienced young boy, Bennie Smal.

With our last bit of money we had the kombi repaired and took the long road back to Cape Town. It was very hot. It was Tuesday 28th February. We drove in silence. We couldn't speak.

We'd already passed Riviersonderend before Jerry said: Not with a bang but a whimper, eh?'

I felt my eyes burning, but I was grimly resolved not to cry. For if I cried, I'd break down completely.

Bennie was sleeping in the back.

After several minutes I said, looking straight ahead : 'You're still with me, Jerry. We'll start again.'

'No, Capey.'

I looked at him : 'You don't know what you're saying!'

'You don't know what you're doing.'

'I'll go on.' My words came out mechanically, without thinking. 'You can all betray me or deny me, you can all leave me : but you won't destroy me.'

'It's not necessary. You're destroying yourself.'

I didn't answer.

He suddenly put his hand on mine, on the wheel, and held it tightly : 'Don't, Capey. Jesus, man, don't do it to yourself.'

'I'd rather do this than sit on my arse like you.'

'D'you really think I'm sitting on my arse? Then you know me badly.'

'What are you doing then?'

He looked round at Bennie sleeping on the back seat, and replied with an enigmatic smile: 'Something more practical than what you've been doing. Something with which you might help me.'

'What?'

I felt his eyes burning into me, felt the urgent way in which he was weighing me.

'If you have enough confidence in me you'll first say yes and ask questions afterwards.'

I shook my head. 'How can I say yes if I don't know whether it'll be worthy.'

He laughed with a note of bitterness: 'Capey, one's got to reach a moment when you no longer ask or search or plan or think of worthiness or shit, but where you're prepared to blindly do something. Because there's no other option left. And I thought you'd reached that moment now.'

'Violence?'

'Does it make any difference?'

'It's important to me.'

'Don't you know what happens to people who shrink back from violence when it becomes inevitable?' he asked angrily. 'Don't you know? Have you forgotten how Gandhi died? Or Martin Luther King, or your friend Dulpert?' He broke off; slowly, more restrained, he asked: 'Tell me: do you still believe in virgins?'

'Of course not.'

'Then it's time you read Malraux again: "A man who hasn't committed murder yet, is a virgin." '

I took a long time to react. The road was winding through the hills. Only when we reached the open plains beyond Caledon, still without looking at him, I said: 'Murder is too terrible a word for us, Jerry. What we've got to do, is to try and survive.'

'If life means enough to you you'll be prepared to fight for it.'

'There are more ways of fighting than one.'

He made an irritated gesture: 'How often must I tell you: your neat contrasts between culture and revolution, love and violence, and God knows what else . . . they're formalist and false. Leave it to the White Liberals. You're worth more than that.' And after a long pause: 'My God, man, don't you know the terrible words: "What times are these

370

when a discussion about trees is almost a crime because it implies silence on so many wrongs?" '

At the beginning of Houwhoek Pass, changing the gears, I said: 'I'm not silent on anything of importance, and you know it. You also know my way of fighting. To make sure that there'll always be moral bases from which the soldiers can advance.'

'A base is a luxury: it's too easy to fall back to it. What we need is an army without bases. Like a man without buttocks: unable to sit down, all he can do is to move on.'

'I don't think any of us has got buttocks left.' I intended it flippantly, but it sounded different.

This time he didn't answer.

I asked: 'Does it mean that you're also going away now, Jerry?'

'Unless you're coming with me.'

'I can't.'

We went up the incline of Sir Lowry's Pass. From the top the wide blue crescent of False Bay lay below us, crystal clear, with a summery sparkle, reaching to the distant Table Mountain opposite. I stopped. I didn't know why. I was afraid to drive on. The Cape was so close now.

After a while he put his arm round my shoulders.

We didn't speak.

I turned the key again and we went downhill. All the way to Cape Town we were silent, and his arm remained round my shouders.

After unloading our things at Aunt Lallie's house we drove back into town to find a second-hand-car dealer. The highest offer we could get for the kombi was six hundred rand. We accepted it; we had to pay our debts. I gave Bennie what we still owed him; Jerry didn't want anything. After settling our accumulated accounts there was less than a hundred rand left. I wanted to put that away for Doors' appeal. It wasn't enough, of course, but I could still sell my little car; and perhaps Jessica would help us.

Then Jerry went home.

Aunt Lallie wanted to come in for a talk, but I told her I was feeling ill and lay down on my bed. I didn't sleep; I only lay there. I was too tired to get up, too tired to think, too full of dread.

Very late that evening I washed myself from top to toe in Aunt Lallie's kitchen and put on fresh clothes. Then I phoned Jessica.

She couldn't believe I was back: I hadn't told her anything about our problems on the trip before.

'Has something happened?' she asked, worried.

'A lot. I'll tell you everything. I want to be with you. I'm tired.'

She was quiet for a second.

'Is there someone with you?' I was too upset even to use our code.

'No,' she said quickly. 'Of course you can come.'

'Straight away?'

'If you want to.'

Twenty minutes later I was with her. I couldn't believe it. In one moment, just seeing her, holding her face in my gently cupped hands, pressing her frail familiar body against me, the fear oozed from me. She was still there.

We went to the balcony to talk. She listened intently, tensely.

'Don't worry, Little Miss Muffet,' I said. 'I'll start again. I'm tired. But now I'm back with you.'

'How can you start again?'

'I can teach for a while, or do something else to save some money first. In the meantime I'll recruit new actors and train them properly. You'll see.' And then I asked urgently: 'But what about you? I want to know everything that's happened.'

'It's been very quiet. I had to get used to living without you, without Father Mark. It wasn't easy. I read a lot. And he wrote me a wonderful letter, a few days ago, I'll show it to you.'

'What else?'

'Nothing really.'

'Did you miss me, did you long for me?'

'Of course I longed for you.'

I wanted to ask: And Richard . . . ? But I didn't. I suppose I was scared. Or else I didn't want to name him in that first hour of being back with her. Tomorrow he'd be with us again, but now we were together, she and I in the serene night.

'Let's go to bed,' I said.

She hesitated. 'Are you tired?'

'Yes. Aren't you?'

'It's so lovely outside.'

'It'll be lovely inside too.'

We went to her room and she stood in front of me so that I could undo her blouse and jeans and strip her panties down to her ankles.

And then she undressed me, clasping, in her gentle way, my penis between her hands for a moment.

'I'm hungry for you,' I whispered and took her to bed.

The dim light from outside fell over us. She wanted to close the curtains but I held her back: 'Don't. I want to see you. I haven't seen you
for such a long time.'

She lay with closed eyes under my caressing hands.

'Are you frightened again?' I asked. 'Like the first time?'

'Yes.'

I kissed her; then moved my head to take one of her nipples between
my lips. There was a small dark stain on her breast.

'What's this?' I asked, caressing it. 'A bruise? Did you bump into
something?'

'I suppose so.' Her eyes were still closed.

For the first time I became aware of her complete passivity.

With trembling fingers I touched the bruise.

'Tell me, Jessica.'

She began to cry. All the time she'd been struggling against it, fiercely,
desperately, until suddenly, with a gasping, choking sob it broke from
her. Like someone possessed she clung to me. I held her, with that
strange, old detachment as if I were looking down on the scene from
very far; I held her till her hysteria began to subside.

'Richard?' I asked.

She nodded. For a moment she wanted to cry again, then she mastered
it. But she still clung to me.

'Come into me. Don't let it . . .'

She was wildly passionate against me. With a despair coming from very
deep down she clung to me, pleading: 'Come, my darling, come, come,
please come, I want you to come.' But I couldn't. Her body confirmed
Richard: in her he became flesh and blood. And after a long time I
stopped, and remained lying on her, immobile, exhausted. It was night
around us, only faintly illuminated by that distant light outside.

'He's keeping you away from me,' I said.

She moved her head.

'When was he here?'

'Don't talk about him now.'

'It's worse if I don't know.'

She breathed jerkily against my throat.

373

'When was he here?'

'Yesterday.'

'Only yesterday?'

'No.' She was silent for so long that I was beginning to think that she'd fallen asleep. But then she said: 'It wasn't often. Don't be afraid, Joseph. I was so lonely. And he too. And there was no one else. Father Mark had gone; you were gone. There was no one. I didn't want to. And it was horrible. For him too, I think. I can't explain it, I don't understand it. But the first time I realised – that I wanted to be comforted, that I didn't want to go on saying no, that everything had become too confused to understand – I thought: yes, let him take me so that I can be punished for it, so that I can be cleansed for you. I know it's mad. Sometimes I really think I'm going mad. But I was so utterly alone. And there was so much I had to avenge in myself. To *make* myself suffer.'

I moved off her and, holding her in my arm, we fell asleep. But it was a restless night filled with disturbing dreams. Once I woke up; thinking that she was asleep, I cautiously tried to get up to go to the bathroom, but as I moved over her she put out her hands and touched me: and I sank back against her and started caressing her, and she me. It was very dark then, the darkest part of the night just before dawn, and we couldn't see each other at all: we didn't even know it was us. But when I came this time, we were together in that small, fleeting moment of reassurance against the impossible world. Not escape, for we would never again be able to get away; not wholeness, for we would never be whole again. Only a pitiful sharing, a dark grace. We had passed every vestige of romantic love and irrevocably lost something: Fall and Flood were behind us, far behind. But in the new dimension beyond disillusion and shock we could touch one another: beyond guilt and innocence. Paradise had become irrelevant to us – now that we had to live by the sweat of our brow all we had left was the ability to share the compassion of the nights which divided the merciless days. Everything was exposed, everything could touch us. But we were still together. Perhaps we'd failed in all other ways. But we were still together.

XI

I went to Richard of my own accord – driven by what? morbid curiosity? an urge to wound? or to be wounded? He was wearing a red and
grey gown when he opened the door of his flat, clearly surprised to see
me.

'Joseph!' A pause. 'Come inside. I was just going to have a shower.'

'Don't let me disturb you.'

'I'll pour you a drink.'

I didn't really feel like anything, but he brought me a glass. Handing
it to me, he said: 'This is a surprise. Jessica told me you were back, of
course. But I wasn't expecting you here.'

The deliberate reference to Jessica made me clench my jaws, but as
calmly as possible I asked: 'Why not?'

'You've never visited me uninvited before.'

'There's always a first time. For everything.' I saw him cast his eyes
down. After a second I added: 'Anyway, I have more time now than
before.'

'Of course. I don't know what to say, it's awful.'

'It's just a temporary setback.'

'I hope so. I really hope so, Joseph.'

'What about you?'

'I've started on the novel again. It's going a bit better this time. But
very slowly.'

For a while it went on in that polite way. Unless we spoke about
Jessica, I thought, we really had nothing to say to one another.

After some time he got up and went to the bathroom, while I remained behind with the brandy glass in my hand, listening to the sound
of the shower behind the plastic curtain. Now that I was there, I no longer knew why I'd come, and I felt annoyed with myself. And yet it was
necessary, I knew, to see him again, and, through that, to neutralise his
threatening presence.

Ten minutes later he turned off the shower and came to the threshold
of the bathroom, drying himself. Through the movements of the towel
I had brief glimpses of his body. It fascinated me in an unsettling way.
From his hands and wrists I'd expected him to be hirsute, but I was
quite unprepared for that thick mat of blackish, greyish hair covering
his entire body. Actually that upset me more than Jessica's mere state-

ment that he'd been with her. His appearance suddenly became a comment on the nature and the intensity of her anguish : and perhaps a reflection on me. This was the body which had bruised hers. I wanted to
avert my eyes, but I couldn't.

Presumably to cover up his self-consciousness he said : 'I find that
water stimulates my thought processes more than anything else. When
I'm writing I shower four or five times a day.'

If he hadn't been standing there like that I don't think I would have
reacted in that way : but his appearance seemed to goad me into saying :
'Personally I prefer to relax in a bath when I'm thinking. With Bach
in the background, and Jessica with me.'

That caught him unawares. For a few seconds he stopped rubbing
himself and lowered the towel : and I noticed how the hair on his belly
became a curious yellowish red lower down, with his prick protruding,
the loose, veined skin like wrinkled parchment soaked in water. I deliberately wanted to see it as vulgarly, as grotesquely as possible, for at
that moment I hated him. That large ape-like body he'd exposed to her ;
that hideous thing had penetrated her.

'Why do you speak of her?' he asked after a pause, cautiously.

'I think it's relevant.' I raised my eyes from his prick to his face. 'She
told me everything.'

He raised his towel as if to protect himself.

'Now you're hitting a man when he's down,' he said tensely.

'You have a nerve to say that!' For a moment I lost all control.
'After playing your hypocritical little game, waiting for the moment
when I'd turn my back and her resistance would be at its lowest . . .'

'Jessica needed me.'

'She needed help. Not what you gave her. She's not a bitch that gets
on heat and has to be fucked. You exploited her.'

'What about you?' That was the first time he'd ever lost his temper
in my presence. 'Aren't you exploiting her? I'm trying to save her from
drowning. You're pulling her in.'

I put my glass down and went over to him. The room was reeling
before my eyes. For a moment I stood in front of him. We must have
cut a ridiculous pair : if he wanted to hit me he could probably give me
a thrashing. Strange, I might have welcomed it. When he remained
standing without moving, his teeth clenched, I turned away.

'For God's sake go and dress yourself,' I said. 'You make me sick.'

He went to the bedroom. Uninvited, I filled my glass again and gulped

376

it down. Perhaps it would be better if I went home without waiting for him. But that wouldn't resolve anything. Lighting a cigarette I returned to his bookshelves, waiting for him to come back. He stayed away for a very long time. When he finally emerged from the room he was wearing dark pants and a silk shirt, with a cravat tucked into the front. I could smell his scented deodorant; at the same time I was conscious of perspiration in moist armpits.

After he'd poured himself a drink too he looked at me: 'I hope you'll forgive what I said. It was in the heat of the moment.'

I looked at him. His face wore the habitual mask: Richard Cole, author. ('Tell me, Mr Cole, what is your opinion about . . .') I'd hoped that we would be able either to fight it out or talk it through. This politeness merely served to confirm the distance between us. And when I finally took my leave of him, all I was aware of was the growing weariness.

How did we manage to last another month? It doesn't seem possible and I can't hope to explain it. We existed on a very elemental level, barely thinking, breathing in anguish like fish moving in water, with moving gills, primitive and exposed.

There was a continual awareness of change, but without shocks, because there was no real resistance any more, only weariness and resignation. I had no more money and for the moment there wasn't any prospect of a job. The few teaching posts I'd applied for had all been filled: although the same posts were advertised regularly after I'd been turned away. Jessica supported me; I didn't even try to object. Taking the make-believe at face value she offered me a 'loan', with the car as security.

We took fewer precautions to shelter us from the world. We never acted recklessly, of course, but we'd grown too tired to bother overmuch about the elaborate framework of defences we'd relied on before. If the final knock on the door had to come: oh God, then let it come. Sooner or later the end would be upon us. Both of us accepted it now, without any more attempts to hide it. All we didn't know yet, was the form it would take.

Often we resorted to the inevitable by going to bed to avoid having to talk or think, abandoning ourselves to the desperate struggle of our bodies. As in the final act with Ursula and Beverley, years before, the awareness of an end forced us back to the most aggressive explorations of sexuality : two bodies, each celebrating its ecstasy in isolation, every orgasm a confirmation of aloneness. There was a strange urge in us to bruise our bodies, to leave marks with teeth and nails, ephemeral tokens, pathetic souvenirs : it wasn't pain so much that mattered – everything was painful – but the signs as such, to prove to one another, and each to himself : look, we exist; look, we love each other; look, she has my seed in her womb.

There was one final sign we didn't attempt: to make a child.

She wanted to. So did I. It was an almost unbearable urge, a final affirmation, shameless before the world. We often discussed it. Those were among the most beautiful hours of our last month : all the dreams about our children, what their names would be, how we would bring them up, what clothes they should wear. (She said: 'You know, I'd prefer my children to go naked in summer and wear sheepskins in winter.') But we both knew, and that was what made the game so poignant, that it was all make-believe, the make-believe which had become indispensable for living. And at night, as always, she took her pill; and when her period came we grieved – but that too, was part of the game – for our children washed down the drain.

In between the violent bouts of our bodies there were also hours of pristine purity (her voice against my throat: 'Shall we come together this time? Or I first? Or you? I'm so close . . .'); and there was a stiller stillness in the long evenings we spent sitting on her balcony or lying on her carpet reading by candlelight. Then we knew that all our struggles had been nothing but efforts to penetrate an outer crust and reach this inner serenity where we could be together. 'Oh my God,' she whispered in the bath one night, 'it's so terrible : one keeps thinking and struggling and trying to sort things out, hating oneself and fearing oneself and suffering from oneself : all the agony of not knowing who you are . . . And then suddenly you break through and it becomes peaceful again, like now, and you know why it all had to happen.'

These silences were few and fleeting : then we were driven back into the wilderness. Somewhere in the background was Richard. I knew he went on seeing her, pleading and insisting. I don't think she ever yielded to him again. But she might have; and then, out of compassion for me, she would have kept it secret. But such was the essence of our game that we had to go on pretending that there was no threat at all – even though the game depended on that threat for its very existence.

A dream from that month, one of the most disturbing of my life: I'm standing under a shower while she is in a bedroom behind me, lying on the bed. Suddenly, turning round, I notice that she's lying with her legs pulled up, a small camera mounted in the length of her sex: and I realise she's recording all my movements to send the photographs to a secret espionage centre far away.

We were on her balcony, talking about nothing in particular, when unexpectedly she asked:

'Have I ever told you about my grandmother?'

'What about her?'

She laughed softly: 'I wish you'd known her: my father's mother. A minute, meticulous person like a small Victorian doll, a sort of emblem of the respectability of our family. By the time she got married she'd never been alone with her bridegroom before. On the three or four occasions when they'd met, there had always been a chaperone with them. And then, quite unexpectedly – I don't think they'd been married a year yet: it was certainly before they had any children – she ran away to Paris with a young French painter. He was destitute. Many days they had neither food nor money for gas. But for a year she lived with him in his tiny garret, as mistress and model. And then she returned to my grandfather. The only thing she brought back from her year in Paris was one small nude he'd painted of her.

'The whole family was up in arms, but she refused to do away with the painting. In fact, she had it framed and kept it on her dressing-table. For the rest of her days she led an exemplary life with my grandfather. But that little painting remained in her room and it was shown to all her children and grandchildren. Not to boast, and certainly without contrition: I think she hoped that they would understand something about the only meaningful fact from her long life.'

When she had finished, I asked: 'Why did you tell it to me?'

'I don't know, I just thought of it. It's the only nice story from our history: the rest is so unbearably mundane.'

'Do you take after her?'

She laughed.

But I said, gently: 'Your year in the garret is nearly over: don't you want to go back to your family too?'

'Why do you ask?' she whispered.

379

'The little garret is getting smaller and colder, Little Miss Muffet.'

'We still have money for a little bit of gas.'

'Not much.'

'A little bit.'

Why didn't I stay quiet? What was there in me that forced me to ask:
'And then?'

'That's what I've always asked you,' she reminded me. 'And you said:
Don't talk about it. We've still got *now*.'

'The *now* is nearly finished.'

'Don't, my love. Oh don't.'

'One of these days they'll come knocking on the door of our little
garret. Or you'll marry Richard.'

'I won't. I won't leave you.'

'Suppose I went with you?'

'To England? Do you want to?'

I smiled. 'I can't. Don't you know?'

'What else then?'

'Nothing. There isn't anything else.'

She bowed her head. 'I can't bear it, Joseph.'

And then, almost imperceptibly, we'd arrived at the moment we'd
never wanted to admit and which had become inescapable.

It was she who asked: 'Have you ever thought about death?'

'Often.'

'I mean: is it always very painful? I'm scared of pain.'

'I suppose there are other ways too.'

'Like what?'

I reflected, and shrugged, and said: 'Gas or something. In a car.'

'If one's so tired: I suppose we'll just fall asleep and forget about
everything, and not be afraid any more.'

'Why do you say "we"?'

'You said you would go with me.'

Without moving we stared in front of us. It was almost merciful,
like rain, like sleep, like the sea; like the night of St John. So easy. So
graspable.

'I didn't know it was so close,' I whispered. 'I thought we'd be able
to fend it off, from day to day.'

'And now?'

'Now I'm too tired to go on thinking. All I want to do is to go with
you.'

XII

That morning I didn't take Aunt Lallie's string bag to do her shopping downtown as usual : I drove out to Goodwood to buy her groceries and the length of garden hose. It was probably an unnecessary precaution but I didn't want to run any risk of being recognised. Afterwards I filled up the car so that we could reach Bain's Kloof that night. There were no thoughts in me. I couldn't think any more. I seemed to be moving through limbo, timeless and spaceless, all thoughts and emotions suspended. The sedatives I'd taken early that morning made me sleepy and kept everything hazy. The city was strange, all the people were strange, endlessly more strange than the day, coming down from District Six, when I'd been afforded a glimpse of Segismundo's dream world.

And it was raining. The mountain was invisible through the misty clouds, the city a low hum, with the wet hissing sound of tyres. Now and then there was a sudden patch of colourless light shimmering on rooftops and streets. It was like the day old Oom Dirk and I had gone to fetch the pastor on the horse-cart. I remembered his singing :

> *My bonnie lies over the ocean,*
> *My bonnie lies over the seaaaaaa ...*

Indeed, memories were much more vivid than the world around me. Every person, every object was shrouded by the incomprehensible and by the hissing sound of silence.

I'd hoped to take a nap in the afternoon; the day was so endless. But before I could drift off Richard knocked. I was at least as surprised as he'd been on the day I'd gone to him. It was obvious that he was in a bad state, his normally immaculate clothes crumpled as if he'd slept in them. And he was smelling of brandy, old stale brandy, his eyes seemed swollen, and in spite of the cool day and the rain there was an unhealthy film of perspiration on his forehead and his upper lip.

'What's the matter, Richard?' I asked, amazed, yet detached from the situation.

'You should know.' He was aiming this way and that as if he were looking for something, his movements uncertain, almost stumbling.

When he finally turned round to me he seemed to be peering at me through layers of pain. 'I've been walking the streets for twenty-four hours now,' he said. 'I can't go on like this. Do you understand? It's impossible.'

'What are you talking about?'

'What do you think?'

'Jessica?'

'Sooner or later one reaches breaking-point, Joseph. We've tried to treat each other like gentlemen, but it's brought us nowhere.'

'I know.'

'What are you going to do about it?' He reeled, although I could see he wasn't drunk.

'Why me?'

'You're the only one who can do something.'

'Do you think there's still anything any of us can do?'

'I'm not going to allow you to destroy her!'

I started, wondering whether she'd told him anything, but that was impossible.

'You must lay off. If you had a grain of respectability in you, you wouldn't stay with her any longer.'

I wanted to laugh. It was so utterly absurd just then, with the green hose already lying in the boot of my car.

'Jessica has always been free to stay or go,' I said.

'You're holding on to her. You have an evil influence over her. You're clutching her like a spider.'

'Poor Miss Muffet.'

'What the hell do you mean?' he asked angrily.

I shook my head.

He grasped my shoulder and forced me back to him.

'I've tried to be considerate towards you,' he said trembling. 'I used to respect you. I knew what it meant to you. I didn't want to hurt you . . .'

'Because I've got a brown skin?'

'Fuck your bloody brown skin!'

I smiled. 'Why haven't you said it long ago? It must be a hell of a relief.'

'Joseph . . . !' He grabbed me more tightly, his eyes peering at me through heavy swollen lids. 'Don't push me too far.'

'I'm not pushing you at all. You're the only one who's trying to use force.'

382

'And why not?' He shoved me violently. 'You're going to lay off now. I've had enough.'

Placing my hands on his wrists I loosened his grip. 'What happens between me and Jessica has nothing to do with you, Richard.'

'It's got everything to do with me! Do you hear me?' There was a falsetto tone in his voice. 'You're going to lay off, or I'll break you.'

'How do you think you'll break me?'

He was beyond control now. Leaning over me, breathing heavily, he said: 'You've got no right to be with her. You're Coloured. Why don't you stick to your own sort? You don't know your place!'

'Do you think she'll take you if I withdraw?'

'I warned you, Joseph. I swear . . . If you don't move out now, I'm going to the police.'

For a moment I still kept looking at him, before I turned away to the window, laughing. Not loudly, but as uncontrollable as crying. The ridiculous situation, the utter irrelevance of his threat, overwhelmed me. I laughed until I was quite out of breath.

He probably didn't realise it was laughter. After some time I became conscious of him behind me, grabbing me and shaking me, pleading: 'Please stop, Joseph. Don't. I didn't mean it like that. Please stop!'

It brought on a new fit of laughter, but more weary than before.

'Come on,' I said at last, without looking at him. 'I'll take you home.'

'No.'

I walked on; he followed me. In silence we drove on to Mouille Point where I accompanied him to his flat. He was moving with great difficulty, and twice he stopped on the staircase to rest his shoulder against the facebrick wall.

Inside, I led him to his room and helped him to sit down on the bed. He tried to protest, but he was too exhausted.

Pushing him over on his back, I covered him with a rug.

'Now you must sleep,' I said.

'Joseph, I didn't mean to . . .'

'Sleep.'

I drove back alone. For the first time that day the feeling of strangeness left me. I was glad about it. I wanted to be lucid when night fell.

It was still raining when I drove up to Kloof Nek shortly before eight o'clock. I parked the car in front of the main entrance of her building, pulled my raincoat over my shoulders and went inside. There were people in the foyer, but without hesitation, quite openly, for the first time, I went past them and climbed the staircase to the top floor.

I knocked. She opened immediately.

We went to the balcony.

She looked down at the car outside, startled.

'It doesn't matter,' I said. 'Not this once.'

'That's true.' She looked at me, then turned away again.

'Have you brought – everything?'

'Yes. Don't think of it now.'

'How long will it take to Bain's Kloof?'

'Not long. In our little car, in this weather . . . not much more than an hour.'

'It's quick. I always thought Bain's Kloof was very far.'

'No, it's quite near.'

'I'm glad it's raining.'

'Not that it makes much difference.'

'No.' After a while: 'What have you been doing all day?'

'Drove around a bit. I slept this afternoon.'

'I also tried to sleep, but I couldn't. Then I wanted to tidy the flat, it's such a mess, but I didn't get much done.'

Below us the evening was deepening in the rain.

'And tomorrow . . .' Her voice choked.

'No.' I held her tightly. 'Tomorrow is for others. Tonight is ours.'

'Are you glad, Joseph?' she suddenly asked.

'Glad?' Surprised, I looked up at her and smiled slowly, moving my lips down from her forehead, across her small straight nose, to her mouth. 'Yes. I'm glad. It makes one feel so peaceful.'

'Yes.' But my hand resting on her breast could feel the raging of her heart.

Later she stood up to look for cigarettes. The packet was empty.

'Let's go and buy some,' I suggested.

'I'll go quickly.'

'No. Tonight we're going together.'

For the first time, for the only time, we walked through the streets together, in the rain, like any loving couple going to the café: not hand in hand, not touching at all, but beside each other. It was like a feast.

We bought the cigarettes and returned to her flat.

When we arrived there, she was trembling.

384

'Are you cold?'

'No.'

Her teeth were chattering.

'Are you afraid?'

'It's only . . . It's so long to wait. All that distance. And I wanted so much to be brave until we got there.'

I looked at her, discovering anew how frail she was. Her eyes were large and wide open.

'Please trust me,' I said.

'I trust you.'

I opened the door of her flat and closed it behind us. We didn't put on the light. It was just as always.

XIII

Under a heap of wet branches, hidden from the road, against the lowest slope of Bain's Kloof Pass, I covered the car. I had more than enough time. I could come back later. I took the length of hose with me, I don't know why. My thoughts were muddled. I suppose I thought something like: *If someone finds the car while I'm gone at least I'll have the hose.* But I don't know what I could have used it for.

It wasn't raining steadily any longer: just an occasional drizzle. I walked up the road, dodging the sporadic cars by hiding behind trees or rocks, not because I was frightened but reflexively.

Somewhere along the winding mountain road, I thought, Dlamini/ Daniel must have died when he grew too tired to go on. It was becoming something of an elephant graveyard. All of us who grew weary came this way.

When I finally reached the hotel I swerved to the right, following the footpath across the veld towards the deep ravine. But it was too dark to see; I didn't want to plunge down a cliff.

Under a tree, slight protection against the sporadic showers, I sat down. Strange, that one should be able to sleep under such circumstances, but that was exactly what happened, with my back leaned against the trunk and the garden hose across my legs. The first colourless light was seeping through the clouds when I woke up. It was very cold, almost as cold as the night Willem and I'd sheltered under the cliff. But then, at least, we'd had each other to keep warm.

I got up and went on, to get the blood circulating again. Following the stony path, down the side of the ravine, and leisurely upstream, from rock to rock. The day was breaking, but the sky was still grey and humid. I was glad about it, because it was Good Friday, and if the weather had been fine, hordes of picnickers would soon have descended into the kloof. Now I was alone.

I was still not hurried. Time had died nearly twelve hours before. I was free from it.

Actually that was the strangest of all, the lightness in me, that near-carefreeness. I'd passed the ultimate *Thou shalt not,* and now the world of morality had fallen from me : it was like being born.

High up in the stream I found our pool. I should have liked to swim, but it was much too cold. Under a few boulders I tried to make myself comfortable, watching the ripples on the water where we'd dived in a year before. That was where I'd found the pebble with the girlish cleft. 'If I let it drop,' she said, 'it'll endure it, look, it has no pride. It's so completely itself.'

The pebble should still be there, somewhere, unfindable, but equal to itself. I, too, had become like that pebble, as smooth, as whole, as ready to fall, as prepared to endure. For I had nothing left beyond myself. Everything was rounded off, everything had come home to me. It wasn't even necessary to act any more, I'd abandoned my last role : now I'd been peeled off like Peer Gynt's onion, now only the pure emptiness of the heart was left. It was very beautiful.

On the slopes above me I could see the grass swaying in the wind. The wind blew, and blew, the grasses and the heather swayed, just as before, as always. Everything was unmoved and still, like myself.

When it grew dark I went on again, higher, but it was too late to get very far, certainly too late to reach the overhanging cliff. I opened up a hollow in a cluster of shrubs to sleep. At sunset the clouds were blown away for a few seconds so that I could see a patch of sun. Then the clouds covered it up again.

I thought of the old Bushman story about the people without knees living in the west and eating the sun at nightfall, the sun being living flesh. And one day a brave hunter ventured close to them and saw them sleeping in a standing position, for lack of knees, their backs resting against the tree-trunks. We sun-eaters of the west, I thought, we were the people of darkness, yes, and we lacked repose and proper sleep. Without knees, without buttocks, without anything. Until nothing was left of us, until just going on remained. And the stars were the eyes of dead souls.

But there were no stars that night.

At daybreak thoughts began to ooze back back into me. I had to go back to the car sometime. Perhaps tonight.

But if I went, if I did alone what we had planned to do together, it would be something like ultimate defeat. Doing it together would have been different, an act of love. But to do it alone, after what I'd already done : that would be unworthy. I couldn't explain why, I didn't even know why it should still be important to me. But it was; and for her sake too.

I went up the slope, farther away, into the wholly unknown mountains where I'd never been before : walking to keep my body warm, to keep my thoughts moving.

The hosepipe I hurled into the bushes. It was like severing an umbilical cord, the last thing still attaching me to cause and effect.

As evening came on I found a better shelter than the previous night, a shallow cave. The clouds were dispersing, but it was bitterly cold.

It didn't matter. Having lost that detachment of before, the cold enhanced my awareness of a new oneness between me and the grass and the imperturbable mountains.

All through the night I spoke aloud to myself.

If I kill myself, it's an admission of failure. Then you'll believe that you have hunted me to death, that I couldn't bear it. But if I prove myself ready to endure whatever lies ahead, if I give myself into your hands, you can never ultimately possess me. For then it will have been my own choice, part of my liberty.

You have taken everything from me which I've ever had. But if I triumph in the end, you won't retain anything.

She is safe. I can choose to go through hell for her sake. Then it won't be you who force me to, but I who choose : this I. Not blindly or impulsively, but with lucidity, with every thought thought through.

It was getting fiercely cold.

To keep my wits and not to freeze to death, I started reciting passages from my old parts. Only it wasn't as if I was acting : their words seemed to have become my own, and I was my own audience. I recited poetry. Shakespeare's sonnets, Rilke, Donne, anything I could recall. St John of the Cross :

For no one saw it,
Neither did Evil appear;
And the siege was lifted,
And the horsemen
Came down at the sight of the waters.

As the day began to break – it must have been Sunday then, Easter –
I started walking, not back the way I'd come, for I could never turn
back, but on over the mountains and the hills. I knew I had to find
people sooner or later. I suppose I was tired; I must have been hungry;
I don't know.

In the afternoon there was a farm below me. I stumbled down the
last slope and knocked on the back door; when the farmer's wife opened,
I said:

'Madam, my name is Joseph Malan. I believe the police are looking for
me. Would you please telephone them?'

Seven

I

Against the thousand threats which happen or never happen I have no defence. The least can overcome me, for I have put down all arms. There's only one I am prepared for, and that is death. Not because I confront it aggressively, but because I know now for how long we've been living together. It is familiar to me, like the body of a beloved: I know death the way it knows me. Now I'm certain, like the first time she said to me:

'Yes. Come into me.'

During all the past weeks, months perhaps, I've taken, night after night, the pages written under my bare bulb and flushed them down the toilet. And now my narrow, scrubbed table is nearly empty, tidy, bare, like a piece of furniture in a monk's cell. All that remains, in a small pile on one corner, is the handful of sonnets for my guards. I suppose they'll be indignant when they find them, not realising that everything is summarised in them after all. What they were waiting for, like the advocate, was 'my own words'. But as an actor it has always been my function to give life to the words of others. That it should be Shakespeare's, now, gives me a unique sense of satisfaction.

Theatrical to the very end, they'll say. To thine own self be true! I'm no longer so sure about the distinction between act and gesture. In the final analysis we're all just performing our little series of gestures in front of the invisible audience, or the mirror. And the only criterion is whether the acting has been more or less coherent and more or less convincing. A matter of technique. Some live and die better than others. The same darkness overtakes all.

That remains a marvel to me: the suddenness with which night can fall. All day one knows it's coming, yet when it arrives it comes as a surprise.

The jailer came late this afternoon, a middle-aged man, bald and bespectacled, his face tanned, but with a deep groove caused by his hat running across his forehead, and above that it was white; as if he'd been a farmer for years. I can easily imagine him in the elders' pew every Sunday morning. *His* teeth will never be washed away.

'What you sitting like this for, man?' he asked, with deliberate joviality which immediately made me realise what he'd come for.

'There's not much else to do, is there?' I said. 'However, I don't suppose it'll be long now.'

'How'd you know, hey?'

'Isn't that what you've come to tell me?'

He wiped his hand across his forehead, where there must have been an unruly lock of hair years ago. 'Yes, it's so.'

'When?'

'Well you see.' He thrust his hands into his pockets. 'It's tomorrow.'

'Early?'

'Sunrise. Usual time.'

'I see.'

'Now you mustn't let that worry you, man. You know it had to happen sooner or later.'

'That's true.'

'Anyway, we give you enough time.' He took out his pipe and started scratching in it. 'I mean to get everything ready and so on. If you got any special requests, you must just ask.'

'I'd be glad if they could put off my light tonight, if you could arrange it.'

He shook his head, looking deeply unhappy. 'That's against the regulations, man. If I could . . . But then I land in trouble, you see.' He tried to sound jovial again : 'But why sit in the dark anyway?'

'I'm fond of the dark.'

'I wish you could say that to my son, my youngest, he's twelve years younger than his sister. And all the time from his birth he's been dead scared of the dark. I think he got a fright from the thunder or something.'

'I've also been frightened by thunder once,' I said. 'One night in London. I don't think I've ever been so scared in my life.'

At last he managed to light his pipe. 'Ja.' He put the used match back into the box. 'You been all over the world, hey? But I also travelled in my time. All the way from Tzaneen in the Transvaal, I was farming there then, down to Bloemfontein. Five hundred miles. You won't say that if you look at me today, hey? That was when my oldest sister died. Ay, death has taken away the lot of us, it's just me what's left today. But I don't suppose you want to talk about dying and things.'

'It's all right.'

He was getting hurried. 'Well, as I said: if there's anything you want to ask us, then ask. We'll send you a minister in the morning.'

'I'd rather not, if you don't mind.'

'Are you Catholic then?'

'I'm not a believer.'

He took his pipe from his mouth, putting it back after a few seconds. 'Of course,' he said thoughtfully. 'You Coloured people are different from us.' I could see him struggle to find the right formula. 'But our Lord Jesus died for everybody, Joseph. You mustn't forget that, hey. When he was already on the cross he still saved one of the murderers.'

'But the other one went to hell.'

'His ways are different from ours, you see. It's not for us to ask about it.' He opened the door. 'Well, whether you get a minister or not, we still got to wake you up early. Five o'clock. You know, there's a lot to be done.'

'Of course. Please tell me if there's anything I could help you with.'

'No, it's all right,' he said. 'We know the ropes.' He stopped in the doorway: 'Ag ja, and tonight, of course, you can eat like a lord. You just order anything you want.'

'Perhaps some red wine, if it's possible,' I suggested. 'And a slice of brown bread.'

'Brown bread?'

'It's good for the digestion.'

He laughed, discovered that his pipe had gone out and started fumbling with the matches again. Behind his broad back the metal door slammed shut.

So it's tomorrow. After all these nights, only this last one left. I'm sorry I had to disappoint him about a minister or a priest. If Father Mark had been available, I should have liked to have him with me. But perhaps it's better like this, too many people have made use of him in the past. Still, it would have been good. Not to pray together. Only to talk to him for the last time, about Jessica, or his flowerbeds. I wonder whether anybody is watering them nowadays, they're so exposed to sun and wind.

What happens, is good the way it happens. I've never been afraid of

391

loneliness. It was more difficult after Jessica, of course; but it was necessary. It's not a matter of being happy at all, of course. In that respect Jerry was right: happiness is a function of blindness. And yet I look upon the same darkness which the blind do see and find meaning and beauty in it. The night is a great redeemer. No, not happiness: all I wish is to remain open: aware, to the end, of what is happening, denying nothing, excluding nothing.

A man like St John – he stripped himself of all possessions in order to be more completely open to the fullness of everthing. To be naked the way we were in Bain's Kloof, or at night: that was our most complete possession of one another, our ultimate freedom, our only honesty, that meeting of our bodies brown and white. And because we'd dared to be naked together like that, everything else happened. And so I regret nothing. This is love.

Will it all be finished tomorrow?

No, it seems to me it's only a beginning. Not of a hereafter, but of a hereness: not for myself, but for others: perhaps. I was never sure whether I'd be able to endure it all, but I have. I haven't betrayed anyone: neither Jessica, nor Jerry, nor my history. This is joy.

I don't know whether they arrested Jerry. I don't even know what he's doing at the moment. It's of no concern. *If* he is free, he'll know that I haven't been untrue to him. He'll be able to go on in his own way. And if it must be violence, it will be purified by his sincerity, like Yanek's. In that, we'll always be inseparable. This is grace.

When they come to call me tomorrow morning, I shall be awake – I dare not sleep this last night of all, it is too short, too precious. *O night more desirable than dawn.* I want to be awake every hour, I want to know every hour of the dark.

At six o'clock they'll lead me into the innermost circle. And afterwards bury me, I suppose, for there'll be no one to ask for the body.

I wish I'd bought a funeral policy from Oom Appie after all, he would have appreciated it so much. And then I would have been assured of a decent burial, with coffin and mourners and a wreath of plastic flowers, and eventually a headstone, a little milestone on the road of the numerous dead. But I didn't use my opportunity and now it is too late. For where is the grave of little Leah, where did they dig in Adam's broken bits, where lies Moses, or Dlamini/Daniel, or Rachel, or Abraham, where is David, where my father Jacob? Not one of their graves is marked by name or date, so how could I be allowed to presume? One should know one's place, my mother said. Else one only sees one's arse.

My place is with her and the others. I'm not alone tonight, they are all with me, the long dark row. I am not the victim of my history. What happens, has been chosen by myself. I do not undergo it, I create it. I abandon myself to them. I am a smooth round pebble contented in its fall, dust unto dust, true to itself.

This is peace. Not a world-forsaking peace: not the peace of ignorance, of not-knowing. I have probed and explored my night, I love it; in the still heart of the storm it exists, motionless, destined by Jessica – not dependent on her, but freely acquired through her. That serenity, that smile, which I first recognised in Dulpert.

Dulpert

One day we shall succeed in opening his big black trunk. Then we'll see what's inside, and we'll walk through the city with the open trunk, he and I, up towards District Six which will be the way it was before they'd started clearing up. On Oxford Place a mouse will be running pursued by all the children of the neighbourhood, but they won't catch him, no one will squash him under a bloody heel. And Gran'ma Grace will be on her balcony, laughing with her toothless hairy mouth. Oom Sassie will shout: 'Say, Gran'ma, how'se tomato?' And she'll answer: 'Tomato's ripe en' reddy!' She will beckon to us to come up to our rooms. On the table the meang sticks will be burning and Dulpert will squat crosslegged on the love bed humming peacefully: 'Om. Om. Om.' There will be a girl lying in my arm, Ursula perhaps, or Fatima or Sheila, or Beverley, or Annamaria. Perhaps Hermien.

Jessica will be lying in my arm in the evening, in the night, in the familiar dark. And I shall say to her: 'Come, Little Miss Muffet, come, my darling: let us go out into the streets, let us walk through the city hand in hand, don't be afraid, no one will mind, no one will stop us, and the horsemen will descend at the sight of the waters.

Come, my darling. The world is open and the laws are dispersed in the wind. Come, walk with me, naked, on the beach without end. Come to the pool in the sand, let me wash you, your shoulders and your lovely small breasts, your back and your belly and your legs, come let me taste your secret darkness on my tongue. And you will wash me, the way a woman washes a corpse, with love and gentle hands.

And afterwards you'll bury me in the sand and plant a cross between my legs. They will see the cross and think of me, it won't be there in vain, it won't ever be forgotten.

And back at home they will hear the news and have a service in the small white missionary church, and the pastor will read the funeral notice:

It hath pleased Almighty God of his great mercy to take unto himself the soul of our dear brother Joseph Malan: the Lord gave, the Lord hath taken away, blessed be the name of the Lord.

On the contrary notwithstanding.

January 1965 – April 1973

Shall I compare thee to a summer's day?
Thou art more lovely and more temperate:
Rough winds do shake the darling buds of May,
And summer's lease hath all too short a date:
Sometimes too hot the eye of heaven shines,
And often is his gold complexion dimm'd;
And every fair from fair sometimes declines,
By chance or nature's changing course untrimm'd.
But thy eternal summer shall not fade
Nor lose possession of that fair thou ow'st;
Nor shall Death brag thou livest in his shade,
When in eternal lines to time thou grow'st:
   So long as men can breathe, or eyes can see,
   So long lives this, and this gives life to thee.

Love is too young to know what conscience is;
Yet who knows not conscience is born of love?
Then, gentle cheater, urge not my amiss,
Lest guilty of my faults thy sweet self prove:
For thou betraying me, I shall betray
My nobler part to my gross body's treason;
My soul doth teach my body that he may
Triumph in love; flesh stays no farther reason,
But, rising at thy name, doth point out thee
As his triumphant prize. Proud of this pride,
He is contented thy poor drudge to be,
To stand in thy affairs, fall at thy side.
  No want of conscience hold it that I call
  Her 'love' for whose dear love I rise and fall.

Love is my sin, and thy dear virtue hate,
Hate of my sin, founded on sinful loving.
O, but with mine compare thou thine own state,
And thou shalt find it merits not reproving;
Or, if it do, not from those lips of thine,
That have profan'd their scarlet ornaments,
And seal'd wrong bonds of love as oft as mine;
Robb'd others' beds' revenues of their rents.
Be it lawful I love thee as thou lov'st those
Whom thine eyes woo as mine importune thee.
Root pity in thine heart, that, when it grows,
Thy pity may deserve to pitied be.
   If thou dost seek to have what thou dost hide,
   By my example mayst thou be denied!

Weary with toil, I haste me to my bed,
The sweet repose for limbs with travel tired;
But then begins a journey in my head
To task my mind when body's work's expired;
For now my thoughts, from far where I abide,
Intend a pious pilgrimage to thee,
And keep my drooping eyelids open wide,
Looking on darkness which the blind do see:
Save that my soul's imaginary sight
Presents thy shadow to my eyeless view,
Which, like a jewel in the darkest night,
Make black night beauteous and her old face new.
   And thus, by day my limbs, by night my mind;
   For thee, and for myself, no quiet find.

When I consider every thing that grows
Holds in perfection but a little moment,
That this huge stage presenteth nought but shows
Whereon the stars in secret influence comment;
When I perceive that men as plants increase,
Cheer'd and check'd even by the selfsame sky,
Vaunt in their youthful sap, at height decrease,
And wear their proud state of memory;

Then the conceit of this inconstant stay
Sets you most rich in beauty in my sight
Where wasteful Time doth battle with Decay
To change your day of joy to darkest night;
   And all in war with Time for love of you,
   As he takes from you, I create you new.

As an unperfect actor on the stage
Who with his fear is put besides his part,
Or some fierce thing replete with too much rage,
Whose strength's abundance weakens his own heart;
So I, for fear of truth, forget to say
The perfect ceremony of love's rite,
And in mine own love's strength seem to decay,
O'ercharg'd with burthen of mine own love's might.
O, let my looks be then the eloquence
And dumb presagers of my speaking breast;
Who plead for love, and wait for recompense,
More than that tongue that more hath more express'd.
   O, learn to read what silent love hath writ:
   To hear with eyes is part of love's fine wit.

Why dids't thou promise such a beauteous day,
And make me travel forth without a cloak,
To let dark clouds o'ertake me on my way,
Hiding thy beauty in their rotten smoke?
'Tis not enough that through the cloud thou break
To dry the rain on my storm-beaten face,
For no man well of such a salve can speak
That heals the wounds, yet cures not the disgrace:
Nor can thy shame give physic to my grief;
Though thou repent, yet I have still the loss:
Th' offender's sorrow lends but weak relief
To him that bears the strong offence's cross.
   Ah! But those tears are pearl which thy love sheds,
   And they are rich, and ransom all ill deeds.

That time of year thou dost in me behold
When yellow leaves, or none, or few, do hang
Upon these boughs which shake against the cold.
Bare ruin'd choirs where late the sweet birds sang.
In me thou seest the twilight of such day
As after sunset fadeth in the west,
Which by and by dark night doth take away,
Death's second self, that seals up all in rest.
In me thou seest the glowing of such fire
That on the ashes of his youth doth lie,
As the death-bed whereon it must expire,
Consum'd by that which it was nourish'd by.
   This thou perceiv'st, which makes thy love more strong,
   To love that well which thou must leave ere long.

Why is my verse so barren of new pride?
So far from variation or quick change?
Why, with the time, do I not look aside
To new-found methods and to compounds strange?
Why write I still all one, ever the same,
And keep invention in a noted weed,
That every word doth almost tell my name,
Showing their birth, and whence they did proceed?
O, know, my love, I always write of you,
And you and love are still my argument;
So all my best is dressing old words new,
Spending again what is already spent:
   For as the sun is always new and old,
   So is my love still telling what is told.

Since I left you, mine eye is in my mind;
And that which governs me to go about
Doth part his function, and is partly blind,
Seems seeing, but effectually is out;
For it no form delivers to the heart
Of bird, or flow'r, or shape, which it doth latch;
Of these quick objects hath the mind no part,
Nor his own vision holds what it doth catch;

For if it see the rud'st or gentlest sight,
The most sweet favour or deformed'st creature,
The mountain or the sea, the day or night,
The crow or dove, it shapes them to your feature.
   Incapable of more, replete with you,
    My most true mind thus mak'th mine eye untrue.

Being your slave, what can I do but tend
Upon the days and nights of your desire?
I have no precious time at all to spend,
Nor services to do, till you require.
Nor dare I chide the world-without-end hour,
Whilst I, my sovereign, watch the clock for you,
Nor think the bitterness of absence sour,
When you have bid your servant once adieu,
Nor dare I question with my jealous thought
Where you may be, or your affairs suppose,
But, like a sad slave, wait and think of nought
Save, where you are how happy you make those.
   So true a fool is love that in your will,
    Though you do any thing, he thinks no ill.

Farewell! thou art too dear for my possessing,
And like enough thou know'st thy estimate:
The charter of thy worth gives thee releasing;
My bonds in thee are all determinate.
For how do I have thee but by thy granting?
And for that treasure where is my deserving?
The cause of this fair gift in me is wanting,
And so my patent back to me is swerving.
Thyself thou gav'st, thy own worth then not knowing,
Or me, to whom thou gav'st it, else mistaking;
So thy great gift, upon misprision growing,
Comes home again, on better judgement making.
   Thus have I had thee, as a dream doth flatter:
    In sleep a king, in daylight no such matter.

No longer mourn for me when I am dead
Than you shall hear the surly sullen bell
Give warning to the world that I am fled
From this vile world, with vilest worms to dwell:
And if you read this line, remember not
The hand that writ it; for I love you so,
That in your sweet thoughts I would be forgot,
If thinking on me then should make you woe.
O, if, I say, you look upon my verse,
When I perhaps compounded am with clay,
Do not so much as my poor name rehearse,
But let your love even with my life decay;
　　Lest the dark world should look into your moan,
　　And mock you with me after I am gone.